ACCIDENTAL SEAL

SEAL Brotherhood
Book 1

SHARON HAMILTON

SHARON HAMILTON'S BOOK LIST

SEAL BROTHERHOOD BOOKS

SEAL BROTHERHOOD SERIES
Accidental SEAL Book 1
Fallen SEAL Legacy Book 2
SEAL Under Covers Book 3
SEAL The Deal Book 4
Cruisin' For A SEAL Book 5
SEAL My Destiny Book 6
SEAL of My Heart Book 7
Fredo's Dream Book 8
SEAL My Love Book 9
SEAL Encounter Prequel to Book 1
SEAL Endeavor Prequel to Book 2
Ultimate SEAL Collection Vol. 1 Books 1-4 /2 Prequels
Ultimate SEAL Collection Vol. 2 Books 5-7

SEAL BROTHERHOOD LEGACY SERIES
Watery Grave Book 1
Honor The Fallen Book 2

BAD BOYS OF SEAL TEAM 3 SERIES
SEAL's Promise Book 1
SEAL My Home Book 2
SEAL's Code Book 3
Big Bad Boys Bundle Books 1-3

BAND OF BACHELORS SERIES
Lucas Book 1
Alex Book 2
Jake Book 3
Jake 2 Book 4
Big Band of Bachelors Bundle

STAND ALONE BOOKS & SERIES

SEAL's Goal: The Beautiful Game

Nashville SEAL: Jameson

True Blue SEALS Zak

Paradise: In Search of Love

Love Me Tender, Love You Hard

NOVELLAS

SEAL You In My Dreams Magnolias and Moonshine

PARANORMALS

GOLDEN VAMPIRES OF TUSCANY SERIES

Honeymoon Bite Book 1

Mortal Bite Book 2

Christmas Bite Book 3

Midnight Bite Book 4

THE GUARDIANS

Heavenly Lover Book 1

Underworld Lover Book 2

Underworld Queen Book 3

Redemption Book 4

FALL FROM GRACE SERIES

Gideon: Heavenly Fall

NOVELLAS

SEAL Of Time Trident Legacy

All of Sharon's books are available on Audible, narrated by the talented J.D. Hart.

ABOUT THE BOOK

Navy SEAL Kyle Lansdowne, on a mission to find his AWOL Team buddy, is staying at his buddy's home while investigating the disappearance. When someone breaks in, he takes protective measures. He doesn't expect to find that a beautiful young woman is responsible for his teammate's abduction.

Christy Nelson embarks on her new career in Real Estate by holding her first open house. Entering the wrong house, by accident, she finds the nude sleeping body of a young man.

What starts out as a meeting by accident becomes a hot affair neither one is ready for. Kyle is conflicted about getting Christy involved in his mission, but his hand is forced when he learns the same San Diego gang responsible for his teammate's abduction has kidnapped her.

Battling a cadre of dirty law enforcements hell-bent on getting military equipment, especially state-of-the-art firepower, Kyle is forced to admit that he would die to protect her.

AUTHOR'S NOTE

I always dedicate my SEAL Brotherhood books to the brave men and women who defend our shores and keep us safe. Without their sacrifice, and that of their families—because a warrior's fight always includes his or her family—I wouldn't have the freedom and opportunity to make a living writing these stories. They sometimes pay the ultimate price so we can debate, argue, go have coffee with friends, raise our children and see them have children of their own.

One of my favorite tributes to warriors resides on many memorials, including one I saw honoring the fallen of WWII on an island in the Pacific:

> "When you go home
> Tell them of us, and say
> For your tomorrow,
> We gave our today."

These are my stories created out of my own imagination. Anything that is inaccurately portrayed is either my mistake, or done intentionally to disguise something I might have overheard over a beer or in the corner of one of the hangouts along the Coronado Strand.

I support two main charities. Navy SEAL/UDT Museum operates in Ft. Pierce, Florida. Please learn about this wonderful museum, all run by active and former SEALs and their friends and families, and who rely on public support, not that of the U.S. Government. www.navysealmuseum.org

I also support Wounded Warriors, who tirelessly bring together the warrior as well as the family members who are just learning to deal with their soldier's condition and have nowhere to turn. It is a long path to becoming well, but I've seen first-hand what this organization does for its warriors and the families who love them. Please give what your heart tells you is right. If you cannot give, volunteer at one of the many service centers all over the United States. Get involved. Do something meaningful for someone who gave so much of themselves, to families who have paid the price for your freedom. You'll find a family there unlike any other on the planet. www.woundedwarriorproject.org

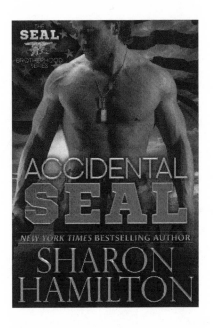

Go here for the video trailer for Accidental SEAL.

youtube.com/watch?v=67Ee5xb5TRM

CHAPTER 1

C HRISTY NELSON WORKED to keep her breakfast down as Wayne
Somerville came lurking around her cubicle. He'd pestered her
every day since she'd been introduced as the newest agent at the
Patterson Realty sales meeting three days ago. His soft, flabby torso
was repulsive, and those distinctive hair plugs, installed at an angle on
Wayne's shiny salmon-colored forehead, were distracting. Her gaze
followed rows of black dots receding into his dyed-black hair. A life-
sized version of Mr. King's Chuckie.

Wayne winked at her again, and her blood turned to ice.

His horse teeth and foul breath could raise the dead. He'd made it
clear he wanted to mentor her, but she suspected he had more in
mind than real estate contracts and short sales. He was persistent,
though. She'd give him that.

He draped his bulky frame against the back of her chair. She wanted to duck for cover. The eerie need to protect her neck put her radar
on high alert as she visualized violence and fangs.

"I've coached quite a few of the new agents over the years."
Wayne's look lasted too long—hungry and inappropriate. Christy
didn't trust one single hair plug.

"Well," she said, resisting the urge to escape, "I do need a good
open house.

Now, why did I say that?

"I've got the perfect one! Great little short sale." Wayne launched into his routine, oblivious to the fact she'd become dizzy from the smell of the garlic fries he'd apparently had for lunch. "The house is a little rough around the edges, but in a super neighborhood. The sellers are about to lose it." He threw her a mock frown. She could see him singing a hymn, asking for money on TV.

Perhaps a second career.

"No sign on the lawn yet and it's not even in the computer," he continued. "You can snatch all those buyers for yourself." He leaned in and whispered as if it were a national secret. "And I could help you with the paperwork. You know, show you how it's done."

Male alert. If he touches me, he'll get a knee to his groin. She swung her chair to angle for quick action.

He stepped back just in time. She exhaled, grateful for the distance.

"Doing short sales is a real art," he added with a frown, stiffening. His shiny suit fit like one of those unfortunate animals in a teddy bear factory, stuffed into its fur. The silver glint of the fabric reminded her of fish scales.

Run, Christy, run. You could be the one who got away…

She had never in her life paid a favor with sex and wasn't about to start. She would hold his new listing open, but only if she could do it without owing him.

Besides, she had to do something to drum up business. Her move to San Diego marked the beginning of her new professional career as a Realtor. Being the top salesperson at Madame M's lingerie boutique on Maiden Lane in San Francisco barely paid the bills. She'd loved Madame and had thrived as a sales clerk, but recognized the time for a real career. She trained in real estate, and then moved to San Diego after her mother passed. Christy inherited the condo.

Though she'd been comfortable selling to the rich and powerful of the City by the Bay, Wayne, even if he was half the success he claimed he was, made her nervous.

This is a very bad idea. Just say no.

"Fine." It sounded like it came from the cubicle next to her.

But then she spotted Wayne's dimples and canines.

Oh. My. God. I've just said yes.

CHRISTY'S RED HONDA looked like a wet cherry lollipop, polished to perfection. Cute and shiny on the outside, but hot and sweltering on the inside. Sitting in the cramped front seat, she stopped and squinted to make out house numbers, comparing them to the address Wayne minutely scribbled on the back of his business card. Then she found it.

The house appeared nicer than he'd described. The advertised price, he said, was the lowest in the neighborhood, going back ten years. Hopefully she'd pick up a young couple out looking for their first home, complete with good credit and a wad of cash from Mommy and Daddy. Wouldn't it be great to make a sale on her very first day on the job?

She parked in the driveway, popped the trunk, and brought out three sandwich signs with the Patterson Realty logo, on loan from Wayne. He was out with his family today. She hoped the Somervilles didn't stop by since she'd feel uncomfortable looking into the eyes of Wayne's wife, a woman he'd probably cheated on and would again if he got the chance. One of Christy's other rules: no married men. She wasn't about to change that, either.

A perfumed late spring breeze blew softly against her face and neck, sending a thrill up her spine. The air ripened with possibility. This was her favorite time of year.

The walkway looked freshly swept. After placing one sign in the front yard, she stacked the other two beside the front door and inserted Wayne's key. While the lock accepted the new shiny silver metal, the tumblers stayed in place, frozen.

Way to go Wayne. Waste my time and give me the wrong key!

Irritation bubbled, ruining her cheerful, spring-induced mood. She yanked on the front handle and pushed against it out of frustration. It opened.

"Anybody home?" her voice wavered like that of a small child. She waited. No answer.

Christy stepped inside, onto a striped cotton rug lying cockeyed behind the front door. The smell of fried food hit her. She walked across the wooden floor of the living room, her stilettos clacking. She cracked open a window. Air scented by fresh blossoms poured in, diluting the smells of ordinary life. She grabbed the newspaper tossed on top of an ottoman and folded the crinkling pages under her arm, aiming for the kitchen to find a trashcan. She passed the dining room table, which was strewn with a map of the area, a couple of felt-tipped pens, and a letter-sized yellow lined tablet. She collected these items as well and made her way to the kitchen.

Christy threw the tablet and newspaper onto the tiled countertop and placed her hands on her hips to assess the scene before her. She squinted at several days' worth of dishes piled high in the sink. Next to it, a large stainless steel bowl sat encrusted with dark green and purple leaves at the bottom, evidence of a salad—several days old.

Maybe Wayne had neglected to tell the sellers about the open house. She decided it was entirely possible. "How can you expect to sell a house this way?" she muttered, then sighed and removed her jacket, slinging it over the back of a clean-looking kitchen chair. She decided to take a tour of the place, checking for other things to clean or straighten before she'd be ready to hold it open.

But this house was such a mess, an uneasy darkness chilled her. She tiptoed down the carpeted hallway, feeling like an intruder, past empty rooms to a closed door at the end.

Probably the master bedroom.

Something about the whole scene was strange. These people left in a hurry without cleaning up dinner from several days before. She'd been told short sale houses rarely showed pride of ownership, but this felt absolutely creepy, like she'd stepped on someone's grave. The hair on the back of her neck bristled as she gripped the doorknob. She lightly tapped with her other hand and then opened the door.

A naked body lay on the bed.

Holy crap.

Hesitant to look at first, she pushed through her fear. She saw movement. Tanned skin, a muscular male chest that rose and fell. Earphones were wired to a phone balanced on his open palm. The man was very much alive, and healthy. Her eyes drifted further down to a dusting of dark brown hair that led to an impossible-to-miss erection. His penis stood at attention, like a deep rose-colored light standard under a matching fireman's hat of deeper pink.

Blood pumped to her ears, making them ring, as her heart raced. A wave of anger coursed over her at the realization she had been the victim of a very sick joke perpetrated by Wayne and one of his disgusting friends.

Christy silently closed the door and tiptoed back down the carpeted hallway, her three-inch heels wobbling on the thick, padded surface. Her knees knocked against each other as she picked up speed, her anger building. She grabbed her jacket, keys, and purse, and crossed the living room, headed toward the front door. She was almost free.

Christy wouldn't give the prankster the satisfaction of knowing she had even seen him. She wanted to stomp her foot and kick something through the window. This was Wayne's doing.

That sonofabitch and his lopsided plugs will pay for this.

She pulled the door handle and was rewarded by the smells of a warm spring day bleeding through the inch-wide crack she'd created. An enormous hand and forearm came from behind her and slammed the door shut. She saw a familiar blue-green tattoo of some animal tracks on his muscled forearm just before his other hand gripped her mouth. Callused fingers pinched the sides of her cheeks. The grip hurt.

She panicked at first; then her self-defense training kicked into gear. She struggled to duck and turn, digging her nails into the man's arm. He locked her tightly in a choke hold, which immobilized her upper torso. She attempted a muffled cry, but the chokehold pulled against her windpipe and allowed her only a weak, high-pitched whine. He was good at the mouth grip, not giving her any room to bite the way she'd been taught. His mountainous shoulders were so large she couldn't find his face to scratch at his eyes.

That left her lower body somewhat free. Christy balanced herself like a stork on one high heel, leaned against the wall of his chest, and dug the other heel backward into his knee. She felt him jerk in a sharp inhale. He didn't cry out. She knew she'd hurt him, but cursed her inability to land the steel tip of her new three-inch stilettos into the soft tissue area of his thigh, going for his femoral artery. Christy moved to deliver a second blow and was pulled backward, tight against his chest. They tumbled to the floor. He took the brunt of the fall, and then pitched her body like a tiny twig in the wind, climbing on top of her.

Though they faced each other, her hair was everywhere, covering her eyes, but by the anatomical placement of his body pressed against hers, she knew he was the naked stranger from the bedroom. It took only one large paw to hold both her wrists and pin them high above her head.

With the weight of his packed and well-developed body immobilizing her, she feared a more sinister intent. She mentally prepared herself for the worst: a brutal rape or murder, or perhaps both.

Think, dammit. There's always a solution.

But the universe remained mute.

Out of options, she vowed deep in her heart she would cause him damage, maybe spill some of his blood so that when the police detectives looked over her lifeless body at the crime scene, there would be forensic evidence.

So this is the way I will be remembered: at a crime scene, outlined in yellow chalk.

Maybe she wouldn't survive, but she would help get him caught and save another innocent woman from this sexual sicko. She couldn't see his eyes, which was a minor blessing. She didn't want him to know her fear.

He adjusted himself and shifted off her lower body. Her skirt rode halfway up her thighs. Christy used the opportunity to maneuver her stocking-covered knee between his legs and punch his groin. To her horror, her knee felt the warmth of his naked skin. His yell, accompanied by a string of obscenities, interrupted her repulsion. She was pleased not all the blood from his cock had drained, meaning the hit had caused him pain. He lifted his hand off her mouth and balled it into a fist under her head, gripping her hair at the scalp.

"You bastard..." She growled from deep inside her chest, surprised at her own bravado, then decided to scream. Immediately, the hand clamped over her mouth again. This time she bit down through the soft tissue between his thumb and forefinger and tasted the warm metallic liquid from his broken skin. But he still didn't flinch and pressed down even harder. His other hand released her wrists and pulled her hair back with a tug at the nape of her neck, forcing her chin up toward the ceiling. She tried pushing him away with her arms, but his were longer.

She arched her chest in defiance, but this gave him a full view of her breasts. The buttons on her sheer ivory blouse popped open. She muttered a curse. The fleeting thought that he would now ruin her two-hundred-dollar bra and be spurred on to ravish her further flashed through her mind.

He immobilized her arms above her head with one forearm and pinned her thighs with his own that were easily twice the size of hers. She had no way to move and no ability to scream for help. But his blood dripped on the wooden flooring, and it coated the inside of her mouth. Maybe that would be enough to land him a spot in San Quentin. Tired and resigned, she sighed, knowing she could not win the physical tussle, and allowed her body to go limp.

He responded by whispering a question in her ear. "Who *are* you?"

For a second, her ears buzzed. Then she mumbled through his fingers, seeking the soft fleshy part of his palm with her canines again, but failing. She was unable to give him an intelligible answer, but if she could, it would be, "*Who the fuck are you?*"

"I'm going to take my hand away, and you will tell me who you are and whom you work for." His voice came across calm and steady. Practiced. Measured. She'd have to say, commanding.

This surprised her, but she still didn't trust him. She gave a short nod, but intended to get away at the first opportunity. He removed his hand and brought it between their bodies. She sucked in her breath and straightened her spine, even though it hurt. She prepared for him to grip her breasts and rip her clothing to shreds. She clenched her abdomen and waited for the pain.

But instead, she caught a filtered view through her tresses of one heavily veined hand reaching to his tensed pectoral muscle, removing her Patterson Realty nametag that speared him there. He sniffed the pin as he thumbed over the embedded letters of her name, and then tossed it. The pin skidded across the floor until it hit a baseboard.

"This gonna make me pass out?" He made it sound like a legitimate question. He touched the pinprick wound on his chest and then yanked back the strands of her hair he still held wrapped in his fist. She couldn't see much of his face.

"What?"

"You an agent?"

"Yes, I'm…I'm a r-r-r…"

"Business or political?"

Christy furrowed her brow, squinting. "Business!"

He reached under her skirt, pulling down her pantyhose so quickly that he got her lace panties too. Cold fear snaked in her belly and shivered up her spine. She shrieked, but it did no good. He removed her remaining heel and then ripped her under things off in one fluid movement. Christy attempted to scream again but was silenced by his hand squeezing her neck, his thumb pressing against her voice box.

"Stop it. I don't want to hurt you."

That's what they say just before they kill you.

She couldn't move. She couldn't breathe and tried to cough, hoping death would come soon, *before* he raped her. But then he relaxed his grip, allowing spring air to flood her lungs. For a grateful few seconds, everything was right with the world.

With his other hand, he took the now shredded pantyhose and

wrapped them around her wrists that he held up over her head. The knot he tied cut off circulation to her hands, but at least she could move her torso a little. Her neck tensed up from the fall, and her tailbone hurt.

"Please, I'm j-just…here…for…the open house."

"What open house?"

"W-Wayne…said…I…should…"

"Who the hell is Wayne? He your handler?"

Now this pissed her off. "God damn it. I'm an independent contractor!" She'd heard it so many times while she was studying for her license that the phrase was the first thing that popped into her mind. "Wayne is another agent. I'm a Realtor."

"Sure you are."

Christy drilled him with a look he wouldn't be able to mistake, if he could see it. Hair still covered her face.

He chuckled. "This part of your sales training? They teach you how to bite men, break into houses, knock out their knees, and puncture them with poisonous needles?" His subtle mocking fueled something bubbling in her stomach.

She shifted slightly, noticing the still rather large package between her legs that might have been welcome in another time and place. She shook her head to the side, clearing the hair from her face with the aid of her bound hands; she then stared into deep blue eyes, a crooked nose, and soft full lips pressed together in a straight line. A tiny scar resided on his high cheekbone just under his left eye.

He swallowed as he looked down on her and watched her follow the trek of his Adam's apple. When she looked back into his eyes, his body seemed to soften. A few errant strands of hair were caught in her lip-gloss. He removed them with two hardened fingers. His eyes explored her face, tracing all her features, as if memorizing every one.

Her heart beat against her chest wall, echoing his, for several long seconds. He didn't look like a criminal. Or a practical joker type. As she studied him closer, she realized something didn't add up.

He righted himself, released his hold on her, and then sat crouched, covering his exposed groin with the throw rug. He seized her purse and turned it inside out in seconds by pulling apart the lining and dumping the contents on the floor.

"Hey! That's a Coach bag, you…"

He gave her another glare, reminding her she was physically out-matched. She closed her mouth mid-sentence, choking down renewed anger. He sifted through the contents, opened a lipstick tube and sniffed the pink shaft, then carefully retracted it and replaced the top.

"Sorry." He directed his apology to the floor and didn't glance up.

That's it? Can't even look at me, you horrible son of a bitch? She decided it was still unsafe, so kept her thoughts to herself.

He's crazy. A psycho. A sociopath. No wonder he has financial issues and has to sell his house.

Christy sat up, her spine ramrod straight, and held out her hands, encumbered by the torn pantyhose that hung like moss from a tree. It was not a beg but a demand to be released of her bonds. To her surprise, he gently leaned over and untied her. She buttoned her blouse, noting before she could finish that his last-minute stolen peek gave him a good view of her lacy beige bra.

She returned a poisonous look she hoped would stop any ideas from forming on his part, and then she noticed a tiny trickle of blood coming from the pinprick in his chest. A much larger ribbon of blood dripped to a small puddle on the floor where her heel had done damage to his knee. Below that was a tattoo of thorns ringing his bulging calf. As if she asked, he raised his palm, showing her a nice bloody semicircle of teeth marks.

"You're lethal," his voice was soft, but measured. He arose, all six-foot-something of him, then fisted the throw rug to his groin. He turned, exposing his muscled buttocks, and looked over his shoulder at her. He shook his head and smirked as he watched her stuff the lining back into her purse and replace the spilled contents.

"I don't think it's funny at all," she huffed. "Get someone else to hold your damn open house."

He didn't say anything but continued staring down at her as he offered a hand, which she refused. She clamored to stand up, barefoot.

"And if you think this is a good way to meet a girl," she said as she wedged her bare feet into her heels, "well, I hope the bank takes your house and I hope your wife finds out what kind of sick games you play."

She headed to the door. She was relieved he was going to actually let her go. Without looking back, she swung the door wide open.

"This isn't my house, and I'm not married," she heard him call just before she slammed the door behind her, finally free at last.

CHAPTER 2

NAVY SEAL KYLE Lansdowne threw down the rag rug and stalked naked to the place where the woman's nametag landed next to the wall. He traced the letters again and examined the nametag's construction, looking for—*what?*

"Christy Nelson," he said as he focused on the indentations the letters made in the smooth white plastic tag. He had the funny feeling he'd met this woman before. Or maybe she reminded him of someone he'd known in his past.

He dropped his shoulders and arched backward to give his spine a good crack. Holding the light plastic badge in his fingertips, he was careful not to let it puncture him again. He leaned forward, aimed for the dining table, and tossed the nametag so it landed in one bounce at the center.

He checked the front window, confirming that the car he'd heard leaving was hers and that he was now alone. He locked the dead bolt on the front door and made his way back to the bedroom.

I'm losing it, man. He cursed himself for his carelessness. The naked meditation he engaged in usually heightened his senses, but this time he'd fallen asleep. Next thing he knew he was smelling her perfume. Still could smell it. Had she not been a woman, he could have hurt her, or worse. On the other hand, if she'd been hired to neutralize him, she could have taken him out in an instant.

His Team buddy, Armando Guzman, was missing. Gone. Never showed up at ProDev. He'd made it out of Afghanistan with the rest of SEAL Team 3, but instead of doing the five days decompression in Hawaii with the rest of the guys, he'd booked a flight to Puerto Rico for some family emergency.

Where the fuck are you?

Mysteriously, Armando met them at the airport in San Diego when they arrived from Hawaii, talking about seeing everyone at ProDev the next day. And then he didn't show. Timmons, their chief, was freaked, worried to hell. It just wasn't like Armando to do this. No way would he disappear voluntarily without alerting Kyle and the chief.

Day before yesterday, when Timmons told him Armando never checked in, Kyle thought perhaps he'd just found himself a lady to share a little time with, disappear for a day or two. Something they were trained to do: get lost. Wouldn't have been the first time Armando had gone to dark. And Kyle couldn't blame him. He'd done it a time or two himself, but never without checking in with his buddy first.

Something is very wrong.

Armando was known all over Coronado as the Latin Lover of SEAL Team 3. So good looking he could capture a girl's attention simply by walking down the street. His linguistic training allowed him to sound Aussie, French, Brit, Eastern European, Spanish, Pashtoon or Afghani. He could charm the pants off anyone on the phone as well as in person. He'd even been "captured" by a Marine unit who mistook him for a foreign interpreter trying to infiltrate the U.S. forces. Some of Team 3 still called him *"Tarjumah,"* the translator.

More than a couple of Senior Officers' wives, took long, dangerous looks at him when he wore his dress whites. He was the Antonio Banderas type of good looking, with a fashion sense and love of stylish clothes that made him look more like a cover model than a SEAL. The Team guys nicknamed him "Armani."

But when Timmons told Kyle his buddy never checked in before he left base, Kyle knew some serious shit had hit the fan. Nobody ever did that unless there was an attitude issue. Attitudes didn't last long on the Teams. Armando had a history from his youth, growing up with a Puerto Rican gang, but the Navy had pretty much drummed that out of him. Legendary for his nerves of steel, Armando could disarm a bomb while blowing bubbles with his bubblegum. Could save the whole team from extinction while thinking about what he would have for dinner that night.

So, Mr. Cool and Lethal wanted to be followed, and found. It was as obvious as if Armando had sent him a registered letter.

"What the hell are you up to, Armani?" Kyle whispered.

He'd spent days buried in sand with the man. They'd put their lives on the line for each other as well as for the rest of the team. Having spent three tours in Afghanistan and Iraq together, he and Armando had survived the battle of Fallujah when their unit reported record kills without losing many of their own. He could practically read Armando's mind. They'd been scared shitless together. They'd cried over a fallen Team guy and still had the presence of mind to jump in and save someone else the next minute. That kind of brotherhood couldn't be taught. It had to be *lived*.

Without Armando as his swim buddy, Kyle knew he never would have completed the grueling BUD/S training, the qualification all Navy SEALs had to pass in order to begin their real training. He owed his gold Trident, the insignia of a SEAL, to this man. Armando's problem, whatever it was, would now become Kyle's problem.

Armando swam like a fish with the explosive strength of a bull. He used to joke with the members of his unit how he could bring a cruise ship to port in his native Puerto Rico by holding the tie line with his teeth.

Kyle and a couple of other teammates had been granted ten days leave, and Kyle intended to spend every day of it searching for Armando. He knew deep in his soul that the guy would do the same for him. Kyle and his chief had a silent understanding. If he needed more time he would have to ask for it, and the request would be denied. If Kyle couldn't find Armando, no one could. But the Navy could hardly afford to have one missing SEAL; two missing men could get a commander stripped or booted.

His thoughts wandered to the girl.

The scent of her perfume lingered on his skin. He couldn't get the little hellcat out of his mind. No denying his body liked what Christy felt like under him; his erection had never fully settled down, even with the pain above his knee. His traitorous body part now started rising again, as if it had been summoned.

Damn. It had been too long since he'd held a woman that close. Was his training such that consorting with females ended up posing a danger to their health? He hated how he'd treated her. He shook his head, thinking of how the woman seemed to be one of those feisty, angry types who wouldn't allow herself to become a victim. This woman, a stealth survivor of the love wars, did a damn good job at self-defense.

Except she shouldn't have experienced this today. She was an innocent. She didn't deserve to be tied and treated like a suspect. The honor in Kyle's chest, the vow he made to protect the innocent even if it meant his own life, was wounded. He'd have to make it right somehow. He'd caused her the fright of her life, and he needed to make amends. Later.

But maybe she *was* somehow involved. Otherwise, why would she break into Armando's house? And why had she mentioned something about a bank and a wife?

Would Armando be losing his house? Kyle didn't think this was possible. Armando was frugal as all hell, even managing to send money home to parts of his family still in Puerto Rico. Kyle also doubted he would sell it.

Who is this Wayne guy? Does he know Armando?

Kyle stepped into the shower and washed the glorious smell of her off his skin, poring over the other questions in his mind.

Enough of that.

That kind of lapse in concentration could get a good squid killed. He needed to stay sharp, not distracted by the fantasy of a woman he barely knew. A woman who he didn't believe was involved in his friend's disappearance. He'd been trained to challenge other warriors, and if his time came, trained to take several bad guys with him. Not like this, mistreating an innocent.

He shut the water off and thought of his deep admiration for Armando. It made no sense that the man would just walk away from his country, his proud heritage, his family, and his SEAL community. Kyle doubted any one man would be able to take Armando down without a big fight, something so high profile it would alert one of their friendlies.

Even on leave, his team would email or text or run into several of their buddies every day. They hung out in the same bars owned by former members, got their tattoos at the same parlors, even picked the same beaches in San Diego to hang out on—away from the base, of course—but never far away from another Team member. The community was their family, and the blood in their veins pumped to protect it. They never even considered the cost.

So something very wrong happened, he thought as he dried off. A quick sniff to the towel told him a tiny amount of her perfume remained a scented shadow. Yeah, he'd wait a day or two before washing that towel. He hung it on the back of the door.

Staring at his image in the bathroom mirror, he didn't see the face of a killer. It was his warrior persona, his part of an exclusive brotherhood. Hesitation had been drummed out of him. Was he succumbing to fuzzy judgment of the female kind? Thank God he'd been able to accurately assess the danger she didn't pose to him before he'd caused her unintentional harm. Other than scaring the wits out of her, of course.

He decided to shave tomorrow. He straightened the bed, then threw on some mid-calf khakis and a green T-shirt. Today was a flip-flop-out-of-uniform kind of day, as it usually was whenever he was home. He had one pair of non-military dress shoes and they hurt his feet. His BUD/S trainers told him he'd develop webbed feet eventually, and although it was a big joke, it had a ring of truth to it.

He completed his dress by adding a sweatshirt hoodie, then took the dark wire-rimmed sunglasses from the pouch in his duty bag and smoothed them across his eyes.

As he left, he noted the two red sandwich signs leaning against Armando's front porch. Then he spotted the one in the front lawn, and added it to the other two, leaving all three of them there. He knew it would be a mistake to try to track her down.

Leave the poor woman alone. He hoped she would come by when he was gone.

Kyle hit the button on his key fob and his black Hummer squawked. It reminded him of a greeting a good horse would make. As if saying the machine was ready to do his master's bidding. He hardly washed the beast, and knew the salt air wasn't a friend, but he just couldn't bring himself to drive something clean and sanitized and smelling like hospitals, the one place he tried to avoid.

He'd parked across and down the street from Armando's house. He'd intended to bring the Hummer inside the garage after dark, erasing evidence he was there in case bad guys watched the house. He'd checked the garage when he'd first arrived. It smelled like it had been a couple of days since a gas-fired engine had turned over there. Armando's Land Rover was missing.

Not a good sign.

Kyle hopped into the Hummer and headed toward Coronado.

He came to the strip, one block off the beach, and passed familiar haunts, cruising past a couple of Team guys watching girls and drinking beer at an open-air cafe. He honked and was rewarded with two three-finger salutes, which he returned. His anxiety lessened somewhat by that quick check-in with fellow Team guys.

Up and down the strip he looked for Armando's Rover, but without any luck. He headed to Gunny's gym.

He liked the iron smell of rusty, well-used equipment that assaulted his nostrils the instant he pushed his way through the glass door and tinkled the bell. But he hated bells.

The DOR, or Drop On Request, bell they used during their BUD/S training didn't survive the class. He'd had his share of looking at that damned thing, tied to the back of a pickup truck that headed down the beach as some poor Team hopeful tried to catch it to end his torment and pain. There was no shame in quitting. Not everyone was cut out to do this job. Even at the beginning of Hell Week, the new class of recruits were one in ten thousand regular Navy guys who would gladly trade places with them for a shot at becoming a SEAL. But, the instructors didn't make it easy to drop out. DOR guys had to chase the damned thing a mile down the beach, catcalls being shouted at them from the back of the pickup, like these hopefuls were sissies.

Not a surprise to anyone that he and Armando had given that bell a really good deep-sea burial. Out of the 190 who started their class, they were part of the twelve who'd successfully graduated. That bell was homage to the 178 brave souls who'd given it a shot. God bless them for trying.

He and Armando worked out at Gunny's almost every day when they were home. The smell of sweat and the ancient equipment suited him just fine. No Nautilus stuff here, no digital anything except a scale that couldn't be rigged. The house rule reigned: when you finished with the dead weight, you had to throw it on the black rubber matted ground so it would bounce, not just place it carefully at your feet. That part he liked best about the place. And of course, he could always spot a Team or former Team guy there.

Gunny had been Marine Recon, a Gunnery Sergeant. He'd gone in just as troops were pulling out of Viet Nam, but saw a little combat at the tail end. He called himself a serial husband, and had a pack of ex-wives and kids littering the whole globe. Some of them didn't even speak English.

Everyone knew, including his ex-wives and their lawyers, that Gunny didn't have anything but his pension and this crusty, run-down gym that barely broke even. Gunny had told Kyle if any of his kids wanted to see him, they'd have to come to San Diego. There were no birthday or Christmas cards exchanged, and as far as Kyle knew, Gunny had never met any of his progeny, except one.

Gunny was known for rescuing Team guys at bars in the middle of the night if they were too drunk to drive. He'd get them home safe, keeping them from the local or military police looking to make a trophy bust. Gunny made sure no one got booted for a DUI or Acts

Unbecoming, and called the MPs and even regular police who were also ex-military "Rent-A-Cops." He held them with about as much respect as he had for security guards. Kyle guessed there would be some interesting reading if he ever got his hands on Gunny's personnel jacket.

Gunny was violating his own sign, a cigarette full of ash protruding out the right side of his mouth. But the gym was empty today.

"Thought you'd have quit by now. You got that scare last year, Gunny."

"Nah, I'm gonna burn it out." Gunny's grizzled gray chin stored a line of sweat in the deep crease under his lower lip.

"But you dodged the bullet, right?" Kyle knew the gym had closed for a week when Gunny went in for lung surgery. Later, Gunny had gotten a tattoo over the scar that read, *I Already Gave*, just in case anyone would have some crazy idea to harvest his lungs and heart upon his demise.

"What do you think, kid?" Gunny gave Kyle a wary look and continued. "Not one of us gets out of this tour alive."

So Kyle knew the rumor was true. They'd opened Gunny up and then put him back together again. No cure. That's why he'd never lost his hair. No further treatment. Team guys had been making bets on what Gunny would look like—maybe pink and hairless like a newborn, since his normal pelt made him resemble a grizzly. Kyle and Armando just figured Gunny's system was too ornery for the chemo to affect him.

"I'm not happy to hear this, Gunny."

"Hear what? I never told you nothing." Gunny grinned, showing his stained teeth, then removed the cigarette and put it out in the palm of his hand. He shook the ashes into a wastebasket by the entry glass display case filled with Gunny's Gym T-shirts bearing the picture of

Popeye holding up a barbell with an anchor tattoo prominent on his forearm.

"You don't look like you're here to work out," Gunny stated the obvious fact.

"No. I'm looking for Armando. You seen him last day or two?" Kyle watched the old man's eyes flash with alarm, and then the older man shook his head.

"Not a good sign," Gunny said as he looked at the floor. "What are you thinking?"

"He's never done this before. Timmons is freaked. Armando left the base without checking in with him." Kyle leaned toward the older man. "And I didn't tell you that, either."

"Got it."

The tinkling bell over the door broke the awkward silence. Two older ex-Team guys entered, carrying their well-worn workout bags. In their late forties, they still bore developed chest and arm muscles, maybe even more than the younger guys. Both of them sported graying ponytails and were covered in tattoos.

"Hey, guys," Gunny said, addressing them.

"Shit, Gunny, you've been smoking again," one of them said as he propped open the door. "All your brains go south on you?"

"There's a reason I have twelve kids and five ex-wives."

Kyle laughed inside at this comment. He knew Gunny well enough to know he married every one of those women before he had sex with them. This was a little known fact he and Armando had been privy to—hardened and tough Gunny was also a gentleman. He'd even married one in a jungle temple in Southeast Asia, the rites performed by a yellow-robed priest who'd painted both the bride and groom with symbols. Gunny told Kyle he couldn't wait and had consummated his marriage on the way back to the family celebration in the covered litter pulled by water buffalo, piloted by his new wife's brother. They had a hard time calming her mother down when she saw the disarray of their intricate face paintings, meant to ensure good luck, fertility, and great fortune.

The two men nodded at Kyle and went about selecting the equipment for their workout. Gunny motioned to the outside, so Kyle followed him through the entryway.

"So, what have you found out?"

"Timmons is tracking down Armando's cell signal. Said it would take a day, maybe two. But this is Sunday and Timmons has to wait until tomorrow to call it in."

"The waiting must be a sonofabitch."

"I don't do 'wait' very well." Kyle thought about the waiting they used to do, buried in sand, perched on rooftops. Waiting for the enemy to show up. Waiting to be told to get the hell out of there. But this was worse.

"Looks like he's trying to leave a trail of breadcrumbs. Not checking in with Timmins might be his first clue. I just don't know where to go from there. I'm missing something important."

"He didn't tell you anything?"

"I'm thinking about the last few times we were together. He got a lot of text messages, but I'm not sure from who," Kyle continued in a whisper, "Now that I think back on it, he didn't look too pleased when he got them."

"Can't get the cell location any sooner?"

Kyle's thoughts exactly. "Timmons says to wait until we have a location. Don't want to alarm the locals or ask them for help."

"Understood. Meantime, you're hoping he'll show up somewhere and it was all a false alarm."

"Exactly."

"Possible he got offed?"

"Nah. No fucking way. Not alone, anyway."

"He have a girl?"

"Between girls."

"Someone who pulled him back into the dark ages?"

Kyle recognized this as Gunny's way of dosing out a bit of his personal philosophy about not getting permanently involved with women. Gunny felt women were the biggest threat to a man's freedom and always told the men to steer clear, advice he seldom took himself. Kyle tended to agree with him.

"No. The only people outside the community who could pull him away like this would be someone from his family in Puerto Rico."

"Then you start with them." Gunny leveled a dead-serious stare. "Kyle, they don't know how many months I got. I never made it to your ranks, but I feel like a father to all you Team guys. If you want me, I'll help."

CHAPTER 3

CHRISTY STRADDLED THE line between fury and fear all the way back to her condo. She checked her rear view mirror every thirty seconds to make sure that cretin hadn't followed her home. Trying to remember evasion strategies she'd read in some of her favorite thriller novels, she'd doubled back, turned right, then drove for ten minutes in the opposite direction, finally headed for her place. She planned never to go back to that damned house or even the street again for the rest of her life. She'd just take that page and rip it from her Thomas Brothers Map Book. She would familiarize herself with all the other streets and buildings of San Diego County except for the ones on page 68.

Then she remembered she'd left all three of Wayne's red Patterson Realty signs back at the house.

"Damn!" Well, it served Wayne right. Christy wasn't entirely sure of Wayne's involvement in this afternoon's caper. *Let him go back and get those signs.* She chuckled at the thought of Wayne finding the naked crazy guy at the front door. Now that would be a sight she would go back to see.

She drove into her condo garage, double-checking dark corners of the structure for evidence of someone lurking there. She'd never worried about this before.

All kinds of possibilities and scenarios ran through her mind as she rode the elevator to her floor. Perhaps Wayne wasn't who she thought he was. Could there be a jealous husband or jilted lover from one of the affairs Christy imagined he'd had?

Wayne must have been the real target, she thought. After all, the worst thing she had done was help some guy max out his credit card at Madame M's lingerie shop. She was the shop's best saleswoman. Last she checked, this wasn't a crime.

Once inside, she put the whole afternoon's incident out of her mind by stripping her clothes and donning her workout gear, and then she headed for the upscale gym on the top floor of her condo complex.

Every area of the complex had a terrific view of San Diego Harbor. A few minutes into her spin class, her body was covered in glistening sweat as she worked out to her iPod playing her favorite *Secret Garden* piece. The beauty of the poignant viola speared her heart. Tears streamed down her cheeks.

Damn, I'm lonely.

All her relationships with men ended badly. And the guy she'd just met had some sort of sick death wish for her. She barely knew him, well, except for how nicely he fit between her legs. Though she tried, she couldn't get that image out of her head. Why were all these weird men coming into her life now, just when she wanted to embark on a professional career?

"You okay, Christy?" Marla, her personal trainer, touched her arm.

Christy realized the class had stopped for a water break. She looked up and saw the concern in Marla's eyes. Christy buried her face in the white towel around her neck. "No. I'm not alright," she said, her voice muffled through the towel so Marla couldn't hear the waver there. Memories flooded in—how she'd tried to scream and how that big hand had covered her mouth, how she'd felt with him pressed down onto her body, and how she'd reacted to those damn blue eyes that seemed to drink in her face. She could easily mistake it for attraction. What was going on?

"Aw, honey." Marla wrapped her arms around Christy's waist. "Take a break. Come on, let's go into my office for a bit."

Christy nodded and let Marla lead her into a private office off the spin room. Marla motioned to a chair in front of her desk, and Christy collapsed there, continuing to wipe her face and neck with the towel. Marla punched the phone and spoke softly.

"Marla here. Hey, can Trey finish my spin class for me? Something's come up." Marla locked eyes on Christy.

"I'm fine. Don't do this, Marla," Christy whispered.

"Okay? Good. Tell him I owe him one." Marla hung up the phone. "Not a problem. Happens all the time." She pulled her desk chair over and held Christy's hands in both of hers. "Come on, spill it. Don't make me dig."

"Today was supposed to be my first open house."

"Yup, you were excited about it."

"Yes, I was…until I got there…" Tears welled up in her eyes and her lower lip quivered.

"Christy, what happened?"

"There was this crazy guy there who was asleep in the master bedroom, stark naked."

"Did he touch you?"

"Yes…" Christy's chest was heaving and she found it difficult to breathe.

"The creep. Did he hurt you?"

Did he hurt me? "He scared me, that's all."

"You call the cops?"

"No. I mean, he thought I was breaking into his house. I couldn't call the cops. Maybe Wayne set it up…I'm just not sure what happened."

"Who's Wayne?"

"The agent whose listing it is."

"Tell me honestly, Christy. Were you hurt?"

"He ripped off my pantyhose and messed with my purse, but no, I'm not hurt."

"Jeez, Christy. What do you mean messed with your purse? Screw the purse. He scared you to death!"

The two women looked at each other. Christy's composure was coming back, but Marla seemed to be losing hers.

"I know. He could have killed me, but he didn't."

"Exactly. And you're giving him a pass for acting like a Neanderthal? Why would he rip off your pantyhose?"

"He used them to tie my hands together."

"Oh, this just keeps getting better and better. That's assault, Christy. That man should go to jail."

"Yes, I understand, and under normal circumstances, I would agree. But somehow I got that this guy was simply reacting to what he thought was a threat. Maybe he's not right in the head. I don't want to have anything more to do with him. I just want to stay away. He let me go and he didn't really hurt me, just scared me is all. I don't know, but I somehow don't feel it's entirely his fault." She looked up at Marla. "Does that sound crazy?"

"Absolutely. You're not thinking straight at all, Christy."

"He secured my wrists to keep me quiet…so he could talk to me."

"That sick bastard."

"No. I mean I was pretty hysterical and I did bite him and even spiked his knee with my high heel. I fought as hard as I could, Marla. He attempted to get information out of me, like he thought I was some sort of undercover agent or something, like I was there to do him harm. His mind had it all screwed up."

Marla nodded.

"Are there lots of paranoid whackos like this in San Diego?"

"Not generally. But then, I don't seem to attract them like you do."

"Thanks a lot."

Marla rubbed her hands with her thumbs. "How did you get hired to hold this open house?"

"Wayne." Christy winced as she forced herself to say the name again. "He told me they were expecting me. I don't want to think he purposely set me up, but you know, I can't figure it out otherwise."

"What can I do to help?" Marla's sincere voice soothed.

Christy stood up and gave her a hug. "Thanks, Marla. You already have." At the door, she turned. "I'm going to report this to my manager tomorrow as soon as I get into the office. If I felt I was in danger now, I would call the police."

Marla shook her head. "I'd say call them just in case, Christy. Don't be a wimp. That's how come these creeps stay out there. Nobody turns them in."

"I'll do it tomorrow, I promise. Tonight, I'm going to take a hot bath and go to bed early. Thanks again, Marla."

Marla handed her a business card with her home and cell number on it. "Call me tonight if you need company. Honest. If you have trouble sleeping, that's a gut check that you need to call the cops, okay?"

THE WARM BUBBLES in Christy's bath sluiced all the tension from her muscles and bones. But every time her eyelids closed and she began drifting off to sleep, she saw those blue eyes staring down at her, his full lips, slightly upturned at the edges, and his swallow that had forced her attention to wander down his tanned neck and rest just under his stubbled chin. She could smell the muskiness of this man's heaving chest as he arched over her while she peeked at the trail of light brown hair that led downward to the place where their bodies touched. When he'd whispered in her ear, asking who she was, he had pressed his cheek next to hers. She'd had to endure his scent all the way home in the car. There was a part of her that wanted to reach up and—do what? Kiss him?

Get a grip!

After the bath, she went to bed with a big glass of warm milk, taking her favorite romance novel with her. The bath had done its job and she fell asleep, waking up at midnight to turn off her reading light.

She lay back again, deciding to put up with the fear while she studied him in her memory—every inch of him, and fell asleep for the second time.

MR. SIMMS CAME in early, so Christy made sure to arrive first, just a little before eight o'clock. She knew no one else except the office staff would likely come in until well past ten.

"Good morning, Christy," he said as he passed by her cubicle. "Nice to see you here bright and early. That's a good sign." He appeared in a chipper mood and Christy didn't pick up any indication he was somehow involved in the fiasco the day before.

Good. I'll just tell him, then.

"Mr. Simms, I have something to speak with you about. It's urgent."

"Oh? Something happen?"

"Yes." Christy was surprised at her forcefulness.

"Okay, come on in." He indicated she should follow him to his office. Once inside, he closed the glass sliding door behind her.

Christy took up a chair in front of the red cherrywood desk. Plaques from various agencies, awards from the Board of Realtors, as well as several service groups, including Rotary, decorated the walls. An impressive collection, Christy had to admit, not quite sure why she hadn't noticed them before.

"Shoot." He waited without expression on his face, hands folded over the calendar desk blotter. On the back credenza sat a picture of a woman, two children, and a black Labrador retriever. A family like she'd always wanted.

"I went to do the open house on Sedgeway yesterday for Wayne. You know, his new listing?"

"Oh, that's a great one. Bank sale, right?"

"Um, yes. Short sale."

"So what happened?"

"Well, I got attacked."

Mr. Simms fell back in his chair and almost toppled over. He righted himself and let out a big sigh. "Did he...did he...hurt you?"

"Yes and no."

"Meaning?"

"He didn't rape me, but he, he..." Christy's eyes stung in reflex, trying to create tears that would no longer come. Her lower lip trembled. Her throat was parched.

Mr. Simms was quick to make it around his desk. He knelt in front of Christy and placed his hands on her upper arms with care, as if he didn't want to appear inappropriate. "I'm so sorry, Christy. Have you been to the police?" he asked, his demeanor genuine and tender. She appreciated that.

"No."

"Why?" He rubbed her arms gently and then took her hands in his. His moist, warm hands were a comfort to her. "We *have* to report this. You know that," he said softly. "Could you identify him?"

Oh yes, I could. I can't get the look and smell of him out of my mind.

"Mr. Simms, I'm thinking there was some sort of a mistake. Maybe even a prank. I don't want to blame Wayne, but this guy was like, waiting for me. He was…he was…naked."

Simms removed his hands from her arms and stood up, shaking his head.

"Bastard. Did he say he knew Wayne?"

Christy could tell Simms was considering Wayne's involvement, which further underscored some of her own hesitation to be anywhere near the man.

"No, he didn't. In fact, the guy acted like he'd never heard of Wayne."

The appearance of a very angry Wayne, puffed up and red, tore apart their conversation. He pulled open the sliding glass door without being given the nod of approval from Simms, and wedged himself into the room, making it feel suddenly very stuffy.

"What the hell happened, Christy? My clients called me, and they're so mad they want to cancel the listing." His tiny bloodshot eyes darted back and forth between Christy and their manager.

"Wait a minute, Wayne." Simms put a palm on Wayne's sausage-shaped chest, holding him back from coming any closer to her. "Christy here was just explaining what went on yesterday, and I have to say, I find it highly disturbing."

"Disturbing? Disturbing? I'll tell you what's disturbing!" Wayne said, looking like he wanted to crash through Simms and grab Christy himself.

Great! Another man wants to attack me.

"I work damned hard to get a good listing, then try to take my wife and kids to the zoo—just try to take one Sunday off to be with them the way I never do—and I drive by the house on our way home and, voila, no open house signs. No sign of Christy anywhere. Then I get home and I get this irate message on my answering machine telling me I'm fired."

"Wayne, you sack of shit." Christy's own surprise wasn't half of what got reflected on Wayne's and Mr. Simms' faces. One of the office staff came running to check the ruckus so Christy toned down her voice. "I was going to hold it open, but there was this naked crazy guy who came after me and...and..."

"What?" Wayne looked genuinely shocked.

Simms interrupted. "Apparently, Christy was attacked, Wayne. That's what she was trying to tell you."

"No way."

Christy hated the man now. Genuinely hated him. His sense of morals, his scheming, his lack of sensitivity to her and what she was going through, and the way he'd pushed his oversized body into Mr. Simms's office. Anger boiled in her stomach. Christy had reached her limit.

"I'm not putting up with this. I quit. No way can I work in the same office with this...this...idiot." She pointed to Wayne, wanting to say something nastier but thinking better of it.

Christy tore around her manager and sneered at Wayne as she pushed him with one hand, which sent him careening against a bookshelf with a loud crash. Christy saw the ruckus had attracted every staffer in the area. Simms bolted past Wayne, who tried to right himself, still thrashing in a nest of books and files.

"Christy," Wayne called after her. "Christy, wait a minute. This is all wrong."

She turned and glared at him. "That's the first truthful thing I've heard all morning."

She dug in her heels and whirled around to exit, then ran straight into the chest of one very solid wall of man, holding a bouquet of flowers in one hand and three red open house signs in the other.

CHAPTER 4

"**Y**OU!" CHRISTY SAID, suddenly aware of the understatement. His blue eyes melted her bones. She needed air and pushed against him to step back a safe distance, if that was possible.

She wondered if he felt the electric ripple that traveled with lightning speed all over her skin's surface.

Probably not.

His face had that soft smirk, and he held his head at an angle. He looked more uncomfortable holding the flowers than the three metal open house signs.

"I came to apologize for the misunderstanding," his deep voice, cracking just a little, was dripped in honey and ensnared her as if he'd tied her up with pantyhose again. She shivered at the very thought that this might be something she could look forward to.

"Good. Saves me the trouble of calling the police." As soon as she'd said it, she wondered why. Calling the police was not what she was really thinking.

"That won't be necessary. Just hear me out first, and if you still want to call them, I won't be able to object. It's your right. But I'm sorry about..."

"This him?" Simms immediately stepped next to Christy, and, after sizing up the physique and bearing of the stranger, pegged him.

"Navy, right?"

"Yes, sir."

Wayne appeared at the end of the hallway, but his ego had turned to pudding. He hovered in the shadow, half protected by a wall.

Simms continued. "I'm Carl Simms, the manager here. Ms. Nelson was just telling me how you terrorized her yesterday. Scared this nice young lady to death. I've advised her to call the police, and if she doesn't, *I* will." Simms delivered this with determination, but Christy noted he stayed a healthy two steps away from the large Navy man.

The visitor had been looking at Simms, but in the silence that followed, his blue gaze turned back on Christy, as if to beg for time alone with her. And damn, she was going to give it to him too. There was something there she needed to find out about. She had too many questions about the day before to be consistently angry. And how could she, when he looked at her like that?

"Why don't we go to the conference room and discuss this?" Christy offered softly.

"That sounds fair to me," the stranger replied. He didn't take his eyes off Christy when he added, "Simms, you can join us if you like."

"Christy?" Simms asked.

"I think I'll be okay. Thanks."

"Can someone take these please?" the man said, holding up the heavy metal signs like they were a carton of Chinese food.

"Those are mine." Wayne darted from the shadows and grabbed them away without looking at the stranger. The signs clattered and he almost dropped them.

"I'm guessing you must be Wayne."

Wayne shot him a murderous look, then adjusted his bravado and walked away, carrying the signs awkwardly in both hands. He was swearing under his breath, his sport coat stretching across his shoulders and his knees bumping the metal signs as he lumbered off.

Christy drew back the sliding door to the conference room as the stranger passed by too close. A fresh soap scent made her eyes flutter and her nose itch. He found a spot at the head of the table facing out to the reception area and remained standing until Christy slid the door closed. When she took the chair at his left, he sat in tandem with her.

He pushed the flowers in her direction across the laminate tabletop. She noticed again the tattoo of footprints from some unknown three-toed creature that traversed up his forearm.

"These are yours. Once again, I am very sorry." His voice, raspy and soft, drew her complete attention. His large hand squeezed the plastic outer wrap with a delicious crunch. The package displayed a colorful spring gathering of daffodils, stock, and baby green chrysanthemums. A few sprigs of lavender had been added for garnish. The glorious smell of the bouquet filled the room. The flowers had obviously been hand selected and the bouquet freshly made. She noticed things like that. Some of her past boyfriends hadn't even bothered to take the price tags off the supermarket bunches. This bouquet probably set him back a good twenty dollars.

A whole lot cheaper than bail. Some of her anger returned, but she gave him a curt thank you.

He pulled his hand back and leaned against the table. He took a deep breath, and then exhaled as he began his story. "My name is Kyle Lansdowne. I am in the Navy. I'm looking for my Navy buddy and best friend, who is missing."

"Okay."

"The house…where we…met…belongs to my friend, Armando. I'd begun to look for him and thought I would start there."

"Naked?"

"Well." Kyle suppressed a grin and nodded his head. "I under-stand this may not make sense, but I actually meditate like that all the time. I didn't expect company." He flashed those blue eyes up at her again.

"Obviously."

"Look, I'm sorry, but I'm really not a weirdo."

Christy knew she had to break eye contact or she would never get through this. She rubbed her temples and closed her eyes.

Mr. Simms popped his head into the conference room. "Every-thing all right?"

Christy realized how weary she must have looked from her night of tossing in her sleep. The stress of the last twenty-four hours had gotten to her. She could barely hold it together.

"It's okay," she said to Simms.

Simms nodded, staring back at Kyle, but leaving them alone again as he closed the door. Kyle rubbed his palm where her teeth marks remained clearly evident. When he noticed her looking at them, he stopped and buried his hands under the table.

"So why the questions about all this covert stuff? The tying me up with my pantyhose? What was that all about?"

"Again, please let me apologize. I thought maybe you were in-volved with Armando's disappearance."

"Me?"

Kyle rolled his shoulders. "I just assumed you might be one of the bad guys."

"You think I look like a bad guy?"

"Of course not. I see that now."

Christy glared at him. She decided he was telling the truth so she backed down. "Well, I still don't see what the big deal is. Maybe your friend went out on a bender—it happens, you know."

"Not to us."

"I'm *sorry*?"

"We're SEALs."

"Oh."

"And we never disappear without someone else from the SEAL community knowing about it. We're trained to disappear, but that's not how this happened. Something's wrong."

"Sounds a little over the top. Don't you guys have a life?"

"That's exactly what we've got."

Christy watched Kyle survey the top of the conference table, his eyes sweeping up to the flowers laying flat against the Formica surface.

"Staying alive is the goal," he said.

Christy didn't know what else to say.

"Well, I've taken enough…" He started to rise.

"No. Wait a minute. That was unkind of me."

Kyle shrugged, and then sat back down. He looked at his lap.

"What can I do to help?" she asked.

Kyle folded his hands neatly in front of him and a crooked smile angled up to the left, causing a dimple. "Nothing you can do. I'm here because you never should have been involved in the first place and I wanted to personally apologize for my behavior."

Some of the pieces started to connect. She rolled her neck back and forth and felt some of the tension leave.

"Did I injure you? I tried not to." His eyes were steady as he raised his brows, forming crease lines on his forehead. "You hurt anywhere?"

Good question. "No. I'm fine." She didn't understand why he chuckled at this and nodded his head twice.

"You're a very strong young lady."

"I've been told that a time or two."

"I can imagine." He scanned her face like he had yesterday when they were on the floor. She could tell he wanted to look at her farther down, but held himself in check. She liked that about him.

He looked to the side as if thinking about something before he spoke again. "I would like to make it up to you, if you'll let me." He turned on the blue-eyed charm again and smiled. "Give me a chance for you to see my decent side, not my animal side."

She was thinking about his animal side. Did he know?

"Well, I don't normally bite people when I first meet them, either." She found it in herself to smile and enjoyed that he returned her smile, focusing on her lips.

An awkward silence followed, but she determined not to break it. His move and how he played it would indicate if she would trust him.

"Maybe I could buy you lunch sometime. Tomorrow?"

She'd been hoping for dinner but knew lunch was the right answer. "That would be fine." She wanted to say "nice" but was pleased she made the last-minute word substitution. No denying her attraction to this man, but it would be dangerous to let him see it.

"Okay, then. Can I pick you up here tomorrow at, say, noon?"

"If I still have my job."

"What do you mean?" he asked.

"I technically quit," she whispered, peering down at her hands. "I thought Wayne did this."

"And so now you know. It was my fault. Entirely."

"Yes, I see that now. Okay, I'll see you here tomorrow."

They stood as she gathered up the flowers, burying her nose in them, inhaling the delicious scent. He caught her little lapse in judgment and smiled.

"I thought you'd like them. They look like you."

CHRISTY DIDN'T REMEMBER when or how she said good-bye. She'd been numbed by his words...*they look like you.* For the rest of the day she operated out of the comfortable cocoon that warm numbness created, that shielded her from ordinary life.

She didn't completely trust or believe Kyle, but looked forward to tomorrow with eagerness she hadn't known in years.

KYLE'S FIRST STRING of second thoughts rushed in before he got into his Hummer. He stopped halfway there, almost turning back to call the whole thing off.

You've got no business doing this. You are one messed up sailor if you think someone like her is fair game.

He wondered why in the world he'd asked her out for lunch. Well, being honest, he knew why. She reminded him of someone from his past.

He couldn't stop thinking about her and the way her eyes held him courageously, staring at the possibility of her own death. She didn't beg—a true fighter.

Just like me.

That kind of a person deserved an apology, and more. Her defiance in the face of mortal danger reached in and grabbed him. She commanded respect. Sure, he was marking time, waiting for Timmons to get the information on Armando's cell phone, but something else was going on, and he couldn't quite identify it. Or, maybe he didn't want to.

He continued telling himself that buying her lunch was the right thing to do, his way of an apology. After all, he'd terrorized her, a civilian, an innocent—something he never thought he was capable of. He was half-surprised she'd said yes.

Hanging around a woman like Christy was dangerous. Would it set things in motion Kyle knew were better off buried? It was difficult enough dealing with Armando's disappearance. Did he need this complication as well?

Despite what he tried to suppress, he realized she enchanted him. There was something about her fiery attitude and that leveling gaze that made his heart drop to his knees. He couldn't wait for tomorrow.

CHAPTER 5

KYLE CHECKED IN with his chief, but was disappointed to hear from Timmons that finding Armando's cell phone location would take at least another day. He bought a sandwich and went out to look at the boats berthed at the wharf. He liked studying the expensive toys of the privileged—no trace of anything military. Being at the water's edge always calmed him, helped him think. It was either watch boats or practice meditation again, but since the last practice hadn't turned out so well, he was reluctant to try again.

He shook his head. *What were the odds his meditation would have drawn such an audience?*

He watched a man and a boy, who was probably the man's young son, coming down the wooden pier. The boy looked about six, skipping along, holding hands and trying to keep up with the man, who rolled a small ice chest down the planks with a bumpity-bump. At one point the boy tripped, getting the front rubber bumper of his tennis shoes caught between a gap in the wood. Before he could skid and get a splintered scrape to his knees, the man hauled him up to safety. The boy squealed with a giggle and then kept up his incessant chatter as they made their way down the dock.

This wasn't anything that happened in Kyle's life. There were no picnics down by the harbor, no father-son outings, no camping trips.

Happy afternoons fishing with his father had never happened as he was growing up. He got other things that made him strong and hard: a leather belt on his rear or the back of his dad's hand. It wasn't until he'd joined his SEAL team that he learned about the meaning of family.

He'd called for a meeting with two other members of Charlie Team, along with Gunny. They agreed to gather early at the Rusty Scupper, which meant the place would be nearly deserted. There were only two reasons the community came into this favorite Team hangout. If a group of Team guys sat out front at one of the tables, tilted on indestructible chairs, they were passing time, watching the meat parade meandering down the sidewalk.

Even high schoolers, totally off limits, of course, but hotties nonetheless, were only too willing to tease them. The skirts got shorter, and the shorts showed everything. Skimpy clothes were worn so tight a guy could tell if they wore panties, thongs, or nothing. Tops were becoming practically nonexistent. Girls wore kids sizes, too, so a firm three- to four-inch swath of tanned skin without a single stretch mark bounced deliciously around pierced belly buttons. Just a hint of a tattoo poking up from underneath sometimes, or perhaps a little black lace. It was distracting for sure, if a guy looked for that sort of thing.

The other reason to go to the Scupper was to plan something without prying eyes. The Scupper's dark corner at the back of the bar was perfect for such a meeting. That's where Kyle sat, waiting for his guys to show up, watching the bubbles traveling up the side of his glass of beer.

His apprehension about Armando grew the more he considered all the clues or, rather, lack of them. He also worried about being too late. He faced the reality that in waiting too long for their only clue, the location of the cell signal, he might have put Armando in further danger. Perhaps grave danger.

Nah. Not Armando. Guy is a fuckin' warrior machine.

Kyle had never had an unsuccessful mission. This wasn't going to be his first. Not today. Not this week. He hoped to God never.

Help me out here, buddy. Give me another sign. Don't try to do this alone, Armando. Kyle knew the missing SEAL would find a way to steer him in the right direction. And he knew Armando still lived. He could feel it in his bones.

Cooper walked into the bar first, followed by his ever-present sidekick, Fredo. Coop, a farm boy from Nebraska, had graduated as the tallest SEAL at over 6'4". He still looked like he walked around in his overalls, had a loping gait, and needed to duck under every door-way in his path. Raised nowhere near the ocean, Cooper still swam second fastest on the Team. Second to Armando. Coop had spent the summer before Indoc learning. Had hired a former Olympic coach who told him he might have a shot at a medal if he washed out of BUD/S.

Fredo, short and built like a soccer player, which was how he'd spent his youth in LA, took two steps for every one of Cooper's strides, but beat the giant and almost everyone else at timed runs, either long or short. Best wrestler on the Team also went to Fredo. And he liked to cheat, touching a guy someplace he didn't want to be touched, causing a serious lack of focus and getting the resulting quick take down.

The unlikely pair of friends hunkered down across the table from Kyle. They were served a couple of beers by the new girl with the nice hands. Cooper ordered mineral water with lots of ice and lime. He told Kyle he'd leave his for Gunny. At last Gunny showed up, red-faced, as if he'd been on a bender. He arrived a full fifteen minutes late, and Kyle suspected he'd jogged to make up time, but didn't have the lung capacity for much of a run.

"Sorry, gents. Got caught up at the gym with a late arrival," Gunny said as he pointed to a beer.

"Got your name on it, Sarge," Cooper said.

Gunny downed half of it quickly. Too quickly, Kyle thought. Gunny must be in some pain and had decided to douse it. He noted Gunny might not be much help on this mercy mission.

"Armando's gone missing."

"Fuck me. When?" Fredo asked.

"Friday night, maybe Saturday." Kyle watched as his words sank in.

"You're just now fuckin' telling us?" Fredo's brow contorted. Prune face, Kyle had said on more than one occasion. But a good question, and one that deserved an answer.

"I wasn't sure. Thought maybe he was having a little honeymoon, without the ring and the preacher."

Everyone laughed.

"That would be Armani." Coop chuckled.

"Timmons asked me to look into it."

"You try calling him?" Fredo asked. Everyone immediately turned and growled at the Mexican-American SEAL, who shrugged his shoulders and added, "I'm just sayin'."

"Timmons is waiting for the cell tracking." Kyle looked at Coop, who had gone alert.

Coop answered. "I definitely can help you there."

Kyle knew Cooper had done a rotation at the CIA and had some friends there.

"I got his number right here."

Kyle handed Armando's number over to Coop on a white piece of paper. "No strings. Invisible."

"Of course." Cooper frowned. "Probably get it later tonight. I'm gonna make the call now."

"Thanks." Kyle watched as the giant SEAL unfolded from the table, stood, and went outside to make the call. Cooper's huge frame completely blocked sunlight from coming through the doorway of the Scupper.

Two young ladies sauntered past Coop, and they must have looked back at the handsome farm boy because Cooper waved, wiggling his fingers and grinning, with the cell phone clutched to his ear.

"What's the plan, boss?" Fredo wanted to know.

"First we get the location, and then we get Armando out. Just like the snatch and grabs we did overseas."

"Sounds cool," said Fredo.

"Got nothin' else to do," said Gunny.

Coop came back. "Take a few hours at the most. My friend in DC will have the coordinates on Armani's cell—if it's still on." He gulped down his water, crushing ice with his molars. "So I suppose now we hurry up and wait?" He dumped a lopsided grin on Kyle.

"Exactly. We've got our team. We go when we get the location. Not a breath to anyone but Timmons. No other Team guys, you got it?"

They nodded in agreement.

"And you get some rest. Not sure what's in store, but we gotta be alert and strong and ready to go. Get your gear in order in case we need it. I'll check back with you boys tomorrow sometime after noon. But be ready to take off as soon as I call."

He watched them leave behind their unfinished drinks. He hoped his call to action wouldn't cost them their careers—or their lives.

CHAPTER 6

CHRISTY KNEW SIMMS wasn't expecting her early, so she slept in. She shaved, oiled her skin after her steamy shower, blow-dried her blond hair, and then curled it in ringlets, extra fluffy.

She pulled out her special Lady Parisienne bra with the skin-like padding and silky butterfly stitching. Madame M gave her the delicate garment as a gift when Christy made that thousand-dollar sale to the San Francisco mayor who bought lingerie for his new girlfriend. He had been one of the shop's regular customers. The mayor liked his girls extra full on top, so Madame M always had a fully stocked DD section with nothing but the most expensive lingerie.

She leaned forward and lifted the soft pillows of her breasts into the creamy cups, leaving just enough cleavage to distract the average male. But Kyle wasn't an average male. She doubted he'd ever seen a woman in a three-hundred-dollar bra. That part about men she could read like a school primer. Her trouble happened with the after-the-first-date-thing. She decided not to fall too quickly for him, even though she already had, and he hadn't done anything but tie her up on the floor with her hands above her head, lay across her body with his package between her legs, covering her chest with his muscled torso, and spread her legs with the strong muscles of his thighs. And then he gave her flowers and asked for a lunch date.

Pretty unbeatable combination.

Her sex quivered in anticipation as she slipped the satin and lace matching panties over her hips and centered the small frilly triangle in front. She applied her makeup with patience and skill, thinking about kissing him, wondering what the feel of his tongue would be like opening her lips and plunging in to play with hers. She imagined what those strong hands could do around her waist, then sliding down the front of her abdomen into her panties.

She sprayed perfume in the air and walked through it, coating her flesh with scent. She was a lethal combination of female determination and need. She would make him pay for yesterday's transgression. She'd make him beg, and then she'd decide what to do next. Logic told her she should hold out and not let him touch her. But her heart and her body craved the caress of the man with three-toed footprints running up his muscled arm.

After she finished dressing, she drove her Honda into the office parking lot. Sounds of sea birds and a foghorn in the distance reminded her the ocean was not far. It never got hot in San Diego. The moist late morning air caressed her cheeks. She turned and found him leaning against a shiny black Hummer, legs crossed at the ankles, arms crossed as well. He'd been watching her get out of the car. She hoped she'd been graceful.

A slight smile lit up his face. She tweeted her car closed, slung her purse over her right shoulder, and walked straight for him without taking her eyes from his. He made no apology for watching every moving body part she had, including her mouth, when she stopped in front of him and licked her lips.

So far so good.

Something registered on his face. A loneliness and hunger resided inside his vacant eyes, something dead and now coming back to life.

He appeared so confident, so well trained and measured. Probably he'd learned to cut off his soft side from his survival side.

She had a sudden urge to soften him.

Where did that come from?

"I wasn't sure you'd come," he said. One eye twitched. His long dark lashes, thick and shiny, outlined the blue gaze he leveled at her. It almost made her faint. Her ears buzzed and her stomach lurched.

"I promised you lunch," she answered. "I keep my promises. Always."

"So do I."

His masculine cologne wafted toward her. Erotic goose bumps slipped down the front of her blouse like cool fingers touching her white flesh. She felt naked and blushed, looking down.

His chest heaved and then stilled. Had he caught himself reacting to her blush?

A man of control.

She read all the little signs of a man's arousal. Even without dwelling on the considerable tent in his pants, she knew she turned him on by her fragrance and appearance.

And she loved it.

He assembled all six-foot something of himself and walked around to the passenger side of the Hummer, then opened the door. She bent her left knee, gripping the chrome handle on the doorframe for the high step. He stopped her with a hand to her shoulder.

"Here, let's use this." He retrieved a white plastic stepstool no larger than a shoebox, bent down, and placed it on the pavement at her feet. He uncoiled his muscled frame less than four inches in front of her and just as slowly let his eyes wander over her body, from her knees all the way up to her chest.

"Better?" he asked with a hint of a smile.

Her knees wobbled, knocking against each other. "Much," she said as she leaned in, almost brushing against his chest, close enough to feel the heat from his body. She was careful not to make contact, though her insides argued with her willpower.

She step-mounted into the front seat of the vehicle. The black leather groaned. His scent filled the air. Smiling, he handed her the seatbelt, tossed the step into the rear, and slammed the door. Something told her life was about to change—for the good.

Strap in and get ready.

They didn't talk as he drove down toward the wharf. She focused on the Celtic ring tattoo that peeked below the right sleeve of his T-shirt. Staring at the tattoo helped with the not-wanting-to-look-at-his-chest-neck-and-Adam's-apple stuff. And it definitely helped her not focus on his lips.

Does he know I'm sneaking little looks?

Maybe he was used to it. Maybe he liked it. Maybe he didn't notice. In any case, he never looked back at her.

They walked into a tiny sandwich shop by the water. Holding out her chair, he stood guard as she seated herself, then he leaned against her back and put a palm on her shoulder as she settled in. On his way to take up position across the table from her, Kyle waved at a couple sitting on the opposite side of the room. The other guy sported a series of ringed tattoos on his forearm, too.

Clean place but not fancy, she observed. The menu specialized in seafood sandwiches and soft shell tacos.

"The turkey chili is what they're known for, even though this is a seafood place," Kyle said over the top of the paper menu. "But you'd probably like the crab salad sandwich." His blue eyes flashed on her and a ripple of energy traveled all the way down her spine. He showed perfect white teeth beneath slanted, full lips, which ended with a curl at one side she found so distracting. He had to be fully aware he was turning on the charm. *The Blue Charm.*

"I've heard about this spot," Christy said. "A few of the Realtors in my office come here for dinner and drinks after work."

"Only if they're single. This place is a real meat market at night," he replied.

"Well, that never seemed to stop some." She fanned herself with the menu as she looked out over the bay.

Kyle chuckled. "I've never seen Wayne here, not that I would notice. But then, this is a pretty young crowd."

"Hmm. Exactly. No, this wouldn't be his kind of place."

"So, you're single then, Christy?" He glanced at his water glass.

"Very much so. And enjoying every minute of it." She'd rehearsed this line in the shower a dozen times just in case it came up. But as she watched him raise his eyes, it sounded ridiculous, but still earned her a smile from his tanned face.

"I catch your drift. I'm the same." He'd turned serious. Honest. Totally kissable.

Their waiter came over and gripped Kyle's outstretched palm like they'd probably done hundreds of times. "You're back, and you don't even smell like a camel."

"Goat. No camels. Goats."

The two men laughed.

"Christy, this is Griz. Griz, Christy. I'm going to taste-test all your food now that I know he's on."

"Bro, I got your back. You've done enough defending the ladies for a while. Time for some R and R." Griz nodded in Christy's direction.

The crab sandwich tasted better than any she'd eaten, but she could only take a few bites. Her anticipation of this meeting completely eliminated her appetite.

The couple from across the way dropped by their table and Kyle introduced them. Without Kyle telling her, she knew the man was another Team guy.

"You seen Armando anywhere?" Kyle asked, adding a quick shrug. The eye contact seemed urgent between the two men, despite what Christy saw as Kyle's attempt to be casual.

"Nope. You try LuLu's?" The Team guy gave Christy a wink, but she could tell all was not well.

"Stopped by yesterday, but they hadn't seen him either."

"Well, look, if I catch sight of his sorry ass, I'll tell him his lover needs to get a call from him, 'kay?" the Team guy said, walking backward, holding the girl's hand. "Nice to meet you." He waved at Christy.

"Later." Kyle waved back.

"So your friend is still missing?" Christy asked.

"Yep. Probably holed up somewhere. When we don't want to be found, nobody can find us."

"But you're worried," she insisted.

"He never checked in with me before he left. We always do that. We talk to each other every day."

"*Every* day?"

Kyle lowered his head. She could see remnants of a grin he didn't want to show her. "Yep. Every day. We're practically married."

Christy's cheeks heated. This was totally unexpected.

Kyle looked up. "Hey! Don't worry," he said. "I only go for the ladies. Please don't get me wrong."

"Sorry. Seems like all the best looking guys are gay…"

"Then I'll take that as a compliment."

His perfect grin made her glad she was sitting down.

She watched him take the final bite of his chili, tipping the bowl to get the last drop into his spoon. She couldn't keep her eyes off him or anything that he did. He must have noticed how she watched him. He took a long time to dab his mouth with the white paper napkin, his eyes averted. He licked his lips and swallowed. She followed his Adam's apple down his tanned throat, and then she fell into his gaze as he searched her face. That smile again—it roped her in.

Get a grip, Christy.

"How long has it been?" she asked. Her face blazed heat involuntarily at the unintended innuendo. But he acted as if he didn't notice. *Or maybe he liked it.*

"Three days. Maybe four."

"So what are your thoughts?"

Kyle leaned in, setting aside his dishes, and rested his forearms on the table. "I know he's in some kind of trouble. I'm sure it's nothing he caused. There's a lot of gang activity here in Coronado, and some of the bangers try to hang around our community, looking for Team guys who might have an axe to grind. Misfits."

"Community? I don't understand."

"Our SEAL community."

"Misfits?" she asked.

"Stress does things to a guy. Makes him question all sorts of things." He looked out at the bay and squinted. "But that's not Armando."

"So you think he's like been kidnapped or something? Held for ransom?"

"Don't know. And we're not supposed to be talking about this."

His blue eyes pinned her again. She'd never felt so good being helpless.

She wiped her hands on the warm, wet washcloth, soaked in lemon juice, and then handed it to Kyle. They touched for a moment and he slid his forefinger along hers in an obvious caress she didn't back out of. They looked into each other's eyes, and something understood passed between them. Then his face formed a question.

"Want a coffee? Like a cappuccino or something?" he asked.

"Sure."

"C'mon. I have a great place in mind, unless you…"

"I don't really know the area well," she interrupted, and then thought maybe she sounded too eager.

He left money on the table. It seemed natural that he put his arm on her shoulder again, which she liked, but then he quickly dropped it. Kyle walked behind as they exited to the salty afternoon air.

"Duckies is just down the street," he said, pointing. "Let's walk. Parking around here is nonexistent."

Rubber duckies of all shapes and all states of dress littered the coffee shop. The barista wore a Hawaiian flowered shirt covered in sunglassed yellow ducks. Jimmy Buffett blared from the speakers. After getting their drinks, Kyle waved to a group of four guys in the corner, who flipped him the bird when they thought Christy wasn't looking. Kyle directed her to be seated in the opposite corner in front of an opened bay window. They both sat just as a gentle bay breeze tickled the back of her neck.

"So, Christy, you from here?"

"No, I've just moved down from San Francisco."

"Just moved down, as in maybe the last three or four days?" he asked.

"Yes."

"I saw you at the airport." He leaned back in his chair and gave her an admiring grin.

Christy remembered seeing that muscled arm with the tats, and how hard his chest felt as she almost fell into him that day at the baggage claim.

Holy Guacamole. It's him. That guy.

Christy regained her composure. Her cheeks flushed recalling the two times she had been so close to him.

Think, Christy. Get hold of yourself. It's just lunch.

"My mother died last year and I inherited her condo, so I decided to try San Diego for a spell. She loved it here, even though she was sick."

"Sorry to hear that," Kyle said with a frown. "Sounds like you were close."

"I have a brother I don't see much. Never knew my dad."

"Well, that sorta makes two of us." He looked out at the water, tightening his jaw.

"How about your mom? Where does she live?"

"She's gone, too. I have no one," he said it to her with a blank look, but Christy could tell he had steeled something inside him. He seemed practiced at hiding, at being private.

"That probably makes it easier to do what you do. I have a lot of respect for your profession."

He nodded into his coffee cup as she said this. He probably got this line a lot and had grown immune to the words, so she decided to add some levity. "Even though we both know you are a dangerous killer who ravishes females and ties them up with their pantyhose."

He laughed. The sunshine of his face warmed her all the way to her toes.

"Not today, though. Don't think you're wearing any." He leveled the blue charm on her mercilessly.

He'd noticed?

His simple comment made her wet. She'd told herself she would let him beg. She would stay aloof, make him grovel to get back in her good graces, but his effect on her was the opposite. Everything he did made her crave more. She even wished she'd worn pantyhose.

The pause became the most awkward since their meeting, more awkward than the position of his body over hers as he'd incapacitated her on the floor of Armando's house two days ago.

"You live here in San Diego, too, right?" she had to ask.

"I'm between places. Was planning to stay at Armando's while I looked for a condo."

His blue eyes scanned her lips and then searched the side of her face. "Maybe you could help me."

God, yes I could.

"I don't handle leases, but if you're looking to buy…"

"I have a bonus coming and I thought now would be a good time."

"The absolute best. There are bank sales and foreclosures all over the county. Even some in my complex."

"Which one is that?"

"The Infinity, down by the harbor."

"Nice place. Too expensive."

"Not as much as you think. I could show you."

Her stomach clenched. She had crossed a line. He'd get scared off now. But she'd wait to see his response before she retreated.

He leaned back in his chair and nodded with a mock frown. "Okay, we could do that. What about this afternoon?"

His blue eyes pierced her again—with what he *didn't* say.

THEY RETRIEVED CHRISTY'S Honda at the real estate office and Kyle followed her over to the Infinity complex.

"Some of these places went for close to a million dollars when they first came up for resale," Christy said as she let them inside the furnished model with her passkey. "My mother was one of the first to buy. She got in under a special housing density program." They both stepped into a beautifully staged great room and kitchen. Through tall picture windows, the bay gleamed as if covered with shattered glass. He opened the sliding glass door and stepped onto the balcony.

"Nice place. Doubt I could afford it." He turned, resting his back against the black iron railing, his bulging package prominent. He cocked his head, removed his sunglasses and asked, "How much?"

"This one's five sixty. But we could make them an offer. It's owned by the bank. If you have some sort of down payment, this could be financed VA."

"Not sure I have enough." He walked past her and waited by the slider opening.

"Want to see the rest of the place? It has a nice big bedroom."

She slipped through the door, close to his body, and heard his inhale. He didn't move out of the way.

"I don't care about the big bedroom. I like a big bed," he whispered, his voice husky.

She melted and didn't dare look back at him, but instead kept walking down a short hallway, past a guest bath, and into a bright bedroom. A full-sized bed, covered with a flowered green bedspread, sat against the far wall. She stopped at the foot and immediately felt his heat behind her.

"Too small," he whispered. When she turned to look, his eyes focused on her lips. Her knees were shaking. She melted when she heard him murmur, "But it will have to do." He leaned in and kissed her.

She raised her arms up over his shoulders and loved the feel of his firm chest pressed against her breasts, the way one arm wrapped around her waist and pulled her to his groin. His other hand fisted in her hair at the back of her head. His wet kiss opened more than her lips. It opened her soul. He plunged his tongue into her mouth, lacing over her teeth, searching. She granted him full access to everything in the moan she couldn't help but give him.

He pulled her tighter against the rock wall of his upper torso. She spread her legs and rubbed herself against his thigh with a need she'd not felt in years. Her fingers entwined the short, curly hair at the nape of his neck, then slid around to trace down under his jaw. She pulled away to look at him, needing to see his eyes.

Without saying anything, she held his face in her hands and stared into the azure sparkles of his soul. One vein pulsed at his forehead as he allowed her to examine the questions written there, the traces of need and pain, of hurt and loss. He let her see it all. And she knew she could heal him.

She stepped on tiptoes and leaned against him again, as his hand slipped under the skirt of her sundress and smoothed over the lace panties she so carefully had put on for him.

He kneeled and buried his head under her skirt, licking the smooth satin fabric and then poking his tongue around the elastic to find the slit of her sex.

"Oh, God, Christy," he whispered, as he sought her nude opening. And then the roughness of his tongue laved her, deepening their connection. She released herself to his hungry mouth.

Her thighs trembled, her hands clutching the hair at the top of his head as she leaned into him, pressed into him, and begged him. She begged him to take all of her, anything he wanted, as much as he wanted.

Anything.

He came out from under the cotton fabric, a wet grin on his face, eyes blazing, and slowly rose, standing in front of her. He slipped her dress off like lifting a piece of tissue paper from a lingerie box, then stared at her bra and panties. It registered what she had done for him. That she anticipated him seeing those lovely lacy things.

And she could tell it thrilled him.

Christy removed his T-shirt, and then let her palms slide over his hairless ribcage and nipples as she squeezed the heavy muscles underneath. His broad shoulders were more massive than she had remembered. Her fingers snaked around his thick neck as she pulled him down to her lips and made him cover hers.

She moved her hands to the button fly on his jeans, squeezing his erection, which earned her another moan. His hands kneaded her ass, pulling her to him and pinning her arms between their bodies, palms to his chest.

"Should we go to my place?" she asked.

He smirked and looked her over as she stood before him, clad only in her lacy underwear, and shook his head slowly. "Too late. Maybe later." He stepped closer, holding her head with one warm palm that turned her ear to his lips. "Maybe tonight. Maybe all night?"

"I might need you all night."

"I can deliver whatever you need. I promise."

She needed his pants off right now. She slipped them down his nonexistent hips and then over huge thighs, taking off his briefs with them. His warm cock bounced to life. She palmed the entire length of his shaft and squeezed the moist tip. She sat at the edge of the bed and put her lips over the helmet of his crown and tasted him.

His breath came harder as she worked on him, his fingers sifting through her hair, pushing her head into his groin. Then he lifted her under the arms and lay her back on the bed. He made short work of her panties, leaving her bra in place. His fingers massaged her opening as he climbed on top of her. His gaze searched her eyes, and then sought her mouth. First one, and then a second finger tucked into her folds and she thought she would explode. Christy stroked his length and helped guide him, pushed the head of his shaft against the wetness of her sex. And rubbed.

God, I need this.

A shrill voice came from the living room. "Okay, now we have this one here. It's a little on the small side."

Christy and Kyle looked at each other in panic as they realized a Realtor was in the next room showing the home. Kyle quickly leapt off the bed and slammed the door, which drew a resounding "Oh" from a female on the other side.

They dressed and straightened the bed. Christy's cheeks were on fire as she looked at Kyle. She swallowed, and then opened the door to face their audience. A portly woman too large for her height stood armed with an expression of surprise and disgust.

"Sorry. We had to use the bathroom," Christy said, realizing too late the water to the unit had probably been turned off.

The Realtor looked at them as if they were road kill, but the young couple behind them grinned from ear to ear.

"Hey, no problem, guys," the man said. "It happens." He squeezed his wife's shoulder.

Christy handed the Realtor the passkey and realized as she did so that her panties hung around her wrist. The older woman inspected her hand and shot back a hateful look with black, beady eyes. "This is way out of line, missy. I'm going to have to report this."

Everyone else but Christy jumped in with a comment. Then Kyle grabbed Christy's hand and they escaped together down the hallway to the elevator.

"I can't believe I just did that," she said, looking at the floor.

Inside the elevator, Kyle took the panties from her fist and buried his nose in them, then gave her a smirk. She grabbed them back, stuffing them inside her bra. He was enjoying her turmoil way too much.

"Regrets?" Kyle asked as he stepped close to her, tracing the form of her right breast with his forefinger and then squeezing her nipple.

She had to admit that even if she lost her job, which most assuredly could happen, it was worth it. She squeezed his package as she pressed herself to his chest again. "Not one. You?"

"Only one, but I'm going to fix that right away." His deep, penetrating kiss turned her bones to rubber as the doors to her floor whooshed open.

CHAPTER 7

KYLE PRESSED HIMSELF against Christy's backside as she worked the lock on her door. He flipped her scented blonde hair off her shoulder and kissed her soft neck. She arched her rear into his groin, rubbing against his shaft. He was so hot for her, he wondered if they would make it to the bedroom.

The door gave way and Christy turned to face him, her eyes fixated on his lips. She then threw one arm about his neck and kissed him. He kicked the door closed and she dropped her purse. Staring at each other, they began to disrobe. He watched her lithe body unsheathe itself from her dress. The bra was his to remove. He pulled her hands from her back and stuck them down his unzipped jeans. Her fingers found him and then pushed his pants over his hips. At last they embraced fully naked, flesh on flesh.

He picked her up and she encircled his waist with her legs, pressing against him, rubbing her sex against his cock, kissing first the line under his jaw and then full, on his lips as he inhaled her.

After he placed her down on the bed, he whispered in her ear, "I need protection. Let me go…"

"Shh. I have some." She arched and rolled over to her tummy, exposing her plump ass as she reached for the bedside table and pulled open a drawer. He could see the little fruit of her sex, hairless and wet.

He rose up and covered her body, pushing his shaft into the crease between her legs, begging for entrance. She flipped to her knees, raising herself up off the bed just high enough so he could slip a hand there and plunge two fingers inside her wet opening.

She gasped and spread her knees out wider, arched up and slapped her palms against the wall. He spotted a red foil packet in her right hand. He removed his fingers, slid his thighs under hers, and pressed his chest against her back. He grabbed the packet and quickly covered himself, while she moaned and leaned back against him, turning her head, giving him a mouthful of blond tresses until her lips found his.

Ready and poised at her opening, he stopped, and then tenderly removed the hair that separated their cheeks and pressed his forehead to the side of her face by her temple.

"Christy, Christy," he murmured. He wanted to be covered in her scent, wanted every part of his body rubbing against hers. He wanted her to rub off all the roughness, all the little scars and nubs of his soul.

Make me clean. Bring me back to life.

He plunged in from behind, watching the long curls fall down the silky softness of her back. He brushed them aside and kissed one vertebra at a time while his cock slowly had its way with her, drawing back and plunging in, back and forth in a rhythm he would not be able to sustain for very long.

She had gone liquid, as if made without bones or cartilage. Her body pressed against him, needing him, drawing him deeper inside her. She gasped for air as he slid to the hilt and then slowly drew out. With gentle rhythms he rode her, loving the feel of her flesh covering his cock, loving how each wave of pleasure brought him to the edge and then back again as he withdrew and plunged again and again.

He clutched her breasts as he pumped her. He held her by the waist and moved her up and down on his shaft as he arched his groin into her. At last, the muscles in her sex tensed and then released as she shuddered. He moved even slower, in and out, as every delicious ripple of her orgasm washed over both of them.

At last he could hold on no longer, and with one last plunge to answer her soft, satisfied whimper, he burst forth and came, rooting and planting himself deep inside her. She squeezed every drop from him as he continued to pump and then lurched one more time. They collapsed on the bed, his body covering hers.

He wanted to be careful with this delicate creature lying beneath him, the one who smelled of lavender and vanilla, of the sweet sweat of her arousal. His hands were too callused to rub across her soft breasts and down her arms, but he needed to feel the smoothness of her skin, as if the more he stroked her, the more he would be healed.

He nuzzled and found the back of her neck and kissed her there, feeling the vibrations of her sigh, her chest moving down into the bed as his body could do nothing but follow her. He continued to nuzzle, kiss and give her little bites, tasting the salt of her skin along her neck, under her ear. His tongue found the upturned curl of her closed lips and he could tell she was smiling. He begged for her to open to him again.

She rolled to the side and faced him as he pulled out and then repositioned himself, covering her chest and lower abdomen from on top. His hands held her face as his thumbs traced over her cheekbones, her lips. He slid his fingers behind her head and cupped her, raising her up to meet his lips again in a long, languid kiss. She studied him deeply and he saw her face was wet with tears.

"Hey. Are you okay?" He wondered if he had hurt her in some way. The glittering moistness in her eyes drew him in and he wanted to forget who he was and where he was. Almost, but not quite.

He could tell she wanted to say something as he watched her

think, but she chose to stay silent. Some day he might want to let a woman tell him things of her heart, but not today. It was way too soon. This was just beautiful sex.

Yet, something had shifted. Certain words would have to remain unspoken for now. But he knew he'd found someone very rare and very lonely, like he was. It would be difficult to let her go, like she belonged to him already. Or maybe he needed something she had. Something he would protect.

They rested, then made love again as the raging orange sunset streamed through her bedroom window. All he wanted to do was watch her face as she came, as he shot her full of his seed. He couldn't be deep enough inside her, touch enough of her skin, or hear enough of her little moans and whimpers as he poured out everything he had. He slid in and out of her and watched her bloom for him, open to him, need him. And he could do this. He could be there for her, could send them both into ecstasy. Every soft brushing of her lips on his flesh brought on a new wave of strength and the desire to own every inch of her body—the desire to give her all of his body in return.

They played in the shower until the hot water ran out, then they dressed and went to the harbor and ate at the Salty Dog cafe that overlooked boats of every size. The moonlight shimmered on the still waters of the inlet.

Kyle turned back to her face, which was lit by the table candle that flickered, sending dancing shadows like a fan dance that first covered up and then revealed her sweet smile. He wanted her all over again, but that was foolish. He braced for the cold blast of reality to follow. This was wrong. He needed to find Armando first. The Navy came second. There was no room for a third option.

So what's going on with you? Wake up, Kyle. You know better. You've warned other men on your team about this. It's nice being with her, but let's not get lost here.

"You come to this place a lot?" she asked, as if testing the waters.

"Actually, I've never been. Don't normally hang out in this part of town. But I can tell you about every dive on Coronado."

"I'll bet."

Two large bowls of seafood chowder delivered to their table broke the silence in the nick of time. The chowder tasted hot and delicious and was accompanied by warm steaming French bread and melted butter, which was the way he liked it. They ate in silence. He'd been starved.

"They fly in the French bread from San Francisco," she said between bites.

"No wonder you like it here."

"It's close. My mom and I used to come here when I'd visit her."

"That must have been nice."

When they finished, he avoided her gaze but could tell she was trying to engage eye contact, so he pulled out his phone and checked to make sure the ring was on. No messages, either.

"It's late and I'm going to have to be going. If you're done, I'll walk you back."

She flinched but seemed to catch herself. Her eyes held lots of questions. Things she had a right to know. A regular tangle of things he wouldn't be able to answer.

Get out before you get dragged in, Kyle.

"I was hoping you'd stay the night," she delivered her words with steely coolness.

She was watching him. He knew it was important how he responded. He sensed she was trying her hardest not to look disappointed. Forced casual.

Here it comes. Damn. This is harder to do than I thought. "Sorry. I don't do the overnight thing…"

"But you said…"

"I'm sorry. I seem to do a lot of apologizing to you." He looked away quickly. Her body shook as he noticed her composure crumble. He saw the glistening tears out of the corner of his eye.

Give her a chance to recover in private. Being direct is being merciful. Don't lie to her. It's cruel to linger. "C'mon, let's get you home, safe and sound."

He felt awkward and ashamed he'd crossed the line with her, that he'd made her think there was more to it than just the sex. The *incredible* sex.

God, I wish there was.

At the lobby of her building, he kissed her. "Thank you. This was nice, Christy."

"I'd like to do it again sometime."

She was masking again, trying not to plead. But damn, if he didn't love the way she wanted him, and how hard he felt she was fighting to cover it up.

Me, too. Fuck. I could do this every night. He shifted his weight and stepped on his own foot to wake himself up—a trick he'd learned in the BUD/S training.

"Let's not get ahead of ourselves here." It hurt to say it, but it had to be said. After all, he was a dog. And she deserved way better.

As she opened the heavy glass door, she turned and asked him a question. "Kyle, *will* I see you again?"

He didn't want to answer it. He didn't want to lie. But what was the truth, after all? He sighed. "I think so." Then he shrugged. "Just not sure when." He looked down at his feet, then up to her face. "Best not to expect too much out of this."

She got the message. He saw it in her eyes, in the flicker that showed she had felt the spear of rejection. He could see she wasn't used to getting it. And she wasn't used to giving so freely of herself.

He'd been honest with her, at least. He'd done what had to be done, no question about it. But he still felt like a complete heel. He hoped her anger would help her forget him.

He knew it would be impossible to ever forget her.

CHAPTER 8

THE NEXT MORNING, Kyle didn't have time for shame. He threw it in the back of his mind like he used to throw his wetsuit and surfboard in the back of the battered old truck with the rusty headlights. His old but reliable vehicle had been crumbling, with parts sloughing off it for years. This flawed hunk of metal had served him well while he became a man. She was always by his side, proving to be much more reliable than any of the girls he'd dated.

His heart hadn't gotten seriously snagged on any of the lovelies from his past. But the truck was different. He nearly cried the day he'd sold her to a friend, the sale signaling the end of his carefree but tumultuous life—the same day he'd reported to the Indoc center. Not once did he ever wash her. She was perfect the way she was.

He took a shower, then checked Armando's refrigerator for something unhealthy. No luck. A little nonfat yogurt and greens. No milk for cereal, if he even had cereal. No bread for toast. He found some cheese and cut a slice. It tasted terrible, like rubber tires. He read the label.

99% nonfat? What the hell is up with that?

Armando was a food Nazi, all right. Kyle grabbed a bruised apple from a bowl on the kitchen counter and walked around, surveying the house, sure he missed something. Armando had nothing frilly to indicate a woman's presence. All hard steel stuff. No pictures of frogmen jumping out of airplanes or US flags either.

When I was a child I thought like a child. But when I became a man, I put away childish things. It was one of the quotes he and Armando loved, and that had sustained them all during his training and during some of the darkest days overseas in the Middle East. On those days he'd look out over the sand and hear the kids playing, the goats bleating, and wonder if this dusty hellhole was going to be his killing field, where he would end his days on earth.

He and Armando had the shared experience of getting up close and personal with Death. And just like at BUD/S, neither of them would quit.

Wherever you are, Armani, I'm coming. I'm bringing you home. Armando had to know Kyle would do this, or die trying.

He thought about the lovely woman he'd shared his passion with last night. How her face was filled with tears from the intensity of their lovemaking. He caught a very brief glimpse of what life would be like with a woman like her. But all too quickly the picture turned, and once more he'd humiliated Christy, exposed her to the dark side of his chosen life. All she'd done was peek her head around the doorway of his vacancy—try to smooth him a bit with that soft skin and those little squeals she made when she came.

He hoped she had a mess of friends to take care of any wounds he couldn't help but create. He didn't want her brooding over something she couldn't control. Hell, he couldn't control it either, and it was damned unhealthy. He hoped she was the kind of woman who could take it like a man. Take the hard truth. He'd let his guard down this time. He'd had no business getting her involved, even if it was only one incredible night of sex. And he'd almost spent the night, even promised her he'd pump her all night long. Not like he didn't want to.

He needed the sex. But he didn't need the entanglement.

He checked his cell again. Still no word from Timmons. He'd have to go see his chief this morning.

Damn. Armani, where are you? The silence didn't reveal an answer. He was alone again, with the visions of a magical few hours of lovemaking and something that couldn't be.

The afternoon and evening with Christy had tipped the earth on its axis for him. Damn, it was a close one. If ever there was a woman for him, she'd look and act and smell and sigh and need just like Christy did. He wished he'd met her about six years ago, before he'd become a polar bear. Before the dinosaur skin. Before he became a trained killer. Before Armando had disappeared. She'd have been a welcome distraction in those days.

She can do way better. She deserves it. Some day. Some day the timing would be right for that kind of woman. In the meantime, it would be best if he left her completely alone. He swallowed, his throat parched. He knew he would never call her back. He knew, too, being without her would get easier every day and week that passed, until he would only have that warm glow and smile at the memory of a really nice time with her. When he couldn't remember what she looked like and how she tasted. When the pain got buried.

He pulled himself back to the task at hand: finding Armando. He flipped open his cell.

Gunny answered after a coughing spell.

"Shit, Gunny. You gonna croak on me today?"

"Not on your fuckin' life. You'll go before me."

"Now, how's that?"

"I should ask you, Kyle. What the hell are you doin'? I got reports from no less than three groups of your webfoot buddies that you found yourself a honey pot and went MIA yesterday. You're not going to find Armando between her legs. Nothing there but pain an' misery," Gunny spewed out.

Well said.

"I had apologies to make. I shook her up a little when she came into Armando's house *by accident* and found me."

"Accident, my ass. You know better than to hook up with a sexy cat burglar."

Kyle laughed, enjoying the banter they shared. No one else except Armando could talk this kind of disrespect and trash to him.

"Well, I was asleep on the bed. Naked."

A series of croaks and wheezes sounded between some Navy swear words, assaulting his ears, words Kyle hadn't heard since one of the early Team reunions. What came next on the other end of the line was not intelligible, followed by deep hacking and a release of some phlegm-wad probably large enough to knock a man down. Gunny's condition was worsening by the minute, and it worried him.

"Heard from Timmons yet?" Gunny rasped.

"Nope."

Gunny let out a series of thick, rheumy coughs that sounded like his lungs had turned inside out.

"You need to smoke more, Gunny. The burning-it-out-of-you isn't working."

"Tell me about it." Gunny wheezed and then continued. "I got Cooper and Fredo waiting until we could find you. Coop's guy got us some intel. We could meet up. That is, unless little miss fancy pants is in heat."

Perceptive. Almost like that. Kyle could see Christy's face as he filled her to the hilt, as he held her jaw and lips with one hand, as he squeezed them into soft pillows he could suck down. He could see her fingernails dragged against his butt cheeks, pulling him into her while he tasted the salty sweat between her perfect breasts. He felt like turning his Hummer around and driving to her house, then taking her again, but that was ridiculous. If he were another man, they'd just ride off together and get lost.

But he wasn't that kind of man.

"No comment. But Gunny, it's all about Armando now."

They arranged a meeting at a local beer pub for later that evening.

Kyle checked Armando's stash of guns in the concealed weapons box he'd built under the floorboards of his bedroom, hidden by the carpeting. Everything looked untouched, as Armando would have left it. The guns were oiled, with hardly a speck of dust anywhere. Clips and rounds were separated from the weapons. Kyle would have to deal with them if Armando didn't turn up soon. Besides, unless entirely necessary, it would be best not to enrage the locals by carrying weapons in his vehicle, other than his own in his vehicle. It wasn't protocol to carry a big stash unless a Team guy was on his way to ship out, but everyone did it anyway.

He found Christy's nametag still on the dining table where he'd tossed it three long days ago. Kyle picked it up again and traced over the indented letters that represented the woman he couldn't get out of his mind.

He released a sigh and put the plastic tag back. He surveyed the dirty kitchen sink and ruled it unacceptable. Adding hot water and soap, he rinsed off the crusty dishes and loaded them into the dishwasher, then turned it on.

Cleaning always helped him center his thoughts. Armando had a vacuum in the storage closet, and Kyle lost himself in the dull buzz of the machine while he removed a week's worth of dust and dirt. He wiped down the countertops, then looked at the damp rag and wet formica surface, wondering if he'd just removed evidence.

Not likely.

If Armando had been taken against his will, there'd be holes in the wall, missing windows, and a few large carving knives stuck into cabinet doors. And there'd be blood. Lots of it. No question.

No. Armando had left in a hurry, but he'd left on his own.

Kyle went back to the table and looked at the yellow tablet he remembered seeing the day he'd been waiting at Armando's. There were scribbles on the top and a folded street map tucked under several sheets. He hadn't noticed the deep grooves where something important had been pressed into a sheet that had been removed. He recognized it as Armando's writing. He became annoyed he'd missed this obvious clue two days ago when he first came to the house.

Rubbing the No. 2 pencil over the surface, he found a phone number with the area code of an adjacent county. He picked up Armando's landline, holding it with a towel, and hit redial. The same number came up.

"Hola? Armando?" said a panicked voice on the other line.

"No," Kyle said. "*¿Está Armando allí?*"

"No, Armando is not here." He did not recognize the voice.

"Kyle? Kyle is that you? Armando is not with you?"

"Ah, Mama Gúzman. Didn't recognize the number."

"*Sí.* I'm at my daughter's. Where is Armando? Please, you will tell me now he is with you and he scares his mama for no good reason?"

"No. Sorry. I'm looking for him too. I'm sure he'll turn up." Kyle wondered if she believed the lie.

Probably not.

"Kyle. I am worried. He is coming to my house, but he never come. I am sick with worry."

"When was this?"

"Five, six days ago. Mia, you know Mia, Armando's sister?"

"Yes." Kyle assumed the stories of Mia's poor choice in men and lifestyles were true.

"Mia is in some trouble again," her voice started out calm, but her strength collapsed at the end, like a row of dominoes. Through ragged catches of breath, the creaking sound of the phone in Kyle's ear told him she was pacing anxiously, beside herself.

"So what happened? Did you call him?"

"Yes. I told him Mia is gone. And now Armando. I am here at Mia's apartment. I have no choice but to go to the police next. But they will laugh at me. And I don't want to tell them about Armando and the Navy."

"No. You did the right thing. We can handle this."

"You think so? He was mad, very, very mad when I told him."

"Mama, what? What did you tell him?"

"Mia is pregnant. She got pregnant with that bastard Caesar. She went off to tell him the good news." She mumbled something in Spanish Kyle didn't understand. "And I think Armando is thinking Caesar didn't take it very well. He has girls all over, but no, Mia loved him, she says. She says he will be different with her, with the baby when it comes."

Not fucking likely.

Kyle knew exactly what Armando had done. Gone dark. But why hadn't he told his mother? This question niggled and worried him. So that was what all the texting was about. Kyle didn't like it either.

"Mama, you need to get back to your own house. What if he's tried to call you there?"

"Yes. Yes, I will do that now. Nothing here for me. I just came to see if they were...here..." her voice trailed off again. Kyle knew Mama Guzman had thought she'd find them in a bloody pile.

"Anything look out of order?" He had to ask it, the picture in his head was too strong.

"No. Looks just like she went to work."

"Best get out of there. I'm not sure it's safe. You need to get home."

"Yes. Yes I will."

"Bring her key, okay? I might need it."

"*Si.*"

"You have a cell phone?"

Kyle heard a streak of swear words he thankfully couldn't understand.

"I'll give you my home number. I don't want to get the ear cancer."

"Mia have one?"

"Yes, of course."

Kyle wrote both numbers down. "I'm going to get some friends, and we're going to go find them. You stay by the phone, okay, Mama?" He gave her his personal cell number, not his overseas phone. "You won't get me, but leave a message there."

He could hear her chicken scratches, mumbling the numbers in translation to herself.

"When I call you, it won't look like a regular number. So, pick up anything that looks strange. Don't want you screening out my call. Leave me a message. I'll get back to you when I can."

"Yes. No caller ID, like Armando."

"Right."

He hung up, and then programmed her home number and Mia's with a quiet code ring and ran to Armando's bedroom to change into some gear and dark clothes. On his way out the door, he checked the phone calls and messages, leaving them just in case the police got dragged in. He noticed the last call out was five days ago, Mia's number. He wrote down the two previous numbers as well and the date and times they were made. He saw the calls from Mrs. Guzman and two blocked calls incoming earlier in the day.

He thought about Armando's stash of guns under the corner in the bedroom and decided against taking them in case his buddy made it back and needed the firepower. He grabbed his black duffel bag that contained everything he'd brought and slung it over his shoulder, then headed to the door.

Kyle looked around to say goodbye to Armando's home.

He might not ever return here. That same thought was always on his mind each time he deployed.

He flipped the lock and almost shut the door, but then remembered Christy's nametag. In three long strides, he reached the table. He grabbed the little badge and placed it in his left breast pocket and closed the Velcro flap.

After leaving the house, he hung out under the darkened overhang to see if anyone watched the house. The quiet street held only a couple of parked cars that dotted the curb, but none of them were close. He made it across the street to his beast and drove away. He had to check in with Timmons back on base.

KYLE SWORE UNDER his breath when he saw Petty Officer IIIrd Carlisle Channing, decked out with his usual asshole attitude, manning the front gate like he guarded the Alamo.

"Well, here he is, the second coming. How many times you jerk off in the bathroom today, sailor? Or do you just whip it out and show all the girls—"

"Shut the fuck up, Car-LILE."

"Need to see your ID, you prick."

Kyle dug out his military issue card. Before Channing could put his well-manicured paws on it, Kyle let it slip through his fingers to the ground.

"Oops. I'm sorry about that," Kyle said sarcastically as he opened the door of his Hummer, catching Petty Officer IIIrd Channing in the groin.

That made the guard hop around. "I'm going to write you up for that," he said as he held himself with both hands.

Kyle knew the Naval police would add the infraction to the other forty they had. Really important ones, like not showing respect to the regular Navy guys. Kyle couldn't hold anything against someone who tried one day of BUD/S. Took balls to even consider going through the hell of becoming a SEAL. So, the ones who thought they'd drawn some kind of cushy police job, trying to hold the real warriors back as if they were a danger to the general public, well, he carried no respect for those assholes.

He'd gotten a dozen slips for riding a bicycle without a helmet after he'd taken his Hummer into the shop for an alteration and it was getting fixed. One slip for scuffed shoes. One for stopping just over the line at the gate. These guys just itched to bust him. Carlisle had a whole six-pack of associate flunkies he terrorized on a regular basis. Like monkeys at the zoo. Kyle felt sorry for the whole lot of them.

"Make sure you write that I hit you in the crotch. My reputation is at stake."

"One of these days, sailor, you're gonna need a friend and I'll be sitting back, watching you squirm, on my way over to screw your woman," Carlisle said as he handed Kyle back his ID.

"Geez, Carlisle, I'd have to wear Kevlar if I had a friend like you." Kyle slipped his card inside the pocket that held Christy's nametag. "And as for the girls, well, I thought you knew I like guys. But in your case, I'd share. All you had to do was ask."

He puckered his lips and blew a kiss at Carlyle, revved the motor, and tore off through the parking lot before he got a dent in his door.

I'll have to tone it down a bit soon. This one is a war without winners. Kyle knew well enough what a man would do if pushed too far, and Carlisle looked just like one of those guys with no control. But he was a comrade, a member of the same Navy Kyle served. And that was worth something, after all.

Another set of amends I need to make. But not today. Today was still all about Armando and getting his ass safely back on base. Kyle marched down the buffed vinyl floor tiles leading to Timmons's office.

Timmons frowned down at a half-inch report, his thick glasses perched atop his shiny forehead, which told Kyle he wasn't reading a thing. Timmons mumbled and tapped his pencil.

"Sir?" Kyle said as he rapped on the open door.

"Lansdowne. You got anything good for me today?"

"Sir? I was hoping you had the last cell coordinates."

"We got some of the best equipment known to man, and we still have to wait on the fuckin' phone company."

"Coop's friend said the signal's dead."

"Dammit, Kyle. I told you not to involve the locals or the Feds."

"It was off the record."

"Sure it was. Nothing is off the record, son. So what good news *do* you have?"

"Wish I did, Mister. I got another number for you to check, though. This one belongs to Mia, Armando's sister. No news at all. Just a big fucking mystery, getting worse."

Timmons nodded his partially bald head, the shiny nut-brown skin of his scalp all too visible and getting more so by the day. Kyle noticed he looked a little pudgy too.

"Why are we tracking the sister?" Timmons asked, staring at the piece of paper like it was a dead cockroach.

"His sister's gone missing. Talked to his mom. She's major freaked."

"So this is some kind of stinking foul play. What—"

"No sir, it wasn't Armando's doing. I'd stake my career on it. He's gone after his sister. Nothing's disturbed at his place and the same for hers, according to his mom. It's like they just walked into the sunset together."

"Except that never happens."

"I understand, sir."

"I don't want to get the local cops involved. Or the regulars either, if we can help it."

"Completely agree, sir."

"How could two people disappear without any clues?"

"Disappearing is what we're trained to do. When we don't want to be found, we aren't found."

Timmons nodded again, then gazed back at his report and pulled down his glasses. Then he yanked them off, leaned back in his chair, and nibbled on a well-chewed plastic temple. "One problem with that fuckin' theory, son."

"What's that, sir?"

"When Armando didn't check in, that's like painting a great big fucking red SOS sign on a destroyer." He leaned forward, his forearms on the desk, and stared at Kyle. "He wanted to be found from the day he left."

CHAPTER 9

C HRISTY TORE INTO cleaning her condo with complete abandon. She'd washed three loads of laundry, including the sheets full of the scent of him. She added five lavender-scented dryer sheets just in case a trace of the man remained.

On her hands and knees, she scoured the bathroom floor. She removed almost everything from her refrigerator and cleaned her glass shelves with hot, soapy water. Searching through her closet, she filled a garbage bag full of clothes she would give away to the women's shelter. Purging her bathroom vanity drawers, she gathered up little bottles of shampoo and soap from her hotel stays and threw them into the giveaway bag.

Damn him. How dare he come waltzing in here, disrupting my life? Everything had been just f—

But no. Everything hadn't been *fine*. Her eyes, already sore from crying, painfully filled with tears again. She felt cheap, furious with herself for allowing a romp in the hay without commitment.

What were you thinking?

After checking her phone at the office for messages, she forwarded calls to her cell. She went online and answered several emails that had piled up over the last two days.

Kyle Lansdowne lacked for nothing, of course—the asshole had screwed her good and plenty and then had left. No way she'd let him treat her this way. Her insides still smoldered, but she'd landed on her feet.

God damn you. Who gave you the right? How could I have felt as if something wonderful was happening?

The option of giving up and going back to San Francisco to nurse her wounds was out of the question. He'd left a rather stern message this afternoon. She needed another cup of coffee to dredge up the guts to return his call. No doubt that Realtor they'd run into at the model had told a compelling story and had probably even embellished it.

Well, she had to just suck it up and deal. They'd all be surprised. She'd throw herself into her work even more than before. Be the best goddamned salesperson in the whole office, if given a second chance. After all, she'd had lots of training selling upscale bras and panties that cost as much as most people's car payments.

She would make it her mission to go looking for someone else to wipe the memory of Kyle out of her mind, someone else to kiss her all over and make her shudder with pleasure. Couldn't be *that* hard to do.

Working for Madame M in San Francisco had exposed her to a clientele of wealthy older men who would often ask her to dinner or the theater. One had even asked her on a cruise. But the answer had always been the same. She'd done her share of flirting, part of her customer service, and Madame M had showed her how the clients liked it. Happy clients bought more things. But Christy never took their interest seriously. She knew they were seeking a replacement to a loss in their lives as the result of either widowhood or divorce. Madame M had called them the "real DDs."

Christy didn't mind being the familiar face associated with happier times when they bought lingerie for their wives or long-term companions. But she didn't want to be a *step* anything, wanting to have her own family someday with someone who hadn't made that choice before. Christy wanted to be someone's *only*.

She sank into her leather couch and leaned back. A cobweb she had missed dangled in the corner, almost winking at her. Christy jumped up and threw a rag at it, then collapsed back into the couch and had a good cry. Although she'd tried, despite all the scrubbing, cleaning and purging, only one man's face popped up on her radar screen—the one with the three-toed tattoo tracks running up his arm.

Get a grip, Christy. Life moves on. Apparently he has too.

But she could have sworn he'd felt something.

She jumped up, stormed into the kitchen, and threw her rag into the suds in the kitchen sink, which sent a splash of gray water all over her countertop and onto the floor.

Maybe another Team guy could fill the bill, someone Kyle even knew. That would get him. And it would serve him fucking right. Let him imagine her screwing the other guy senseless every time Kyle had to look at the guy. Every time they had to go on a training mission.

See how it feels to be discarded.

First things first. She dialed her manager's office.

"Christy. Thanks for calling back. I was a little worried. I hadn't seen or heard from you in a couple of days. You okay?"

"Yes. Been working, but out of the house," she lied.

"Good. That's good. Say, I got this very disturbing call yesterday afternoon from Connie at the Infinity sales office," Simms said.

"Yeah, I thought maybe she would call." Christy sucked it up and just decided to tell the truth. If she lost her job over it, well, she hated hanging around Wayne and the way he stared through her clothes, anyway.

"Mr. Simms." She surprised herself how confident she sounded.

So she turned it up a notch and continued, "I owe you an apology."

"Oh? How's that?"

Christy heard doubt in his voice, and continued. "I was so relieved when that SEAL turned out to be…he had a legitimate reason for being at the house. I was the one in the wrong place at the wrong time."

"I thought it was Wayne's fault. But he insists he gave you the right address."

"Whatever. It isn't important anymore."

"Never happened before here. Very strange. I'm glad you weren't really hurt."

"No. Just scared out of my gourd. But it was my fault, I guess. Anyway, the tension was getting to me a little, and I wanted to give him a chance to apologize. So, we agreed to have lunch. Well, one thing led to another, and…" She had to tell the little white lie to keep her job. "All we did was kiss. I know what you're going to say. It was a complete lapse in judgment on my part."

Simms chuckled into the phone. "Yeah, those guys can get pretty wound up. Nice lookin' fella. I can't say as I blame you. But…Christy…she said it went way beyond kissing. She said…"

"Just how would she know?" Christy interrupted. "I can't deny the fact that we were engaged in a very passionate kiss, but, honestly, Mr. Simms, do you really believe we would… It was the *model*, and, you know… I live right upstairs. If…"

He sighed. "Yeah. Look, Christy. I get it. Older agent versus a new, young, pretty agent. She thinks you get your business by screwing your clients. Unfortunately, I've heard that one before too."

"Well, it wasn't very professional of me. Not right that her clients had to be witness to my little indiscretion."

"Oh, hell, they probably didn't mind it, although she said different."

"They were laughing. I'm sure she blew it out of proportion. I don't even want to know what she told you."

Christy knew Simms was blushing even though she couldn't see his face.

Yeah, the old biddy told him about the panties.

"Well, I'm satisfied. As long as you clarify one more thing with me," Simms words came across short and clipped. Christy braced herself.

"Sure. What?"

"Did you enjoy the rest of the afternoon?" He chuckled again.

"As a matter of fact, I did." She hung up.

TOTAL TRUTH, CHRISTY couldn't stop thinking about Kyle. The hair at the back of her neck and all the way down her spine tickled deliciously where he had kissed her, where she needed him to kiss her now. She stood at a crossroads between spending energy trying to bury her feelings for him and...what?

Oh. My. God. Am I actually thinking about running after him?

Something she'd never done. She wasn't going to beg. Besides, he'd made it clear. For her sake, he would say no.

He'd walked right back into her life with those damned red signs and the flowers, and had made a nest in her heart. And then something had made him stop. Something Christy knew she didn't cause.

What?

Maybe if she could find him, they could talk it over. Take it slow. She could tell him she didn't expect a lifetime, just a casual friendship. A *little* relationship, not a big one. A friendship with benefits.

How do I do this? Where do I find him? He knew how to reach her, but she had no clue how to find him. She couldn't just hang around a bunch of bars, hoping for him to show up.

Could she have offended him in some way? Had he misunderstood her? She just couldn't let it go. She didn't do "wait" very well. Wait until he decided to waltz back into her life?

Never! But if she didn't talk to him perhaps he would ship out or worse, find someone else.

No.

She'd have to go back to that street Armando lived on. Back to the page of the Thomas Bros. guide she had already mentally ripped out of her book.

Though she was nervous, she had to go back to Armando's house to search for some evidence of where Kyle was staying.

Christy's red Honda puttered down the tree-lined street of Armando's neighborhood. The sun hung low and on its way to retiring. She drove by the house quickly at first, making sure there wasn't a car in the driveway. A vacant brown beat-up Buick was parked down the street two doors away. Other than that, the neighborhood seemed empty. A jet streaked across the sky and sent a rumble through the air.

Fly boy.

Christy pulled into the driveway in case she needed to make a quick exit. The front door to the house was locked. As she walked around the side, trying the wood sash windows, she heard something inside clatter to the floor. She listened through a window that had closed drapes, but heard no other noise.

She continued along the side of the house to a wooden gate leading to the rear yard. She pulled a wire latch, and a shallow garden oasis with a lap pool came into view. Everything was neatly maintained, although the grass looked a little long. A few dozen leaves floated in the turquoise water, out of place.

A pair of concrete steps on the back porch led her to the rear sliding glass door, and, to her surprise, the door was unlocked. She slid it open without making a sound.

As soon as she stepped into the large open kitchen, she knew she'd made a mistake, but her curiosity had been piqued. The house had been ransacked. Things had been tossed everywhere; a chair left upended, cabinet doors flung open, and several dishes lying smashed across the kitchen floor.

She turned and went down the hallway leading to the now-infamous rear bedroom. Inside the room she found all the sheets had been ripped from the mattress and tossed about. The mattress top was sliced open. Clothes from Armando's closet were strewn haphazardly all over the place.

All of a sudden, she heard the front door open and slam shut, and then heard footsteps running outside. Through the living room window she saw two men jump into the brown sedan that had been parked down the street. They pulled a U-turn and left the area.

Christy quickly checked the rest of the house without touching anything. She was alone. A message light blinked on the phone machine. Using the edge of her jacket, she pushed the button to play it back.

"Amigo," a thickly accented voice said. "Thirty minutes. Foothills. Smell fire. They got at least ten. Loaded. Left…" The line went dead. Christy knew she'd just heard the voice of Armando, and he sounded stressed. He'd spoken in some sort of code. She didn't have time to put together the pieces, but she knew she had to get the message to Kyle right away. Something told her it could mean a matter of life or death. She jotted down the words, replaying the message until she got it right.

Would Kyle believe her? Well, yes, if he heard the message. But knowing he wanted to disappear, would she even be able to find him?

She remembered what he'd told her about the community, and how the buzz traveled like the Underground Railroad. Everyone knew about everyone else somehow. So, if she gave one of the Team guys a message, Kyle would come. She was counting on it.

Christy drove to the Golden Bear Café and searched for square-shouldered, stern-looking men with tattoos and didn't spot one. But she saw the cook Kyle knew. Griz. Maybe he'd have a suggestion.

Griz's unshaved chin was heavily scarred on the right side. His steel blue eyes wandered carefully up and down her torso with a glint of appreciation for another man's lady. At least that's how she interpreted it, anyway.

"Well, hello there. You flying solo today, or is he meeting up with you later?" Griz asked her while wiping his hands on his stained apron.

"I was hoping you'd remember me," Christy said as she looked down at her sandaled feet with the pink toenail polish, and then back up to his face before her tears burst loose.

Damn those pink toes.

"You're not exactly easy to forget." He smiled, but didn't look at her cleavage, though she could tell he wanted to. She liked that part about this community, the respect they showed her. The direct look without flinching, not hiding the effect she had on him.

"You wanna beer?" he finally said.

"No, thanks."

"Well then, Missy, what can I do you for?" He chewed on a toothpick as he nodded to a couple just entering the diner.

"I'm looking for Kyle. It's important."

"Well, I haven't seen him since yesterday. With you. Doubt he'll be here tonight either. Not his scene."

"If you could put the word out. I need to talk to him about a friend of his."

"Um hum. This a message he's going to want to hear?" The man pinned her with his eyes, being careful, protective of Kyle.

"Yes. He's looking for someone. You know, Armando. I may have some information."

"'Kay. So you have some information about Armando. Where should he contact you *if* I hear from him?"

Christy fished out her business card. "My cell phone's at the bottom."

Griz flipped the card back and forth against his other thumb, obviously thinking. He looked as if he wanted to say something, but stopped himself. Christy felt the awkwardness of the two of them standing in a nearly empty room.

"Well. I've got to go. I'm going to drive around and see if I can spot his Hummer."

He nodded. "You two have a little tiff?"

"That's an off-limits question."

"Could be, but then Kyle's a special operator and we look out for each other."

"I know about that. Any idea where he's staying?"

"You're asking me? I'm surprised he let you escape."

Griz grinned full out, but lopsided and apologetic. She saw the heart of gold inside the rough-hewn man of steel.

Christy scratched the back of her head, hoping to break the tension and change the mood. "I'm sorry I bothered you. I'll be off now. But if you think of anything, please give me a call."

Christy's shoulders stiffened as she drove back and forth along the strip lined by little shops across the street from a white expanse of beach. Several times she thought she felt eyes watching her, but upon checking in the rear view mirror, she found no sign of the black

Hummer. She ran into three young men in shorts and flip-flops with matching wrap-around sunglasses that screamed military issue at the frozen yogurt stand. She also gave them one of her cards since they hinted they might know Kyle but said they weren't sure.

They're lying.

She checked her phone to see if she'd missed a call, but her voicemail was empty. The afternoon wafted away from her, so she decided to return home. She hoped to see a black Hummer inside the automatic gate at the underground garage, but no such luck. She stepped into the elevator after parking and made it up to the four-teenth floor.

A maid vacuuming the hallway nodded a greeting as Christy let herself in the condo.

Dropping her purse and kicking off her shoes on her way to the bathroom, she automatically massaged the back of her neck, which was still so tight. She recalled how Kyle had protected her head when he leveled her to the ground that first day. This must be some result-ing swollen tissue, she thought.

She slipped off her clothes and prepared a bubble bath. She placed her cell phone to the tub's edge and picked up a current romance novel she had yet to finish. She'd just submerged in the warm bubbles and lain back against a towel when her cell rang. A strange combina-tion of numbers, not from an area code around San Diego, appeared in a sequence on the screen.

"Hello?"

"Hi, Christy."

A shot of electricity traveled down her spine. She'd done a pretty good job of thinking she could maintain her composure until she heard Kyle's voice. Her will turned to butter.

"I know you don't want to have anything to do with me, but—"

"That's not true, and you know it."

Damn the man.

"I went over to Armando's house today," she said.

"Now why would you go and do that? Not very smart."

"No. But then you know how smart I am, don't you?"

"I think you're one of the smartest girls I've ever met, but it was dumb to go over to that house. You must promise me you won't do it again. Ever. It's dangerous."

"I think I know that now. Don't worry."

Kyle paused. In a soft voice, he asked, "What are you saying?"

"There were two men there."

Christy moved around in the water.

"Where are you?"

"In the bathtub."

"Oh." He paused. "So, what did the men look like?"

"Dark-haired. Young. They ran out the front when I went in the back."

"You went into the house?"

"Yes. The place is a mess. I think they were looking for something. But I scared them off."

Kyle chuckled at that. "I could see how you would make a man go weak at the knees. Even two men. Two very bad men."

"Not funny. Don't make fun of me."

"I'm not. So after you scared them off, what did you do?"

"I listened to Armando's phone message on the answering machine."

"What the hell? Christy, you have no business getting involved. You stay out of this, understand?"

"So do you want to hear the message?"

Kyle hesitated, breathing hard into the receiver. God she wished he was breathing against the side of her face, kissing her there, looking at her and touching…

"Yes."

"He said 'Foothills and thirty minutes.' Then he said 'Got ten loaded.' He started to say he *left* something and then the line went dead."

Christy could hear her heart pounding, wondering if he heard it too.

"Thanks," he whispered.

More silence. She would make him talk next, if he wanted to. That's what she needed to hear. Did he want to or not?

"I understand you went out of your way to find me. I appreciate that."

"Because it's the right thing to do, Kyle." She hoped it didn't sound too strong, so she added as soft and sexy as she could muster, "Because it was important to you."

There, she'd said it. Time to figure out if she would have to do a rescue mission on her own heart. A girl's night out? A romantic movie that made her cry all night long?

"Well, I thank you."

She could tell he had difficulty saying it.

"So, if you're free tonight, I am." God, she hoped he'd say he was.

"No. We have things we have to do. I'll give you a call sometime."

Her heart fell to the bottom of the tub. That was the answer she had expected. At least her attempt had been worth the try.

"Okay then, sailor. You know where I live." She found the courage to hang up on him first. She lay back in the tub and placed a wet washcloth over her eyes, which absorbed the welled-up tears and those continuing to fall.

No, she didn't do "wait" very well. She needed to move on.

CHAPTER 10

KYLE STEPPED INTO Jimmy's, the place where the Wall of the Fallen took Kyle's breath away every time he saw it—all the faces of young, handsome men, cut short in their prime. He usually looked at every one of their pictures as if he were looking right into their eyes, and said a thank you.

Every time.

The inscription in the middle, translated from a rough-hewn carving by some anonymous artisan at the graveyard on Iwo Jima read:

When you go home,
Tell them for us, and say,
For your tomorrow,
We gave our today.

As tough as he knew his community was, he didn't know a single Team guy who didn't choke up reading that.

Being a SEAL wasn't all about rah rah or politics. Wasn't about highs and lows of armed warfare, man on man. Wasn't about knowing your limits or having a band of brothers. It was about life and death.

When he and Armando got their very first tattoo together, his the band of barbed wire thorns around his calf, the old artist looked Kyle right in the eyes and said, "So you want to make friends with death, son?"

He could answer the old man today. But not that day.

Kyle sat and waited for his team to arrive.

"I'VE TALKED TO Armando's mom," Kyle began, after the group had gathered, "and I think he linked up with this guy, Caesar, who Mia has been hanging around. Apparently, she's pregnant. Armando went to go find her."

"That could be good news. Maybe this asshole won't hurt her," Fredo tossed that statement into the mix.

"Can't count on that, Fredo." Kyle worked to keep panic out of his voice.

Gunny swore and shook his head. "The man must be an animal. I'd say put him down."

"Whoa! Gunny. We're not talking about doing anything like that," Kyle shot back, alarmed.

"Be doing the female population a favor, you ask me. But then you didn't, did you?"

Cooper narrowed his eyes at Kyle and then winced. "You think they're still in the area?"

Kyle nodded. "The message said something about the foothills and thirty minutes away. Said there were ten. Well-armed." He sighed. "Can you get your friend to track this cell phone?" Kyle handed Cooper a yellow Post-It note with Mia's cell phone number.

"Sure. No problem. How old is this?"

"I think only a couple of hours. This morning there was nothing on the answering machine. But…" He didn't want to tell them how he got the message. "Well, the message came in sometime after noon. I'm guessing he used Mia's cell phone, since they took or destroyed his."

"You listen to it?" Fredo asked as Cooper got up, presumably to call his friend in the DOJ.

"Nah. Someone else did. And there's another thing. Armando's house has been trashed."

"Hey, boss, you got someone else working on this job? Someone we need to know about?" Fredo asked.

Kyle looked down at his folded hands. He wanted a beer, but he knew he'd need his wits about him in case they got a location. "The lady I was with yesterday afternoon came looking for me." He didn't want to make eye contact.

"Uh huh. Like I said, you gotta start thinking with your other head, boss."

"I never had that problem," Gunny inserted, laughing at Kyle's obvious discomfort.

"So Gramps, you knew about this too?" Fredo asked.

"Shit, yes. My gym's like a fuckin beauty parlor. I learn everything about the crap you guys get into just from keeping my ears open. Always some newbie or wanna-be who is only too quick to tell me about all your dumb-ass moves." Gunny coughed. "Although this time, he gave me a full description of the lady in question, like she was naked."

Kyle almost grabbed Gunny by the shirt collar. He drank water and crunched on ice cubes instead.

"So Kyle, I gotta ask. Are you okay?" Fredo looked at him hard.

Not the question he wanted to hear. Were they feeling him starting to slip? Was he starting to slip? Was it wrong to want to feel the soft flesh of a woman next to his and not be able to get her out of his mind?

No, it wasn't wrong. It was right. But it interfered with his mental clarity, and was so unfair to her.

"No worries, gentlemen. I'm right as rain. Got all the cum lovingly worked outta me real good last night. Now I'm ready for a fight." Kyle hoped they believed him.

"Sounds like she didn't get enough, though," Fredo barked.

"Oh, yeah she did." Kyle grinned. "She just wants more."

Finally Fredo laughed and nodded his head. "Tell her I'm available."

Kyle punched Fredo's bicep, this time a little harder than usual.

Coop returned with the news he'd left a message for his DOJ friend in two places. "He'll call me back, I hope tonight."

"Okay, so now that we know Armando's alive, we're gonna only have one chance to break him out. I want this kept tight, just between us. And when we're ready to roll, we go."

The team nodded in agreement.

"Gentlemen, we got only three days to do this. Then I'll go it alone," Kyle said.

"The hell you will. I'm with you all the way," Gunny said.

There was a pause as Gunny looked back into three cowed faces. Nothing more needed to be said. "Fuck it, fellas, I can drive a car, shoot a gun, I don't wear glasses. And the ladies don't distract me like some people sitting at this table."

Everyone laughed, except Kyle. He was thinking of the way Christy's breasts filled his palm, how she tasted under her ear, and how he'd tried to sleep with the largest boner he'd ever had just from the feel of her hair on his chest as he snuggled next to her in bed. The mere memory of her scent had kept him awake all night.

Gunny snapped his gnarled fingers in front of Kyle's face. "You've got it bad, kid. That kind of a lapse in concentration can get you killed, you know."

A harsh thing to say, but it was the truth. Kyle looked at the pockmarked and ruddy red complexion of one of the ugliest men he'd ever met and knew Gunny would give his life to protect him. Gunny had a heart the size of the Pacific Ocean and wanted to go out like a hero.

But Kyle hoped he wouldn't have to.

KYLE DECIDED TO get a motel room and watch movies all night. He knew he wouldn't be able to sleep. He couldn't get drunk or go clubbing because he had to be able to hear his phone. There were some nights he couldn't wait to press his body into a throng of strangers and dance to oblivion, but tonight wasn't one of them. He knew what he wanted to do.

If you're available, I'm available.

It wasn't the right thing, but it was the *only* thing he could think about. How she whimpered under him, how he loved to watch her and feel her shuddering with climax. He loved watching how he made her feel.

A really good guy would stay away.

But I'm just a man. A dog.

So he turned around and headed off the island toward Old Town.

CHRISTY HEARD A knock at her door. She'd fallen asleep and the bathtub water had turned ice cold. She got out of the tub and quickly dried off, her heart pounding in her throat. With hair still dripping wet around the sides of her face, she slipped on her flowered silk robe, headed down the hall, then viewed Kyle's face in profile through the peephole of her front door.

She quickly ran to her bedroom and made her bed, throwing her clothes behind the closet door. She put on some hand cream and then wished she'd gotten her legs and feet as well. She applied cherry lip-gloss and a spritzer of *L'Interdit*.

He came back.

She slowly walked back to the front door, took a big gulp, and pulled the door open, raising her gaze from his beltline up the hard chest encased in a baby blue T-shirt, up the thick clean-shaven neck to a square jaw, to the full lips and two light blue eyes. He stared back at her like he had the first time they'd made love. His need came across stronger than his control, and seeing that, she felt hope.

In an instant, he'd moved through the doorway and had kicked the front door closed behind him. His hands were suddenly inside her robe, exploring her flesh and igniting her passion. She tugged at his pants, and then kneeled to unbutton his fly. He stripped off his T-shirt and removed his shoes. She kissed the head of his cock, and then took his full length into her mouth, peeling his jeans down his tight cheeks to his ankles. She sucked him hard as he pulled her robe away and threw it into the corner. He leaned over her kneeling form, running his hands down her spine, over her shoulders and under her chin as she worked her tongue over him.

He moaned something she couldn't make out.

He withdrew and kneeled in front of her. She didn't care that she showed him how much she'd missed him.

"I can't seem to stay away, Christy. You ensnare me and I willingly go…" He stopped speaking to plunge his tongue into her mouth, seeking hers, commanding her heart, and pulling it out of her chest.

"I don't want you to stay away, Kyle. I want…" She stopped before she said something she'd regret.

His hands grasped her jaw as he searched her eyes. Christy's breasts rubbed against his hairless chest, nipples against nipples, and lazily moved one hand up and down his shaft while the other cupped his balls. His thumbs moved on her cheeks, then down to her lips as he bent and kissed her long and carefully, as if she were a China doll.

He picked her up with one arm under her knees and the other behind her shoulders. She buried her head in his neck, kissing him, biting him there. He placed her on the bed, then moved up to spread her legs and put his lips on her sex in one fluid movement. She offered no resistance, wanting him there. Her fingers dug into his thick brown hair and then moved behind his ears as his tongue pleasured her, licking her folds and sucking on her bud.

She asked to be found, and he found her, right there, between her legs, breathing life into her soul with his tongue and his hot breath.

Bending one knee and slipping her thigh in front of her, she turned to her belly to let him lap at her sex from the side and then behind. He placed two fingers deep inside her. She clutched the pillow and groaned into the fresh lavender linen, knowing he could see her face in profile. With her sighs and moans, Christy told him of her need and how beautifully he satisfied it.

She forced her rear up in the air, begging for penetration, and he pressed the crown of his cock at her opening. He slid inside her slowly so her body stretched and accepted his wide girth.

Bracing her arms in front of her, she placed her thighs outside his and arched her back up, then down as she impaled herself on him and ground into his groin He encased her back with his chest, whispering something in her ear and holding her breasts with his palms, letting the pillows of her flesh overflow between his fingers.

"I love making love to you, Christy."

Not exactly what she hoped to hear, but close. "Yes, Kyle. Oh…"

"Not possible"—he said between thrusts—"to stay away. Not possible."

She shuddered and exploded in a warm, fluttering orgasm that shook every cell in her body. At the same time, his spasms filled her in more ways than one.

ONLY A FEW minutes had passed, and Kyle was still embedded inside her where they'd collapsed on the bed.

"Thank you," Christy said as she turned to touch the side of his face with one hand, then trace over his lips. He bent and kissed her shoulder.

"I'm sorry I sent you away. I am so sorry."

Christy snuggled against his chest, her fingers lacing over his lips. "I'm glad you came back." Her hand reached down below and she found him nearly hard again.

"Oh, my," she whispered to his belly button.

KYLE LAY BACK, staring at the ceiling. Satisfied. This was the way it was supposed to feel. He'd finally found a woman who loved sex as much as he did.

Christy had fallen into a deep sleep, which surprised him. He loved the feel of her inhale and exhale, craved the sound of her gentle reverie. He drifted off, thinking about his other teammates.

Praise the Lord, Cooper would say. He smiled as he recalled the time when Cooper had told him how hot it made women when he read them the Love Chapter from Psalms.

He'd asked the guys to call him when they heard back from Cooper's friend. Then he pictured Armando's house and hoped it was not part of a crime scene investigation. He wondered what the intruders were after.

Probably guns.

He was the only one who knew about the hiding place in the corner of Armando's bedroom—enough guns to start a small war. There'd be time to get his friend's gear out of there later. This break-in meant Armando hadn't given them what they wanted, unless they'd just found the guns. But Christy didn't say anything about the floor being ripped up, so hopefully Armando still lived. And Mia as well.

Christy had cuddled herself under his chin. She awoke and stretched, then began stroking his chest with those nails of hers, tracing over a few scars, most of them from surfing. A few jagged ridges were from knife wounds due to close encounters with some pretty sorry-assed bad guys, not all of whom had lived to tell their side of things.

He knew she waited for him to say something. Like it or not, she *was* involved, *wanted* to be involved. He hoped like hell she knew what she was doing. He sure didn't. He'd never felt this way about a new relationship.

"Thank you, Christy."

"For what?" She turned and gave him a crooked, wide-eyed smile.

"Thanks for the intel," he whispered to the top of her head. He got back the warm scent of lavender.

"Oh." She giggled. "No problem, sir. Anything else I can do for you?" She gripped his thigh between her legs.

A damned comedian, funny as hell. *Is this how life with her would be?* He studied her face, tilting up her chin, losing himself in the sparkle of her deep brown eyes. "No. I think you've done quite enough." He saw the beginnings of a lusty smile form on her lips and knew it wouldn't take long before he felt his own need growing. Again.

"Can I ask you what the message means? Or will I have to torture you to find out?" She kissed his left nipple and then licked it, swirling her tongue.

"Ah, not fair. Not sure this is in keeping with the Geneva Convention."

"Shall I beg?"

"Please, no! I'm not sure I can get it up any more. I mean, my mind's willing, but my body…"

She continued stroking him. "Please."

With those eyes of hers, who would be able to deny her?

Hell, what would it hurt? He'd be telling her all sorts of things in a minute if he weren't careful. "He said…" Kyle's voice grew husky and ragged, but he continued, "He was trying to tell me he's okay for now. But he's heavily guarded, and whoever has him doesn't mess around."

She tensed, and he knew he'd lost her again. He read her fear. She was afraid something would happen to him.

Do I want to know this?

"There are things you just should not know about. This is what my work is all about, Christy. All the time."

"Yes. I understand."

But did she, really?

"So you forgive me for breaking into your friend's house and listening to his personal messages?" she teased.

He chuckled, grateful for her humor. "No, I didn't say *that*." He paddled her rear in a mock spanking. "I'll have to punish you further, and…" He scanned her face again. "Make you tell me all your secrets." He kissed her wanton lips, murmuring to them, "And extracting how you cleverly wound me around your little finger so easily."

"You'd make me?"

"I could. I'm very good at interrogation," he whispered in her ear. He followed up with a kiss below her earlobe and felt the rumble of her moan.

"How would you get information from me? How would you *make* me tell you?"

"I'd improvise. Think of something." He rubbed his lips against hers, biting her lower lip.

"Improvise?" She arched to press her breasts against him.

"Use things at hand."

"How would you use these things?"

Kyle smiled. Her naïveté to the ways of the warrior community thrilled him. He stared into her lusty eyes. He wasn't quite sure what to say.

"I might have to use pantyhose," he said to her lips.

Christy's eyes drew wide and she arched again into him, rubbing her sex against his thigh. "You'd tie me up?" she said breathlessly.

Kyle started. *Was she asking for this?*

She sighed and whispered, "I want you to improvise. On my body. Make me tell you something."

"Ah." Kyle searched her face and then decided. He glanced at the floor beside the bed, reached over, and picked up the silk sash from her robe. He drew both her arms above her head while he kissed her underneath her jaw. Holding her wrists together with one hand, he wound the sash around them, binding them gently. Her lidded eyes told him of her pleasure. He wanted to kiss her all over her body.

He could feel her heart beating against him. He felt her moist arousal as he lazily fingered her bud and she moaned into his ear.

"Tell me, or I won't let you go," he said.

"I don't want to go."

"Yes you do. You want to squeeze your breasts. You want to pull me into you again," Kyle answered. He avoided her mound searching for his groin.

She started to move her arms down to encircle his neck and he stopped her.

"Bad girl. Tell me how you managed to capture my heart?"

"My name is Christy Nelson. I am a Realtor. That's all I'm going to reveal at this time."

"I think you'll reveal more," he said as he inserted two fingers into her wet sex.

"Ahh." She opened her eyes. "No. I won't tell." Her breathing was ragged. It looked like she was suppressing a smile.

"You must tell me." He pushed the head of his cock into the soft folds of her opening.

"Take me, Kyle. I am yours. All of me."

God, I wish I could have you totally, Christy. What would that be like? He realized he lived and died in her eyes. Could he have this forever?

"Tell me, Christy. Be a good girl and tell me how you manage to bewitch me so that all I think about is making love to you."

Had he ever said something even close to this before? Holy...

"I think of your hard places. I think of how I can wrap my softness against your hard body and make you need me. I try to get under your skin."

When he looked her in the eyes, tears had pooled there. If he put himself inside her, he would be lost forever. And that's what he wanted. He pressed his hand over her bound wrists and plunged into her.

"You have captured me again," he said as he stroked her insides. Her face was urgent. Her fingers curled into his and squeezed.

"You're a willing victim."

She sighed and gripped his thighs tighter with her knees, then opened herself wide again and let him plunge deeper.

"Yes, I am. Indeed, I am."

KYLE BASKED IN the scent of her spent body. Her breathing had calmed. Was she asleep?

Would it always be like this? With her the world was righted. He knew there wasn't anything this perfect in reality. But in the fantasy, everything seemed as it should be between them, which thrilled him.

And was so damned overdue.

And now so dangerous, because he'd formed another reason to live. Something he feared losing, like everything else in his life that meant anything.

Something had been lurking outside his consciousness, waiting for a dark moment to rush in. What?

And there it was again.

Life isn't this perfect. Nothing lasts forever. He remembered being a young boy of fourteen, like it was this morning. All the pain and uncertainty came flooding in.

What have I done?

CHRISTY HEARD KYLE'S heavy breathing and was thankful he'd fallen asleep. He tossed about, talking in his sleep. No sweet erotic dreams, like the ones she'd been having. His forehead creased and his lips pursed.

Maybe he's just not used to sleeping with a woman. She remembered the first few times she'd spent the night in a strange bed, in the arms of a lover. Every touch of Kyle's body heightened her hunger for him. This strong man with arms and shoulders that could hold the whole world, cared for her. Quiet and strong. Ever the gentleman, until she got him into bed, and then he consumed her. She'd never known a man who needed so much passion. He demanded her body perform for him and she would do it. Loved doing it. She even loved letting him bind her hands above her head while he pumped her silly.

Last time, he'd brought her to the brink of ecstasy so many times, then had held her still, only to fall into the crest of the wave of her passion. He rode that wave with her. Watching her. Attentive, but unyielding. She doubted she would ever be able to make love to a man again and not think of Kyle.

God, she hoped she didn't have to try.

She found the warm place beneath his chin and buried herself. Inhaled his musky scent and drifted off to oblivion. Tomorrow she'd worry about the future. Right now, her future lay in the warm body of this man, the one with whom she could easily spend the rest of her life.

CHAPTER 11

K YLE WOKE UP with a start and couldn't get back to sleep. He sat in Christy's living room as the dark night became early morning. He usually loved this time of day. Everything was so quiet, peaceful. He could think better when it was like this.

He should have taken off last night, just left, but that wasn't the way to treat a lady, and Christy was that, with every luscious inch of her. Could a man be blamed if he wanted to spend just a little more time in her arms? Christy had obviously felt a connection. Hell, he'd felt the connection too. But that was before common sense took over and he realized he'd made a huge mistake. He had to face the music and fix it. It would be hard, but it was up to him to do the right thing.

He'd gone to see her at the realty office three days ago just to say he was sorry. But when he saw her fingertips touch the flowers he'd brought, he'd lost his head and asked her out to lunch. What did he do that for?

You know better than to get involved. You don't do "relationships." You get in and get out before they get too attached.

He shook his head. He was indeed a dumb ass. Was he still mourning the most important woman in his life? Could that be why he had such a hard time staying away from Christy? Was he that damaged, that out of control?

His mother died when he was fourteen. She had cancer. The disease had spread quickly and she was gone within weeks, despite the surgeries that tried to stem the tide. He'd told himself this meant she didn't suffer too much. At least, not until the end. But the speed with which the cancer overtook her didn't give young Kyle time to pull together his feelings and say a proper goodbye. It remained an unfinished chapter, an open wound.

Kyle knew he had been the light of her life. He remembered her laugh, how intently she would watch him and cheer at his soccer and baseball games. She was there when he was discouraged. Still, he felt somehow responsible for her cancer, and he would have done anything, even traded places with her to stop it.

He'd wanted for nothing, although it was clear his father resented having to work so hard and complaining about the expensive traveling tournaments, special camps, coaching, and expensive equipment. His mother ran interference, but young Kyle heard the arguments behind closed doors at night. She was devoted to him, almost at the cost of her failing marriage. Kyle's older sister, just one year his senior, was totally boy crazy and working on getting herself a fast ticket out of the hell that was their family.

He couldn't remember a single game his father went to—couldn't remember him ever being even slightly interested in what Kyle was doing. He would come home in a sullen mood and would say nothing at dinner except to pepper the conversation with his irritation, regardless of his wife's attempts at conversation. His father would drink wine until he fell asleep in front of the TV. After that, he'd go off to bed early. Some nights when Kyle stayed up to do his homework, he'd get a gentle kiss from his mother before she turned in for bed, but he'd hear her softly cry herself to sleep. It broke his heart.

Light was beginning to shimmer, a deep purple on the inlet. He liked the view of Coronado from this side of the island. It gave him a different perspective on his life in the Navy. He looked at the cold outlines of the destroyers in the early morning light and took strength from the cold, gray shadows they cast on the murky inlet.

The machines and hospital stays his mother had undergone scared him. He was afraid she would never open her eyes again each time he visited her, especially toward the end. She insisted she was getting better, but he could see that was a lie. He realized that nothing he could say or do could protect her, and she slipped away one evening while he was out of town at a soccer tournament. She'd made him promise to go. Told him she'd be stronger the next time he saw her.

She died alone. In the dark. He'd been told of her death on a cell phone call from his father. He'd been sitting on the second seat in a Suburban, driven by one of his teammate's moms, surrounded by seven other sweaty kids.

The bastard couldn't even wait until I got home to tell me in person.

That night Kyle didn't say a word to anybody. He stared out at the rest of the world going by, resentment making a home in his chest. How could everything go on just like nothing had happened? He knew he would never heal this loss. She'd been the only one who'd believed in him.

Things changed at home after his mother's death. There were no more camps or elite sports teams. Kyle focused on his studies and worked hard to bury the love for his dead mother and the ache of her leaving him. His father became even colder and more distant, and they rarely talked. Kyle hung out at the library or with friends who didn't play sports. It was a bitter year, and just as he was beginning to feel some hope for the future, circumstances conspired against him.

Kyle had met a nice girl, Judy Dobson, and had asked her to the prom. She was crazy for him, which annoyed Kyle sometimes. But she was a good girl—the pretty one everyone else overlooked because she wore huge, thick glasses. They were going to ride with his older sister and her current boyfriend, but at the last minute, his sister wanted to go alone with her date. Kyle suspected they were going to skip the dance altogether and get a motel room.

He and Judy had barely gotten to the dance when the police arrived, telling him his sister had been in a life-threatening car accident. Kyle spent the rest of the night in the emergency room, in his tux. A friend took Judy home. She'd wanted to stay, but Kyle wouldn't have it. He and his dad sat across from each other all evening, except for the times when his dad snuck out to the car to drink. They spoke not a word.

Near dawn they got the bad news. His sister was dead.

Kyle thought maybe his father would stop drinking, maybe start taking care of himself and pull things together. But that wasn't in the man's nature, and his father retreated further into his alcoholism.

And now Kyle hadn't talked to him in six years. He considered his dad dead.

At eighteen, the week after he'd graduated high school, Kyle reported to Indoc and joined the Navy, with an eye on trying out for the SEALs. His mom had wanted him to go to college on an athletic scholarship, but that wasn't in the cards. The Navy took him without any promises, and then he got his chance. One out of ten thousand was the odds of being allowed to try out for the Teams. But Kyle got his spot. The Navy became his new family, and it served him well.

Armando was in that famous class that almost was a complete washout. Out of the 190 men that started, only twelve graduated. Of the twelve, four were officers, which was unusual. He and Armando were the only ones without a college degree, but they scored higher than the rest academically. They were closer than brothers.

They would gladly die for each other. That got battle-tested during their first deployment in Iraq when they survived the battle of Fallujah. Their unit ran into more than 259 Tangos in a narrow street that wasn't anything more than an alleyway. They were being shot at from all sides, including above. After the mounted guns ran out of ammo, they used their personal assault weapons. And when those ran out they resorted to their sidearms as they scrambled to a safe spot until the extraction team could get them out. A few good men died that day. A record number of the enemy had been killed, and the SEALs would be up for some medals, which would be awarded in private. His friendship with Armando, forged in steel, would be with him forever.

So now he'd let this beautiful young thing into his world. She had no idea what she was getting into and deserved way more. What in the hell had he been thinking? He had to stay focused on finding Armando first. This had to remain his number one priority. Besides, his getting her involved in this mission was dangerous for her too.

How in the world could he have been so stupid?

CHRISTY AWOKE AND felt the bed cold behind her where a warm male chest had been. Being alone this morning, after yesterday's love making, scared her. She should have been able to start her new day in his arms, where she hoped she would remain until her last breath.

She sat up, naked and a little sore in wonderful places, still groggy from little sleep. Then she smelled coffee, and that made her feel better.

He's still here.

She rose and put on the flowered kimono-type robe her mother had left her and cinched the sash that brought back wonderful erotic memories. Fluffing up her hair, she looked in the mirror and yes, she looked like "the wreck of the Hesperus," as her mother would say.

Mascara pooled under swollen lower eyelids, which covered faintly bloodshot eyes. Her stomach twitched, as if starved for food. But it wasn't that. She was in love. That new, wonderful feeling that came when she met someone special and the whole world became a possibility instead of an obstacle course.

And Kyle loved her too. He didn't say it, but she knew he did. Just remembering those kisses emblazoned on her flesh last night in the moonlight made her wet. God, she'd fallen hard for this guy. She was normally slower to make a judgment about dating someone, but here she'd hopped into bed with him several times in three days. This relationship had started off as a safe lunch, but had become so much more.

Half the time they were having unprotected sex. She was never this casual with her body. Was she being foolish? Was her unbridled passion going to get her heart broken again?

She hoped not, but it wasn't going to change one iota of the way she would play it out.

God, it would hurt so bad, this one. He's so perfect for me.

She put her hair up in a ponytail and stepped into her oversized ivory tumbled granite shower. It was what she loved best about this beautiful condo her mother had left her. She soaped off, used the shower wand to softly stimulate the swollen lips of her sex. It felt good to be exhausted, to have been covered with his hard body, have him breathing and groaning in her ear as he took her. He liked to make love with her hands above her head, the sash forming invisible handcuffs. He'd press her palms to his and wouldn't let her move except to wrap her legs around his slim waist and arch to receive him, to let him plunder her again and again. And whenever she'd opened her eyes, he was watching her, as if the look on her face was what fed him and made him the man he was.

Am I up for a man like this? Can I be the woman he needs?

She knew, remembering the first time they had been together, when he tripped her to the ground and immobilized her with her own pantyhose, that he was not going to be an easy man to love. He was complicated and secretive. Would she be able to keep him satisfied without getting herself hurt? Was she strong enough for this?

Drying off with the oversized fluffy white towel, she felt courage and hope for a beautiful new today. Maybe not tomorrow or the next day, but today she could be the woman he needed. Tomorrow would have to take care of itself. And she didn't want to ponder the "what ifs" any longer.

Showtime. She splashed on a little French cologne, brushed her hair back into a clip, donned her sexy silk robe, then put on light pink cherry lip gloss and a tiny bit of mascara. She could face anything after a shower. Well, almost anything.

When Christy walked into her living room and saw him out on the balcony, bent over her railing, fully dressed, sipping a mug of coffee and looking out over the inlet, she knew today was not going to be a continuation of yesterday's lazy bedtime caper. There was something hard about him she couldn't identify. His armor was in place and locked down.

God help her if he said they were moving too fast toward a relationship he wasn't ready for. Would she have to play the casual game, pretend it didn't matter? She'd heard all those excuses before, after the dinners and the dating, after the mating dance of a first kiss and the first fall into deep, dark, uncharted waters. Passion plays, all of them. Then came all the reasons why it wasn't the right time. Half the time, she was the one doing the leaving. And of the ones who had left her, if she were to be honest with herself, she was secretly happy for the ending.

But this one, the one with the strong back and straight shoulders, with that tight little ass so clearly delineated for her as he bent over and searched the water and harbor below like a hawk looking for prey, this one would hurt her.

Big time.

"Hi," she said in her best Marilyn Monroe voice. He turned to face her and she let the tie to her robe slip loose. She twirled the smooth silk with her fingers and saw the flame in his eyes, a slight flush of his cheeks perhaps at the memory of her hands bound above her head. The flowered silk parted and she stood like a deer in the forest, caught in a ray of sunlight, unable to move.

His gaze traveled down her body, focusing on the triangle at the juncture between her legs, and then worked back up to her lips. He smiled, as though he remembered pleasant things about the night before. But he was holding back. It would have warmed her heart if he'd grabbed her, just picked her up and made love to her anywhere. But his restraint was dominant over his desire. She saw just the faint flicker of something burning in his eyes when he swallowed.

"Good morning."

His words were soft, but efficient. And he didn't come to her.

"Can't a girl get a morning kiss?" She toyed with him enough to get a reaction, but not the one she was hoping for.

"Sure," he said, and kissed her on the cheek. Then he grabbed her hand and tugged her inside, closing the sliding glass door behind them. "We have to talk, Christy."

So here it comes. The big talk. Is this the part where I want to throw myself over the balcony, where he can watch me die as he tells me he never meant to cause me pain?

She wondered why she saw so much blood and gore. Or was it rubbing off him and onto her? Was this his legacy, what he would bring to her life? She inhaled and tried to steady her nerves, prepared to face whatever he was going to dish out.

"Am I allowed to have coffee first," she delivered in her most sultry voice, "or do you normally continue to keep your prisoners up, sleep deprived, and without the aid of caffeine?"

He came over to her, but she slipped away and quietly darted to the kitchen, padding in her bare feet with the ridiculous hot pink toenail polish. She felt like crying, realizing it was such a stupid color. The happy pink was out of place this morning.

He rounded the corner. "It's not what you think."

"Oh?" she said as she rummaged for some cream in the refrigerator. "You need a fill up or are you done with this pit stop?" She held up the pot after pouring coffee into her half and half.

"It isn't a pit stop and you know it."

"I see. Well then, sailor, suppose you tell me exactly what it is," she said as she looked over the top of the steaming mug, into his eyes that weren't afraid to stare right back at her.

"I'm not sure I can do this. Or, what I really mean is, I'm not sure I'm any good at this."

So, he's not used to begging. She knew he was trying hard to cover up something. She liked it better when his control waned.

"Oh, sure you can. Just say thanks for the hot sex, Christy. Maybe we can do it again some time. That sort of thing…"

She turned and took her next sip of coffee so he couldn't see the tears breaking free and running down her cheeks.

Christy heard the flinch and his instant reaction toward her. He slipped his arms around her waist, one hand sneaking inside the delicate silk with a soft brushing sound like leaves in the fall as he spooned her back into his stunning chest she hadn't had enough time to study, and whispered, "It isn't like that, and you know it." His voice was soft, but urgent.

His fingers massaged her breast as his tongue traced along the curve of her earlobe, driving her crazy for him again. In spite of it all. Even if it was going to be the last time she'd ever see him, if he asked, she would fuck him silly and make him think about her and wish he'd stayed.

Damn the man. It was going to hurt. Maybe this one would be lethal.

She set her coffee down on the countertop and turned to face him straight on. The side of her robe had brushed open and her naked body was against his fully clothed one. The next thing she knew, he was kissing her neck, then her mouth. She was unbuttoning his fly, finding his erection. She was a woman without pride, on a collision course with a man who was practiced at getting in and out without being noticed. Well, she'd make him pay. She'd make sure he never forgot how much she needed him and how good it felt to be inside her.

She nudged a toe behind a cabinet door and stepped up to sit on the counter while he dropped his pants to his ankles. She pulled his T-shirt off and spread her palms against his smooth, warm chest. She let her knees drop to the sides and he urgently impaled her. She lay back among the clean dishes and glasses, which she knocked to the side. He mounted the countertop and pressed down on her. Dishes were falling, breaking. A glass shattered as it hit the floor, but he didn't flinch and he certainly didn't have any intention of stopping. He rode her, obsessed with something raging inside him.

He brought both his thumbs to bear down on her nub and she thought she would go insane with pleasure.

"Oh, Kyle. I..." She bit her hand to keep from saying the words. She wouldn't tell him she loved him, because he wasn't going to tell her that either.

It was over quickly, except that she was still vibrating from the deep thrusting. He pressed his shaft against her insides and came in huge explosive grunts, as if his climax would never end. She was already rubbed raw and perhaps lightly bruised inside from his ministrations the night before. She quivered like a puddle in an earthquake.

"This is not a pit stop," he whispered as he bit her earlobe.

She wanted to believe him. Deep down inside, she thought that she could.

"But...?"

"I need this...maybe too much."

"Is that possible, Kyle?" She looked into his blue eyes and thought she could see his pure white soul. But it was terrorized by something dark that she could not see.

Another glass fell to the floor. She laughed at the fact that this was going to be their last time and he was breaking her things. He'd fucked her on the countertop, of all places. No one had ever done that. "That's one way to get out of doing dishes."

He pulled up his pants with one hand and carefully lifted her up off the counter, then took her to the living room couch, saving her delicate feet from harm. But she was disappointed he did not bring her to bed. She'd been right. He was leaving, after all.

She sat snuggled in his lap, running her fingers over his chest, memorizing every bulging muscle, the size and feel of his nipples, the way his Adam's apple moved when he talked or swallowed, the size of his full lower lip that she traced with her index finger. He covered her mouth with his, then drew back and held her face in his palms.

"You are so..." he started. "I've never met anyone like you."

"Same here. I've never had so much fun in my kitchen before, either. You do this sort of thing often?" She could show her thick skin too.

She got an angry glare back.

"Are you going to walk away from this? Isn't there anything I can do to convince you to stay?" She had looked down at his chest as she'd asked the question, but he continued to hold her head between his hands and made her look at him.

He searched her eyes, and for a second she thought perhaps he would say something else, something she would like, but then again the control came back and his eyes died right along with her heart. It was no use. He dropped his hands and sighed.

"I said some things last night I shouldn't have."

"No," she said, turning her head from side to side, rubbing her forehead against his jaw. "No. Don't you dare say that. Not now." Tears began to form. Hot tears.

"I have no right to—"

"That's for damn sure. You have no damned right to come waltzing in, saying things you don't mean so you can get into my bed. Or in this case, on my kitchen counter."

It felt exhilarating to let the anger spread. It was stuffy in her condo.

He got up abruptly and fastened the top of his pants, leaving her disheveled, and her robe gaping. She quickly covered her body and wiped her eyes, hoping he couldn't see her tears.

"I'm going to clean up the mess in the kitchen," he said. He looked like he was ten years old and had just broken his mother's cookie jar.

"Don't be ridiculous. Who the hell are you? One minute I see glimpses of a man I could love, and the next, a cold, calculating—" She teared up again.

"I'm sorry."

"Leave. Just go."

It hurt to say it, but her pride and what was left of her self-esteem was at stake. Better if she sent him off.

"Christy. I really enjoyed our time together."

"But not enough to stay."

"There's no future here," he said, tapping his chest with his tattooed forearm, the one with the little three legged creature prints. He squinted his eyes.

"Guess not. Maybe someday when I'm not naked and just been given the goodbye fuck you could tell me what you meant to say but didn't."

"I can't promise that. I'm afraid this is all we have. I'm sorry."

"Will you stop saying you're sorry? I would have preferred, 'I can't,' before you screwed me."

He turned and walked out of her life.

She was in shock. She could still smell him in the air, on her skin. She could still feel the touch of his fingers and his thumbs as he'd played her, as he'd snagged her heart and then ripped it right out of her chest.

CHAPTER 12

K YLE SPENT THE morning gathering equipment. He put things together to make small IEDs, bought and borrowed ammo, and purchased thin razor wire. He ran into Cooper, who was stocking up his medic kit. The tall SEAL held up a plastic tube.

"You wanna know what we use these for in Nebraska?"

Kyle had no idea. He welcomed any conversation as a distraction from the hollow cavern in his chest.

"Mom said her dad, when he got older, wouldn't want to come into the house when he had to pee if he was way down plowing his fields. Used to keep one o' these tucked into the brim of his hat."

Kyle wasn't sure where this was going. But he knew he was going to wince.

"Granddad's solution was to shove this thing up his unit and he'd spew like Yellowstone. Became the only way he could pee during the day."

Kyle frowned, worried his friend was perhaps on a bender. And Coop didn't do benders anymore.

"Not very sanitary, and it would hurt like hell," Kyle finally said. "Something wrong with just whipping it out and peeing on the ground? He enjoy the pain and irritation it must have caused?"

Cooper shrugged. "Damn straight. Exactly what I thought. Mom said he was always on penicillin. I think he had a low-level bladder infection and had to pee constantly. Happened all during my younger years until he died. All those farmers did in those days. They didn't go to a doctor, they went to their vet."

Kyle shook his head.

"And here I am, using these as chest compression tubes. The very same stuff. Goes to show how some things change and some things stay the same."

Cooper wandered off down the aisle, in search of something else. Kyle was in awe of how the farm boy knew so much about mechanical things, both gas-fired and human. Cooper just knew how things worked in every sense of the word.

All machinery.

And Kyle knew Cooper was probably an expert with the ladies, due to all this knowledge of working parts.

Then Kyle remembered about Christy. He got hard in spite of himself.

Damn. He felt bad about how he had treated her. But it had to be done. And she'd made it easy on him. She'd asked him to leave. He wasn't half sure he would have if she hadn't insisted on it.

But what a way to break it off. Fuck her on the countertop amongst the dishes.

You are a goddamned dog. That's all there is to it. You're the same man as your father. Add a little alcohol, and hell, you are *as mean and uncaring as your father.* He was glad she got away. He didn't want to make a woman as miserable as his father had made his mother.

He called Timmons, who had no news. The chief was near hysterical.

"You better get me something quick. I'm starting to smell here in this office. Hard to cover up shit like this."

"Copy that. Armando was alive yesterday, that's all we know. Co-op has a friend at DOJ, off the record. He already found out Armando's cell is whacked. Gonna see if AT&T can give us the location of his last call. But I doubt it will be helpful. Too old now."

"I was afraid of that."

"But Timmons, we got Mia's cell. I think I'll have the locator on it today. Armando left a message on his answering machine yesterday afternoon from that number. Told us we've got three or four days. I'm thinking three."

"Damn it all. I'm going to go talk to my liaison with the local PD. Maybe they can help."

"Good idea. You can pull rank, and remind them to play nice."

"Well, they won't play so nice if this caper doesn't get solved right away."

"Roger that. Doing the best I can, under the circumstances. Not like we can break down doors and start laying traps."

"Fucking A. You need anything?" Timmons asked.

"A miracle."

COOPER AND FREDO were waiting for him at the Scupper. Gunny was on his way from the gym.

"Timmons is going to ask for some backup for us." Kyle's stare drilled a hole right through their heads. "We need to get this done before any of the locals catch wind of this."

The hard look he got back from Fredo and Coop told him they got the message. Their ability to move unfettered would be greatly curtailed if they had to ask for permission and wait for jurisdictional etiquette. It would be a cluster fuck, and might cost Armando his life.

Fredo swore, but Cooper just looked back at him, chewing on a toothpick like one of his family's Herefords in Nebraska chewing on a strand of hay. The farm boy took a slip of paper out of his vest pocket and pushed it with his long fingers across the greasy table with a squeaking sound. "Here's the address. That cell phone has been there two days now. The friendlies at DOJ are watching it for us."

"Thanks, Coop."

"My guy said someone's been nursing the battery. Turning it off and on. Trying to make it last and sending out a signal every few hours."

"That's got to be Armando."

"That's what I told him."

"Think your *Babemobile* is ready for a little undercover work?" Kyle dropped this bomb on Cooper, but again, the farm boy didn't flinch. Cooper lived in the converted and customized motor home at the ocean, but they'd never used it for a domestic mission like this one. Built to look just like an old fisherman's motor home, Coop had installed state-of-the-art surveillance equipment so he could monitor the whole area. It also contained arms stored in hidden compartments, and half a dozen drones he'd picked up overseas on the black market.

Cooper kept the beast clean and stocked with fresh flowers nearly every day. He'd told Kyle that he never knew when his walks on the beach would produce a young lady willing to share his bed for the evening. He didn't have far to go, so when the urge overtook them, he had a pleasure palace outfitted with candles, music, and clean scented sheets, not to mention the flowers, which the girls always loved. It sure was a damn sight cheaper than a motel room. Kyle halfway admired the boy for his frugality, which was legendary among the Teams.

"She's ready, boss."

Fredo chuckled and finished his beer. "I sure hope you changed the sheets..."

"I'm not sleeping with you, Mr. Beans-And-Tortillas-For-Breakfast-Lunch-And-Dinner." Cooper gave Fredo a twisted grin. "Besides," he said, showing off his straight, oversized white teeth that obviously had cost his parents a small fortune, "I'd rather smell the sheets than your sorry little ass. Little Miss Saturday Night likes Chanel No. 5, and it's growing on me."

Kyle watched as Fredo gave Coop a punch in the arm that almost sent the giant sprawling to the floor.

"Okay, gents. Showtime." Kyle was impatient to begin.

All three got up. Cooper dumped the last of his fries and some packets of sugar and salt into a napkin and wadded the top closed. He never left a morsel on his plate, or anyone else's either.

"Supplies," Coop said to Fredo's frown.

Kyle felt like two people who inhabited the same body. One side heard and was entertained by the shit talk between two best friends who were closer than blood brothers. His other side was worried about what would happen at Christy's condo while they were off during surveillance. And he couldn't deny the fantasy of slipping his long frame against her warm supple backside and riding her all night long.

Be safe, Christy. Be smart. Don't want to lose you.

He wished he could be the last thing she saw at night and the first thing she saw in the morning, for however long he was given the opportunity.

What am I doing? Wake up, sailor.

They found Cooper's wheels in the parking lot adjacent to the beach, amid trucks and vans loaded with surfboards and marine toys. The Navy gave the farm boy a sizeable housing allowance since he did what most of the Team guys did, choosing not to live on base except for specialized trainings. Instead of procuring an expensive apartment, he'd bought the smoking ten-year-old toy hauler, and chose to get around town on a bright red scooter he kept well secured in the rollup compartment at the rear. What would have been a problem to tinker with and maintain for the average guy was hardly a challenge for Coop, who spent most of his youth on his back fixing his father's tractors and trucks.

When Kyle followed Cooper's bony ass up the metal pull-down steps to the motor home, he noticed a new hand-painted sign to the right of the small front door curtain window: "Mi Casa Es Su Casa." Kyle chuckled and thumped the tiny daisy drawn below it on the painted aluminum frame. It was someone's calling card. From the style and lettering, Kyle recognized it as being done by Daisy, the buxom blonde from one of the tattoo parlors they frequented.

Son of a bitch. He's nailing her.

Sometimes Coop just outdid himself. Every Team guy who was single and half the married ones were trying to get into that young lady's pants. Leave it to Coop.

The small space did smell flowery. Fredo was swearing and holding his nose.

"Lose the air freshener, man. It's just gross, man."

"After an hour it'll smell like your pits, and then I'll have to wear a mask."

Kyle had to admit, the smell was a little obnoxious. "I can't believe they actually like it this way. You better open some windows or we're gonna pass out," he said.

Cooper opened a window over the kitchen sink. "That's all I'm doing, since it takes a boatload of gas to run the heater."

Fredo tossed the bouquet of flowers out onto the parking lot, then poured the remaining water on top.

"Hey, you owe me five bucks for those, Fredo," Cooper lashed out, grabbing back the vase.

"Got hay fever. Don't you ever listen? Asthma too. I wind up at the ER and you're gonna pay for it."

Kyle knew it wasn't true. No way the Navy would have cleared him for SEAL duty with asthma or a severe case of hay fever. Every cell of Fredo's body had been inspected and none had been found lacking.

Except for maybe some of his brain cells.

Cooper crawled over the dinette seat and inserted himself into the driver's console. The passenger seat door was wired shut, so Kyle followed Cooper's ass and dumped his bones into the passenger seat next to his teammate. Stuck to the dash were glued plastic dinosaurs and some of his favorite childhood toys like Skeletor, He-Man, and Conan.

The *Babemobile* spewed smoke out the back and coughed a few times before reaching a safe cruising speed of twenty-five miles an hour. By the time they got to Gunny's, a trail of more than a dozen cars were backed up behind. When they pulled up to the curb, Cooper got honked at and was given a generous serving of one-finger salutes.

Cooper looked as if he hadn't paid attention, but Kyle knew better.

Gunny was at his front door, locking up early.

"You ready to ride, Gunny?" Kyle said through the open window.

"You bet. Halfway thought you guys'd leave me behind."

"Nope. Need a chaperone for these two." Kyle tilted his head back as Gunny climbed aboard.

Gunny sat at the built-in dinette table with Fredo while Cooper punched the address into the GPS unit, then turned over the motor, which was reluctant to start. The machine backfired, sending two Team guys on the street horizontal on the sidewalk. With a slow rumble and another backfire, the beast took off on its secret military mission, the sun just setting in an orange puddle on the inlet.

They drove up the coast for nearly half an hour, heading north, and then turned inland.

Kyle got his sat phone out of the black duty bag he'd brought, along with his night vision goggles and other equipment. "Reception here is terrible, but I got it boosted." He showed the wire antennae running down the inside of his jacket. "The computer will track everything too." He pointed to the MAC plugged into the center console.

Coop was focused on driving, but nodded to the roadway, which had grown twisty. They were headed into small foothills.

"Coop, you're gonna have to talk to your friend when we get there."

Kyle got more nods.

Fredo looked worried. "So, Kyle, what are they looking for?"

"I'm thinking guns. Guns they can't buy on the street."

"But why take the girl?"

"I don't think they wanted her. I think they want something from Armando."

"Can't believe he'd let himself get caught like that."

"I think his sister told them about Armando. She's less than discreet. I'm being kind," Kyle said.

"Kid's had it rough, from what I hear," said Fredo. "Raped at fourteen. The dude woulda died, too, if the cops hadn't gotten there in time and stopped Mama Guzman. That woman's a pistol."

Cooper laughed. "Well, no wonder you're scared shitless about asking Mia out to dinner, Fredo."

"I never said that," Fredo's defensive tone gave him away. Kyle hadn't noticed this little soap opera. Knowing Fredo, the athletic SEAL had a personal reason to protect her from the lowlifes she'd been hanging around with. That would be like him. But only if her mama approved.

They drove for another few minutes in silence. Kyle thought out loud. "I think Armando didn't expect to meet anyone but Mia. Otherwise, he would have been more prepared." It was the only thing that did make sense in this scenario.

"Except that he didn't check in with you or Timmons at ProDev," Cooper yelled over the noise of the engine.

"Exactly. He knew I'd go look for him if he disappeared."

"I don't like it. Going after civilians," Fredo said.

"Don't have to. We can let you out right here, if you want. You're either in or out."

"No. I'm in. I just don't like it."

"They're dangerous, bad people," said Kyle. "They kidnap and terrorize innocents like some of the guys we saw overseas, except these guys do it for the money. No religious morals here."

Fredo nodded his head. "Yeah, and they expect to live about as long as the sand rebels do."

"Without the glory," Kyle added.

"Or the virgins." Cooper turned and grinned at them.

Kyle was thinking about Mia and what her mother had told him. Pregnant with the bad guy's baby. That made it more complicated. He hoped none of his Team would have to sacrifice their lives or sustain major injuries just to save Caesar's offspring.

What a fucked up twist of fate that would be.

The motor droned on with mind-numbing vibrations. Kyle lost track of time. They turned off the main road and onto a dirt trail that wound through a dense, unmarred forest of small saplings. A young branch slapped the side of the aluminum shell, sounding like a gunshot, sending all of them but Coop to their feet. Cooper allowed the beast to idle in a crawl. The hauler snaked through the foliage, which grew sparser.

Kyle leaned back and stared at the ceiling. It had gotten dark outside. He'd been lulled to near sleep by the bouncing and rocking of the clumsy vehicle.

"Coop, how come you know about all these places?" Fredo wanted to know.

"Boy Scouts. This was an old scout camp. I came every summer. That's how come I wanted to join the Navy. I saw those guys one day running down the beach and thought to myself, that's what I wanted to do."

"Yeah, being a SEAL is all beach and babes, right?" Fredo gave a smirk.

"Little did your parents know," Gunny added.

"Yeah, they freaked. Thought I'd get excited about the San Diego area and decide to go to college here. Maybe settle down. They always wanted to retire here. Farming is a hard life."

That was an understatement, Kyle thought, recalling some of Cooper's stories.

Fredo closed his eyes and tried to doze off. Kyle thought Gunny was in pain from the jostling around and couldn't fall asleep, so Kyle took advantage of a few minutes rest. It felt like he'd just closed his eyes when he heard a thump.

They had stopped.

"Okay. We're a click away." Cooper turned and faced the trio. "I'm gonna call Morris."

Cooper got out and slammed the door, rocking the aluminum frame, which startled Fredo fully awake. He looked in panic at Kyle, his hand instinctively reaching for his Benchmade knife.

"Coop's calling his friend," Kyle said.

Fredo seemed relieved, but stayed alert. Both of them looked outside the windows. No lights were visible anywhere.

"Black as hell out here," Fredo said.

"Black is beautiful," Kyle said. Using state-of-the-art night vision equipment would give them a real advantage.

Before Fredo could respond, Cooper was inside the cabin. "No change in the position of the cell phone. Battery still sending out signals." He looked down as he slipped the phone back into his pocket. "We gotta plan for the possibility that perhaps she's dead. That could be why the signal hasn't moved."

"Don't think so," Kyle said. "If Mia were dead, Armando would have done something to draw attention. He's being stealth because they're alive and he wants it to stay that way."

"He'd have taken out a bunch of the bad guys," Fredo added.

They pulled into an abandoned campground a few hundred feet from the turnoff. Small shacks were built around a half-acre open area with an old, crumbling stone fire pit built in the center.

They transferred their gear from their duty bags that had been stored below the couch cushions to backpacks.

"Okay, Gunny. You stay with the ship," Kyle announced.

"Not sure I can get into that seat," Gunny said as he pointed to the driver swivel chair that looked more like his dad's old La-Z-Boy. When Kyle was a boy, his dad wouldn't let anyone else sit in it. But then, after all the drool and vomit Kyle's mom had cleaned off the surface over the years, no one had wanted to.

Cooper was helpful. "No problemo, Gunny. You'll not have to drive it. But I'm leaving the keys, just in case. Just watch her for me a bit. I'd offer to load up some triple Xers on the CD player here, but the battery is acting wonky. Don't want to chance it."

"I don't watch the stuff anyway."

Kyle knew the only TV Gunny watched was the Military Channel, which ran 24/7 at the gym.

The three SEALs put on Kevlar vests and blacked their faces. They positioned their night goggles after killing all the lights. Cooper had obtained a 9mm SigSauer P225 for Kyle. Fredo and Cooper had their H&K "USC" .45.

"Gunny, if I hear you honk the horn twice, I'll know we can't return, got it? Need to know if we're walking into something," Kyle said to his older and unofficial fourth member of the Team.

"That I can do."

"That means you're on your own. And the first call you should make is to Timmons."

"Will do. But you come back soon, 'cause I'm fucking scared of the dark."

Everyone chuckled. Then it was down to business. Kyle and his team finished their preparations. No one spoke. The hauler was filled with sounds of zipping and Velcro being separated and smoothed over.

Gunny picked up a paperback book that had a near-naked man on the cover. "Shit, Coop. I didn't know you was gay."

Cooper grabbed the book, obviously embarrassed. His face was a shade of peach Kyle had never seen.

"It's a romance novel." He pointed to a woman standing behind the hunk on the cover. "See? Besides, it isn't mine. Someone left it behind."

"Uh huh. Sure," Fredo added.

THE PLAN WAS to go in quietly, now that darkness had fallen, and grab Armando and Mia, if she was there, and then get out before anyone found them. Kyle knew they had to avoid any big firefight. And they absolutely couldn't get captured.

They left the cab of the hauler and dove into the forest with less noise than an owl's wing flap. They jogged for nearly twenty minutes.

The trio traveled through low-lying brush, using their night vision goggles. Eyes of small animals and one pair of deer flashed before them as they kept to occasional outcroppings of rocks and tree stumps. The area had been forest at one time, but a recent fire had eliminated any semblance of the lush wilderness it had once been. Kyle could still smell the charred remains of scorched trees.

They came upon a clearing and a lighted cabin, with gray smoke barely visible snaking up from the chimney behind. Two black Suburbans were parked out front, along with Armando's Land Rover. There was no sign of the brown sedan. Kyle wasn't happy with this.

The front door to the cabin opened and a male figure stepped out, profiled by the warm yellow candlelight from inside. The man, with an AK-47 slung over his shoulder, scanned the darkness. He unzipped his pants and urinated. The three of them stayed very still, waiting until he finished his business. He went back inside and slammed the door shut. They heard the click of a lock as it was secured.

Kyle went around the back of the cabin as Fredo and Cooper waited in place, scanning for new arrivals. He pulled up his black facemask to cover every inch of exposed skin. Coupled with the goggles that covered his eyes, nothing of his skin showed in the dim light of a half moon beginning to travel above the horizon. His shadow crouched at the backside of the structure as he slowly looked through one window. He caught a glimpse of Armando, asleep, his hands in handcuffs, chained to a large metal hook drilled into a four-by-eight wooden beam. He'd been beaten; his usually handsome face was swollen around the eyes and cheeks. A bloody slit extended from his lower lip down to his chin. But Kyle didn't see a puddle of blood anywhere on the floor or blood sprays splattered along the wall, which was what he'd been half expecting, and he was relieved.

A male figure entered the doorway to the room and Kyle ducked just in time to avoid looking into the man's eyes.

Kyle peered back into the window. The man was administering a shot to Armando. Kyle suspected it might be heroin, or something to keep Armando quiet or unable to plan an escape. He could see the disgusted expression on Armando's face as the drug took effect. His eyes opened just slightly wider, two little sparkling slits of dark pain. Armando's gaze connected with Kyle's and registered. Armando's smile was wide as he bobbed his head to the left to let Kyle know he saw him.

"You like this shit, don't you, hero boy?" The heavily accented man kicked Armando in the gut.

Armando retched, and then raised his head up with another wide grin. "Oh, yeah. I like it all right. I'm dreaming of peeling your skin off in strips and cooking it like bacon, man."

Armando got another kick in the gut for that one.

"Yum," Armando said, and then spat out blood onto the man's shoes.

Kyle figured Armando was going to get a fist and probably more kicks, but the phone rang, and the man went after it. Left alone, Armando nodded to his left twice in quick succession, indicating Mia was probably in the next room.

Kyle silently crept to the other window and saw Mia, her arms cuffed up over her head and her ankles spread and cuffed to the iron bed frame. She was covered with a dirty blanket. Her sleep was deep.

God, hope they didn't drug her too.

Kyle thought he heard a vehicle in the distance. He adjusted his goggles and scanned the forest, but couldn't detect a light source. He ran near soundlessly through the brush until he reached Cooper and Fredo.

"You hear that?" he asked.

"Yeah, sounded a ways off, though. Came from there," Coop whispered, nodding toward the motor home. Kyle recognized a slight waver in his buddy's voice. The last time he'd heard it they'd been lying on their bellies on a rooftop in Afghanistan.

Kyle knew if something happened to the motor home, they'd have to wing it in the woods. But they had gear and had been trained to improvise, to use what was around them. It would be a minor inconvenience for them, but might put Gunny in harm's way. But wasn't anything he could dwell on right now.

At least they weren't in the frozen tundra in Alaska, where they'd been trained.

Kyle began making a plan, assuming there were at least two bad guys in the house. Perhaps more in the woods. Definitely more coming. Though outnumbered, at least they had the element of surprise on their side. And so far, they didn't have anyone shooting at them.

Something whizzed through the night air. Three definite taps hit the tree right behind Fredo and splinters of pinewood flew in all directions. Kyle recognized silenced automatic fire.

CHAPTER 13

C HRISTY HAD SPENT a restless morning cleaning her condo. Again.

Twice in one week? I'm turning into my mother.

But she knew she'd have to step outside her cocoon eventually and face the real world. She wouldn't be looking for anyone to take the SEALs place. Just something to distract her thoughts until her heart could heal.

If that was even possible.

She thought about calling Marla, but didn't need the questions she knew would come. She needed an intense workout, though, and Marla, the toughest of the personal training staff, would push her as hard as she wanted to go. And then ask all her questions.

So be it. Christy really didn't want to be alone. And maybe after the workout, she'd even think up some answers that might make some sense.

Marla agreed to meet her at the gym an hour before closing. She put off the trainer's sharp queries, promising to catch her up later.

She grabbed her keys, loaded her gym bag for later, and left it on her bed.

Though she knew it wasn't wise, she needed to go look for Kyle. He was probably occupied with searching for Armando, but she hoped for a chance encounter. Or perhaps word would get back to him she was looking for him again.

Will this send him away permanently? She decided it didn't matter.

Her hallway was deserted. Downstairs in the garage, it was deathly quiet. A pair of finches had traveled into the huge underground structure and made a nest. She heard the peeping of young life echoing faintly in the cold, gray cave of the bowels of her complex. It took away some of her apprehension.

Why can't I relax?

It wasn't as if she was in any danger. Kyle was the one who was doing all the exciting stuff. Christy was a Realtor. The only thing she had to do was land on her feet after a rocky first week at the company. Time would heal her jitters. If Patterson Realty wasn't going to start getting comfortable right away, she'd move on. She would try another office. Make another fresh start.

Or I'll quit and go back home to San Francisco.

Her Honda was still clean after last Sunday's bath. When she'd been ready to launch her career. Been dressed to the nines. Hopeful. All this had been just four little days ago, back when all things were possible. Before the guy with the three-legged tattoo had wound her pantyhose around her wrists and challenged her very existence.

As she exited past the lumbering automatic rolling grates of the garage, afternoon sunlight caught her like a blast from a furnace. Her eyes hurt from all the crying she'd done. One look into the rear view mirror told her it showed. The car had no forgiving light fixture like the one in the bathroom. Harsh sunlight showed every wrinkle, every bloodshot vessel in the whites of her eyes, every part of her puffy red eyelids. Crying and lack of sleep made her look ten years older, she thought.

Come on, Christy. Get yourself together. Focus.

Nothing looked familiar yet in San Diego. Every street was new.

Every building, office, or restaurant was more eye candy. The colors of the bay, the clouds in the sky—everything was different from San Francisco, a city she knew so well. A city where she'd felt safe. Not like here, although San Diego was probably safer with all these hunky guys running up and down the beaches. The only constant was that she felt she didn't belong here yet.

Her Honda pulled up outside the sandwich shop Kyle had taken her to on the island as if she'd willed it that way. She'd traveled without being conscious of where she was driving. Over the Coronado bridge that always scared her just a little bit. She hadn't noticed.

Why?

Though Kyle was the biggest asshole she'd ever met, he was also a complicated package doing a hard job. She was collateral damage. Plain and simple.

The thought didn't help her as much as she wanted it to. She'd wanted to be more than collateral. That was the whole point. She wanted to be the center of someone's universe. And she knew with Kyle, that could never be. His duty, his job, would always come first.

My own damn fault. That's right, Christy. You knew it would hurt. Well, babe, you were right.

God, how she hated to be right, especially when she didn't listen to herself.

"Fuck it," she whispered as she exited the car and tweeted it locked.

The grill was hopping, with a full crowd. Too early for happy hour. She spotted a table full of America's finest, eating hamburgers and drinking shakes. She knew, just knew they were SEALs. They were all dressed casual, with their hair a little longer than regular military, and even a couple had moustaches. Their muscles were bulging and from what she could see, she figured that among the eight of them, there were probably fifty tattoos. She didn't want to stare.

But she did.

Almost on cue, all of them turned and quietly assessed her. They looked in her eyes, every one of them. She could tell they were scanning elsewhere, but wouldn't show it, with that damned peripheral vision Kyle used.

Did they know she'd been with Kyle here? *No way.* How in the heck could they tell?

She nodded in their direction, smiled, and took a flying leap of faith. Her legs automatically took her to their table's edge and she addressed them.

"Hi there, fellas."

"Afternoon, ma'am," one said. Several of them stood.

"No. Stay seated, but thank you."

"You like to join us?"

God, he was good looking. Dark, almond eyes and light, coffee-colored skin. They all were specimens. She smelled something familiar in their group.

Confidence.

"Well, I…"

"Sure she will, gents." Griz came over and handed her a menu. "I'm giving her this, but I already know she likes the fresh crab sandwich." He winked, and several of the men nodded.

So that's how it's done. Griz just let them know she'd been there with someone. Didn't matter who. Someone had claimed her.

But do they know he's dumped me?

It probably didn't matter. She could tell she was permanently off limits. And it wouldn't be the first time an ex-girlfriend…and *what in the hell are you thinking, Christy?*

I'm no ex anything. I was a two-night stand. Nothing more.

That did it. Her eyes stung because the tears were being dredged up all the way from her feet. She'd cried so much last night she was plain out of tears and hadn't recovered, probably wouldn't recover for days.

She shoved the menu against Griz's chest, chanced a quick glance into his puzzled eyes, and then took off. She ran. She ran down the sidewalk three blocks, hoping the wind would take the tears away before she felt them running down her cheeks.

And then she stopped.

What am I doing?

She'd run past her car. She saw water glistening on the inlet and she walked toward it, down to where the waves were lapping on the shore. The sand was warm under her feet. A couple of little kids were playing in the surf. The beach was dotted with visitors.

Christy turned to the left and saw a portion of the beach roped off in orange. Out in the bay several gray boat crews were bobbing up and down, their oars dipping deep into the murky water, held by muscled arms. It kept them from being pulled onto the rocks ahead of them on the shore. Another small crew of men ran in tandem down the beach, carrying a rubber boat over their heads, looking like ants under a bulky sausage. A lone man with a bright orange vest was shouting through a white bullhorn. He stood atop the large boulders of the breakwater.

She walked closer to the spectacle. A small crowd of tourists was standing outside the orange zone. As another crew passed them, someone shouted, "Smile, gentlemen. We got pretty girls ahead."

Half of the men didn't look up, but the handsome boat crew leader showed off his pearly whites to a couple of well-tanned lovelies in their all-too-skimpy bikinis, each holding up their iPhones to take pictures.

"Bet he won't be smiling tonight," someone said in the audience.

Another instructor with a bullhorn shouted behind one brave soul, who was limping.

"I said sandy. Good and sandy, mister."

The whole beach could hear him.

"Yessir."

"Don't yessir me. Get sandy, sailor."

"Yessir." The recruit did somersaults all the way to the edge of the surf, where he lay back and allowed the little slapping waves to cover him. He threw wet sand over his camis and boots that were laced up mid-calf. The young man looked up to see where his tormentor was.

"Did I say you could raise your head, sailor?"

The recruit put his stubbled head back onto the wet beach and continued to splash water and wet, sloppy sand on his own face.

Christy heard the bullhorn blurt out something toward the waiting boat crews on the water, and she watched as one crew cheered and began paddling in. Reaching the rocks, they dismounted, held their boat above their heads, and inched up, painfully slow, as one crab-like animal. They brought the precious boat up and over the rocks without damaging it. They cheered, as they must have been rewarded with something the instructor said. They ran the rest of the way to take their positions next to another crew, who was sitting on the edge of their boat, sunning themselves. Waiting.

So this is what he did.

She'd seen the TV programs. She was touched that this little routine of triumph and defeat was so openly visible for everyone to see. If someone failed today, some of the people they were supposed to defend were going to witness it.

Have I ever faced that kind of reality?

She had to say yes. She'd come during her mother's last days, taken a few days off from the lingerie shop in San Francisco. When her mother died, she felt totally alone.

The first few days after her mother's death, she didn't even cry. It wasn't until her mother's pastor stopped by to visit, as she was boxing up some of her mother's things she was taking to her brother or to donate that she'd collapsed against his chest and let loose. Was that all it took? Someone's big strong arms to hold her so she could free herself of the pent up grief and loneliness? Someone to help her feel what it was like to be truly alone?

After that, she'd taken a breather from packing, and for the next two days she'd walked down to the water's edge, watching the boats. She had watched the sun setting both nights. On the second evening, as the pink and orange sky turned purple, she'd decided she'd stay in San Diego. Something in the water called her.

She dialed Madame M and told her she wasn't coming back to the shop after all.

"Ah, ma chère, I feel a great adventure awaiting you. Is there a man, perhaps?"

"Hardly. Unless he's the doorman, or a driver for Goodwill."

"No romantic dinners by the water's edge?"

"No."

"Galleries. They have wonderful galleries. Not as great as here, of course."

Nothing was ever as good as it was in San Francisco. Madame squealed about every new yogurt shop or cupcake bakery that opened. It was their secret mission to visit all the new ones within the first week of their opening.

"And then there are the boys on the beach. The ones that run bare-chested."

"I've not even seen them."

"Then you must. In fact, I will never forgive you unless you do."

Christy knew Madame would be stressed and shorthanded with her absence. But while the woman knew her customers, she knew her staff even better. There'd be nothing she could say to change Christy's mind.

Christy had intended to transition to work for a wealthy San Francisco developer and customer of the shop. He'd been delighted when she told him she'd passed her test.

She called Tom Bergeron's office and told his secretary she was going to hang her new license somewhere else, and would be permanently relocating to San Diego. The secretary feigned disappointment, but Christy knew the older woman was secretly jealous of the attention the handsome owner paid to her. At least he did before his recent public spectacle of a wedding to the famous international supermodel. Married on the bay, on a full moonlit night. She'd watched the couple and hoped someday her wedding would be just as beautiful.

If she could only meet the right guy.

Mr. Simms was going to be the Realtor she had selected to sell her mother's condo, but when he offered her the job instead, she took it. And that was how she got here, on the beach. Watching some poor mother's son get wet and sandy.

Finding out where his limits were.

And where hers were, as well.

Christy left the beach and returned home. In her dusky-lit condo, Christy made some client calls and then checked her emails. She checked her cell. Nothing from Kyle, of course. She fixed herself a salad and ate alone on the balcony, watching the sunset over the channel.

She wondered what he was doing. If he was safe. If he'd found Armando.

Stop this. Not good for you.

The orange sunset reminded her of that first night they'd shared together. His dark hair had a red streak to it in the sunlight. Even the hair on his thighs and calves had orange tips, like they were on fire. She'd looked down and touched him there at their joining, then had drawn her hands up over his flat abdomen, drifting over the smooth muscles that moved under his warm skin as he made love to her. His body had undulated close and then apart as he'd thrust slowly and completely in and then out, ministering to her, giving her something she'd never had.

She'd wanted to see it all. Wanted to watch what they looked like making love. Then she'd felt his gaze on her as she looked up to his face. He'd stopped. And as they'd shared the gaze between them in the quiet afternoon, he'd entered her deep and stayed there, and filled her.

Something had happened. She knew it did. Did he feel the same?

Her face was warmed as she stared out at the glistening water. If she thought very hard, she could still feel his lips on hers. Her body responded. She remembered what it felt like to touch his chest with her nipples and arch up to his warmth and see his pleasure in those blue eyes.

It was going to be another restless night. Maybe her workout would sweat it out of her.

Maybe not.

CHAPTER 14

KYLE AND THE team took off, running toward the cabin to do a snatch and grab on Armando, but a rain of automatic gunfire from that direction stopped them. Caught between the cabin and their safe house on wheels, they elected to go off toward the road and lead their pursuers away from the van. Then they slipped back and waited.

"They've got some decent equipment," Fredo whispered.

"Ex-military?" Cooper asked.

Kyle nodded. Whoever was hunting them had night vision too, so their advantage of surprise and their equipment had been equalized. He decided the best method was to retreat and sneak back later. He wasn't sure who was lying in wait for them. Perhaps it had been a trap—one they'd walked right into.

Every few yards they stopped to listen. Nothing was moving. No animals, no sounds from anything. Just rustling wind. It chilled Kyle to the bone and worried him.

You don't worry about the animal sounds around you in the jungle. It's when there's no sound it's the most dangerous, Gunny had told him.

Cooper tapped him on the shoulder and pointed west. Kyle turned and saw two heavily armed men, wearing all black, running between rocks and trees, using them as cover. He motioned for Fredo and

Cooper to split up. The three of them would come at the men from behind.

Fredo set off a small timed IED under a tent of charred branches, and then the three dispersed. In thirty seconds, the explosion echoed throughout the forest and up into the foothills above them. While the men were focused on the blast, Kyle and Cooper came up behind them and with quick jerks to their neck, rendered them unconscious. The team tied the pair up back-to-back and added strips of heavy military duct tape across their eyes and mouth, and then secured their wrists and ankles with zip ties.

The team waited for evidence of more gunmen, but all was silent. Coop injected something in the men to make sure they remained passed out.

"That buys us an hour," Coop told Kyle.

They returned to the clearing with the cabin. This time the brown sedan had just pulled up alongside one black Suburban, and two occupants jumped out. Armando's Land Rover was parked off in the bushes to the side.

Dust from the off-road trail was settling all around them. Another vehicle approached—a Jeep. Its engine whined, then sputtered to silence behind the Suburban. A single male occupant in police uniform, armed with an automatic strapped to his chest, got out of the Jeep and headed for the front door of the cabin. Kyle realized they were out-gunned, maybe three to one.

Not bad odds, if there were no wounded.

Heated voices came from within.

What Kyle and his team heard next froze them to the ground. A hail of bullets came from inside the house, along with a woman's scream.

Mia's emotional pleas were difficult to understand, but Kyle could hear the occasional "No." That meant the men were doing something horrible to her or to Armando. After the expended rounds, her sobs pierced the otherwise silent and dark night.

Kyle's eyes filled with water as he drew on one horrifying thought: Armando might be dead.

Fredo and Cooper checked Kyle's expression before he quickly sent them off. Practiced at reading each other without words, the team made their way to cover the house, Kyle in the rear, Cooper up front, near the porch overhang, hidden behind a water tank, and Fredo on the side of the house, where he hopefully took up a vantage point by the living room window.

Kyle looked into the first bedroom and saw the two men kicking someone he thought was Armando at first. But he soon realized his buddy was handcuffed to the doorframe, looking more out of it than before. The man on the floor had been the one who had injected Armando with the junk. From the blood pooling around him, Kyle figured he'd been shot. The smoke from recent gunfire wafted through the room like incense. The man on the floor put up no resistance to the barrage of kicking and fists pummeling his body. Kyle knew the man was probably dead.

The policeman was at the doorway and swore when he saw the corpse.

"What the hell were you thinking, Caesar? You're gonna fuck us all," he shouted.

"He pumped Armando so full of junk he didn't even know Mia's name. And just now I caught him going down on Mia, the sick fuck. She's my woman. And Armando has told us nothing," Caesar answered. "I caught this guy yesterday with his hands all over her ass."

"The girl means nothing except for him," the dirty cop said, nodding to Armando who remained motionless, eyes closed. If he was awake, Kyle couldn't tell. Bloody drool was dripping down his chin and onto his stained white T-shirt. Maybe a bicep flinched in response to information about the man's attempts with Mia. Maybe. Kyle couldn't be sure.

Caesar was glaring at the policeman, keeping one hand on the knife strapped to his thigh.

"You gonna use that? You fucking dickhead. We're gonna have to torch this place. The squad will be here any minute with all that fucking gunfire. Can't leave evidence."

The cop gave instructions in English to two huge guys. The pair dashed off to the Suburban.

Caesar swore and left the room.

Kyle couldn't get Armando's attention, so he moved on. Mia was whimpering in the next room, sobbing uncontrollably. Her body jolted in rhythm with her sobs as she writhed on the dirty mattress, trying to dislodge herself from the restraints. She seemed beyond hope, naked and beside herself.

Caesar was wrapping her dirty flesh with an old quilt, trying to calm her sobs. She raised herself up as far as she could and spat at him, earning her a slap across the face that sent her back onto the dirty mattress, where she lay still. Kyle gripped the handle on his sidearm. If it weren't too dangerous, he'd put a bullet through the guy's skull, but it was too risky.

Caesar checked Mia's pulse and swore.

"We gotta go, Caesar. Cops are on their way," the other man said.

Kyle had every reason to avoid the cops as Caesar did.

"Give me a hand, Zario. I gotta get her unhooked."

"He says to leave her," Zario answered.

"What the fuck?"

"Leave her," Zario repeated.

Kyle could smell gasoline.

"No, man. She's carrying my kid. I can't leave her."

"So Caesar, you gonna think with your dick or with your brains? She's baggage, man." The cop had appeared at the doorway and shoved the other man away. He leveled his gun at Caesar. "You wanna die for her, hmm? That what you're saying? 'Cause I'm not."

Kyle thought Caesar would make a run for the cop's throat. Caesar seemed to be seething with hatred, barely able to control the blind anger inside. There was no way both of them would be alive by morning.

"Give her a chance," Caesar said.

"No. We go. Now." The cop was smart enough to wait for Caesar to leave the room first. "Zario, go get the stuff."

Kyle joined Fredo on the side and watched as the men loaded Armando into the brown sedan's ample trunk. He saw Fredo write down the license plate number for both the vans.

Kyle briefly considered launching an attack against the bad guys, but he couldn't risk further injury to Armando and Mia.

Zario disappeared into the house for a minute, and then brought something out. Kyle saw a homemade IED that Zario set on the porch by the open front door. In a matter of seconds the place was going to blow, depending on the timer. Kyle motioned to Fredo to take cover behind a boulder. Fredo stood in his tracks and shook his head.

The jeep and brown sedan turned and took off down the dirt road, in the direction of Gunny and the van.

"I'm going in to get her."

"No. You stay put…" But Kyle doubted Fredo even heard him.

The explosion rocked the house, sending sparks into the forest, igniting trees like matchsticks.

Water from the tank adjacent to the building spilled all over the yard, partially putting out the resulting fire. Kyle hoped Coop had been safe behind the ruptured tank. Through the burning timbers he and Fredo found Mia, who was badly burned and bruised, and thankfully unconscious. She'd been covered with the thick quilt and curtains as well as other debris, which had probably saved her life.

They couldn't remove her shackles, but the bed frame was so rickety they could detach her, and so they brought her outside, slung in the bed sheets. She was breathing. Fredo poured water on a strip of cotton and wiped her face as Coop checked for further injuries. Fredo offered her a drink from his pack. She moaned and spit up blood.

"She's got something internal going on," Coop said. "We gotta get her to the hospital."

Sirens were getting closer.

Kyle nodded.

"We could leave her with them. They'd take her," Coop offered.

"Nah, can't risk it. Remember, she might be able to ID the cop."

Kyle pulled a folded tarp from his pack, and they placed it under the sheet to make a sturdy sling to carry her. They took off toward the van. It was slow going through the brush, and they alternated two at a time so one could concentrate on lookout and cover, but they ran as fast as they could. Thank God Mia was a little thing. It would have been faster to drape her over a shoulder, but Kyle couldn't risk exacerbating her internal injuries in doing so.

In the direction of the roadway came the sounds of other engines. Two RTVs were snarling and echoing off the rocks in the night air. They reminded Kyle of the sounds of chainsaws he'd wielded working the logging camp one summer between his last two years of high school. The sounds were getting closer.

The three men set Mia down under a small madrone and some brush. Kyle rigged a catch with lightweight razor wire from his pack.

They wrapped it around two outcroppings of rocks. Someone was going to have to be bait, Kyle thought as he looked at his team. No one said a word, but Cooper ran up through the brush and conspicuously stepped on a fallen tree branch and fell, expelling a scream on purpose. Kyle and Fredo moved to either side of the rocks, the razor wire wound several times around the boulders between them. They hoped the person on the RTV would be attracted to their buddy like a fly to shit. Cooper would light up like a Christmas tree, but Kyle was hoping whoever was after them would miss seeing the wire.

Both RTVs came at Cooper's direction. He lay centered about thirty feet from the trap, holding his leg like he had twisted it. Just as he saw the headlights of the vehicles reflected on Coop's face, Kyle saw him check to make sure his flak vest was secured. Kyle checked the taut wire. Cooper flashed light in the two driver's direction, distracting them enough to miss the trap.

It worked.

The first RTV ran right into the razor thin wire, knocking the rider off. His limp body lay motionless where it fell. Kyle and Fredo kept the wire taut. The second rider tried to stop, and as he slowed, Fredo lurched at him, tackling him off the whining machine. Cooper went to switch off the first engine, but Kyle stopped him.

Fredo wrestled the other driver, who was considerably larger than the SEAL, and seemed well-trained.

Probably ex-military.

The man crashed against a boulder, and Kyle heard the familiar snap of a bone breaking. Fredo bounced up and immobilized the unconscious man with zip ties on his wrists and ankles. Kyle hogtied the other one, who still hadn't regained consciousness.

"He's got a busted shoulder. Bad break," Fredo said. "He'll be screaming his lungs out when he wakes up."

"Someone will find them. Let's get out of here."

They quietly covered up their footsteps and picked up Mia.

"Whoever is out there will be listening. They're gonna know if the drivers don't come back," said Coop.

Kyle answered him by sending off a few rounds of fire from the weapon he'd ripped from the bad guy's fingers. He tossed the other automatic to Coop. He signaled, and farm boy took one RTV, mounting it with glee.

"Always wanted one of these."

Kyle shook his head. "You and your toys." He turned to Fredo. "Can you handle Mia for a bit? I guess you've got five hundred yards or so to go."

"No problem, boss." Fredo held Mia's dead weight against his chest and took off. Kyle hopped onto the other coughing RTV. He and Coop zigzagged through the forest to distract any other snipers out there, giving time for Fredo to get the girl to the hauler.

A few minutes later they stopped and fired off a few more rounds. They headed back toward the hauler.

When they found Fredo hiding behind a large rock outcropping, they shut the motors off.

"Someone's pulled up. Heard maybe three trucks pass by," Fredo whispered.

"The Suburbans?" Kyle asked.

Fredo shook his head. "I think these are local law enforcement. Must have been running a roadblock or were headed out to the cabin. They'll send a chopper too."

Mia started to moan. Cooper pulled her away from Fredo's chest to check her, but the SEAL possessively wouldn't let go.

"I got to check her, dumbass. She's not your girlfriend."

Fredo shot him a warning look. Coop knew he'd embarrassed the man. Had singed his pride. Fredo defiantly held Mia's hand during Kyle's examination. A thin trickle of blood poured out of her mouth.

"Keep her warm. Jeez, I hope we can get her in the van soon," Coop said.

"She gonna be okay?" Fredo asked.

"If she gets help. I can't tell what's going on inside, except for this." Kyle pointed to a thread of fresh red blood running down her bare leg.

Mia was losing her baby, Kyle thought.

Cooper looked at both teammates. "The body does what the body does."

"We'd better go the rest of the way on foot," Kyle changed the subject, not wanting to look in Fredo's eyes. They covered the RTVs with branches, Cooper taking one last long look before covering the red one. Then they moved out.

The forest was erupting with lights and sirens, and the smoke from the cottage fire had plumed up into the air about forty feet. Just before they came upon the toy hauler, they heard the horn honk. Twice.

"Shit," Kyle said under his breath.

CHAPTER 15

B ACK AT HER condo, Christy had decided to eat dinner, then sat at the dinette table, staring into space, until she dropped her fork. It clattered on the glass top, the sound bringing her abruptly back to reality. She'd been sitting there. In the dark. All alone. What was she looking for?

Enough.

Checking the time, she noted she'd be a few minutes late for her workout with Marla.

She took the last of her unfinished salad and water to the kitchen and dumped them in the sink. Her appetite was gone.

In her bedroom, she shed her clothes and put on her workout sweats. She still felt Kyle's kisses at the back of her neck, the touch of his fingers as he'd moved down her spine and kissed every vertebra. She'd never felt so worshiped. And so abandoned.

She tied her shoes and put her hair up in a scrunchie, then gave herself a good hard look in the mirror. Some of the puffiness around her eyes had calmed down.

She slung her gym bag over her right shoulder, grabbed her keys, and walked down the silent hall to the elevator for the second time today. The gym was on the top floor. It was going to close in an hour, so she'd have just enough time for a quick workout with Marla and maybe a sauna.

Then maybe she could sleep tonight, after all.

She didn't know why the hair at the back of her neck prickled as she walked toward the elevator. She couldn't remember a time when the condo had been so quiet. The art deco doors opened and she stepped in, then pushed the black up button for the gym and common area. The elevator rumbled, as if asking her if she wanted to change her mind at the last minute. Took forever. Were the lumbering doors always this slow?

What am I afraid of?

The gym was nearly empty. Marla wasn't there waiting for her, as she usually was. A new male employee with the Infineon's green polo shirt logo was wiping down the weight machines with a white towel, using a spray bottle of emerald green cleanser. He held the bottle up to Christy in a salute.

"Marla here?" she shouted.

He shrugged and held up his hands again as if he didn't understand.

"I'm going to do some cardio first, then I might come in here," Christy shouted out to him over the classic rock and roll. The music blaring throughout the gym was a little too loud, and it was irritating.

"Suit yourself," he shouted back. "We're open for another hour and twenty." His British accent bothered her. And she hadn't recalled the gym being open so late before.

Why? No one was here. She looked down the hallway of offices. Marla's door was closed, but a light shone under a crack at the bottom.

Probably on the phone.

Christy thought perhaps she'd take her sauna before a quick workout to relax, but didn't want to miss Marla. She headed for the cardio room. Her body flinched at every little creaking door, and at the sound of howling winds whipping around the glass corner windows that overlooked the dark sky. Lights twinkled on hanging streetlamps at sidewalk level below. Some of the boats in the inlet had strings of lights illuminating their masts.

She slung a towel around her neck, put on her headphones, plugged them into the elliptical machine and clicked the TV on the wall directly in front of her. Two other TV screens mutely flashed ads and programming down at the end of the room, playing to ghosts of workout patrons who had long since vanished.

She clicked through her choices until she found a movie channel and started playing an old Rambo film. Kyle's biceps weren't as big as Stallone's, but she liked them better. All alone in the cardio room, Christy became absorbed in the movie as she coursed through her three-and-a-half mile routine.

Until images of a fire in the Santa Nella forest flashed on the screen of the TV furthest from her. A reporter was in a helicopter as the overhead camera zoomed in on a burning cabin. She switched her channel changer to listen to the newscast on the screen right in front of her.

"Police and fire crews are still trying to determine the cause of the blaze. The bodies of three men some half-mile away have been found, dead under what the coroner has called 'unusual circumstances.'"

That got Christy's attention. But why did she suddenly feel like Kyle had something to do with this? Would she always wonder if Kyle was involved when she saw a news report about an unusual occurrence? Is this what came with the territory: feeling afraid to watch the news? And why did it make her fear her own surroundings?

She hated being afraid. When she was little, her biggest fear was of drowning. She'd developed this fear after she'd had a close call at a neighbor's pool. Although now a good swimmer, it had been a whole four days before she would jump into the pool with all the other youngsters during summertime swimming lessons after her near drowning. But once she got the knack of it, she became the fastest swimmer in the class.

She used to lock up Madame M's store at night in San Francisco dozens of times, and she wasn't as apprehensive then as she felt tonight.

This was something she'd have to fix. Being with Kyle was giving her the heebie-jeebies. And that wasn't good.

She switched back to her movie and completed her forty minutes. No one else came in during that time, which she thought was odd. Marla must have gotten involved in something else, probably left her a message she'd get later on her cell.

Someone was cleaning out the garbage in the weight room, but still there was no sign of the other staff or other patrons. Christy decided she'd take a sauna in hopes it would quiet her nerves.

In the changing room, she slipped off her workout pants and sports bra top, left her shoes underneath the clothes peg in her locker, wrapped herself in the oversized white fluffy towel, and stepped to the sauna area. Just outside the glass door she found a water bottle steeping in a bowl of half-melted ice cubes, along with a rolled-up washcloth. She grabbed them and stepped inside the warm moist enclosure.

She poured water on the artificial coals to create steam inside the chamber, spread her towel down on the cedar planks, lay on her back, and placed the ice-cold washcloth over her eyes. The wet heat soothed her bones. Her skin loved the moist womb of the sauna.

Raising her knees, she felt the little bruises left between her legs from her night of heavy lovemaking. She had the urge to place her own fingers there, but decided against it.

Someone walked past the door.

In pants.

In the women's wet area?

Christy sprang to the glass door, pressing against it, and peeked out, but she could not see anyone else. She threw the towel around her, opened the sauna door a crack, and then quickly made it to the dressing area, where she dressed. Without taking the time to put her shoes on, she ran out through the women's side lobby, clutching her shoes by the laces, and into the reception area next to the weight room. The phone was ringing, but no one was manning the desk. Through the glass wall that divided the reception area from the weight room, she could see the bottle of green spray and the towel the staff member had left on one of the padded benches. The garbage can in the corner was tipped over.

She hit the heavy glass doors of the gym and discovered they were locked. She turned the heavy metal lock, pushing on the door handle. She burst into the hallway, running to the elevator. As she stepped in, she heard the gym doors open. She pushed the down button multiple times as she heard the sound of footsteps running toward her.

Christy flattened her body against the right side of the elevator car as the doors slowly closed. She half expected someone's hand to separate the doors and come after her, but the elevator began its slow descent to the fourteenth floor. Once again, she was safe for now. But what awaited her at her condo? It took forever to get there, and luckily, the compartment hadn't stopped.

Again, the hallway was deserted. After checking both right and left, Christy dashed to her condo door and scanned the pad with her room card, which released the latch. She slammed the door behind her.

Home.

Any calm she'd achieved with her workout and the sauna had been shattered by the fear that someone was after her. Images of the last hour flipped through her mind. Sure, she'd exercised by herself before, especially late at night. She'd been the last one in the gym several times. Maybe this was just her crazy imagination.

Where was Marla? The other staff? Why was the garbage can turned over? And why wasn't anyone at the desk?

CHAPTER 16

GUNNY HEARD THE explosion and knew nothing good was going to come of it. Then cars pulled up all around the van. He wasn't going to go for his piece, which was tucked in a plastic bowl and covered with a tea towel. There were too many of them. He heard the familiar clicking sounds of rifles and weapons being readied.

"Please step out of the vehicle with your hands up," the stern voice yelled. Bright light shone through the small portal of the front door. Gunny swore loudly so the men outside could hear him, and acted like he'd fallen, hitting the horn on the steering wheel to give the signal. As he slipped his pants down, leaving just his shorts in place, he swore again even louder and looked around, wondering if it would be the last time he'd see the cabin, then slowly pushed down on the door lever and stepped outside into the blinding light with his hands up.

He saw outlines of sheriff's hats and some baseball caps. No military, he was relieved to note. But then, the only military he was worried about would never let themselves be seen.

He placed the back of his arm against his forehead to shade his eyes.

"Turn around slowly," came the next command. Gunny lowered his hands and started to turn.

"Hands. Get your fucking hands in the air."

Gunny complied. But he turned his head as his wrists were jerked down by a uniformed officer and handcuffed together with two cuffs, due to Gunny's girth.

"You wanna tell me what I've done, officers? Is there a law against camping?"

As he turned back to face the light, he heard someone whisper, "That's Gunny."

So someone was military, or at least they hung out with military.

"You're no fuckin' camper. Where are your friends?" the officer asked.

"Back at the gym."

Someone in the crowd snickered and was silenced.

"Mind telling me what's going on?" Gunny persisted.

"There were two murders out this way we're investigating."

"Gents, do you mind? I'm not a well man. I'm standing here in my underwear. You caught me taking a piss, and then I was going to go back to bed and sleep off a hangover." He squinted and nodded at the array of lights. "I sure as hell didn't kill anybody. At least not tonight, anyways."

Gunny was glad he had thought to remove his pants down to his aloha shorts. Barefoot and bare chested. Hardly a threat.

"Fellas, I've had a bad day. I'm a little plastered, and no threat to anybody."

"That's for fucking sure." A smooth-shaven, handsome, square-jawed officer in a light tan uniform strode to up to Gunny and gave him a sniff. The officer waved and immediately half the lights cut out. "You don't smell like you've been on a bender, Gunny."

"I'm sorry, do I know you?"

"Not nearly as well as you're going to." The officer exhaled and stepped back, looking Gunny up and down. "You like pain, Gunny?"

Gunny tried to stand as straight as he could, but the cuffs hindered him. "I'm Gunnery Sergeant First Class Joseph Hoskins to you, sir."

The officer hit Gunny on the kneecap with his baton. Gunny went down like a sack of bricks, hitting his head in the gravel, which caused a gash on his forehead just above his right eye.

"Hold on, Warren. You got no cause to do that. He's a local and well known to have no ties to any drug dealing."

Gunny didn't recognize the voice, but the boots told him the man was not military, but local law.

"Well, he's in the wrong place at the wrong time," the lawman they called Warren noted.

"I'll admit that. But we might need his cooperation."

Red lights flared as a black Suburban pulled up. Two dark-clothed ATF uniformed officers got out and ran up. The three of them conferred, then broke. The two new men took Gunny into custody, pulling him up and placing him in the second seat of the Suburban.

"Can't I have my pants? Maybe some shoes?" he yelled from the open door.

"Sure, I'll get them." A minute later his clothes were placed on the bench seat next to Gunny, who was still handcuffed, but now seat belted in. Before the Suburban backed up, Gunny heard the special agent tell Warren to wait for someone to come back and claim the *Babemobile*.

"I already know who it belongs to," Warren said.

"So why didn't you tell me? This guy owns this rig?" the ATF officer asked.

"Nope. It belongs to Cooper, one of Kyle Lansdowne's friends. And Coop was seen driving it off the base tonight."

"We got to get back to the fire. Don't touch anything inside. If they don't come in an hour, see if you can secure it and get back to town."

"What if there's another homicide at the fire? I got jurisdiction."

The agent stepped to within three inches of Warren's face and chest. "And how the hell would you know there was another body at the fire?"

"That's no fire, and you know it. That was an explosion. Like a military explosion."

"Fine. You wanna go back to the fire with us? Okay by me. But in your position, I'd be pretty darn pleased with the opportunity to catch up on my sleep. This hits the press and tomorrow you won't have two minutes to yourself."

"I'll post a guard. But I think I could be more help to you at the scene. Who knows, maybe Gunny will start to feel talkative."

KYLE COULDN'T BELIEVE they were all leaving. All except one young deputy sheriff, who looked like he belonged in one of Cooper's scout troops. The kid was barely legal age and skinny as the saplings they'd been hiding behind.

After a quiet darkness descended on the area, Kyle got up behind the young lawman and whispered in his ear, "I don't want to hurt you. Just going to tie you up."

The kid tried to turn around, but Kyle had him in a choke hold.

"Nah, uh, uh. That'll get you into trouble. You're going to see my face soon enough, but not tonight, hear?"

The kid nodded.

"Good boy." Kyle patted his head. He had already secured the boy's wrists with a zip tie. "You remember when you used to play Pin the Tail?"

The boy nodded.

"Just like that. Although I trust you, I'm going to make sure you don't cheat." Kyle applied a black nylon tape across the boy's eyes. "Sorry, but it will pull out some eyebrows. Keep your eyes closed and it won't get your eyelashes. They don't grow back."

Kyle could feel the kid flinch at the thought of going through the rest of his courting life like a hairless freak. He sat the boy down next to a tree stump, then removed his service revolver and knife.

Cooper was going to say something, but Kyle put his finger to his lips. He brought his two rolled up fists together, then pointed to the van. Cooper climbed inside to jump the vehicle for their getaway.

Kyle and Fredo carefully lifted Mia into the back, placing her on the bed. Fredo looked down on her as though it were the first time he'd seen a naked girl. He found a clean sheet, placed it over her brown flesh, and patted her thigh.

"You're safe now, honey. You warm enough?"

She nodded, but was shaking and biting her lip. Fredo placed a blanket over her, and she smiled back up at him.

Kyle and Cooper ran back to where they'd left the RTVs.

Cooper was walking around the little toys, their shiny surfaces glistening in the moonlight. Kyle could tell he was admiring them. The Nebraska Team guy was a man who loved his toys and gadgets even more than his women, Kyle thought.

"We can't bring them."

"How about one?"

Kyle thought about it. He'd seen a steep drop around one of the curves Cooper had driven past on their way out. "Okay, one. But one we gotta dump and burn."

He knew it was going to break Cooper's heart to see a perfectly good vehicle ruined, but there was no way around it. They needed just a little time as well as the possibility of sending a message to Timmons for help, maybe draw off some of the heat. A fire would do that.

"I'll need a ravine, Coop. Something flashy," Kyle said.

"Got just the spot." Cooper started his RTV and took off. Kyle was glad his started right up because Cooper was already out of sight. He followed the filtered headlight he saw through the trees.

Coop revved up the RTV and sent it over the edge with a small explosive charge on it. When it hit the creek bottom it burst into a fireball, sending a long fiery tail up into the dark sky.

Kyle hopped on behind Cooper, and they hauled ass off toward the hauler.

Time to get the fuck out of Dodge.

Everything was quiet when they got back, except for the hauler's purring motor. They could hear Mia, inside, talking to Fredo. She was fully awake, but seemed to be in pain.

Cooper lowered the rear of his van and pulled the other RTV inside, then pushed the button to roll up the door. Kyle saw the look of appreciation on the farm boy's face.

"Thanks, boss. You let me have the red one."

"Sure hope it was the right choice." Kyle laughed as they ran to the door.

"Don't matter," Coop said as he resumed his driver duties. "It was a steal."

The hauler came to life, and they motored out of the forest without revving the engine. They had parked on a slight knoll, so they were able to slide down the hill quietly and drive away to safety.

Kyle observed Mia's skin began to peel and bubble from the bomb and heat of the fire.

"Coop. I need you to look at her. She's blistering and starting to shiver. I think it's shock," Kyle shouted up the aisle to Cooper. They switched places just before they hit the main road. To the right were some distant lights. Kyle donned his night vision goggles, killed the hauler's headlights, and turned left, back toward the coast. With the goggles, he had no trouble following the road and saw every raccoon, deer, and possum along the way.

A half hour later, they pulled up to San Diego General Hospital emergency room. Kyle ran inside, then returned, followed by two attendants with a gurney. Mia was carefully unloaded to the gurney and taken inside.

"We gotta split. Can't have us here like sitting ducks," Kyle said. "I'll call her mom and get her over here."

The horizon was beginning to glow, indicating sunrise was a couple of hours away, as the three Team guys drove toward Coronado. Kyle started to feel the weight of their nearly twenty-four-hour shift. But it was a momentary lull. He'd learned in his training he could stay up for as many as three or four days in a row with just a couple of catnaps in between. Trick was to push through the low-energy phase until he got his second wind back. And it would come back. It always did. He would need it today.

Kyle dialed Mama Guzman on the phone while Coop drove the *Babemobile* to where Fredo's car was parked along the strip. He'd left it in the two-hour parking in front of Jimmy's Bar and Grill. Sure enough, Fredo had earned a ticket, just like they'd planned. Fredo and Kyle got into Fredo's car and headed back to base, Cooper tight on their tail in the hauler. At the base, while Cooper waited in the van down the block, Fredo and Kyle drove Fredo's car past the guard shack to check who was on duty.

They were in luck. Carlisle wasn't around anywhere. They checked through, drove to the parking area, and waited for Coop, who passed through the guard gate without incident and parked the van where he usually did, then secured it. He wore Fredo and Kyle's duty bags on him as if he were hauling a couple of spare oars on his back. Behind the locked and guarded gate, local officials would have to maneuver through the minefield of the Navy's paperwork to get permission to search the vehicle. And Timmons could perhaps run interference, delaying the process further.

There wouldn't be any evidence of foul play since Cooper had sent the bloody sheets with Mia to the emergency room. Kyle figured nothing else there would tie them to the firefight or rescue.

They stopped near the beach at a breakfast café that catered to surfers and an occasional Team guy still up from a night of raising hell. The sunlight shining on the water hurt Kyle's eyes. He wanted a shower. He wanted to be tucked in and warmed by Christy's smooth flesh.

God, it had been hours since he'd thought about Christy. And he couldn't help it now. This was the quiet before a shit-kicking storm that was about to come down on all of them. But one look from her, one kiss, would sure feel nice. She was good for *him*. Just that he was bad news for *her*.

And that was exactly why he needed to stay away.

He dug into his Mickey Mouse pancakes, delivered with a smirk by the waitress named Dottie, who could have been their grandmother. Fredo and Coop took turns punching him in the arm.

"Glad you're back to your old self," Cooper said. The cook had learned long ago Kyle loved pancakes with mouse ears and chocolate chips. And four extra mini pitchers of syrup. He ate lots of chocolate and sweets when he was stressed.

Fredo was having huevos rancheros, while Cooper stuck with his usual: oatmeal and a bacon and egg scramble.

The coffee was thick like oil, but it tasted good, and they knew the caffeine would keep them awake until noon. That and the sugar rush.

"You gotta call Timmons, man," Fredo said.

"I intend to."

"He's probably worn a hole in that floor by now."

Kyle nodded and considered Fredo's statement. "Hope he hasn't gotten any flack from upstairs. We aren't the most popular team around, you know."

"Wonder how Gunny's holding up," Cooper said, hanging his jaw in a frown. He motioned toward the last pitcher of syrup which had been only half drained.

Kyle nodded. "Best thing for him is to learn we made it out alive," Kyle said.

"I'll do that," Fredo eagerly volunteered.

"Fredo, you and Gunny mind meld or something? Where the hell are you going to find him?"

Fredo stretched and then rolled his head, setting off several loud cracks from the back of his neck. "I'm feeling the need for a workout, boys. They'll know down at the gym."

"Without him, it'll be closed."

"Nah, he'll ask someone to open it for him. He won't let the boys miss a day of PT. He lives for that shit."

Fredo signed the "loser" signal with his thumb and index finger attached to his forehead, then got up and left the café. Cooper was scooping the last of Kyle's maple syrup into his yogurt with a knife.

Cooper looked up at Kyle and said, "Can't give you a lift anywhere, unless you want to ride with me on the scooter."

"No worries. I'm walking, not going far."

Kyle looked out at the water. He'd have liked to spend the day in the warm sand with Christy, holding hands and anything else he could get away with holding. Kissing her and making her blush, making her moan.

He'd bring her here. Watch the wind in her hair and wipe the sleep out of her eyes. She'd look beautiful in that crazy-tired way. They'd have explored each other's bodies all night and not tired of it. They'd feed each other as if they had a million golden days like this left. As if their pasts didn't matter. As if everything was in the future.

Cooper's clicking fingers brought him back.

"Fredo's right, boss. You're dreamin' all the time now. She that special?"

"Yeah, she is. More than I deserve." Kyle took his last huge bite of pancake that dripped with syrup. It was almost too much to swallow at once. "And I treated her like shit."

Cooper's blue eyes studied Kyle's face. Kyle could feel the examination, the evaluation going on. Did he look like a fuckup now to this loyal Team member? Did Coop doubt Kyle had the stones to see this mission through? Now that he might have something else to live for?

No. Cooper still believed in him. Probably more than he did.

But now it was time for work. "I better call Timmons," Kyle said.

AFTER KYLE'S BUDDIES took off, he called his chief.

"Kyle, I got incoming from all directions," Timmons said. "They've got three fucking bodies and even the Feds screaming at me, telling me I got a rogue killer on my hands. Tell me something I'm not going to have to resign over."

"Only one body that I know of. He was killed by his own men. Who are the other two?"

"Two shot in the head, out in the forest. One in the house, burned all to hell. Can't make out ID yet."

So they offed their own gunmen. That would cost them some loyalty, if anyone left had any balls at all. Leaving a man behind was bad enough. Killing your own men to set someone else up, unthinkable in the SEAL community. A desperate act.

"Timmons, there's a dirty cop involved. You need to be very careful who you level with."

"Shit, Kyle. Don't fuckin' tell me who I can and can't talk to. Where the hell is Armando?"

"I don't know."

Timmons swore, then Kyle heard a crash and shatter. Timmons probably had kicked the frog statue the Team had spent $300 for last year at Christmas.

"Mia is safe, sir."

"Mia? Armando's sister?"

"The same. She was in the explosion. Not in real good shape. But we got her to the ER and I called her mom."

"Good work, son."

"Gunny's been arrested."

"Fuck me. He's on his own. Nothing I can do about that. How did that happen?"

"We went in for Armando and left Gunny with the van. The ATF took him. Not that I like it, but I think he's safe in their custody. Can you find out where he's being held?"

"I'll try."

"The dead guys. Can you find out who they are, Timmons?" He gave his chief the license plate numbers from the Suburbans.

There was silence on the other end of the line. "Have to be careful," Timmons finally said. "You don't want anything to get through to Carlisle, right?"

"Carlisle? What's he got to do with this?" Kyle couldn't imagine the guard would be anywhere near anything dangerous. And this situation was fucking dangerous.

"Got himself assigned to the local squad as the Navy liaison. I'm supposed to go through him, can you imagine it? That asshole? Fancies himself as a policeman some day. He's making real nice with the County dudes."

"I'll bet. Can just see him busting sailors' chops and getting paid for it."

"I'd like to find him dirty, Kyle. He smells dirty. We could get him bounced. He has been a pain in my side for years. And for every one of my guys. Especially my guys."

"What's the story?"

"Not today. Someday I'll tell you. So, what's the plan?"

"I gotta get back to my Hummer." But then Kyle thought about the night before and of the man shot in the cabin. "The dirty cop's name is Warren something. I'm thinking now he shot that dude with an MP5. I think these guys are hooked up with some ex-military. They've got equipment."

"This Warren shot the one in the fire?"

"Yeah."

"How does Armando look?"

"He's messed up. They injected him with heroin, I think. And beat him pretty bad."

"Wonder what the hell they want."

"I'm guessing his cooperation. You know they're recruiting from the Special Forces. Recruiting for gang members to help run drugs, train the bad guys, get the special equipment. With Armani's history..."

"Yes I thought about that. Last time he was busted for being drunk in public, it nearly cost him his position on the Teams."

"And I'm glad for my sake you went to bat for him."

"You think his past has caught up to him?"

"Nope. I think it's for Mia. Armando is solid as a rock. But he'd do anything for his family."

"That should worry you."

"It does, but he'd sacrifice rather than cave in to them. If he had a choice, I mean."

"Cocky as hell, right to the last, huh?"

"I'm guessing these guys know him. Trying to turn him. Fredo told me a little about it in Afghanistan this last tour."

"Shit, Kyle. This is sounding worse by the minute."

"Just what they do, Chief. They hit guys in their weak spot."

"No way any Team guys would do that."

"They're recruiting kids that have a beef with the military. Their way of getting even. Fredo says they don't even care if the guys don't speak Spanish. They want the military training."

"What kind of a fucking world is it coming to?"

Kyle thought about the question and then answered Timmons. "I can't stop them all. But we're going to stop these bastards. No way they're going to take Armando. He'd rather die than be used by those guys."

"Then you better hope they don't tell him his sister's safe."

Kyle knew either way would be bad news. It didn't matter whether Mia was dead or safe. If Armando found out, he'd not worry one whit about his own safety and might do something stupid.

Unless I can get there first.

CHAPTER 17

I N BED, CHRISTY opened her eyes and took stock of her room, of
the sounds around her, and of the smells.

No coffee.

So the dreams about Kyle last night had been just that. Dreams.
She'd gone to bed scared to death, but sleep came crawling, and with it
the erotic dreams. Things they had done, things she wanted to do.
Maybe if she fell back asleep, the dreams would all come back. She
could be in his arms. He'd be kissing her.

She rolled her naked body to her side and hugged the pillow he'd
slept on, needing just a hint of the man she knew she craved. The man
she probably loved. The man she might never see again.

Fatal love. She knew it was a really bad idea to cling to something
she could never have again.

She closed her eyes and willed the sun to go back down. Willed the
world to swing back and replay Wednesday night. Every glorious
detail of it. Every kiss. Every stroke.

Damn. Sleep was lost to her. Sunk to the bottom of the ocean like
a lead anchor.

Several times in the night she'd awaken, having heard some sound.
She'd hoped he'd somehow returned and would slide that wonderful
hard body of his against her backside and let her melt into his arms as

they pulled her to him. She could feel his kisses on her neck and shoulders, could feel him roll her over and spread her legs for him, could feel him coax her sex to make love to his fingers while he watched, until she was close to a climax, until she wanted him so badly she could not stand another minute without his shaft ramming inside her to the hilt. In her fantasy she knew he wouldn't do it just yet. While she was spiraling into oblivion, he'd bend down and lap her juices, kiss the pink lips of her sex, and beg her to give his tongue entry.

And then he'd climb her and ride her hard, watching her, bending to kiss her neck and whisper in her ear, take the moans from her mouth with his own. He'd call her name, and she'd listen for the three little words he'd not said yet.

I am your willing prisoner, Kyle. Give me those little words and I'd gladly give you my life too.

She opened her eyes. Her wet fingers remained between her legs as she gently massaged herself there, and then stopped.

I'm being stupid. I'm lost in some fantasy. Truth was, Kyle didn't want anything more to do with her. She was a pit stop fuck on his highway to heroism. Why, she wondered, had she made an emotional investment with this man? Would it ruin her? Or would she recover?

And she knew it didn't matter. She was going for broke. Whatever it took. She had no way to stop it.

Please come back to me. Give me another chance. I can handle it, handle whatever you can give me.

The room didn't answer. Sunlight was a stubborn friend, unrelenting, unforgiving, and invading everything about the place. There would be no going back to bed.

Maybe he'll show up this morning! The lingering worries from last night seemed like a distant memory. Things were much better, much safer in the light of day. She'd been ridiculous. Her imagination had gotten the better of her, she decided.

She bounded out of bed, ready to start a new mission, then ran naked down the hallway to the bathroom and turned on the hot steam shower. She shampooed, soaped, and shaved everywhere, working quickly as if he would arrive any minute. But she was thorough. She wouldn't miss a hair or forget to wash a crevice or cave. The lavender conditioner sluiced down her skin, over her pert nipples, and made purple ribbons down her smooth legs and over those damned pink toes.

When she stepped out of the shower, she thought she heard a tapping sound. She dabbed her face with the fluffy peach-colored towel and listened. She heard the sound again, so threw on her old terry-cloth robe that hung at the bathroom door hook and stepped to the hallway, rubbing her wet hair with the towel, and listened. Someone was tapping on her door.

Dashing to her bedroom, Christy put her pajama bottoms on and an oversized sweatshirt. Excitement brewed as she was sure it was Kyle. She wasn't going to check the peephole, just open the door wide and kiss him to oblivion.

Thank God. He's come to apologize.

"San Diego PD. Please open up."

Her heart raced, and her mouth became parched. This wasn't a very good sign. What had happened? She was going to say something, but all she could do was wheeze.

I'm having a panic attack!

"Just a minute. I'm coming," she managed to call out weakly.

She opened the door to greet four officers—three men and a woman.

"We need to come in, ma'am," the eldest of the males commanded as he held up his badge.

"Sure." She stepped aside and the four burst into her condo hallway, and then began a casual visual search of her living room and kitchen area. Before closing her door, Christy took a quick peek out toward the elevators and saw her neighbors, an elderly African-American couple wearing their slippers, standing just outside their door two units down. The man was in a robe, holding a drink in one hand and the paper in the other.

She waved to them both, having just met them a week ago. Mr. and Mrs. Jefferson. They didn't move, but Mr. Jefferson shouted down to her, "They came here first."

"Everything's okay," Christy replied. "Don't worry. Another mistake." She shrugged and that seemed to satisfy the couple, who nodded and went inside.

The older officer flew past her and into the hallway. He turned back to her. "Who are you talking to?"

"The neighbors you terrorized." She enjoyed the words.

It wasn't fair to take her anger out on the police, but since Kyle was MIA, she couldn't scream at him.

Maybe he joined his friend. Two missing SEALs now.

"That kind of language is not smart, missy. I need you to get back inside. Now." He grabbed her arm firmly but without violence, and wheeled her inside, slamming the door behind him.

Christy yanked herself free. This picture was all wrong.

"He's not here, sir," the policewoman said what was obvious.

"Who?" Christy asked, pouting.

"You know damned well who, young lady. Your boyfriend, that's who." The older officer was annoyed.

She snorted. The situation would be funny if it wasn't so sad. *Boyfriend?* "He's not my boyfriend."

He leaned his tall frame into her bedroom, eyeing the tussled sheets.

Christy's cheeks flamed and she looked down at her bare toes with the bright pink polish. Her eyes began to well up with tears. Damn, she was going to have to change the polish. Every time she looked at her toes now, she cried.

She steeled herself, looking straight into the woman officer's face, letting her tears spill over and trace down her cheeks. "It was a good-bye fuck."

The woman officer's eyes grew round and she gave a hint of a nod. Christy saw traces of some pain on her face. But immediately a mask developed and the woman looked away.

"So, where did he go?" The senior man had graying sandy blond hair and clear blue eyes. Despite his age, he looked to be in great shape. Well defined muscles and a proud carriage. More military than police. Christy wasn't done testing the man.

"Out," she answered.

The lead man looked up to the ceiling and shook his head, murmuring something. He sighed and gestured for her to sit on the leather chair she still thought of as Kyle's.

"I'm Sergeant Mayfield, and these are officers Jones, Thiessen, and Woodward."

The woman was named Woodward, Christy noted. Christy crossed her arms and legs as she sat, not about to offer them coffee, tea, or water. They'd have to beg for it. And even then, she'd think about it.

Once everyone was seated, Sergeant Mayfield began. "We are looking for a man named Kyle Lansdowne. We know that he spent some time here."

"Yes. Is it a crime to date?"

"Look, I've reminded you before about your attitude. If you cooperate with us, there's no need for you to get mixed up in this mess."

"And I should believe you why?" Christy fluffed her drying hair.

"Unless you'd prefer to answer questions downtown. And of course, if you refuse, we could hold you."

"What questions? I don't know anything. I meet a cute guy, he came over here and we…you know…" She looked at the female cop, who immediately averted her gaze. "We had a good time. I'm single. But I don't know anything about him."

"Except you know what he does for a living," Mayfield persisted.

"Yes. He told me that."

"And why?"

Christy thought about their first meeting, and no way was she going to tell them.

"He returned some signs I had left at an open house. And he asked me out. Simple as that." She measured Mayfield's expression and found a hint of kindness there, not the bravado he was trying hard to portray. She addressed his ramrod chest. "Don't you tell a girl what *you* do for a living?"

The three younger officers looked briefly to their sergeant, then away. One tapped his foot. Woodward looked out the sliding glass doors to nothing but blue sky, and the third one examined his fingernails.

Christy could see she'd wounded the older man in some way. He was probably a lot like Kyle. A loner, except for his brothers in blue.

Mayfield cleared his throat. "I want to know everything he told you. Start to finish. From the top, missy." The look he delivered told her he could be nice, but only for so long. She'd better comply. She sighed, watching him pull out a notepad from his vest pocket.

"He's looking for his buddy, his teammate. He's gone missing, and

Kyle thinks it isn't voluntary. That's all I know."

"Where is he looking for him?"

"I'm sure I don't know."

"Who does he think has his friend?"

"I don't know. He hasn't said, and I don't think he knows, either."

"Why does he think the guy has been taken against his will?"

Christy had to think about what Kyle had told her. "Armando is his friend from the Teams…" She could see Mayfield picked up on her words right away. "Armando's sister is in some kind of trouble, and Kyle thinks Armando went to find her."

She watched as he scratched notes in his notepad.

"These aren't the bad guys here," Christy continued. "Except for the fact that they are known for their one night stands. But in my case it was two, thank you very much." She placed her palm against her heart and closed her eyes. She'd seen by their squirming none of the officers wanted to be there. "I doubt he'll ever come back here again, so you're wasting your time questioning me. The bad guys are the ones messing with Armando's sister."

"No, missy, I'm afraid I can't agree with you entirely," Mayfield said.

"How so?" she asked.

"We're not in Afghanistan. We're in the U S of A, and *here, we* take care of the bad guys. Kyle and his SEAL buddies don't get to act on their own just because they think it's a good idea. They're not supposed to interfere with local authority. They're supposed to cooperate."

The argument was valid. No one said a word. Christy didn't want to look at any of them. But that same question had gnawed a hole in her stomach.

Mayfield flipped out a business card and passed it to her between two fingers.

"And now we got three dead bodies. Men brutally murdered. I think Kyle had something to do with those murders. That makes him one of the bad guys."

AN HOUR LATER, Christy nearly jumped out of her skin when she heard her cell ring. She didn't recognize the number at all.

"Hello?"

"Christy? Everything okay?"

Kyle's voice sounded far away. She worked to stay cold to him. *Self preservation.*

"I think it's a good idea if you leave me alone." It was true, but so painful to deliver.

"I'd have to agree with you there. But things have escalated and I just want you to be very careful. We're dealing with some people who have already killed. I don't want you anywhere near them."

"I would have liked a nice talk like this yesterday morning. Seeing as how you're so concerned for my welfare. But the slam, bam thank you ma'am thing…"

"No. That's not me."

"Oh, really? You have a multiple personality disorder? One minute you're fucking my brains out and the next…"

Careful, Christy. Don't say something you'll regret.

"Look, I'm sorry about how all this happened," he said.

Christy lost it. "You know what, Kyle?" Here. It. Comes. *Don't do this, Christy!* "I'd say as a lover, you're probably an eight, eight and a half…" *You're such a bad liar.* "But as a hero, and I thought all you SEAL guys were heroes, you're a fucking zero." She hung up.

She counted to ten. No return call. She took the battery out of her phone so she wouldn't know if he tried to call her back. She ran for the shower, stepped in, and turned on the warm water, drenching her pajama bottoms and sweatshirt.

THIS IS FOR *the best.* Kyle wanted to call Christy back—heck, he wanted to do way more—but he knew this mission was probably not going to have a happy ending. He needed to walk away from Christy. Better to involve only those people who had fully signed on for that kind of danger. Let Christy live with the illusion that life was fair and filled with good people. Sure, she'd be nursing a broken heart for a while, but that was being kind, he told himself.

Just focus on the mission. Don't let it get complicated. Then throw everything into his workup for the next deployment.

If they don't boot my sorry ass outta the Navy.

And that would depend on whether or not this mission succeeded.

CHAPTER 18

MAYFIELD WAS FILLING out reports from the interview with Christy Nelson that morning. She hadn't been much help, and her attitude had been irritating at first. But he understood her motivation to protect a man she clearly trusted. He couldn't fault her for being loyal. And more important, he knew she was honest. He'd believed her story about her SEAL. He'd known a few SEALs, even tried the BUD/S course during his ten-year stint in the Navy. But since he wanted to fly jets, he wasn't too disappointed when he washed out. In the end, he'd had to give up flying, too, due to his eyesight.

The SEALs he'd met socially, in the Navy and through his line of work, stuck together and usually cleaned up their own messes. This was all too public and out of control. Something was wrong with the picture. It was starting to smell, too, as the body count was increasing.

This investigation was just not making sense and was going in circles. He'd watched the news report this morning about the late night fire, and it really worried him. That's probably what prompted the call, before he could finish breakfast. He was asked to bring lots of backup and to be armed.

No, the deeper he investigated, the more things didn't add up.

The task force, made up of members of the ATF, SDPD, and the San Diego Sheriff's Department, plus a Naval Officer he'd never met before, had three murders to investigate now, and for some reason, he felt there would be more. That was definitely not going in the right direction. His superiors were screaming at everyone, indiscriminately, while publicly and on camera telling the media they had utmost faith in their men and women and that the perps would be caught. The public was now aware of the Navy angle. He wondered how they had gotten wind of that particular fact. Feeling in the San Diego area ran either hot or cold for sailors. Not much left in the middle. He didn't want those emotions tainting his investigation.

He looked up to see Sherriff's Deputy Warren Hilber stride through the office doors and glamour the staffers and officers as if he were a vampire at a sweet sixteen ball. Mayfield didn't like him and he sure as hell didn't trust him. Hilber's sidekick of recent was that jerk-off from the Navy, Carlisle with a big fat III after his name, the one who wanted to join his force some day. Mayfield would never allow either the deputy or the Navy tin cop anywhere near his squad if he could help it.

Only, he wasn't sure he could help it.

He knew they were coming in to see him. Every time he talked with Hilber, he felt like punching his lights out, effectively ending his own career. Something dirty about the man.

Warren knocked on Mayfield's opened doorframe. And then he smiled.

Shit. Let the games begin.

"Come on in, fellas. You guys off today?"

"No sir, we're just getting revved up. Got real close to catching that rogue SEAL and his merry band of men last night." Warren was eager.

"Don't tell me he got away." Mayfield leaned back in his chair.

Now why does this make me a little happy?

He laced his fingers behind his head. He needed a haircut. And now, at the stench these two gave off, he needed a shower.

The smile was wiped off Warren's face like cold cream wiped off a whore's red lipstick. Warren was sizing him up, and Mayfield could tell he wasn't intimidated in the slightest. This made Warren and his Petty Officer Carlisle the III dangerous. And desperate.

"This time. But we arrested an accomplice," Warren Hilber said.

"And who would that be?" Mayfield asked.

"Sergeant Wilbur Hoskins, retired."

"Gunny. You got Gunny. Good job, boys. I hear women halfway around the world have been looking for that son of a bitch for years." Everyone in San Diego knew about Gunny and his legendary gym. He wasn't much as a husband, preferred his wives to not speak English, but he was still a hell of a guy and a rock in the community. Mayfield wished he were a cigar smoker. He'd have lit one up in celebration and laughed these two out of his office.

Carlisle piped up, "Detective Mayfield, I got it on good authority Gunny is aiding and abetting these criminals, these rogue SEALs."

"Well, Carlisle," Mayfield said, as he stood up and looked out the window, showing his profile to both men standing before him. He knew it wasn't lost on them that Mayfield was almost a foot taller than either of them. He intended for them to squirm a bit. He looked down on Carlisle as he finished his sentence. "I've never heard Gunny pick a fight in the twenty years since I've known him. In fact, he's the one the guys call to stop the fights, or to come clean up the pieces. But aiding and abetting? That's a stretch, don't you think?"

He finished, looking out the window. When he turned, Warren was peering down at his report. Mayfield sat down and put a file over it. A slight frown fell over the deputy's face.

Warren and Carlisle looked at each other. Mayfield continued his lecture. "Fellas, it's like firing the school janitor if the students' test scores drop."

Mayfield could see it got to Warren, who was trying to make nice, with a wolfish grin that was all mouth and no eyes. Lots of attitude oozing through.

"Sir, I understand he isn't the primary target. But I think we can use him as bait. Lansdowne will have to surface. He'll contact Gunny. The Feds are releasing him this afternoon, just holding him as long as they can. Everyone Kyle knows should be under surveillance."

"Well, we've talked to the girlfriend, and I don't think she knows anything either, Warren," Mayfield said. At the expression on Carlisle's face, he wished he hadn't revealed so much, and Hilber had been way too interested in that report lying on his desk.

"That where he was last seen, at her place?" Warren asked.

"Yes. Nearby." He didn't want to give the girl's location, specifically. He hoped Hilber hadn't read it on the report sheet. His antenna was beginning to trace.

"He's going to want to go back," Carlisle said. "He's a real ladies man."

So Carlisle thought he was aiding the investigation and was trying to earn his stripes, a way to get on the police force somehow. Mayfield saw his hatred of the young SEAL as plain as the tattoo of an anchor he wouldn't let his wife get years ago.

"And just what are you talking about, sailor?"

That actually made Carlisle blush. Warren kicked him in the shin and saw the man start.

His words directed more at Hilber, the Navy man tried to explain further. "They all do this, hang around the ladies. Drinking and raising hell. No sense of decency. I've had him cited for service unbecoming for years. The Navy's just looking for an excuse to boot his sorry ass outta here."

Mayfield wondered what in the stars was out there to get young Lansdowne in the crosshairs of so many assholes. Why were these two so anxious to bust him? Why was he in the middle of shit between the Feds and the Navy?

All he had to do was put in another five years and collect a good retirement. He needed all this controversy like he needed another ulcer. Or another girlfriend.

Maria, I'm so sorry you had to hear that. He spoke to his beloved dead wife, only gone ten months now. Mayfield felt she saw everything that rattled around in his brain, including his need for some recreational female companionship.

"We've got some work to do, sir. And I can see you're busy and got your hands full with the press. We'll get out of your hair." Warren gave a bitter smile and dragged Carlisle out through Mayfield's door.

A pair of regulation assholes.

Mayfield had the sense that if he didn't solve this case soon, there would be further violence. Something that wouldn't reflect well on the Department or the Navy. Something that could affect his retirement.

Big time.

CHAPTER 19

K YLE WAS TEMPORARILY holed up at Fredo's apartment, trying to stay out of sight. He'd sent Fredo to go on Gunny, who had sustained some injury and was being held overnight at the hospital. A morning paper had been delivered, so Kyle was reading an article about the explosion at the cabin and the purported murders. He knew they were murders. He didn't like the fact that members of a SEAL Team were implicated. Although the article didn't mention him or his team by name, he knew it was only time before he was found to be a link. If the local authorities knew about the SEAL connection, they'd get to him sooner or later.

His cell rang.

"Gunny's pissed he has to stay longer. They're not going to release him today like they promised," Fredo squawked on the phone.

Kyle nodded. He'd guessed as much. "How long?"

"They're running tests. Doesn't know."

"And so that means we break him out, right?"

"Damn fuckin' straight. He said tonight, when they change shifts."

"He hooked up to anything?"

"Heart monitors, things that drive him crazy. He tries to take them off and then the nurses come running in, thinking he's having a heart attack. Has nothing to do with what they did to him last night.

They've found something else."

"If Cooper says he's okay, then we take him. Tell him that, Fredo. I'm not taking him if it's going to risk his life."

"Roger that. I'll tell him. Not that it would make any difference."

"Not going to happen. Don't care how much he begs. I'm not going to have his death on my conscience."

It was one thing to have the deaths on his hands of the good men he led into battle, but then they'd signed up and knew the risk. Another thing entirely to have a civilian suffer. Someone who'd already paid his debt to his nation. Who'd earned his retirement.

Fredo had obtained Gunny's truck keys. They made plans to meet up with Coop, and the three of them would go to Armando's to retrieve his stash of weapons. No need having that potential discovery adding thickness to the goo they were already in. But first, Kyle had a number of things to do before they carried out Gunny's mission of mercy.

He called Cooper.

"Did Fredo say whether or not he is under house arrest?" Coop asked.

"Nope. I'm guessing yes, but really depends on who."

Cooper whistled. "That's a fact."

"Fredo will follow in his car. I'm going to get the beater. Pick you up in about twenty?" Kyle asked his medic.

"Roger that." Cooper hung up.

IT SURPRISED KYLE there wasn't anyone guarding Armando's house, or at least no guards that they could see. He doubted the guys who had trashed the house earlier in the week would resort to anything complicated, as far as surveillance went. That meant this wasn't an organized unit.

They parked both vehicles on the block behind and made short work of slipping along the side of a house that was vacant and for sale, then over the rear fence to Armando's rear yard. They disabled the slider lock and stopped inside the kitchen, listening for anything.

Deathly silence greeted them. The mess all over the house was just as Christy had described. Coop and Fredo were swearing. With their gloved hands, they began picking up some of Armando's broken picture frames and things that might have been important to the man in happier times.

"Don't get your aprons on yet, ladies," Kyle said. It earned him the finger from Fredo, whose idea of housework was moving to another apartment rather than cleaning.

Kyle made it back to Armando's bedroom with images of that day he'd been naked on the bed when Christy found him. That was barely a week ago, but how things had changed.

No time for those thoughts.

He sprang to the corner, relieved nothing looked disturbed, and peeled back the blue carpeting, revealing a square cutout with a metal loop handle embedded in the plywood underlayment. He opened the two-foot-wide hatch and flashed his penlight into the cubbyhole, revealing black powder-coated weapons and boxes of ammo. Fredo and Cooper were right behind him as he carefully extracted the weapons, including an .88 Karl Gustav rocket launcher. One at a time, amid admiring whistles and profanity from the two Team guys, they reverently lay everything on the bed. Enough fire power to start a revolution.

Start one. But couldn't finish the job without help.

In Armando's closet was an empty duty bag. They loaded the equipment, except for the Karl Gustav, which had to be wrapped in a camouflaged laundry bag, and then carefully put back the hatch opening and carpeting.

Kyle searched the street through the closed living room curtains and didn't see anything of interest. All of a sudden, a San Diego police car cruised by, but the two occupants were not slowing down and kept looking straight ahead. He took it to mean a random coincidence.

In the hot afternoon sun, they silently made their way alongside Armando's pool. Kyle noticed the buildup of leaves had gotten worse. Once over the fence, they checked the street again and found nothing that interested them, so they remounted their vehicles, Kyle stashing the bag of weapons under the rear seat in Gunny's truck. The launcher was precariously laid on the floor behind and he threw a windbreaker over the protruding tip.

Except for the grinding of gears and the lugging of an overworked motor, they left the neighborhood quietly.

They stopped by Kyle's Hummer that he'd left in an alleyway behind a local warehouse for lease. There were no windows from which anyone could watch them transfer Armando's firepower into the Hummer. Kyle wasn't comfortable with letting them out of his sight, and stored his own gear there all the time. With two locking steel boxes bolted to the frame beneath the second seats, unless they were looking, there'd be no way to find them. The Gustav was another problem, and they had to resort to keeping it wrapped, lying on Fredo's rear seat, fully covered.

They parked Fredo's car in the garage at his apartment complex, unloading the CG and stashing it in Fredo's locked gun locker. They took Gunny's beater over to the base. Cruising past the guard gate on their way down the strand, they could see that Cooper's motor home seemed untouched.

"If they was looking, they'd have everything out all over the tarmac," Cooper said to Kyle.

"I don't think Carlisle has seen it back in the lot. But he will."

"Yup," the farm boy replied.

Kyle's thoughts drifted Christy's way. He wished he could clean up things with her. Maybe he would give her a call later.

Maybe not such a good idea. He shelved that pleasant thought for now.

COOPER WAS TO go into the hospital first. He wore a white lab coat and stethoscope around his neck, and was using his military nametag from his rotation at the burn unit in Texas. He wasn't going to say he was a doctor, but his height and confident good looks, Kyle knew, would help give him the air of authority. Kyle wanted him to look like he belonged strolling down the corridor.

Kyle and Fredo watched him go, then they turned into one of the housekeeping closets and were in luck to find several stacks of scrubs. They picked ones big enough to go over their clothes. Fredo found a box of paper caps, along with some foot dusters. Kyle couldn't help but whisper, "I'll have two tacos please, amigo."

"Yeah, you get the one I spit in, man." At Kyle's chuckle, Fredo added, "They do that, man. Got a cousin who works at a hospital in LA. You wouldn't believe what they put in the food sometimes."

"Confirms my thoughts about hospital food."

They walked down a deserted hallway, looking for signs of a police presence. Luckily, Gunny was on the first floor, just around the corner.

Fredo stopped Kyle as they passed by a room with an opened door. He pulled out a wheelchair that was collapsed just inside the doorframe. "The nurse's station is at the end of the hall before the turn. We gotta go one at a time. Here," he told Kyle. Fredo handed his LPO a tall plastic garbage can on wheels. "You take this and walk up and down the hall while I go toward the room. If anyone comes, pretend you're changing the plastic liner."

"Fredo?"

"Uh huh, boss?"

"How much time you spend in hospitals?"

"Don't ask. More than your average Mexican."

Kyle would leave it at that. Although they shared personal details of their past, there were some things that would be left unsaid. It wasn't helpful to say too much. Those who felt the need to spill their guts never made it through the training.

Fredo made easy work leering at the nurses as he walked past the station. He had a way of making women turn away from him as he focused on their body parts, on purpose this time. He rounded the corner and Kyle didn't hear a flutter.

Within five minutes, Gunny was grinning from ear to ear, seated in the wheelchair, followed by his personal physician with a metal clipboard, and pushed by a Mexican orderly. Cooper nodded to the ladies.

"Taking him to X-ray."

"Hold it. You mean that way," Kyle heard.

"Nope, going to take him by the service elevator. Hallway's jammed up there," Cooper answered without stopping.

Kyle abandoned the garbage can and pushed the automatic doors open to go get the truck. He pulled up and Fredo immediately helped Gunny into the rear seat, while Cooper argued with a very large, belligerent head nurse who seemed to know the picture was all wrong. She was pointing at his nametag, saying, "If that's even your real name."

Cooper barely had time to step inside the truck before they sped off in a cloud of dark gray smoke, leaving a bevy of white uniforms behind.

"Sorry, Gunny. But sure as shit they've got your license plates."

"Hey, you hear me complaining? I'm so fucking glad to be out of that house of pain and death. That was a close one."

"You feeling up to this?"

"You kiddin'? All I need is a pair of pants."

Kyle hadn't noticed Gunny was in his shorts, having tossed the hospital gown.

Fredo added, "And man, a T-shirt, too. No way I'm gonna stare at those tits of yours, Gunny."

"Your fuckin' body will do the same, Don Juan." He sighed. "I got extra clothes at the gym. I'll quickly grab them."

"So why were they keeping you?" Fredo asked.

Kyle exchanged a look with Gunny through the rear view mirror.

"Something," Gunny began. "They found something they didn't like."

No one said a word. It was Gunny's information to share, if he wanted, and Kyle knew he didn't want to.

"You know how it is, fellas. The mind is willing but the body has other plans."

Coop and Fredo nodded while Kyle shared another look with Gunny in the mirror but kept his mouth shut.

"So, after I get dressed, where are we going? Where are they keeping Armando?" Gunny asked.

Kyle had no idea.

CHAPTER 20

C HRISTY HAD JUST returned from the gym. She'd asked for Marla, but no one had seen her all day. The light under the trainer's locked office door had been turned off, however.

So was everything else just part of Christy's active imagination? Being in the gym in the middle of the afternoon didn't scare her at all, but she was going stir crazy seeking answers to all her questions about the news reports of last night and today.

She was missing her extra passkey, and it bothered her. She looked through her gym bag and all her sweats, but came up short.

She needed a couple of things at the store, but she liked the safety of her place.

Still in her workout gear, she made herself a turkey sandwich and checked her emails. There were a couple of property searches she completed and sent off to clients. Then she updated her database for search matches against new listings. She heard another tap on her front door.

Now what?

Through the peephole, Christy saw two men in different colored uniforms. The blue Navy camis didn't catch her eye, but the gold badge did, so she slipped on an oversized sweatshirt to hide her skimpy workout wear. Opening the door, she hoped they'd have news about Kyle.

He was barely taller than Christy, dressed in a wrinkled sandy-colored shirt and matching pants with a beige stripe—the uniform of the local Sheriff's Department. He looked as though he was coming down with the flu. His eyes were rheumy and red. Or maybe he was a drinker. His holstered gun was snapped in place. He held a small sheaf of papers in his right hand. Healthy and freshly rested, he might have been a handsome man, if she liked short ones, but there was something about the way he looked at her she did not care for. Sort of feral, predatory.

But then, she didn't like the way most men looked at her. Especially now, in her exercise pants that hugged her ass like a second skin.

"Ma'am. Sorry to bother you," the deputy said. Regular Navy looked directly at her rack. She knew those kinds of guys couldn't help themselves. Gentlemen who knew it was inappropriate and didn't care were the truly scary ones. This guy had a gun too.

This is definitely about Kyle.

"I'm Deputy Sheriff Warren Hilber, and this is Petty Officer Carlisle."

Christy didn't want to look at the Navy guy any more than she had to. But she wouldn't trust turning her back on him, either. "I would like to get dressed first, if you don't mind." She pulled at the sweatshirt and pointed to her black yoga pants.

"Of course, we'll just wait…" He started to walk past her into the hallway, but Christy put a palm to his chest before he could take more than a step.

"You'll wait outside, or I'll call security." She wrinkled up her nose and whispered, "They have guns too, but you're probably a better shot."

She slammed the door in their faces. And locked it.

Jerks! First the SDPD and now the Sheriff's Department and the Navy. Who's next? The fucking FBI?

"Give me two minutes, 'kay?" she said through the metal door.

There was no answer, so she dashed to the bedroom and quickly slipped on a pair of tan khakis and put back on the light yellow oversized sweatshirt. She brushed out her wet hair and pulled it in a scrunchie. She decided against makeup. No body-enhancing underwear either. No reason to encourage either of them, but especially the one called Carlisle. In her bare feet, she unlocked and opened her front door, greeting them with as much of a smile as she could muster.

She was regarded carefully. She could see Warren was the smarter one, and for now, the leader. She stepped aside and they both walked past her. She leaned out into the hallway and found Mr. Jefferson standing, a puzzled expression on his face.

She waved to him, but he just stared back at her. He was still wearing slippers. She quietly closed her door.

"Please," she said as she motioned to her couch, where they both sat side by side. She took up a position in Kyle's leather chair and assumed the pose she'd taken when she'd talked to Mayfield this morning.

"I've answered all the San Diego police's questions this morning. I know nothing about all the murders on TV, if that's what you're here about."

"You're Kyle's girlfriend, then," Warren said, his lips slanted at an angle while he examined a piece of lint on his starched but wrinkled pants. His shoes were dusty too. Christy knew he'd been to somewhere probably Kyle had been. And that place wasn't in town.

"Right now, I'm not quite sure what I am. Why don't *you* tell *me*?" she asked them.

"Well, you could be an accomplice, perhaps an unwitting accomplice. If you help him in any way or impede our investigation, you'll be charged just like the rest of them."

"Them?" she asked.

"I'm sure you know he leads Teams for a living," Hilber began. "Special teams that do things most people would find offensive. And dangerous." He smiled and she got the chills. "We'd be grateful for your help. Thought perhaps we could strike a little deal with you."

The brittle smile across his face didn't seem natural to him. He didn't seem very practiced at making it look sincere.

"A deal? Why would I be interested in a deal, or even need one?"

"Well, right now there's a shoot to kill order, since your man here is armed and dangerous. If you help us catch him, I'll do my best to bring him in alive."

"Surely you are joking."

"I'm afraid not, ma'am."

Carlisle inserted himself in the conversation, apparently having waited long enough. "You may not know this, but Kyle is about to be booted from the Navy. I've been watching him for a couple of years now. I have reams of violations he's been written up for. He's coming unhinged. Very unstable."

She dismissed his comment as if it were the sound of a garbage truck.

He continued, "I've seen things he's done you don't know about. You're lucky to be alive. He's a dangerous man."

He is dangerous. His kisses are dangerous. The way he loves me with total abandon is dangerous. It's dangerous how much I need him even now.

Warren said, "He's a real smooth one. The ladies love him, and—h" he waited until she looked up at him "—he's loved a good many of them in return." He winked, stopping to watch perhaps a flicker of pain cross her face? Christy hoped she'd properly masked it.

The idea that those tattooed arms would ever hold another woman was a nightmare she did not want to endure. But worse was seeing the satisfied look on Warren's face when he realized he'd hit pay dirt. He'd gotten to her. And she knew it was probably all BS anyway, but it got to her, nonetheless.

Warren shook his head. "You know as well as I do, he's married to the SEALs. They are his family. You're baggage." Warren skewered her with a direct stare she couldn't escape. "Only a matter of time before he takes out the garbage. No offense, ma'am."

Again he had misjudged her.

"You're wrong."

"Am I?"

She worked on her composure. This man knew right where to hit her, where it hurt the most. She sucked it in and continued. "He's looking for his friend who's been kidnapped."

"Kidnapped? You believe that?" Warren looked at Carlisle and they chuckled and shook their heads, as if it were some private joke.

"I'd say more like he wanted in on Armando's golden goose. Armando's dirty. Running drugs and guns for a gang here we've been tracking for some time."

Christy's cell rang from the kitchen, sending her leaping to her feet to retrieve it. Before she could get there, Hilber picked it up off the kitchen counter. He looked at the display, then frowned and tilted his head to the side.

"Wayne Somerville? You holding out on Kyle?" he asked, handing her the phone. Even the beefy Realtor she loathed was a welcome distraction.

"H-hello?"

"Hey, Christy, you all right? I've been worried about you. Everyone here at the office is curious as hell…"

"I'm fine." She closed her eyes and wished she could will it so.

Wish I were on someone else's radar.

"Well, that's good to hear. I'll tell everyone."

"Do that."

"Hey, Christy, I wanted to apologize for, well for getting you into this mess you're in. It was an honest accident, giving you the wrong address, but I'm real sorry…and I…"

She needed to prolong the call. Anything to keep her away from the two men in her condo. Hilber and the other one were scanning her living room. She felt undressed.

"I don't know what you're talking about, Wayne," she said into the phone, but she didn't take her eyes off the two men.

Warren began to pace back and forth. He seemed nervous about something because he kept checking his watch.

"I been reading the papers, and, well, I think this guy who attacked you is the one running around killing people. You should have some protection."

Then she understood the purpose of Wayne's call. This was his not too smooth way of inviting himself over for a cuddle and whatever else he could get away with. "Well, Wayne, right now I have protection from Deputy Sheriff Warren Hilber and Petty Officer Carlisle. They're standing right here in my condo, talking to me." She decided it was a good idea to let someone else know about the two jackals in her home.

Hilber winced as Carlisle looked on sheepishly.

Christy had an idea. "I actually think you could tell the whole office these guys are here to protect me right now. Please tell Simms too. I don't want any of you guys to worry."

"Oh, that's good, Christy. Do you need anything? Simms says

you're taking a few days off."

"That's right. The stress has been almost too much. Had a bit of a rocky start and all." She looked at Warren. "But I'll tell you what, could you come over in, oh, say an hour? I need a couple of things from my desk."

"Sure. Happy to help. In any way," he lowered his voice and her stomach turned.

"I have two buyer files I'm working on. They're inside my middle drawer. Could you bring them over?" The files wouldn't be too hard to find. They were the only two in her desk.

She didn't look at Warren but saw him flinch.

"Maybe I'll detain these two nice gentlemen so you can see for yourself how well taken care of I am. I think one of them is looking to buy a new home. And I'm going to be tied up for a few days."

Carlisle was looking up at Warren with a pained expression, holding his hands out, palms up, and shrugging.

"Sure. Sure I could do that, Christy. Anything else?"

"Ask Simms to call me later tonight, okay? I have some questions."

"Yeah. I'll be over in about an hour, maybe less, if it's okay."

"Fine by me." She paused, sucked in her gut and said, "Come over as soon as you like. Thanks, Wayne. That's real sweet."

She couldn't help but gloat when she hung up the phone.

"Well, officers. I need to get this questioning over with so I can get ready to receive company. You're welcome to stay, of course. We were discussing cooperation."

"If Kyle calls you, we want you to let us know," Hilber blurted out.

"Gee, I would have thought you'd have gotten a wiretap by now."

"The man can't be trusted, miss. Do yourself and everyone else a favor. Don't let him con you like he's done others," Carlisle said without expression. "You're in way over your head. Don't risk it for a little…a little…fun." His right eye flinched when he said this.

"Well, suppose you leave me your cards so I'll have your numbers handy." She looked back and forth between the two men. Carlisle turned to face Warren just a little too quickly.

Warren patted down his breast pocket and then the seat of his pants. "I'm fresh out of cards, miss."

Christy took one of hers out from a box next to her chair. Flipping it over, she handed it to Warren, with a pen. "Why don't you just write your contact information here? Do you check emails?"

"Yes, I do," he said, with a lopsided smile, looking up to her looming over him. She didn't trust the man. It was more than the creep factor she had with that dog Wayne. This man was pure cold evil. With authority and a gun.

He wrote his phone number and email address neatly on the card and handed it back to her. Again, his cold stare chilled her.

"Now your turn." She presented the pen and card to Carlisle, who leaned back so as not to touch it.

"It would be better if you just contact Warren. He's lead on this," he said, his eyes not returning her gaze.

"Um hum. Just give me your contact info anyway. Humor me," Christy insisted, her head cocked at an angle. She smiled to let him know she knew he was struggling and was asking anyway.

"I'm sorry, ma'am. That's classified."

"Then next time, you can stay outside, sailor." She put the card and pen on her kitchen countertop next to the stove. Warren was fidgeting, looking unhappy.

"If you will excuse me." She motioned to her front door.

The two men exited. Warren turned before he closed the door behind him. "We're going to catch him and all his team members. Even you can't deny that a rogue SEAL with a boatload of guns and explosives stashed everywhere is a danger to the good people of San Diego County. Way too dangerous for you to be playing with. You don't want to get scooped up in this net. Trust me, you don't."

I already am. Nothing I can do about that now. Only person who can pull me off is the guy with the three-toed creature tattoo.

THE SECURITY DESK downstairs in the Infinity office rang her phone about a half hour later.

"We got a Wayne Somerville down here. Says he has an appointment with you," Jerry's usual friendly voice was stiff and oddly cold.

"Sure, send him up."

Jerry didn't say anything before he hung up. She was going to thank him but got a dial tone in her ear.

When she heard the ping of the elevator, she opened her door and watched as Wayne lumbered down the hallway in a suit that looked a size or two too small and that showed off his midsection girth. The difference between the layer of blubbery fat jiggling as he moved and Kyle's measured strides and chiseled abs was laughable, but she held it in and risked him thinking she was glad to see him.

But in a way, she was. She'd been surrounded by men the last twenty-four hours, and there was only one man she wanted to see.

She smiled and said, "Thanks, Wayne," as he handed her the files. "I really appreciate this."

"No problem. I was going to bring you some flowers too, but thought it would, you know, remind you of the incident and of that bad guy."

She knew he was making excuses for being cheap. Why bring flowers if you weren't sure it was going to pay off?

"How thoughtful. Thanks again. You want to come in?"

"Sure." Wayne's eyes bugged out of his head, growing to saucer size.

"You want some coffee?"

"Sure, Christy. Thanks," Wayne said as he poked his head in her bedroom doorway, and then did a 360 in her living room. "This place is really nice. I've sold a couple of units here, but I think this one is way better."

"Yeah, my mom left it to me." She started grinding coffee beans.

"Free and clear?" He whirled around to look at her.

She was offended, of course, that he wanted to know how well off she was, but today she felt generous and had already dished out her quota of frost this morning. And Wayne didn't really deserve the sharp end of her patience.

"Yes. I have no mortgage." She smiled to the brewing coffee—that pleasant smell she'd loved while lying in her bed when she knew Kyle was in the next room, waiting for her to awaken.

"Wow. That's nice. Wish I had a rich relative." Envy lurked like a snake between his words.

"She wasn't rich. It was the only thing she had, and she'd saved her whole life to buy the place. Used some money she got when my dad passed away."

"Oh. Good for her," he said distractedly as she handed him his mug. He peered down into the creamy brew. "Thanks for the cream."

"Two lumps of sugar too."

"You remembered. That means a lot to me, Christy," he said as he lowered his voice, his gaze lowering to her chest.

"Funny how I remember little details like that." She sat on Kyle's chair. "Have a seat."

Wayne repositioned the pillows so his hefty frame would fit on the couch and then sat, leaving little space for another person.

"Who was your mom's Realtor?"

"She bought it from the builder. A grand opening special, I think."

"Jeez. Talk about timing. Good for her…and for you too."

She was letting his lack of transparency amuse her this morning, a morning without very much good news.

He sipped his coffee and put it on the table in front of him. Leaning forward, he pressed his palms together. "I'm sorry we got off to a difficult start. I was hoping we could be…friends." He had blushed, and Christy thought it looked more like unwelcomed sunburn.

Everyone wants to help me. Do I look that helpless?

Yes. She decided she did. Damn it. That was going to have to change.

"I suddenly have lots of people offering to help me."

"Oh, yeah? Who?"

He was probably wondering if another Realtor was in the picture.

"Well, there's the local police, and the San Diego County Sheriff's Department, and some Naval policeman or something. Forgot what they call him."

"MA. Navy term for MP. Wonder why all of them are so interested. I mean, I can see why they'd be interested in you, but…"

"The triple homicide."

"You were unlucky. I'm sure they'll figure it out soon enough." Wayne frowned and added, "They think he'll continue to strike until he gets caught. Death by cop sort of thing, I guess."

This worried her.

"Just how well do you know this guy, Christy?" He squinted his eyes and waited for her answer.

"We're friends."

"Be careful. You're playing with fire, Christy."

Tell me about it.

CHAPTER 21

IT WASN'T WISE, but Kyle knew he would call her. He wasn't even sure which was more important, his worry over her safety or his need to talk to her for his own personal reasons. And it didn't matter.

She picked it up on the first ring.

"Christy's house of good times."

Kyle didn't quite know what to say. He heard the bitterness in her voice, but something else.

Pain.

He remembered himself, and his reason—at least the reason he'd given himself—for calling. "Christy, I apologize for my behavior."

"You seem to be repeating your sorry routine an awful lot, sailor. I'd say you're pretty practiced at it. Impressive."

"Actually, I'm not. I don't usually have to."

"Well, you don't have to now."

"What I mean is, I don't usually get involved."

Now it was Christy's turn to pause. "Is that what we are? Involved?"

"Yes." There. He'd whispered it. Had she heard? "I told you before, this wasn't a pit stop. You're a nice lady. You deserve more than I can give right now."

"So exactly what is *this* thing between us that you won't describe—

this thing that isn't what you can give me right now?"

"I care about what happens to you."

"Get in line."

"Excuse me?"

"Let's see. Where do I begin? I get scared out of my gourd at the gym last night with some strange guy walking past my sauna door when I'm lying there buck naked. I decide maybe I'm being foolish, but no, the San Diego PD is here this morning asking questions about some fire and a triple murder, thinking you're involved. *He* wants to help. A deputy sheriff stops by with one of your Navy buddies…"

"The Sheriff's Department was there?" This wasn't a good sign. But what did he expect?

"Yessir."

He'd been a dumbass. Stupid. Why hadn't he thought about Christy being questioned?

"Can I come over and talk to you?"

He heard her sigh into the phone, clouding the reception.

"Which Kyle is it who is coming over? The one who screwed me on the countertop and said he wasn't ready for this, or the one who just wants to talk?"

"I promise. Just talk." It wasn't much, but he'd take it. If she'd let him.

WHILE WAITING FOR him to arrive, Christy wished the chatter in her head would stop. Her pulse had quickened. She was beginning to sweat again and knew she didn't have time for another shower. In spite of what she told herself, she'd put on makeup, just a little of Madame's perfume, the cherry lip gloss, a little mascara. She brushed out her hair, and then she heard him, the relentless tap tap tap on her door like the beating of her heart.

Bad sign, girl. Here you go again.

Kyle had arrived at her door so fast she'd barely had time to finish getting on decent clothes.

Damn. Even his knock was sexy. She inhaled a big gulp of air and opened the door.

She was doomed. He stood, leaning against the doorframe, one forearm resting against the trim, his hips at an angle, his smile at an opposite angle. And the crease at the side of his lip. On the left. Did he know?

Did it matter?

Oh, hell no.

His hard chest was against her, his arms tight around her waist. The force of his lips as he kissed her instilled courage and resolve. She'd been ridiculous, of course, but she was so far over the edge for this man, even if he had done what they said he'd done...

Christy, what in the world are you doing? The guy could be a cold-blooded killer.

"Where's that little talk we were going to have?" she said to his hungry mouth. God, she needed that mouth on her right now. She stepped on tiptoes and pressed her lips hard against his. His tongue plunged in deep. His hands found her chest and snaked under her bra, squeezing her breasts. Was that her moan she heard, or his?

He stopped, dropped her from his arms, and looked to the floor. He took a step backward into the opened door to the hallway.

"I'm s..."

She couldn't stand to hear another "I'm sorry" from the man.

"Oh, shut up and fuck me," she said as she slammed into his chest, pushing the door closed. His expression turned from apology to fire.

She leaned into him, wrapping her arms up and around his neck. She liked the feeling of relying on his strength, how hard he was, how sure of himself. How his hands found their way to her, wanting flesh. He picked her up and brought her to the bedroom.

At the foot of the bed, he set her down and kneeled. He shed her pants, then stood and pulled off her pink T-shirt. He looked at her breasts as his hands cupped around them, thumbs rubbing over her nipples through the silky peach satin lace of the bra. She loved how he always seemed to be seeing her for the first time. He smiled and said, "I love your body, Christy. I thank God every time I get to hold you."

But do you love me, Kyle? Tell me.

He kissed her. Christy's hands smoothed over the ripples in his chest, touching the scars and kissing every one of them. Her hands traveled around the backside of his waist and down further to his butt cheeks and she pulled him to her. She ground her pelvis against his hardened shaft, undid his button fly, and slid his pants down. She took hold of the length of him and squeezed, then reached to find his balls and squeezed them as well.

He kicked off his shoes and stepped out of his jeans as she came to her knees. She took him inside her mouth, massaging his sac. His precum relaxed her. His musky scent made her cream between her legs as she worked his shaft, sucking, licking, and inhaling him.

He was beginning to jerk and Christy could tell his climax was close, so she stopped and looked up at him, kneading his cock in the palm of her right hand.

He quickly picked her up and placed her back on the bed. She moved aside several pillows to prop her head. He pulled one of the pillows away and shoved it beneath her hips, raising her sex to him, giving him a deep angle for penetration. God, she needed him inside her. Deep inside her.

She knew he was rock hard and ready to spurt, but he spread her knees and watched his fingers move in and out of the lips of her sex.

Then he bent and kissed her there, lapping her juices, rubbing a thumb over her nub and sending little sharp spasms up her back and down both legs. Her whole world lay open to him, to his slick tongue that pushed in and out of her opening, his hot breath on her waiting womb.

She moaned as delicious ripples of pleasure overtook her. Kyle covered her now, kissing her lips and face.

"I need you. Oh God, I need you," she whispered. Her sex felt vacant, wanting.

Kyle's cock teased at her opening, and then he thrust deep inside, the angle set up by the pillow forcing him against her soft tissues. It sent her muscles into contractions as she tightly held him, refusing to release him as he pulled back before plunging in again. She grabbed the pillow at her side, arched, and cried out. Her body jerked, consumed with the magic of his slow and deliberate motions. His back muscles worked in tandem with the tensed muscles of his ass. She felt his cheeks go soft and then flex and as he ground against her, as he filled her and demanded more.

She vaguely remembered being scared. But not now. Now she was being pleasured by the man she loved, would always love. She dug her heels into the bed and raised her pelvis as he plunged in and out, deep.

A few strokes later, he turned her body to the side by rolling over one thigh. She tried to raise a knee, and he smiled and stopped her. He wanted the deeper penetration as he kissed the sides of her face.

Still inside her, he pumped her from behind as he spooned himself to the backs of her thighs, her back. He pulled her down onto his shaft. The pillow was between her knees as she pushed her rear against him, allowing him deep. He kissed her neck, found her ear, and whispered, "Need you, Christy. I…" But he stopped. He didn't say it.

And it was all right that he needed her. A man who didn't need anything or anyone and he now needed her. And that was going to have to be enough for now.

"I'm yours, Kyle, all of me."

That seemed to drive him crazy. Her body responded, exploding in her own pleasure, clenching down on him. He lurched inside her and she heard the familiar groans of his passion as he filled her with his sperm. She drew him in, accepting every drop, until he fell against her back with an exhausted sigh.

He stayed inside her as they rested. His hands caressed her nipples and breasts while he kissed her shoulder and down her spine, one vertebra at a time.

"I love this," she said. Then she turned her head. He saw it there, she knew it. He saw what she wanted to say, but wouldn't until he did.

"Anything is possible, Christy. Anything." He buried his head at the nape of her neck and pulled her against his chest and held her tight, but didn't look at her.

A minute later, she heard him snore, sound asleep. For some strange reason, the idea that he was so relaxed that he could fall asleep thrilled her. He was totally vulnerable, totally at risk to her. He had bared his soul. The words would come. She knew they would.

A HALF HOUR later, she pulled the blanket over them so Kyle would sleep longer, but he jerked awake. He'd fallen asleep inside her and began to pump her from behind again.

"Hmm. I've missed this so much." She leaned back into him.

"Me too," he whispered. "Sometimes I think about you, like this, and I can't concentrate." He thrust up into her.

"God, that feels so good."

He continued. He propped himself up on his arms, letting his groin have its way with her. She rose to receive him. "Yes," he said.

"I just want all this…agh…past…to be over with, so we can get on with our lives," she whispered between his kisses.

"Me, too." He rubbed his lips against her neck, tipped her head back, and kissed her under her chin. He pulled her lower torso to him, his fingers finding the spot between her legs as he touched their joining. She matched his hands with hers and they touched together, lacing fingers. It was more than sex. Way more than sex. For the first time in her life, she was making love to the man she loved with all her heart.

His hot kisses made her cheeks and chest flush. Her insides began to glow with fire. She was going to explode.

He held her as her body jerked. "Yes," he said as she gave him her climax. He held her tight, pressing with his fingers, pulling with his forearms.

She was spent at last. He continued kissing her until the very end, when he thrust, arched up, and groaned.

She turned to face him. He touched her face, fingers brushing over her lips, thumbs smoothing over her cheekbones. He planted another gentle kiss under her chin. His warm blue eyes searched hers.

She saw he wanted to say something. She wasn't going to ask. When he did speak, it wasn't exactly what she was expecting.

"You may never know where I am or what I'm doing. I won't always be here to help you with the nerves. And you've got to get used to the fact I might not come back."

That filled her eyes with tears. "No, Kyle, I can never get used to that idea. That just isn't something that is going to happen."

He smiled down on her. "Well, then, hold on to that thought. It'll be my homing beacon. Just remember how nice it is when we're together. I have no right to ask for anything else."

Her heart was aching. If there ever was a time she wanted to hear that he loved her, it was now. She knew he cared. But she wanted to hear it. She was looking for the man who could tell her he loved her. He wasn't there yet. But she would wait. She'd do it. She'd try.

HE HELD HER hand as they meandered down to the marina and the Salty Dog restaurant. He sat next to her so his thigh could be pressed against hers, and he took every opportunity he could to inhale the wonderful warm scent of her. His left arm encircled her waist while he tried to eat with his right hand.

She was looking out over the boats, her brown eyes sparkling. Her face was flushed, hair with that just-fucked look that made him hot for her all over again. The whole afternoon had been one turn-on after another.

Did she feel as good as he did? Did she feel the connection, the mating that could be for life, if there ever was such a thing possible?

He told himself the answer was yes. As incredible as it was, he believed it had finally happened to him.

She turned, and her eyes were hungry as she leaned into him. She pressed the nipples of her breasts against his chest and softly kissed him. She was telling him the space between her legs needed to be filled again, that she needed his tongue there and then needed to be filled with his aching erection. She didn't have to say it. She was ready to go home and give herself to him all over again, all night long. She didn't have to say it. He could feel it hitting his face and chest like a blast furnace.

After they finished their chowders, she led him down the walkway by the boats and out along the promenade. Bells in the distance, a foghorn and lapping water, were all familiar sounds of this place that had molded him, had made him a man among men. These things sang to him. The familiar chilly saltwater mist heightened the warm feel of

Christy's velvet smooth lips on his neck, working their way down his chest, as they sat on a bench overlooking the water. She unzipped his pants and felt inside to grab him. She squeezed her fingers over his shaft, up and down, ending with her thumb rubbing a drop of precum over his crown. She straddled him, slipped aside her unnecessary panties, and impaled herself on his cock.

God, he loved how much she needed him.

Her elbows squeezed her breasts together, pressing the firm mounds against his pecs. Her warm ass was a handful in each palm. He lifted her to rub a thumb over her nub as she rode him, and gasped with an "oh" from the sudden jolt of pleasure. He could watch her do that all night. He would surprise her, take her in his mouth, and push his way inside her from behind and deep, from the side at an angle. He wasn't going to stop until his body gave out. He'd trained well for this mission, and he wasn't going to end his pleasuring her until she was unable to walk, and then some.

She was riding him deep, her back arching as he lifted her and pulled her down onto him. He ground against her in the darkness, and then let her free only to have her sheath him again. He felt her thighs rub against his jeans as she moaned and fluttered her eyes. He started spurting first, and then she shivered and came on top of him. He wanted to reach inside deep, press against her womb as she rubbed it over the head of his cock and jumped with every little spasm.

"God, I could just sit here all night," she whispered. She lowered her lips to his and ground her pelvis.

"I wish you would. I'm a polar bear."

"You can keep me warm, then. I don't like the cold."

"Yes," he said as he moved against her. He was fully spent. "I can do that. Give me an hour and I can keep you warm all night long."

"Kyle, I feel like I've known you my whole life."

Me, too.

She leaned into his space and he held her tight, encircling her back and shoulders with his arms. He fell into the rhythm of her breathing and felt the tiny flutter of her heart against his chest. She had fallen asleep. He loved the feel of her warm breath against his neck. She murmured something.

"Are you warm enough?" he whispered.

She nodded and then looked at him. Her hair was messed up and covering her face. He smoothed it to the sides.

"I was having a wonderful dream just now," she said.

"God, I *hope* it was me you were dreaming about." He smiled and was rewarded with a smile in kind. He started to say something perhaps he shouldn't, but he couldn't stop himself.

"Christy, I…"

"Shhh." She put a finger to his lips. Her eyes sparkled with the reflection of lights from downtown behind him. "Don't tell me the bad news. Tell me how right this feels. Tell me you won't ever go."

"No bad news," he said, touching his forehead to hers. "It's all good here. All of it. I want it all, Christy. I want all of you."

And there. He'd said it.

She leaned back and searched his eyes. He had put himself out to her, and for the first time, he felt totally at a woman's mercy. She could end his life with a word. With a frown.

Tears formed in her eyes. She nodded. "Me, too, Kyle. Me, too."

Nothing more needed to be said. A perfect moment, a perfect evening.

CHAPTER 22

IN THE MORNING, Christy got up first. Kyle knew he had to get going. But hell, he'd be back. She'd tried to let him sleep, but the sounds of her doing things in the kitchen and the smell of fresh coffee kept him awake. He heard her take a shower, thought about the texture of her silky skin as he massaged warm steamy bubbles over every delicious part of her. But as nice as the vision was, he had a job to do and needed time to think.

The waiting was getting harder. And, damn, so was he.

Not again.

She finished getting dressed and puttering in the kitchen. He pretended to be asleep when she climbed back into bed with a steaming mug of coffee for him.

She might have known him better by now. He wasn't at all interested in the coffee.

He took the mug from her fingers, took a sip, and watched the need in her eyes fan his own desire. Oh, the things he was going to do to her this morning. There'd be time later for their little talk.

KYLE STARED AT rays of sunlight that filtered through a palm tree outside, making patterns on the ceiling.

Armando? Where the fuck are you?

"Kyle." Christy was awake and had been watching him think. "There was a report on the news about a fire in the Santa Nella forest. You know anything about that? About a couple of dead guys?"

"Had nothing to do with us."

She sighed. "I want to believe you."

He thought about that. Good that she trusted him. But should she? He knew the pause told her things. Things she didn't like. He sat up, eased off the bed, and pulled on his boxers. If he stayed in bed with her a minute longer, they'd be into another lovemaking session. A long one.

She donned her robe and followed him into the kitchen. He could feel the questions mulling around in her head. Questions he wasn't ready to answer yet. There were no answers in the refrigerator.

She handed him the yogurt mixture he was looking for.

He thanked her. "I can't tell you things because it's safer if you don't know. You must promise me you'll not go anywhere for a few days."

"But I will have work. I told them I'm taking a couple of days off, but I can't afford not to work, Kyle."

"Exactly. Stay in place for now. Work on the computer from home. *Live.*" He stepped to her, slipping a hand under her robe. "God, I love this robe."

"I love the tie," she whispered, pressing her breasts against his bare chest.

Kyle leaned down and kissed her softly on the lips. He felt her breath catch as he eased one hand down to her rear. "I do, too." He couldn't get enough of her.

"I promise to wear it 24/7 then." She kissed him again. She pulled back and smiled. She handed him fresh coffee, then tiptoed to whisper in his ear, "And nothing else."

His one free hand roamed her backside, then felt her wetness and her need. "Wish I could do this all day, but I can't." Her lips were soft and hard to tear away from.

"Well, sailor, I'm totally at your beck and call. You can come here morning, noon, and night. I'll just be waiting here, in this robe." She fingered the tie. The silk robe parted so he could see the little triangle at the apex of her thighs he loved looking at. That place he could lose himself in.

It almost worked.

She fluffed her hair and licked her lips. She hadn't given up. But damn, he had to.

Kyle didn't try to cover up how she made him feel. And how he hated to go. But the urgency of finding Armando crept back in. He was tired of waiting. He knew his buddy would send another sign. And he would have to be ready to go.

Somehow.

With regret, he dressed in two minutes. She'd made him a turkey sandwich, tucking it and an apple in a brown paper bag she handed him. He'd finished off his coffee and the granola yogurt mixture.

"So, when?" she asked as she fingered his T-shirt that ribbed at his neck. He could still feel her pert nipples through her robe through his tee.

"Can't say. But I'll call you."

She nodded.

"Christy, you have to be very careful. Watch everything. Notice everything. I don't want something to happen to you while I'm gone."

She nodded again. "Promise." She cocked her head to the side and smiled. "But I like being punished when I'm a bad girl." She held up the silk tie.

Her eyes stopped sparkling when she saw his serious expression.

Kyle saw she was waiting for her dose of medicine.

"Honey, I don't want you anywhere close to danger. You've got to stay away from Armando's house, maybe even me for a while. They could be following me. And now, they could be following you."

"How do you know this?"

"Well, look at all the attention you've attracted already."

She nodded. "Because of you."

"They want something from him, and yes, maybe from me, too."

"I don't understand."

"If they'd wanted to kill him, they would have. We'd already have found his body by now. Those guys always leave a calling card like a neon sign for anyone else to read. There's something else they want."

"What?"

"I can't say. Please, it's not that I don't want to tell you, but I need to keep you out of this."

"Do I have to stay physically right here?"

"With the gates and guards, this is probably the safest place to be."

"How about the gym?"

"I'd say no."

"But it's inside the complex…"

"Christy, someone could have gotten a temporary pass key. You were right about that place. I can't defend you if you're not right here."

"I'm sure it was my imagination. This place is tougher than Fort Knox to get into."

"I got in without any trouble."

Her eyes grew wide. "How?"

He pulled out a spare scan key from his pocket. "I took the Realtor's key she left in the door when she was distracted with your shameful behavior."

"That's where my other card went. She must have mine."

"Promise me you won't go anywhere for a few days." He leaned in close, next to the side of her head, and said softly in her ear, "Please? Just for a little while longer. When this is all over…"

His cell phone chirped.

"Hey, Fredo. What's up?"

"Not good. Not good at all. They want you for questioning." Fredo's voice was calm, measured, but laced with tension. It brought reality back like a cold wave.

"What about the help from locals?" Kyle asked.

"Not even on the horizon until you answer their questions about the bodies."

"They really think a bunch of SEALs would off some local muscle? Besides, those thugs who took Armani used to be military. I'm sure of it."

"Who the hell knows?"

Kyle scanned his choices.

"So what now?" Fredo asked.

"Well, I'm not about to oblige them. I'm not going anywhere near a police station."

"Thought you'd say that, boss."

Kyle felt his choices drying up by the minute. *Armani, anytime now. Another message would be great.*

"Boss, something new. Coop got intel from his Fed connection there's a gang working with some Special Operators, bringing in some illegals, drugs, and guns. There's a hint that there's some official cooperation for protection."

"Not possible it could be Team guys."

"You and I know it and Cooper knows it. Timmons is shit-kicking mad and says you gotta comply. It's bullshit, man, but hey, the locals are working with the Navy regulars. Having some jurisdictional catfight I'd actually like to see."

Kyle thought about the thorn in his side: Carlisle. He could smell the ill intentions of this cretin from miles away. And Carlisle wasn't stupid, either. He'd heap it on, for sure. Tell them what a fuck-up Kyle was. How many reprimands and citations Kyle had been issued. How Kyle was such a loose cannon. Yeah, he could see that happening.

"Only one thing to do, then."

"Yup," Fredo agreed.

"Meet me at the Scupper in a half hour."

"How you gonna get there?" Fredo asked.

"Fly. What do you mean?"

"They impounded your Hummer, Kyle. Found all your gear, filled with enough guns to worry the locals. Shoulda brought 'em with you, bro."

"I was entertaining a…" Kyle looked over at Christy. Her body spilled out from the silk robe she'd neglected to secure. She was watching him, her smile as missing as water in the Sahara.

"Well, it's not looking good, man. Maybe they know about her too. You better think about that, man." Fredo's staccato burst of words hit Kyle. Square in the middle of his gut. Christy said there'd been *two* sets of officers, regular SDPD and a deputy sheriff.

Damn. How did this happen?

"You gotta get out of there, Kyle, before they come in and get you. Get you both."

"Thanks. I'm on my way." He was about to hang up when he thought of something. "You bring the razor wire back, or was that in my bag?" Although he knew he'd wiped the metal down as best he could, he didn't recall putting it anywhere. It wouldn't be good to have blood in his bag match the bodies.

"Dude, you don't remember that?" Fredo sounded irritated with him.

"No, I don't. I think I stuck it in my bag."

"Then the cops have it. You're in some sorry shit, man. You better get your ass over here."

Kyle hung up and wanted to throw a chair through the window. How could he have been so fucking stupid? And it would be only a matter of time before the cops came for Christy too. His prints and hair were all over this place.

Christy came up behind him and leaned into his back, wrapping her arms around his waist. He stiffened. She jerked in response and abruptly stopped stroking his chest. He grabbed her hand before it could start to travel again down to his groin. He turned around to face her. There was going to be no easy way to tell her the bad news and he had no time to do it properly.

"I screwed up, Christy. They want me for questioning." He saw her eyebrows rise up into little tents, saw creases form in her forehead. She cocked her head, and then shook it from side to side.

"Just level with me. Tell me what's going on."

He could see the beg on her face, the urgent plea to become part of his life. *All* of his life.

"I can't. I can't get you involved."

"But I *am* involved, Kyle. Can't you see that?"

He walked to the sliding glass door, but didn't go out on the veranda. He spotted two police cars with lights flashing down below. Several others were approaching, with sirens wailing.

"I gotta go now. The guys are waiting."

Kyle picked up his keys and jacket, turning to face her. He placed his palms on either side of her face. "I'll call you. Stay here. Don't go out."

"What if the police…"

"Obey the police, but no one else, you got it? I'll try to call you on your cell. And don't talk about me to anyone. Anyone. Only the San Diego PD."

He was out the door and on the fire escape when he heard the elevator doors ping open in the background. He ran down the stairs all the way to the street level.

Kyle burst into a lobby full of police. Outside the building, police cars had been parked at odd angles, as more were expected to arrive. A crowd was gathering, along with a news crew. A white coronor's van was parked nearby, its doors open. Something awful had happened, and Kyle knew there was a dead body somewhere in the building. Although he wished he could stay, he knew leaving was the best thing he could do to protect Christy.

CHAPTER 23

KYLE RAN A full mile and then hailed a cab to the island, headed for the Scupper. Once there, he found the SEAL bar dotted with tourists, taking pictures of all the SEAL memorabilia and of themselves in front of Team insignias. Later on the joint would fill up, like any good meat market, revving up to go on until the wee hours of the morning. Weekends were when the locals liked to think they could safely mingle with his crowd. The wanna-bes. Truth was, most of the real Team guys would never be caught there on Friday or Saturday nights, except when they needed an emergency pickup to push something out of their minds. Kyle had done it a time or two. Amazing what an anonymous night of sex could do. And the girl usually liked it, as well.

He scanned the room, catching a few long, lusty looks from several of the female population and "man up" gazes from some of the guys, but he didn't catch the eye of anyone familiar. He heard a whistle over the din, and then saw Cooper, his lanky frame towering a good foot above everyone else, near the exit sign in back.

"We were beginning to get worried," Cooper said as he backed through the rear door, ducking.

Kyle shook his shoulders and checked the sky. It was refreshing to be outside again. Even the brief crowd of innocents made him nervous now. Being in the Scupper felt more like spending time in a jail cell. And maybe that's because he worried he'd be landing there very soon. Until the Hummer had been hauled off, at Christy's condo, no less, he'd thought they were close to ending the caper. Mia was safe. All they had to do was find Armando. Now a whole new chapter had erupted. Things were spiraling out of control.

Think, dammit.

Kyle saw Fredo and Cooper leaning against the block wall of the vacant warehouse behind the Scupper, watching him, arms and legs crossed in an exact mirror image of each other.

"Dude. You have shit for brains, man," Fredo began. "Never seen you so spaced. Whatever she did to you, carve it out right now. No place for it here, or you're gonna get us all killed."

Fredo spoke the truth. It wasn't fair these two would suffer for his lack of judgment. They had to have their wits about them, like they did on the job overseas.

"Let me just say one thing—"

"Shut up. Let's get going," Cooper said as he punched Kyle's arm. "What's the plan?"

Plan? What fucking plan? How could he plan when he didn't know what the fuck he was doing? He'd spent the last twenty-four hours dreaming of a life he could never have. For the first time in his career, he had no plan.

Well then, make one up, asshole. He knew if he could just get into action, readjust his course, it would be easier to correct any mistake he'd made.

"First, I got to tell you something's gone wrong at Christy's condo. I passed a flock of black and whites." He scanned Fredo and Cooper. "And the coroner is there."

Fredo whistled. "Your lady know about it?" he asked.

"Not when I left her. But I'm betting they'll make sure she's fully clued in."

Both of them stood with their legs wide, arms folded on their chests. Watching him. They wouldn't ask and he wasn't going to tell them what they wanted to know. Just like he wasn't going to tell Christy what was really going on, either.

"If it goes bad, I want you guys to know I'll take the fall, and I'll say I acted alone. I don't want you two or Gunny mixed up in this."

"That's the most ridiculous fucking thing I've heard you say," said a voice from behind him. Gunny joined Fredo and Cooper, and now all three regarded Kyle with suspicion.

"Gunny, you shouldn't be here." Kyle didn't need another innocent's blood on his hands.

"Shut up. You're wasting time," Gunny barked back. "Cooper asked you already. What's the plan, boss?" Gunny's eyes looked surprisingly clear and blue.

CHAPTER 24

CHRISTY LEANED AGAINST the door she'd just shut and closed her eyes, reliving the sight of Kyle jumping into the stairway.

He's gone.

When the knock came at her door, she almost opened it without checking, hoping Kyle had changed his mind. Through the peephole, she saw Sergeant Mayfield's large frame, along with the woman officer, Woodward.

She cinched her robe, put on her game face, and opened the door.

"Morning, ma'am." Mayfield was all smiles today. A little apologetic, she thought.

"Sergeant. You two like to come in?"

"Yes, ma'am," he said as he passed her. The creak of leather from his belt and all the equipment he wore sent a shiver up her spine. Woodward whispered a curt "thank you" as she passed by. Christy could smell cigarettes on her clothes.

"I made coffee a bit ago. Let me go make some more…"

"That won't be necessary, Ms. Nelson." Mayfield looked ridiculous, armed to the teeth, in the middle of her living room. His flack vest looked uncomfortable, with his arms and legs protruding from under the heavy layer like the parts of a turtle protruding from under its shell. Unnecessary protection. He didn't seem happy to be there.

"All right." She joined them and motioned for them to sit down, which they both ignored. "Okay then, would you please tell me what this is all about?"

Mayfield took out the little book from his vest pocket and flipped through white lined pages. "You know a Marla Cunningham?"

Christy found Kyle's chair and sat. Her stomach felt vacant. Her heart pounded. Little black dots began swirling around, clouding her eyesight.

"I can see you do." Mayfield was stern. Suddenly unfriendly.

"She's my trainer," Christy said as she looked up to his face. She felt all the blood rush from her cheeks.

"When was the last time you saw her?"

Christy had to think. It had been after the open house. "Sunday night. I took a spinning class from her."

"Seems that she called into a crisis hotline to report a possible attack."

"When?"

"Two days ago."

"Oh."

"You know about anyone who had a thing for Ms. Cunningham?"

"No. We never talked about *her* personal life. Just about mine."

"And so now I gotta ask you about yours. Your SEAL boyfriend…"

"Look, he's not…" But she was lying now. Kyle had said cooperate with the police. "What does *my* personal life have to do with…just what exactly are you saying? Is something wrong with Marla?"

Did she want to hear this?

"She's been found dead."

Christy's chest caved. She couldn't find the air to fill her lungs. Black spots played checkers before her eyes, obscuring the large officer and the lady.

Dead?

She pulled herself back together. They had not offered condolences. Both of them were watching her. She wrapped her arms around her torso to stop the shaking and the buzzing in her head that was like a dentist's drill.

"Where?"

"And what difference would *that* make?" Mayfield was cool as he frowned. Woodward was checking out Christy's pink toes.

"Well, I was supposed to meet her at the gym Thursday night. She never showed."

Mayfield and Woodward looked at each other.

"She was found in her office," Mayfield answered.

Now Christy remembered the light under the office door. Poor Marla might have been fighting off her attacker at that very moment. Christy could have helped her. But instead she'd run. Run to safety. And now her friend was dead. She had to ask the question. "And why do you think Kyle is involved?"

"I can't say, exactly, due to the investigation." Mayfield put his forefinger into his collar and stretched it loose. "Seems Marla kept a journal of her activities and sessions at the club. Her entry for Sunday night was interesting in light of what we found today."

Christy looked at the woman, who was having difficulty keeping eye contact. This was going to be bad.

"She wrote that you'd had an altercation yourself. That a crazy showed up and restrained you, and then let you go."

"It was a misunderstanding," Christy said, the defiance in her voice putting a chill in the room.

Woodward shot her a look that told her the officer had heard it before and hadn't believed it then, either.

"We're thinking it was the same person." Mayfield let it sink in. Christy was starting to get sick to her stomach.

"Why?" She had to force herself to ask it. This was not going to be something she really wanted to know.

"The method of restraint. The man who killed Marla used pantyhose."

CHAPTER 25

MAYFIELD WAS SURPRISED to see Deputy Hilber at the crime scene, since it wasn't the sheriff's jurisdiction. The little prick from the Navy was dutifully at Hilber's side. Mayfield hoped like hell the man never applied to work in his department, and he made a note in his book to check the test roster to see if he'd qualified for consideration. Had to be some way to lose Carlisle's application, if he was stupid enough to have submitted one.

"I imagine this is a little different than checking cars at the guard shack on base, sailor." Mayfield had years of practice looking stern. The young MA might not pick up on the twinkle in his eye.

"Fascinating, sir, watching them work," Carlisle said, scanning the crew from the coroner's office, the photographer, and the forensic team. "Just like on TV."

Mayfield made a mental note this time. The guy was digging the gore and the details of a murder.

Hilber was another story. He was admiring the angle of broken fingers protruding up from the body of Marla Cunningham, whose hands were secured in place by a pair of black pantyhose. He noticed the pantyhose were tied in a bow.

Calling card.

This was someone who was begging them to chase after him. Well,

Mayfield might just have to comply.

The coroner's assistant came over and asked Mayfield to step aside so she could take another picture of the hands. She must've seen the same thing Mayfield did.

"These were tied together after death, am I right?" Mayfield whispered to her.

She nodded and clicked the camera, which set off a bright flash.

"I know you can't say anything officially, but how long has she been dead? Guess."

"More than a day, probably two." She pointed to the excrement and fluids leaking all over Marla's desk chair, which had formed in a puddle on the floor. Marla's purple lips and chalky white skin were ghastly enough, but the white coating over her eyes was something right out of a horror film. If the perp had known her, he would have closed her eyes. With no apparent mutilation other than the fingers, it appeared this wasn't personal. And too many clues had been left to be professional.

Marla had been chosen because she'd had information. Information on Christy.

Woodward stood next to him, a handkerchief over her mouth and nose. Mayfield watched her bring out a small brown bottle with a lavender label that read *Clarity*. He'd seen several of the officers with this womanly brand of smelling salts around at the station.

"Who found her, sir?" Woodward asked through the hankie.

"The manager, when he opened this morning. I'm guessing the smell probably tipped him off."

"She died the night she made the call?"

"April here thinks so. More than twenty-four hours ago, and that was the last anyone heard from her."

He collared the coroner's assistant again. "Can I see the journal?"

The book had been wrapped in an oversized clear evidence bag, left open on the same page it had been opened to when it had been found on the desk. Mayfield put on gloves and carefully removed it.

The assistant frowned.

Hilber had lost interest in chatting up a female reporter. "What's this?" he asked, looking at the journal.

"The lady's notebook."

Hilber blanched, then furrowed his brow. "She able to name her attacker?"

"In a manner of speaking." Mayfield showed him the passage.

"*Raised security concerns today on deaf ears. Now they've gone and hired a new janitor and not told us...,*" Hilber recited.

"No. That's Thursday's entry, which she didn't finish. Look at the one for Sunday."

"*Christy Nelson has been attacked today by a crazed psycho who tied her up with her pantyhose. I tried to get her to call the police, but she seems to think there is an explanation for it. Though this happened off site, I'm going to bring it up at the next staff meeting, without naming names. Security has been lax lately.*"

Hilber beamed after he read it. "You're right. All we need to do now is find the guy who attacked Christy. This lady was directing us right to the guy."

Mayfield watched Hilber's back as the man chuckled his way out to the hallway, too happy with this finding. And a long way from his jurisdiction.

He looked for the Navy guy and didn't see him anywhere.

The sergeant flipped through the day planner's address and phone numbers carefully. He found a listing for Christy Nelson, including her cell phone number and email. And her condo number: 14J. Checking back on the monthly calendar, he saw her name in the box for Thursday. And it wasn't crossed out.

He looked back at the journal entry. Would Marla have had the strength to get the book, open it up, and leave it perfectly centered on her desk, just before she died? And after the torture she'd been through, with the broken fingers, which was a specialty of the local youth gangs, would she have had the presence of mind to do this?

He thought not. More than likely it was the recipe the killer needed to stage it to look like the other attack.

Biggest question in Mayfield's mind was why Hilber was so pleased with it.

"Make sure I get prints on this," he said to the assistant as he placed the book back in a new evidence bag she handed him.

The attractive coroner's assistant stood a little close beside him, holding out her clipboard so he could deposit the cellophane wrapped package on top. He'd known she had the hots for him, but he pretended to not pay attention. God, why were women always trying to ease his pain? And they were younger women too. Still, her perfume was a welcome reprieve to the dastardly smell of rotting flesh and bodily fluids released after death.

"I can get you a copy of the report tomorrow morning, unless you need a phone interview."

"Thanks, April. I appreciate that." He did. But he didn't look her way. Wasn't fair to give her hope. Her eyes on his face and chest were soft and dewy. And dangerous. At least the part he could see. He smiled and whispered, "Thanks," to the floor.

He motioned Woodward to leave with him. They stepped out into the hallway just as Hilber ducked into the elevator. He'd just hung up his cell phone. He didn't hold the doors for them, pretending to try to push the buttons a little too late. It was a complete act. Mayfield could see Hilber shrug as the elevator doors closed and left him and Woodward standing in the hallway.

He cursed and heard Woodward giggle at his side.

"Sir, if it makes it any better, I can't stand the guy either. I mean, why is he even here?" she said.

He appreciated her sentiment.

"Probably because he's got the Feds convinced it has something to do with his murders in the Santa Nella forest. And I'm sure they are linked. Just not sure how Hilber's putting the pieces together."

"Understood, sir. So can I ask?"

"You honestly think I know?" He was pleased she thought so, but everything was swimming around and he didn't know where it landed.

"Yes. I think your instincts are the best I've ever seen. That's why I'm here. To learn, sir. If I became half the cop you are, I'd consider myself lucky."

"I thank you." He looked down at the top of her head. He'd never noticed how pretty her hair was—and what the hell was he doing? How easily a woman could get to him, still.

"I want the trash searched. Probably won't be in the gym area, but I'm guessing there's a cardboard or plastic wrapper for those pantyhose, and if I'm not mistaken, they would be a medium, the size Marla would wear. I don't know about the black, but maybe she liked the color. Someone would know. Ask her friends at the gym. They might have seen her dress up to go out. Most women would have a pair of flesh-toned hose around."

"Very good, sir. Consider it done. How about the girl? Christy. Should I ask her?"

"Nah, I'd leave her alone for now. She's spooked out of her gourd. I need her cooperative."

IN THE EARLY afternoon, Mayfield got a call from Woodward. They'd found a trash bag in the back of the complex. It contained a cellophane wrapper with one pair of black pantyhose remaining, size medium. It had been a two-pack.

And there were dustable prints all over it.

HILBER DROPPED BY Mayfield's office, without his buddy this time.

"You guys done with the Hummer yet?" Hilber looked as though he was trying to whistle or do something to look as if he wasn't as interested as he clearly was.

"Haven't heard back from forensics. Should be soon, though. Maybe tomorrow morning."

"And I'm guessing no one's called about it?"

"You mean called to claim it?"

"Yup." Hilber checked his fingernails as he leaned into the doorframe.

"That's a Roger that," Mayfield returned.

"All his equipment still logged in?"

"Everything I was given." Mayfield wondered why Warren was concerned about the guns and shit.

"Got the coroner's or crime scene reports yet?"

Mayfield wasn't going to tell him about the pantyhose wrapper they'd found. He leaned into his desk, throwing down a pen. "Hilber, suppose I refrain from asking you what the hell you're doing over here, sticking your nose into *my* business? How about you quit interfering? You'll get your goddamned report soon enough."

The cold blue stare Mayfield got froze his bones. Given the chance, this man would put a bullet in the back of his head rather than get caught.

"How did you boys in the Sherriff's Department manage to get the impound order?" Mayfield asked.

"Jurisdictional hospitality. You scratch my back, I scratch yours." Hilber had leaned back. Mayfield didn't like the man's sneer.

"Who signed it?" Mayfield wanted to know who Warren's accomplice was. He could check the records, of course, but he wanted to see the man spew it out.

"Carpenter."

Now there was another man Mayfield didn't trust. Carpenter was known to be a little heavy-handed, especially with the swabs, but he was hell on wheels with the ladies too.

He was beginning to understand the real enemy in this game.

CHAPTER 26

T HE LITTLE TEAM was driving through a seedy part of San Diego. Fredo had given Gunny the directions to his informant's neighborhood.

"Not sure it's a good idea to be seen talking to him. Might make him shy," Fredo said.

"So call him," Cooper squawked.

"Oh, yes. Let me just call 4-1-1 and see if AT&T has the numbers to the Gang Information Directory."

"Think we'd better drop you off a few blocks away," Kyle offered.

"That's what I was thinkin'," Fredo replied.

"You wired, Fredo?" Gunny asked.

"Got my Invisio right here." He flicked his finger hard on his right ear. Coop jumped in his seat, swearing. "And Coop has the earphones, as you can see."

Cooper bore an expression as if he were going to eat the earphones or throw them out of the window.

"Ladies, please," Kyle pleaded.

They passed over several railroad tracks filled with rail cars spray-painted with colorful gang graffiti artwork. A local news crew had done a series on street art. Some of the members were talented and could have made a living as artists if the drug money wasn't so lucrative.

Surrounding buildings were in a sorry state. Everywhere there was rubble: broken bottles, broken windows. In spite of it all, a small group of five and six-year-old boys was trying to play soccer in one of the alleyways they passed. Laundry hung between windows. Dogs were barking inside apartments that had bars over the windows, many of which were boarded up or coated with tinfoil. It reminded Kyle of some of the killing zones in Afghanistan, except without all the incessant sandy dust that seemed to blow right through him. Kids played soccer there too.

But there were not many dogs. People had goats, but those weren't pets.

Gunny parked the beater where Fredo indicated. Fredo exited the truck and wandered through the rubble that was the sidewalk.

Cooper slouched back in the seat, donning his baseball cap, which covered the earphones. Kyle used a small set of binoculars he'd fished out of his pocket. Without his usual uniform, including his bullet-proof vest, he felt hairless and naked. He didn't like the feeling one bit.

"You got me?" The small radio speaker squawked. Cooper was hearing it in stereo and recording it.

"Yeah, you little spic. You know there's a hole in your jeans right where your butthole is?"

Cooper and Fredo had a routine that kept them from getting nervous.

"Musta been that quickie last night." Fredo exaggerated his hip swing.

"Nah, I think it was your farts, Taco Man."

"Well, even rotting goats smell better than yours. Too many vitamins."

"I'm going to break Gunny's record. I'll be getting it up when you can't see yours."

"Okay, ladies. We got incoming," Fredo whispered.

Fredo spewed off Spanish slang no one could follow. The guy could talk faster than an automatic. He spliced in some English, and as the other speaker followed suit, they continued in English.

"Yo. I got some Franklins here for you. Thought you might want a little party. Thought I'd make a donation to your college fund, or an investment in your future," Fredo said.

"What'd you have in mind?" the male voice asked. "Minding the girls, Fredo?"

"Nah. I got that covered. Too much, as a matter of fact."

"Ain't no such thing."

"I hear you. Okay, now for the reason I'm here. Word has it you got some information, and I'm buyin."

"Didn't take you for a buyer."

"Information."

"No ladies, man? We gots the best."

"I'm saving money for a little chiquita I knocked up in LA. You feel me?"

"Shit, Fredo. It's free. They got a free clinic here."

"No free clinic. She's not legal. And I'm having this baby."

"You're having it. Thought the lady did all that."

"You know what I mean. Trying to get respectable. Make an honest woman of her."

"Get in line. They don't even ask, if you want to go the other way."

"I'm not doin' it that way. Don't want any complications. And I love the chiquita."

There was silence for a minute. Fredo pushed, "Hey, sorry man, if you're not comfortable with this. I'll just move on. What was I thinking?"

"No, it's cool. Who're you lookin' for?"

"Calls himself Caesar. Runs girls, and guns too, I hear. I need to find him, man."

"I don't know no Caesar."

"Right. And I'm not Mexican. How much?"

"Three, maybe four."

"How about one to start and then if you got more, you get more."

"Okay. He works out of his bar, the Los Ladies."

They could hear Fredo peeling off a bill and handing it to the informant. "Here's a Franklin. What else you got?"

"I'm not too comfortable with anything else. There's a guy you might want to talk to."

"He buying?"

"Maybe. He works out of Los Ladies."

Kyle rolled his eyes as he looked at Cooper. The topless bar that specialized in bathroom sex, forged papers, and drug deals. Quite the place.

"I've been there a time or two."

"But you don't ask for Caesar. You ask for his woman, Mia."

The team heard Fredo stutter. "Mia, is it? Sure, I'll ask for her."

Kyle heard the banter in Spanish and a slapping handshake. They heard the familiar crinkle of paper.

Makes two hundred.

Fredo questioned the male. "Hey, when was the last time you saw Caesar and this Mia?"

"Haven't seen Caesar for a few days. I've only seen Mia at the Ladies. She dances there sometimes."

"Uh huh." They could hear Fredo breathing fast.

"He's been flashing around some green. Had a very successful few days, I'd say."

"So if he wasn't at the Ladies, where would he be? I'm kinda in a hurry."

"That's an expensive question."

"How much?"

"Another two at least."

Fredo sighed, breathing heavy into the microphone. He lowered his voice and, in a whisper, added, "Okay, this better be good. I got three hundred here. Where does the dude live?"

"He lives with his mama, and don't the fuck tell him I told you. The yellow house on Greenwich."

"I know it," Fredo said. Kyle did, too. It was a block away from Armando's mother's home.

"If you boys are smart you'd get in on this. Gonna get yourself rich, man."

"What do you mean?"

"I just thought you were going to sell something to Caesar. He's buying. Big time."

"I considered it."

"I'll bet you did. Hell of a lot more than Uncle Sam pays. You military types are sitting on a gold mine. Caesar buys the stuff cheap too. Sells it back to the gangs and makes a buttload of green."

"It's a good business model."

"Might as well secure your retirement. War's going to be over soon. You guys will be out of a job."

Not in your dreams, dickwad. Kyle was amazed how naïve people were, even gang-bangers.

"That's for sure." Fredo played along.

"Thanks, man. Be safe."

Kyle was worried he'd already asked too many questions. Now that they knew where Caesar was, finding Armando might not be hard. He hoped. He heard Fredo whistle as he walked back and came into view. Kyle covered him with his sidearm just in case. The informant did not accompany him.

"Gunny, get in the passenger seat. Now," Kyle barked. Gunny's frame barely made it by the time Fredo opened the driver's side door and got in.

Fredo fired up the beater, which backfired. They turned around and went back the way they'd come in.

"They're buying guns and shit all right," Fredo said in disgust. Everyone was quiet for what they knew was coming. "And they're using Mia." Fredo turned and looked at Kyle over the back of the seat. "You think she's back there already?"

"Fredo, she made her bed." Kyle said the obvious.

"The woman's like a cat with nine lives, and wasting all of them. All at once."

"Some people do that." Kyle added, "Can't help those who don't care."

Cooper was carefully winding the wires of the headset around a white plastic cone. He positioned them inside a small case that held the miniature recorder. He leaned against the window. "So what's up now, boss?"

"I gotta make a couple of calls."

KYLE HAD BEEN places that had scared him shitless. This was even more frightening. He dialed Christy, who picked up on the second ring.

"Hi there," he said.

"Kyle! Oh, my God, are you okay?"

"I'm fine." He hoped he didn't sound as nervous as he felt.

"I was worried. I still am."

He had to be careful. "I told you not to worry. I said I'd call you."

She was sniffling on her end of the line. He heard the strain in her voice as she tried to settle herself. "When can I see you?" she whispered. Her need poured all over him.

He inhaled. This was more difficult than he'd thought. Thank God he had enough sense not to go over to her condo. "Better for you if I stay away. Just didn't want you to worry."

"But the police, the sheriff, and even the Navy—everyone's been saying some…very disturbing things. I'm…"

"Don't believe them."

"But you said to cooperate with the police."

"Look, Christy, things got kind of crazy. I'm afraid I've made a terrible mistake getting you involved."

"Kyle, don't…"

"I wasn't using my head." He could do this. He told himself it was better if she got hurt now. Maybe it would send her back to San Francisco. Best place for her. Safest place right now.

"Don't say that. You know I don't feel the same way about this. I *want* to be involved."

There was no easy way out of the box he'd put himself into. Only one right thing to do, and damn, it was going to hurt her in the short run. But way better for her in the long run.

"Christy," he began, "you've got to just forget about all this. I've changed my mind about us."

The deafening silence on the other end of the phone gave him the shivers.

He continued, "I need to focus on finding Armando before it's too late."

The phone went dead.

CHAPTER 27

EXT MORNING, CHRISTY tried to focus on anything other than
Kyle. She cleaned her condo thoroughly, even scrubbing her
toilet. She cleaned her oven, which had hardly been used over the past
few weeks. She tried to read one of her romance novels, and threw it
across the room when she came to a love scene. She cranked some
Candy Dulfer sax music up until she got a call from downstairs telling
her to lessen the volume, and even kneeled on the floor and gave in to
the need to just sob, to get it all out. She knew that, in time, it would
get better. Everything got better in time. But today she had to occupy
herself with awful things she hated doing. Just get through today.

To her amazement, she started to feel better as the Sunday morning dribbled away.

But then she got stir crazy. How long would she be confined to her
apartment now that Kyle had given her the brush-off yesterday? Just
because he said so, was she really now no longer involved? It sure
seemed to her that the SDPD or the Sheriff's Department would still
be interested in what little information she had. She had taken the call
with Simms last night and had told him what had happened with the
authorities and that she was done with the Navy guy. She said she
would be back at work soon. He told her to take as much time as she
needed and that he was sorry.

Sorry didn't begin to describe how she looked, she realized, as she washed her hands in her bathroom lavie and re-tied up her hair. She thought she had aged ten years since last she'd last examined her face. But again, she knew it would get better.

Maybe she should leave San Diego. Would she ever see a Navy jet or a ship or those well-developed bodies running down the beach and not think of him? Wouldn't it be easier to just get away from any memory of him?

But no, she wasn't made of that kind of stock. She had never been a quitter. San Francisco was a one-way street going nowhere. Her mother had given her a ticket to paradise. She'd just have to find it alone, and not in the arms of the most handsome, wonderful guy she had ever met.

There must be someone else out there for me. I thought it was Kyle.

But no. It wouldn't be Kyle. Not now. And this time, even if he did come back to her, she'd have to say no and mean it.

Though he was the bastard who broke her heart, she still couldn't see him as a rogue killer, like the cops said.

No, couldn't be. I just can't go there. For as much pain as she was feeling, she just couldn't see him killing for sport or profit. She couldn't see him killing at all. He was dangerous, yes. Dangerous in all the ways—and *here it comes again.* A flood of tears sprang up and she gasped.

Damn. Her mother would be furious with her. Look how she was treating her mom's gift.

Maybe she knew this would happen. Maybe she had even caused it, thinking how much it would hurt if he left. And now he had, and so it hurt. But she knew she'd survive.

Somehow.

Her phone rang.

"Hello?"

"Cheríe?" Madame M's voice cheerily greeted her on the other end of the line.

"Madame! How wonderful to hear from you. How have you been?"

"Oh, très bien. Very well. Business has begun to pick up. I'm flush with customers."

Christy had a brief moment of regret for having left the woman behind. She was like a second mother to her. And now the closest thing to a mother she would have for the rest of her life.

"Christy? You are well?"

"Yes. Yes, Madame. I'm very well. My mother's place is just perfect for me. I'm enjoying real estate," she lied. "I'm still, you know, getting settled, but it's coming along."

"Oh, that's too bad."

"Excuse me?"

"Well, I was hoping you could come up here and help me for a bit."

"Oh, Madame, I can't." Then Christy thought about it.

Why not? Kyle has just turned me out to pasture. Why shouldn't I get away from all this? If it gets worse, a little break would do me good. If it improves, well, it sure as hell wouldn't have anything to do with her. So why not?

"Cheríe, I have to go in for some surgery. I have no one here who knows our shop like you do. You should know I've not really been able to replace you…"

"Madame, that's nice of you to say, but…"

"It's true. You know my customers, you know the business. My reps still ask about you."

Christy was silent, collecting her thoughts, remembering the happy days there, those days sandwiched between the lonely ones when she knew there was more to life than catering to a bunch of rich men who bought beautiful lingerie for the women in their lives.

"Is this surgery serious?"

"Non, ma chère! Just a little female work."

Approaching sixty years of age, Madame M was the most striking older women Christy knew. How she managed to stay single after the death of her young husband, years ago, was a mystery to Christy. Madame M had offers for dates and expensive travel with eligible, wealthy men whom she turned down frequently.

"I'm holding out for a duke, a prince, or perhaps a king!" she would tell Christy. And they would laugh. Madame would ask her sometimes, "And you? Who are you waiting for?"

Well, she knew the answer to that one. She didn't expect it would hurt this much, though.

"How long will you be out?" Christy asked, not wanting to know the answer.

"Not long. About two weeks. First week I will be in hospital. Next week I must be home and then I can go back, although the doctors want me to be off for a month. Mon Dieu! I can't be gone that long."

"Do you have anyone in training now?"

"Yes, I have two very nice girls. But they are young, ma chère. Very young."

And what am I at twenty-six? Am I old now?

"They work for me while going to college. Neither one of them wants to go into the business."

"Ah. I see."

"Cheríe," Madame M began softly, "have you ever thought about returning to San Francisco?"

"Not really." Christy's stomach clenched up. She knew there was an offer coming she would have difficulty declining, but also knew she would.

"Would you consider coming to help out while I am infirmed, and then possibly taking over the shop some day? I would be happy to give it to you, if it became too much for me to handle. I am not a young woman any longer, you know."

That told Christy the "surgery" was more serious than she was letting on. But she had to be honest.

"Madame, there is no future for me there. I wanted a fresh start."

"I understand. I think the difference between an older woman and a younger one is an older one knows how to think practically. Young ones always go looking for love and think that will save them. The cost is too great, cherie. Take it from me."

Christy knew exactly what Madame as saying.

"There are lots of attractive, older men who frequent my shop, and several of them ask about you. I think even one or two have come in just to see you. They could make your life comfortable and aren't so bad to look at, either. Money can heal a lot of loneliness."

But not for me. There isn't enough money in the world to heal my wound. I have to do this myself.

"Have I offended, ma chère?"

"No, Madame. I take no offense. I just am not interested. Can I think about this for a day or so? When is your surgery?"

"Two days. Not to worry, I have already begun to tell people the store will close for two weeks. Perhaps this is why I have been so busy lately." Madame giggled like a little girl.

Christy saw another phone call was coming in. "Madame, I must go. I'll think seriously about it and then will call you back later tonight. Is that all right?"

"Call me tomorrow?"

Christy pushed the button for the next call, but had just missed it. She hit redial. A crusty voice answered on the other end.

"Security."

"Jerry, is that you?" Christy asked.

"Oh, yes. This is Ms. Nelson?"

"Jerry, it's Christy. Is there something wrong?"

He cleared his throat. "Uh, Ms. Nelson," he started, ignoring her comment, "we've gotten some complaints, and the Co-op Association has asked me to call you about it."

"Complaints? Complaints about me?"

"Yes, ma'am."

"I'm sorry, I don't understand. What complaints?"

"You know about Marla?"

"Yes, the police were here today."

"Seems there's a sort of criminal element hanging around here since you moved in."

Christy felt like throwing the phone through the opened sliding glass door to shatter on the ground below.

"I had a chance encounter with someone…I met a man who…" Everything she started to say was wrong. "The police and the Sheriff's Department have questioned me about someone I met quite by accident." She remembered the feel of Kyle's hard body against hers as he immobilized her knees, her wrists. The smell of his faint cologne, the way his kisses tasted, the words he whispered in her ears— everything came flooding back to her.

"See, Ms. Nelson…"

"Christy. Please, Jerry, are you interrogating me too? You know who I am, what I'm about."

"Look, I need this job. They just want me to deliver a message. They're going to take a vote. I have no say in the matter. Some of the older folks are staying elsewhere. They're afraid to even return back here."

"I see. But this isn't anything I've caused."

"The police have been asking questions about you everywhere. It makes folks uncomfortable."

"Jerry, you know me."

"Like I said, I have no say so here. It's up to the Association, and they have the right to ask someone to leave if that person is attracting a criminal element." He sighed and then gave her the punch she was expecting. "They're going to vote in two days. I'm supposed to let you know they will probably be asking you to leave and that you should prepare yourself accordingly."

"They can do that?"

"Come on, Ch...er... Ms. Nelson. You know they can. Or they can make it expensive for you if you fight them. You're a Realtor. You know the CC&R's."

"But what would I do? Can they force me to sell?"

"No, but they can bar you from living here."

And there it was. Suddenly the place Kyle thought she was safest at had turned out to be the place she had to leave—*might* have to leave.

That made Madame M's offer more attractive. Only question was, would she be able to come back here? Some day?

CHAPTER 28

S ERGEANT MAYFIELD LOOKED at the flashing line on his phone that indicated he had voicemail. He hated voicemail. Reminded him of how he'd spent most of his days behind a desk. Maria would have liked the fact he was now out of harm's way more often than not, but there was that part of him the Navy hadn't drilled out of him, about wanting to be where the action was. That's why he'd wanted to fly jets, but he couldn't pass the vision tests.

He'd gone to BUD/S too, but didn't make it past Hell Week. He wondered how his life would have changed if he could have stuck with it. But he'd had a good life, even though he and Maria had never had kids. Although his current work wasn't the SEALs, he took some pride in seeing to it that young recruits turned out to be fine cops. Honest cops. And he'd seen a few of the other kind, dirty cops, where just one or two bad apples could demoralize a whole battalion. Never thought he'd have to look over his shoulder, but he learned he had to be careful. Everywhere.

Having the desk job gave him the occasional chance to right a wrong that had been done, either by one of his own or a member of the public, or on behalf of someone who'd been victimized by the system. He didn't know why, but he felt Kyle Lansdowne wasn't one of the bad guys. Christy Nelson believed in the Team guy. Mayfield saw it in her body language, as well as in her eyes. And those eyes were not the naïve doe eyes of someone with nothing upstairs. This girl was quality. Someone he knew Maria would have wanted him to find. Not this young, of course, but someone who had the same strength.

So it was a pleasant coincidence that the voicemail message was from Miss Nelson herself.

"I'm going to leave San Diego for a couple of weeks. I can still be reached on my cell." There was a pause. He could tell she didn't want to leave the message. And it wasn't really for him.

"You never told me I had to check in with you, but you seemed the only one I could trust."

Mayfield wondered what was up with that. Whom else had she talked to? He'd have to ask Jones, Theissen, and Woodward if they'd done a second round of questioning. He doubted it, though.

"A friend of mine is sick in San Francisco, and I'm going to go there and run her shop while she's recovering. I'll be staying at a little cottage at 484 Stanyan Street. My cell is the best way to reach me, though." She left her cell number and hung up.

He smiled. San Francisco brought wonderful memories of the honeymoon he and Maria had there, back in the late eighties. He could have lived there, but Maria didn't want to be far from her family in Mexico. Even after many of them came to the States or had died, his career was in full swing in San Diego, and then *he* was the one who didn't want to move.

He marked down Christy's new address on his vest pocket notebook, then programmed her number into his cell in case she called back. He didn't want to leave a written copy of that around. For some reason, he felt protective of her.

The second voicemail was from a Chief Petty Officer Timmons, Kyle's boss.

"Got a couple of things I need to discuss, off the record. If you don't mind calling me back on my cell..."

Now that was interesting, he thought. He knew he was about to find out for sure whether Kyle was a good guy or a bad guy.

THEY'D AGREED TO meet at Jimmy's. Mayfield knew it well, although not entirely on nostalgic terms like some of its patrons. He'd done his share of arrests for drunk and disorderly conduct, but mostly he'd cleaned up the civilian garbage and let the Navy take care of theirs. But there was always some guy who thought he was better and stronger than a soft-spoken SEAL who shied away from local conflict. All the same, there was a limit, Mayfield knew. And once that line was crossed, well, someone would go to the hospital, and it usually wasn't the swab.

That's why this situation bothered him so much. Bodies. Not your normal Navy incident. So Mr. Lansdowne was either a very misunderstood guy or one hell of a bad dude. Either way, this was messy. Too messy for a guy who needed his pension to retire on in five years.

But, he'd always taken the high road. And Maria had often reminded him why she'd married him: he always did the right thing, even if it wasn't always the smartest in terms of his career advancement. True to her word, her last words to him were, "I love you. I will miss you May Day." She knew he loved to hear her call him this. Her private name for him, stemming back to the first time she'd seen him. She'd told him she knew instantly her life would never be the same afterwards.

God, I miss you too, Maria. But he'd promised her he wouldn't mope around. He wished they'd had children. She was insistent it was something wrong with her, but he had his doubts. He'd figured it was something related to his Navy service. She never once complained about being "unfulfilled" like other women would say on TV. If it was a burden to her, she carried it alone.

But he wished something of her remained. Just something.

Soft rock and roll was playing on a radio back in a dark corner. Posters and pictures of Teams on the beach and in Africa, original artwork, and T-shirts signed by Teams all adorned the lower part of the walls. Above all the memorabilia and posters, now occupying both sides of the narrow bar, were row upon row of flags with pictures underneath them. "Fallen Heroes," the sign read. As he studied the faces in the mostly black and white photos, he noted how good looking almost every single one of those men were. And how young. Heck, they looked like kids he'd played football with in high school. Kids he could have had.

But that was because he was in his fifties, and war was a young man's sport. And these young, brave men had given their lives so he could have a desk job in the sunny warm weather of San Diego, so he could finish out his life in comfort and retire to contemplate the death of his wife. So he could have a future he wasn't exactly sure he wanted anymore. But because they gave up theirs, he would do the best he could.

Timmons looked like he sounded on the phone, gnarly and mostly grumpy, with a ruddy pockmarked complexion and beefy hands with sausage fingers. His biceps and shoulders hovered like the guns they were, perched over rock-hard abs. He didn't seem to be the kind of man you wanted to be around when he wasn't having a good day. Mayfield shook hands with him and realized that, under different circumstances, they could have been brothers. Mayfield's fingers got crushed in the vise grip Timmons delivered without flinching or straining a muscle.

"Thanks for coming, Mayfield," Timmons said while he hailed the waitress. "I know you're busy, so I'll buy you a burger and a beer if you'll share one with me."

"No thanks. I had a peanut butter and jelly sandwich at my desk. And I don't drink on duty." Mayfield studied the bluish purple bags under Timmons's eyes.

"We gotta talk," Timmons said after he ordered a cheeseburger and fries to go with the beer he had started. He nodded to two muscled young men who walked in and took up a seat at the bar to watch a game on the big-screen monitor.

"I've never had a SEAL turn rogue. I've trained some crazy-assed men, though."

Mayfield nodded and sipped on a diet Coke the waitress brought.

"Despite what the papers have said, I don't think there's been more than a handful. Certainly nothing like any of the other branches," Mayfield replied.

"None of these special ops guys go evil, but they do get snagged with money problems occasionally. Compromised, but not often. I worry about the ones who almost get through the training and then quit. Not because they can't do it—they quit sometimes because they decide they don't want to. And there's no shame in that. There are a few where the training just picks a scab, opens up an old wound, and they are so filled with hate they can't function and are never the same. We get only a few a year. And it's the part of the training I don't care for. Letting those young guys loose on society."

"Those guys become my problem," Mayfield said.

"I'm sure they do."

"So you called me over this afternoon to apologize?"

Timmons chuckled and cocked his head, as if regarding Mayfield's casual demeanor. "I met you once before, you know?"

"Sorry. Don't remember."

"You'd come by to pick your wife up at the hospital where my kid was. Your wife took real good care of my Cassie when she fell from a horse and broke her arm."

That had been another irony. Maria had worked as a nurse on the children's ward. It was difficult for her when she lost one of her charges, Mayfield thought, almost as bad as losing one of her own. He didn't remember meeting Timmons.

"I'm sure she did a great job. She was known for it."

Timmons looked up at him quickly. "Was?"

"She died almost a year ago."

"I'm sorry to hear that."

"Don't be. Got almost thirty years with her. I'm the lucky one."

Timmons mumbled something before he took another sip of his beer. Mayfield got the impression his marriage wasn't as special. But the man had a kid. And that was something he could take pride in. And live for.

"We could sit here and reminisce, but there are people after someone you and I both know will need help if he's to get out of this jam," said Mayfield.

"So you believe Kyle." It was more of a statement than a question.

"Never met him. But I saw his lady. She's a nice package. Perfect for him."

"And I've never met *her*. I'm sorry to say he's had to distance himself from her," Timmons said flatly.

"I know about it. She told me the same."

Mayfield looked at the walls around them, the history of the lives lost and lives lived to the maximum, the rush of history and years of joy, years of pain. There they were, two men with very different tastes, needs, and desires, on two different career paths. But both with the same focus.

To get Kyle out of this mess. And find his Team buddy.

And like members of his team years ago when he was running little boats down the beach, Mayfield knew the team he and Timmons had set up today was dependent on both of them giving their all for the cause.

And that would be the only way any of them would survive.

CHAPTER 29

THE DRIVE FROM San Diego to San Francisco was easy, especially since Christy decided to break the monotony of the nine-hour trek by listening to a book on tape. It was a steamy romance by one of her favorite authors. She was in tears when she pulled up for gas midway, as she had just listened to a breakup scene. She knew the reason the story had affected her more than it might have ordinarily. Kyle was probably history, a not-too-pleasant part of her past, when he should have been the best part of her future.

She couldn't stop herself from missing him and felt her wound get deeper the more she thought about it.

Four hours later, when she arrived in San Francisco at the huge house on Stanyan Street, she felt a part of her had arrived home. Tom Bergeron kept this place for clients he entertained who came from outside the country. He'd agreed to let Christy stay there until she got herself settled—whatever that meant.

Tom was one of the handsomest older men she had ever met. He frequented Madame M's shop, which had become kind of a liaison between eligible men and the young ladies looking for them. That was part of the service Madame loved: being a matchmaker. Everyone on the Peninsula knew Madame liked to keep her customers paired with partners who liked expensive lingerie and a healthy sex life. It was, after all, good for business.

Tom was in his mid-fifties, had graying hair, a trim physique, and a nice, soft-spoken, well-educated style. He could afford the finer things in life. He'd made no secret he liked Christy, but he had just married a former model and had a lavish yacht wedding on the San Francisco Bay. Over the three years Christy had worked at the shop, she would hold up little frilly things he bought for some of his gorgeous, high-profile girlfriends, and later, his beautiful wife. But he always flirted with Christy, making her blush. She actually enjoyed it.

"You're a good girl, Christy. I hope you find someone who will treat you like the lady you are," he'd said one day as she wrapped a lacy purple bra and thong set in matching purple tissue. When she'd looked up into his cool blue eyes, she'd known he would be someone she might have broken the rules for. Maybe marrying an older man could work, she'd thought that day.

But then she'd realized that was folly. She wanted a family.

Since Tom was now happily married, staying at his cottage behind the main house on Stanyan Street didn't pose a problem for her. Though she didn't need it, the thought of having a protector was a pleasant one. She trusted Tom.

She parked her red Honda on the street, the hood pointing downhill, the tires curbed. She removed her bag, then walked up the brick and cobblestone steps alongside the driveway and rang the doorbell at the main house. The front porch was the size of her condo's kitchen; its large columns and half-walled wooden railings allowed an expansive view of the bay below.

Tom came to the front door, barefoot and in jeans and a light blue shirt, which was buttoned a little low, Christy thought. He had a glass of red wine in his hand. As he opened the large glass and metal sculptured door, she heard jazz coming from inside and caught the faint smell of fresh soap.

"Christy. Lovely to see you again." He took her hand and kissed it tenderly.

Her back was ramrod straight as her knees buckled from his attentiveness. She was conscious of his breathing, the tanned skin with a light dusting of hair on his well-formed chest.

"Thank you, Tom. I appreciate this."

"Please," he said as he gestured to the rest of his kingdom. He grabbed her bag as she passed him.

He collected grandfather clocks, and the incessant clicking of small metal pieces inside massive wooden chests was both stimulating and reassuring. Measured. Organized. Tom had an attention to detail unlike any other man she had ever met.

Except one.

Across thick deep burgundy carpeting, she walked down the walnut-paneled hallway and into the kitchen at the rear, which overlooked a peaceful garden with a running water fountain. The music, the bubbling water, the smell of basil and tomato coming from the stove, all felt like a stage had been set. And so she asked.

"Where is Johanna?"

Tom's back was turned as he got down two plates from his upper cabinet without asking Christy if she wanted supper. He was going to make it for her anyway. "Gone," he said to the cabinet.

"Gone?" she asked.

"She's left me, Christy."

"I'm so sorry, Tom."

"Don't be." He looked up and smiled. "She was not wife material."

Maybe Christy's radar was set higher than normal, but there was something else behind his eyes that he did not say.

Christy stumbled on a couple of responses she couldn't finish.

Tom interrupted her. "She neglected to tell me she intended to keep one or two of her close girlfriends, and I didn't want to share."

"Girlfriends? You mean boyfriends, right?"

"No. You heard me right. Guess I didn't do a very good job qualifying." Tom sighed. "Remember when I taught you about qualifying being the most important part of the sales process?"

Had she asked the right questions of Kyle when she'd had the chance? The vision of Kyle's tattooed arms holding another woman's body loomed large and she felt her stomach lurch as tears painfully forced their way to her eyes.

Tom was perceptive. In an instant he was in front of her, holding her face between his massive warm hands, wiping her tears away with his thumbs. "Madame M has told me about your SEAL, Christy. Perhaps…" His hands were trembling slightly. He licked his lips and continued. "Perhaps we could heal each other…" He bent to kiss her in what she knew would be a tender kiss, but she just couldn't do it. She turned away from him and broke free.

"Sorry. If…if…Madame…," she began.

"No. That was me, just being a man seeing a beautiful woman in pain. I want to help." He went back to the plates, turned, and said softly, his eyes downturned, "Forgive me."

God, there was nothing to forgive! Was she nuts?

"Thank you, but your apology is not needed. I'm overly sensitive right now. But I'll land on my feet eventually. I always do." She gave a brittle, victorious smile he didn't buy, and watched him dish up a tossed green salad next to a red pasta dish.

"Come. We'll eat, have a glass of wine, and then I'll take you to the cottage so you can take a hot bath and fall asleep, okay?"

Of course she was okay with that. Who wouldn't be?

They ate at the formal dining room with large picture windows, overlooking the sight of the city at dusk. It was unusually fogless. Lights began to twinkle as the sky overhead turned deep turquoise.

The food was perfect. The wine was perfect. The man sitting before her was perfect, except he wasn't Kyle. She wondered why she couldn't just lose herself in the moment, let Tom care for her, heal her, as he had said. But she couldn't.

"So, how is your real estate career going?" he asked as he looked at her lips from across the table.

"Good. I was just holding my first open house—well, it was actually sort of a fiasco—I mean…" She couldn't finish. "Oh, I've just been making all the mistakes a newbie agent makes."

"Then you are learning, if you know they are mistakes."

"It is a cutthroat business. People are only too kind to let you know when you've screwed up," she finally said.

"I understand completely. When I was actively selling, I knew how those offices could be. Can't say I miss it."

"Once I build a little confidence, I'll be okay. I'm just not sure what I'm doing yet. I don't want to waste someone else's money."

"Yes. I used to tell people I'd made all the mistakes with my own money first, so I ought to be good with theirs."

Christy laughed.

"You have a condo, Madame M tells me."

"Yes. My mother left it to me. It's a nice place, overlooking the water, the boats, Coronado Island."

"And you will think of your SEAL friend when you look at the island?"

Christy blushed and looked down at her lap. Her fingers smoothed over crease lines of the ironed linen monogrammed napkin that matched the tablecloth. Her fingers couldn't stop the little tenting of the fold. She felt the heat from her body radiating through to her palm. She looked up and Tom was studying her, his head slightly tilted. Handsome, available. Waiting for her move. She smiled as she thought of Madame M's favorite saying, so repeated it to him.

"Better to have loved and lost than never to have loved at all."

At first he didn't react, but after noticing an extra flutter of his eyelids, she could see she had speared him in a most delicate place. Where he hurt. He inhaled and raised his crystal wine glass to her.

"To our broken hearts, then."

IT WOULD HAVE been easy to fall into the rhythm of this household, she thought as she walked into the two-story living room with her glass of port. The antiques, the clicking of the well-timed clocks, the sounds of foghorns over the bay, the glistening lights of the bridges and water at moonlight were pleasant details of a life she could have. What was there not to love about the man who stood behind her, but just far enough away so as not to intrude? She could feel his heat, feel his desire, and knew she could heal him at the cost of herself.

But that is what this relationship with Tom would be, sacrificing herself for something that didn't make her whole. She'd always had her standards. But now she had a taste of what her life could be like, and this wasn't it. She could pass all this up for a picnic on a park bench or a ride in a rusty rowboat powered by arms she longed for to hold her. For a cup of chowder or sandwich at a bar that held pictures of fallen heroes on its walls.

"I'm tired. I'd like to turn in," she said.

His grave response was, "Yes."

He followed behind, carrying her bag as she walked the brick path to the cottage. The fire was lit. Through open French doors, she couldn't help but notice the bed had a centered view of the flames. She heard her bag drop to the floor. His hand was on her shoulder, and he turned her, but did not step closer.

"If you change your mind, I will leave the back door open, Christy," he said softly. He bent, held her face between his hands, and kissed both cheeks. "Goodnight."

And he was gone.

Her fingers fumbled as she placed her bag on the bed and started to unzip it. She removed her toiletry kit, and then hooked it on a custom gargoyle loop above the white marble vanity top in the adjoining bath. She poured a generous portion of lavender bath gel into the two-person tub and turned on the water. She stripped off her traveling clothes, then walked naked to her bag and took out her sets of black pants and stretchy tops like Madame M liked her to wear and hung them up. She put her hair up in a ponytail and stepped into the warm bath water, and melted.

The full moon hung heavy over the arched window as she lay her head back against the cool marble. It was the same moon Kyle would see.

If he looked up.

CHAPTER 30

KYLE BROUGHT THE Karl Gustav and its deadly ammunition to Gunny's gym to stash in an old bank safe he kept there. They were running out of places to stay. Coop's motor home was under surveillance, Gunny's truck was going to be impounded sooner or later, and Gunny was a fugitive from the hospital, thanks to the trio. They were running out of time.

Fredo's apartment was in a low-rent district down the strand, under the freeway. They sat out on his veranda amid the deafening sound of cars while they ate pizza Fredo had ordered. Kyle looked up and noticed the full moon in the cloudless sky. He couldn't help but think of her. And wondered what she was doing right now.

"I guess Mia's going to be okay," Fredo started in.

"Yeah? How'd you find that out?" Cooper said.

"Stopped by today. She looks good, man."

Kyle smiled. He was sure Fredo was recalling what Mia had looked like naked, even though she'd been suffering from the burns of the explosion. Fredo was smitten. No doubt about it.

"I'm sure she appreciated the company. How was Mama?" Kyle said to Fredo's smirk.

"They were arguing something fierce when I walked in. Cops were interested in her too, until she told them I was her cousin."

"Kissing cousins, I'd say," Cooper continued.

Fredo threw his wadded napkin in Cooper's face.

"Gunny, you want some pizza? Better hurry up, or it'll all be gone," Kyle shouted over the traffic din through the opened sliding glass door. The older man had locked himself in the bathroom and was coughing.

Gunny's hacking and coughing continued, accelerating.

"He's not too well," Fredo announced.

"I think we should take him home. I don't want him to drive," Kyle said.

"I heard that," Gunny said as he approached. "You boys are going to nursemaid me to death. I'm fine. I think we need to start focusing on Armando."

Kyle told them about the conversation he'd had with Timmons after Detective Mayfield's meeting. "They think he's still alive, but the gang will step up the play. They haven't gotten what they want yet."

"What does Timmons think they want?" Fredo asked Kyle.

"Not what. Who. He thinks they want me."

"That explains why Carlisle is so interested," Coop added.

"You think they trashed Armando's house for the guns?" Gunny asked.

"Absolutely. And I think they want more. Think I'll trade them guns for Armando."

"He'd never let that happen," said Fredo.

"And that's why we have to get to him first."

Kyle's cell phone rang. He didn't recognize the number. "Hello?"

"Kyle Lansdowne?"

"Yes."

"This is Detective Mayfield of the San Diego Police Department. I've spent most of the morning working on a case I think you're involved in. There's been a murder in the gym at the Infinity Building."

Kyle's stomach churned. He stood quickly. "Who?" He didn't want to know, but he had to find out. He noticed Cooper and Fredo had locked eyes with him.

"Not her," Mayfield said. "The deceased is a trainer, name's Marla. You know her?"

"No."

"I think she was a friend of Ms. Christy Nelson. I'm sure you know her."

"Yes. Yes, I do."

"Look, Mr. Lansdowne, I've spoken to Timmons. We're all on the same team here, but I got people all over my ass. This is the fourth body to show up, and you are the prime suspect."

Kyle took a big breath and then exhaled. He didn't know what to say. Cooper and Fredo were still on alert.

"But I'm not buying it, son," Mayfield continued.

Kyle was relieved. "Thank you, sir. So what's your theory?"

"Rather feels like flushing a rabbit out of a briar patch. They're trying to scare her, make her do something stupid. I think they're hoping she'll go find you."

"Ain't going to happen," Kyle said.

"Come again?"

Kyle looked at his buds and then answered Mayfield. "They won't find me through her. We broke it off."

"You know that, Timmons knows that and told me the same. But they don't."

"I thought her condo at the Infinity was the safest place for her."

"I'd normally agree. But these guys aren't amateurs. And they don't care how much publicity they stir up or who they hurt."

"Why are you calling me?" Kyle wasn't sure he could do anything to help. "You know I shouldn't go near her. Even with the murder, I still think that building is the safest place for her."

"Yeah. Except she isn't here."

Kyle swore under his breath. No one else said a word or made a sound.

"Where is she?"

"I'm not going to say. Not sure it's safe. Besides, you just said you shouldn't be anywhere near her. Let's just keep it that way."

"So what are you proposing?"

"You need to get yourself caught. You gotta be the bait."

"No way."

"They're going to find you, Kyle."

"Not unless I find them first."

"Son, you are thinking with the wrong part of your anatomy. If they don't find you, they'll get her, and if that fails, they'll kill her and your buddy too. She's safe right now, but I'd say you've got about twenty-four hours. That's it."

"Where is she?"

"Not telling."

"She in San Diego?"

"She's not at her condo, if that's what you mean. Someone has been, though. The place is a mess."

Kyle looked at Fredo and Cooper. Both SEALs were watching his face. Ready for anything.

"Look, Kyle. You've got to stop thinking about rescue here. Leave that to us. That's why I'm not telling you. You need to get yourself caught so we can track you. Can you do that, son?

"I'm not sure."

"Well, get sure. Find a way. I got no other way to do it."

Kyle knew he needed to find Christy. If they couldn't find him, they'd go after her. Mayfield was wrong. Christy was the bait. And he wasn't anywhere around her now.

That was going to have to change. Nothing he could do tonight. He'd go see Simms in the morning. If he couldn't get Christy's location from Mayfield, Christy might have told her employer.

Gunny's lumpy couch was going to be home tonight. As he stretched out, he stood up and looked at the almost full moon, bathing everything in a chalky highlight that glowed. Blue-white flashes from the television inside Gunny's added strobes of light to the outside porch. He knew she must have gone to San Francisco.

But where?

IN THE MORNING, Kyle woke up with a sore back. Gunny was sawing logs and had fallen asleep in the recliner with all his clothes on. They had stayed up to watch some wrestling show on late night TV since Kyle couldn't sleep.

He left a note for Gunny and took the beater off the island into San Diego, pulling up to the Patterson Realty office at eight-thirty. In the parking lot across the street he sat and watched, noting Simms was the first to arrive and was checking his watch. Kyle slipped in behind the man, causing Simms to jump as Kyle addressed him.

"Hello, Mr. Simms. I'm looking for Christy."

Simms scurried backward until he slammed himself up against the reception countertop.

"Look, I won't tell a soul you were here. Please, I have a family…"

Kyle swore. "I'm not here to cause any problems for you. I want to protect Christy. She's in danger."

"That's because of you."

"No, that's because some people are trying to mess with me. But I think they'll go after her next."

"Look, I don't know anything."

Kyle stepped closer to the man, who looked like he was going to pee in his pants. "I think you do. I think you know exactly where she is. She has no idea she's in danger."

"Well, why don't you call her then, if…if she'll take your call?"

"I'd like to do that from your phone, if I may." He directed Mr. Simms to go down the hallway, following behind.

"My phone? Here?" Simms asked at the entrance to his office.

"Yes."

"So she'll think it's me?"

"Yes."

"She said you two had broken up. She wouldn't be seeing you anymore."

"That's true."

"You'd better leave all this to the police. They're after you, you know. Came in here with questions."

"I'll bet."

They could hear one of the secretaries arriving. She busied herself, humming a tune, and began brewing coffee and turning on lights. She stopped short when she saw Kyle's hulking frame leaning against the doorway of the manager's office.

"Morning, ma'am."

She blushed, flustered and muttering something to herself, and then headed in the opposite direction.

"I'm not here to hurt anybody," Kyle repeated.

Simms pushed his phone across the desk so that the keypad faced Kyle. He had her cell number memorized. He dialed, heard the familiar ring. When he heard the recording of her voice, his throat became parched. He hung up right after the beep, not leaving a message.

"She'll call you back. Ask her where she's staying. I'm going to call you later and you're going to give me that address, Simms."

Simms frowned.

"For her own safety, you'll give me her address. I swear to you I would never hurt her."

Simms fell back into his chair, resigned. "Give me your number. I'll call you the instant I hear from her."

"Thank you." Kyle wrote his published cell number on a slip of memo paper. "I don't usually answer this, so leave me a message. If you get a call from me, it won't look like any number you're used to."

"Got it."

If he couldn't get it from Simms, he'd have to try to convince Sergeant Mayfield. But he wanted to stay clear of the locals. Now the hard part was starting. The waiting.

CHAPTER 31

S IMMS WAS RELIEVED the SEAL was out of his office. He waited until he saw the soldier exit the parking lot in an old green truck with red Forest Service logos. He locked the front door.

"Stacey, I'm calling the police. Let in only people you know."

"And the police," she quipped.

He didn't have time for her backhanded challenge today, but made a note to talk to her about her attitude. He went straight to his office and picked up the phone. He fumbled a card from his middle desk drawer and dialed.

"Yeah?"

"This Deputy Hilber?"

"Who's this?" The deputy said without confirming.

"This is Carl Simms. I'm manager at the Patterson Realty office in San Diego. You asked me to call you if I heard from Kyle Lansdowne."

"Yes. So I take it you have?"

"He was just here."

"Where's that exactly?"

"Here. In my office. I'm the *manager* at Patterson…"

"Yes, yes," Hilber interrupted. "I *got* it now. Okay, what did he want?"

"He wanted to know where Christy was."

There was silence on the other end of the line. Then Simms heard a woman's voice in the background and the sound of what could be rustling sheets. He continued, "I'm sorry if I woke you up, sir. I get into the office early and…"

A hand muffled the phone, but Simms could hear the deputy swearing at someone, and a woman giggling in response.

Probably caught him having sex with his wife.

"No problem, Simms. I'm all ears now. So, he asked about… Ouch! God dammit. Fucking stop that." Hilber lowered his voice and said, "Excuse me," to Simms. "Having a little problem here on the home front, if you catch my drift."

Simms got quiet. Maybe he shouldn't have called. He'd never spoken to his wife like that. Ever.

"Officer Hilber, Lansdowne doesn't know where Christy is. Neither do I, but I can find out, and he wants me to. Didn't want to call from his own phone. Used mine here at the office. That sound fishy to you?"

"Absolutely. Do you have the number he called?"

Simms pushed down on the silver button at the middle of the headset. A phone number displayed in red digital numbers. He recognized it as Christy's cell. He gave it to the deputy.

"Good. This helps. When you find out her location, let us know first, okay? We need to give her some protection before he gets to her. It also would be a great way to catch him."

"You think he would harm her?"

"Look Simms, he's already killed four. He has the taste of blood in his mouth. He'll do it again."

"But I think he cares about this woman."

"I'd say more like he's obsessed. And maybe he's trying to cover his tracks. God only knows what info she has on him. Look, Simms, I don't think I have to tell you that these men are trained dogs. They are trained not to care about anything or anyone in order to do their jobs. But this isn't fucking Afghanistan."

It was partially true, Simms thought. But he'd never seen a SEAL member hurt a civilian. There were some stories about it, though, especially among the haters in the San Diego community. There were always a few of those.

"Anything else?" Hilber sounded impatient.

"No, sir. Just trying to be a good citizen," Simms answered. "What do I tell him when he calls?"

"Don't give the address to him when you get it. Don't call him back. Just call me."

"Oh. What happens if he comes back over here?"

"Call the locals. Geez, Simms, use your fuckin' head. Look, I gotta go. You got more questions than a schoolgirl on her first date."

"Just trying to cooperate fully, as you asked."

"Well, we thank you for that. Talk to you soon, then—oh, say, did you happen to notice what car he was driving?"

"Truck. Green truck with a red official logo on the door. Never seen it before today."

SIMMS GLANCED OVER contracts he was supposed to review this morning. He couldn't concentrate and had to read over everything twice. He'd wasted five minutes. He was seeing letters and numbers, but none of it was making any sense. Like this situation with Christy.

The secretary appeared at his doorway.

"There's a crowd outside the front door. They're wondering if we're going out of business."

"I told you to let in people you knew. Christ, I don't want to lock out my own agents."

Simms was irritated. He needed this little wrinkle like he needed the mumps. He made a mental note to fire Stacey at his first opportunity. After all this crap with Christy was over.

Stacey was still looking down at her shoes.

"Well, go ahead and let them in, or is there something else?"

"I want a word with you later, Mr. Simms."

Fine. Leave me alone. He grinned. "I'd be happy to speak with you after I return a few phone calls and review these contracts." He pointed to a stack about a foot high, all files he was supposed to review and sign off on.

He heard her heels *clickity-clack* down the tiled hallway and then heard the turn of the lock on the Patterson Realty front door.

Simms poured himself into the contracts again.

Christy was such a levelheaded lady, he thought. Not one to pick some loser rogue military guy. She seemed to be able to slice through people nicely without them knowing they'd been outmatched. Wayne Somerville had discovered that. Yet, she did it in such a way that Wayne was only too willing to come to her beck and call the instant she requested it. There was talent there, strength of personality and something else sorely lacking in his profession: she cared about people.

The phone rang and it startled him.

"Mr. Simms, this is Christy. You called me this morning when I was in the shower. Your message didn't record."

Of course she would assume it was an error, not a trap. Her basic faith in human nature was key to who she was.

"Christy, I gotta have your address, since you're not sure how long you'll be gone. I could use the address of the shop, if you want." Simms felt like a complete jerk.

"No. No, I don't want Madame M to get mixed up in this, and somehow that will happen if I start giving her address out. I'm staying at 484 Stanyan Street. I think the zip is 94117."

"Great. Thanks. I'll keep it in my file here in case I need it. So how long do you think you'll be, or do you know yet?" He asked this for his own sake of mind.

"Haven't talked to Madame M this morning. She's supposed to pick me up for breakfast."

"Oh, great. So you are okay?"

"Yes." She paused. Would she feel obligated to further explain? Something else was there, in the tone of her voice, as she continued, "I think the change of pace will be good for me right now."

"Much as I wish you were back here, I have to agree with you," Simms said. "You need any help on any of your work?"

"No. I gave Wayne my two buyer leads, but would you check on him? I'm thinking he won't be the exact fit for those clients. He's so different than I am, you know."

Tell me about it.

"Christy, why didn't you call me? I could have helped."

"Fact is, those two guys from the Sheriff's Department, well one from the sheriff's office and one Navy guy, surprised me. Just showed up on their own without announcing themselves. I just felt a little uncomfortable with them, being alone."

"So you called Wayne? Not me?"

Christy gave a nervous laugh. "He called me." Her voice faded on the other end of the line, then returned. "I asked Wayne to come over, sort of for protection. I knew he'd come right away. And I know how busy you are…"

"No problem. Just call me instead, okay?"

"Thank you. It's nice to know I have people around me I can trust."

Simms had a sharp pain in his gut. Felt like a hot poker of regret.

And shame. He didn't want to tell her about Kyle, but felt he should.

"Christy, I haven't been entirely honest with you. Your Navy guy made that call."

"What?"

"He came by this morning, telling me you were in danger."

"And?"

"He demanded to know where you were."

Cold silence.

"Mr. Simms, I have to go. But please, please do not tell him where I'm staying."

"Don't worry. I won't. You can count on that."

"Don't even tell him I'm in San Francisco, or he'd figure it out."

"Right."

"Thanks for telling me. Keep the address private. Tell no one."

"I won't," he lied.

"Thanks for looking out for me. I appreciate it." She hung up.

Simms tapped the pad that had her address written on it. He had a choice to make and neither option facing him was good. One got him more involved and perhaps put Christy in danger. The other allowed someone he clearly didn't trust to have information he wasn't sure should be given out. He'd always believed in law enforcement. Maybe this sheriff was just a quirky guy with some unusual habits. Maybe that was what he was picking up from the man.

But one thing was for sure. He didn't want to mess with the Sheriff's Department. And the Navy should be taking care of their own. He dialed Warren Hilber.

"Got the address." He gave it to Hilber and got a curt thank you. Before the phone went dead, Simms knew he'd made a big mistake.

CHAPTER 32

C HRISTY DRESSED AND waited. She'd decided to wear her new black stretch pants and a new pair of patent leather, four-inch spiked heels. When she used to work at the little shop, walking all day on tiptoes had made her top heavy and she had to press out her chest to keep her balance. By the end of the day her calves would ache, but she loved the way they felt.

She recalled what Madame M had said when she first told her of the shoes requirement. "I like the high heels because it simulates a woman's legs in orgasm. It brings sexual tension, and sexual tension is good for lingerie sales."

At first, it made Christy blush. But she eventually got comfortable with the look and feel of the shoes.

Madame was right about the impact it had on shop sales. The male customers didn't seem to mind when she accidentally bumped her chest against them.

To complete today's outfit, she wore a red stretch oversized top that showed off her soft ample bosom and matched the color of her flaming red lipstick.

She observed Tom's kitchen door was open, revealing a shiny inner screen door.

Inviting. Welcoming her to come into his house. She hadn't taken him up on his offer of last night.

Her cell phone chirped.

"Hello?"

"Cheríe, are you up? Refreshed?"

"Yes ma'am. Been up for awhile now."

Madame giggled. "I am so glad you are in town. You have spent some quality time with Mr. Bergeron?"

"Yes. He cooked me dinner last night. I was tired and turned in early afterward."

Madame giggled again.

"Alone. I went to bed alone." Christy didn't want to offend her former boss, but she needed to make it clear where she stood. "You didn't tell me about his divorce."

"Oui. I thought he should be the one to tell you, if he wished. And I see he has."

"Yes."

"C'est bien. I will be over in about twenty minutes. Tom told me he is cooking breakfast for us, if that is all right with you. I am running a little late, and a restaurant trip would make us even later."

"Fine." But Christy couldn't deny the knot in her stomach.

She walked across the brick patio that gurgled with water sounds from two fountains. Bright multi-colored lilies stood at attention along the path and gave off a heady aroma. She stopped and inhaled the glorious scent, filling her head with toxic thoughts of Kyle and how much she missed his hard flesh next to hers. How much she missed his kisses. How much she missed the way he used her body to bring them both such pleasure.

She opened the screen door and stepped into a kitchen filled with cooking smells and the light lacing of jazz in the background. Tom was in faded blue jeans with another blue shirt, buttoned low. But he had a flowered apron on, and that made her chuckle. He turned and flashed her a smile right out of GQ, holding a green spatula in his right hand.

"Wow. You are a vision, Christy. I'm…I'm speechless." He took a long, lingering look down the entire length of her body and back up, his eyes hungry. She hadn't dressed for him, but for Madame M's customers. But she liked it that he found her attractive. She couldn't help it. He wasn't bad to look at either.

She smiled, which pleased him.

"Thanks for cooking breakfast for us. Madame M just called. She's on her way now."

"Yes, I know. She called me too." He remained fixed in place, the utensil held like the Statue of Liberty's torch.

Christy cocked her head. "You guys are conspiring. I can tell."

He set down his spatula and stood in front of her. She could feel his body's heat. "It's a deadly game. I needed her help."

"You?" she asked, stepping back to a cool distance.

He looked at his feet and slid his palms into his front pockets, then shrugged his shoulders. "I had hoped you would come see me last night." He raised his blue eyes to hers. They watered. He licked his lips and focused on hers. She wished now she was wearing pink, not red.

"Tom." Christy stopped. Her words were going to come out harsh, and that wasn't what she wanted. "Look, I thought I made myself perfectly clear last night. I'm not interested in a relationship right now."

"But we already have one."

She looked down.

I've used this line. Places reversed.

She looked back up at him and studied his kind face. She could have loved him, at another time and place. But not now. Not after meeting Kyle.

"Yes, and I'd very much like to keep that friendship, if that is possible. I'm grateful for your generosity, Tom, for letting me stay here. But let's not get carried away."

It was hard to look at him. His tanned and lean body came close again. He held her face in his hands as he bent down. She was afraid he would kiss her, and she knew she would break away. Could he feel how her spine went stiff?

"I'm sorry, Tom." She placed her hands over his. She tried to reflect back to him the kindness she saw in his eyes. Without the need.

He pulled her body to his chest and embraced her. "Not to worry, Christy. Just know that I am here." He kissed the top of her head, and whispered, "But just give me a chance to make you happy."

She nodded to his chest. But these were not the arms she wanted to be enveloped in.

Will I ever be able to forget him?

They dropped their arms and the awkward silence forced them both to smile. Something was smoking on the stove. He ran to the smoking pan of bacon, which was spattering all over the stovetop. He reached up and turned up the six-foot stainless steel commercial hood fan.

"I know this isn't good for you. But I love bacon for breakfast sometimes," he said.

"Yes, thank you. I'm somewhat of an expert on things that are bad for me."

With the smoke under control, Tom fired up his espresso maker, busying himself with making her a cappuccino. He delivered the little cup and saucer filled with foamed half-and-half and garnished with a little nutmeg—just the way she liked it. And he smiled as she took it.

"Thank you. This is perfect."

"I am a student of what a beautiful woman desires." His voice was low and raspy.

Where had he learned she loved cappuccinos? She slipped by him and planted herself at the eating bar. The espresso drink was indeed as perfect as it looked. He'd even sculpted a heart into the creamy foam on top.

Why couldn't this be Kyle in the kitchen? Why couldn't we be here, thinking about what we could do today? We could go to Chinatown. Walk along the piers. Eat oysters and warmed olives. Sip wine and watch the Marin Ferry go and come.

Tom turned and she could feel his eyes on her, though her gaze had traveled out the windows toward the bay watching all the little sailboats already out on the dark blue water.

"It's going to be a lovely day. No fog," she said as she sighed.

"I ordered it special," he answered. "There isn't anything I wouldn't do to make you happy."

Christy sipped her cappuccino. "You don't make it easy, Tom."

"Nor do you. I look at you, and, well…I think to myself…"

"Are you sure it isn't just loneliness, Tom?"

"Does it matter?"

Oh, yes. It matters.

Christy couldn't answer him. She now knew it was not a good idea to stay here. Tom was not picking up the message like she'd hoped. She stood and walked with her cappuccino to peer out the front living room windows. She heard the slam of a car door down below. Madame M's driver in the black Lincoln was rounding the rear. He stopped, got out, and then opened up the passenger door. Christy noted how frail the older woman was as she extricated herself from the rear seat, refusing assistance from the driver.

Madame M sighed and looked up at the long bank of crisscrossed stairs leading to Tom's front door. Her initial expression of concern changed when she saw Christy's face. Her mask, that impenetrable face of steel, came back, and she took to the first few steps like she was a triathlete. But she soon tired. Eventually she made it to the top, even accepting the driver's assistance.

They ate spinach and mushroom omelets, buttered cranberry-orange scones, and drank more cappuccino and fresh orange juice. Though Madame M was several years older than Tom, the banter between the two was passionate, with all statements taking on a double entendre. They continued with their sexy word play all during the breakfast. Christy found it lightened her mood, took her mind off all the problems that were looming on the horizon. She imagined Madame M had been quite the tease as a younger woman and wondered why she spent so much of her life alone. She'd have been a great partner.

They were ready to leave. Madame M had checked to make sure her driver hadn't left.

"Tom, could I trouble you for another cappuccino for the road, for Carlo?"

"No problem. Christy, you want to take one, too?"

"No thanks, I've had plenty."

Tom prepared Madame's espresso drink in a white mug, without the nutmeg sprinkles, and handed it to the older woman with a bag containing the remaining orange scone.

"Just send the cup home with Christy tonight," he said.

"Oui, *certainement*."

Christy found it difficult to look into Tom's blue eyes knowing he would be again asking her to share his bed this evening. And again she'd have to turn him down.

"What time will you return?" he asked, right on cue.

"Oh, well, perhaps six or seven, what do you think, cheríe?" Madame asked. "You want to go to dinner afterwards?"

"No, I'll just pick something up on my way home," Christy said.

"I was hoping to be prepared. I wanted to cook for Christy again. I've bought everything I need."

"I will have Carlo deliver her promptly at six, then. That settles it."

Christy knew Tom was watching her as she stepped out the front door behind Madame M. She hadn't said goodbye to the man she was going to have to turn down tonight. And this time, she'd have to take the gloves off, to make sure he understood there wasn't going to be a sexual relationship brewing.

ON THE WAY to the shop, Madame M leaned against Christy's frame. They were seated together in the back of the black car. Familiar buildings flashed by the window. Christy hadn't realized she missed the city so much.

"I don't understand you, my dear. You could do much worse than Tom. And I think he likes you."

"You think?" Christy frowned. "I don't want to involve him."

"You already have, cheríe. I can smell a man in love a block away."

"I'm not ready for all that."

"Then tell him to wait. Give him one sign, a little hope, and I think he'll wait. But someone is going to land a very nice future with a handsome billionaire."

At Christy's surprised expression, Madame M continued, "Oh yes, he's now a billionaire. It was in Baron's. One of the top 100 in the U.S. now."

"Good for him." It mattered little to her. "I'm sure his ex wives would be grateful."

"Ah, cheríe, that's not kind. He has only one ex, as you know. And she, well, she…"

"He told me about her."

"He has no children. I understand he wants them now. That means he will be looking for a younger woman."

"Please, Madame M. Don't do this anymore. I'm here to help you."

THEY SPENT THE morning going over shop procedures. Traffic was very light. Christy found herself back in the rhythm of the little place on Maiden Lane, with its exotic French Lavender fragrance, the Piaf music playing softly in the background, and Madame M's murmurs in French as she sorted, checked off lists of orders, and poured her arthritic hands over the lacy fabric of pretty things.

Christy found a new boxed Parisian couture bra and panty set made of light rose-colored gossamer and embroidered in tiny white and light pink flowers that was exactly her size. The retail price was over three hundred dollars for the pair. Madame M caught her drooling over them.

"Take them. Just wear them for something special." She pushed the box into Christy's chest. "I insist."

"You mustn't spoil me this way, Madame."

"Now, my dear, you must learn to say thank you. That is all I require." Madame had her hands on her tiny hips, tapping the floor with the black toe of her ballet slipper.

The door behind Christy tinkled as someone with heavy footsteps walked in.

CHAPTER 33

KYLE CALLED SIMMS four times. As one hour turned into two, it became clear to him the man was ignoring him. He jumped in the truck and headed for Patterson Realty.

The receptionist gave him a squinting frown like the vice principal at his school had all those years ago when Kyle and his buddy Marc tried to skip class. They liked to hang out behind the gym and watch the girl's volleyball team practice. Marc was dating the captain, a long-legged giraffe of a girl who was about two inches taller than him. Kyle loved looking at the black spandex and blond pigtail of his favorite girl. Way more important than History or English.

"I'm Kyle Lansdowne. I've left like several messages for Mr. Simms, and I know his car is here. Can I see him?" He tried to soften her sharp inspection with a killer smile that usually worked. But the woman was hardened. Not exactly unattractive, but damaged somehow.

"No. He's asked not to be disturbed."

Just then Wayne Somerville came into the lobby, carrying an over-stuffed briefcase and a load of manila files. His white shirt was overstretched across his chest. It wasn't as big as his fleshy belly. One of the fake pearl buttons was about to pop at any moment.

"Hey there, Wayne. Remember me?" Kyle was watching the receptionist out of the corner of his eye. He needed to have an excuse to be here, to talk to Simms.

The startled look on Wayne's face told him Wayne had remembered the encounter days before. Kyle continued, "Christy was showing me condos, and all of a sudden she's disappeared."

"Uh huh," Wayne said, juggling the files under his left arm. He leaned back and briefly looked at the receptionist standing at Kyle's back.

Kyle continued, "Don't know what the protocol is, but I got a bonus coming, and if she's not available, I was wondering…"

Simms entered the lobby area. "Stacey, I'm going to step out for some…" He stopped in his tracks at the sight of Kyle, and uttered a soft, "Oh."

Wayne was quick on his feet and launched into his salesman persona. "It's okay, Carl, he and I were just talking about real estate things. I got it." Wayne winked at his manager. "Kyle, let me put these down at my desk and we'll…"

"Just one second, Wayne. I need to talk to your manager first. Give me a card. I'll call you later on, if that works for you." Kyle could see Somerville's blood pressure was rising. A fat vein pulsed at the side of his thick, deep, pink neck. "I promise. I will call you later on." He didn't think Wayne was dishonest. Just gutless.

Wayne glared at his manager, then nodded. Repositioning his files, he produced a card from his shirt pocket and handed it to Kyle.

Kyle put the dog-eared card in his back pocket and turned to Simms, ignoring Somerville. With a firm hand on the manager's shoulder, indicating he wouldn't take no for an answer, he said, "I'll buy you a sandwich and we can talk." He leaned into Simms' personal space and whispered, "You got the address?"

"Not yet."

Kyle knew it was a complete lie. "Hear me out, first. It's a matter of life and death," Kyle whispered.

Simms turned and glared at the receptionist. "Hold down the fort for a half hour. I'll be right back."

The lack of response from the receptionist made the room seem small. Kyle pushed Simms out the door and toward his truck.

Once outside, Simms backed up and put his palms out toward Kyle, distancing him from the SEAL. "Look, fella. I don't want any trouble. I've already talked to the authorities."

"No trouble. Not here to make any trouble for you or anyone," Kyle whispered. He opened the driver door to the bench seat of Gunny's truck. "Get in. Now."

Simms hesitantly looked around first, then climbed into the cab and scooted over to the passenger side. His brown Oxfords were nicely polished but didn't match his grey suit, Kyle thought. The flesh appearing over the tops of his socks was pasty white.

He took Simms to a Burger Palace and paid for their order. He sat across the man and dipped fries into a little white paper cup of catsup.

"The fries are the best here."

"Um…"

"So why won't you give me Christy's address? I know she called you."

"How do you know that?"

"You just told me."

Simms muttered, shook his head, and looked to the left.

"She is in danger. She trusts some very bad guys."

"No doubt. I think I'm sitting across from one."

"Come on, Simms. If you really thought that, you wouldn't be here."

"I have a healthy respect for your profession. But I've been told…"

"Who told you about me? Besides Christy." Kyle couldn't help but blush.

"Well, let's see. I got a visit from a Deputy Hilber and some other Navy MP guy with an unpleasant demeanor. I've received a couple of calls from the San Diego PD I haven't returned. There's you. And of course Christy."

"Look, I don't know how to make you believe this, but she really is in danger. I'm trying to protect her."

"That's what the sheriff's deputy said too."

"Yeah, and he's dirty."

"And that's what he says about you."

"Not a chance in hell. This guy actually killed one of his own men. I saw it."

"So why aren't the cops out looking for him instead of you?"

"I don't have all the answers. But the only reason they want Christy is to get to me. They're not really interested in arresting me."

Kyle and Simms shared a look. Kyle could see Simms was thinking over his words.

The two men ate in silence. Kyle wiped his mouth and fingers on the thin white napkin. He took out a small notebook from his vest pocket, wrote a number on it, along with a name. He tore the perforated page off and slipped it across the table to Simms with one finger.

"Call him. He's my Chief. He'll vouch for me."

Simms took the paper, but shook his head as he slipped it into his wallet.

"You gotta hurry up, though," Kyle continued. "We are running out of time." Kyle saw fear written in the man's eyes. A second later it was gone.

"Take me back to the office. Now." Simms's burger and fries were half eaten.

"WHERE THE HELL you been, Kyle?" Timmons barked into the receiver.

"Talked to you yesterday, sir."

"I got people all over the place looking for you. This is no good, son. You any closer to finding Armando? I'm going to have to pull rank here to keep myself out of the wringer now."

"Sorry to hear that. Look. I think this Deputy Hilber guy is after Christy now. Her manager, a Mr. Simms, won't give me her address, but I understand this guy has been snooping around, looking for her. Saying he's trying to protect her from me, of all people."

"That's becoming a common thought every time another body turns up."

"I asked him to call you, sir. Did he?"

"Hilber?"

"No. Simms."

"Nope."

"Shit. I gotta find her before Hilber does."

"Well, what about Armando?"

"He's trained. He's going to have to go it alone for now. He'd be onboard with protecting an innocent."

"This is ill advised. Never should have gotten her involved in the first place, Kyle. What were you thinking?"

"You know what I was thinking, sir."

"I don't like it when the public gets involved. You should just concentrate on Armando, son. I thought I'd made myself clear about that."

"Timmons, I'm the reason she's in danger. I can't just walk away and pretend it doesn't matter if she gets hurt."

Kyle felt tightness in his chest. His voice waivered, his eyes felt like they were suddenly filled with sandpaper. He inhaled trying to calm his insides. It worked.

"Goddamn it. You guys are all alike. Thinking with your small head. Don't go bringing that shit down on me too, Kyle. I can protect you only so far."

"Understood. If it comes to that, I'll take the fall. All of it." It was what he'd told his team. Timmons didn't jump in and offer to share the burden, but that wouldn't be fair anyway. "We need to get that address. I'm not going to beat it out of him. But if we don't, Timmons, I know she'll get hurt. These guys don't care about anything. Pure rogue." Then Kyle remembered the call from Sergeant Mayfield. "There's this SDPD guy, Mayfield."

"I met him. I think he's okay. Why, is he in on this thing?"

"No. I think he's clean. Did me a favor and called me about the murder…"

"Another murder?"

"In Christy's condo complex yesterday. A trainer in the gym."

"Okay. He call you again?"

"No, but he told me he has the address where Christy is staying."

"I'll get it, then. I know the sonofabitch."

Kyle wondered what Timmons had up his sleeve. He only hoped he'd get to Christy in time.

KYLE MET UP with Fredo and Cooper at Fredo's apartment. They were arguing over how many dryer sheets Fredo was using. Kyle knew that meant they were using Coop's box of fabric softener, since he doubted Fredo even used the stuff.

"You know what the problem of living with you is?" Fredo was standing close to Coop, head leaned back to all six-foot-four of a towering farm boy in front of him.

Coop stood his ground. "No, but you're gonna fuckin' tell me. So hurry up and get it over with so we can get your panties washed."

Kyle knew they would shout, yell, and curse. But neither one would touch the other. Not in anger. Jesting, joking, yes. But you don't touch a SEAL in anger. Then you'd deserve everything you got.

"You're wired up so tight," Fredo said. "You'd have a heart attack if you won the lottery. Who gives a shit if I use one or three dryer sheets? You fuckin' offered, man. So I grabbed a handful."

"They cost one point four cents a sheet."

"Incredible. You're never getting married, man."

"Don't plan on it, Frodo. But at least I smell good."

That nearly earned Coop a punch. Kyle stepped in between them.

"Hold on, ladies. Are we really arguing about laundry?" Kyle said, looking from one set of dull blue eyes to another set of dark squinting eyes.

Fredo swore and left the room. Kyle heard the dryer door open. He came back with a fistful of sheets, more than three, and thrust them at Cooper's chest.

"Here. I don't want your fucking jasmine breeze sheets. I'll pay you back next week. All five cents of it."

Coop took the white squares and did count them, which got Kyle laughing inside. To Fredo's back, Cooper whispered, "Five. You took five."

"We go shopping. He gets the two-day-old meat and the no-name stuff from the little Super Saver. He even buys bruised bananas in a bag. That's sick, man." Fredo began to curse in Spanish.

Kyle knew they were nervous. All of them. The waiting was killing them.

Kyle spoke to break the stalemate. "I got Timmons getting Christy's address. She's not at her apartment. I'm guessing she's in San Francisco."

"Frisco, huh. We going to Frisco?" Fredo asked.

"Not *we,* just me."

"Like hell you are. And Gunny won't like it either."

"First I got to get an address. The sheriff we saw at the cabin is after her. I think he's already on his way."

CHAPTER 34

TIMMONS CAUGHT THEM a ride on a Navy transport plane to Moffett Field. Gunny couldn't fit into any of the cami shirts they had, so they let him go out of his uniform disguise, which raised some eyebrows. After landing in Mountain View, the foursome hitched a ride to a rental car agency on El Camino Real. They got caught in commuter traffic to the city.

They arrived at the house on Stanyan Street at seven o'clock. Timmons had told him Christy was staying in a cottage behind the main house. As he looked up the tower of stairs to the side of the big Victorian, he couldn't see the cottage. But he noticed the front door of the main house was wide open.

And gray smoke was coming from the rear. Kyle's blood pressure rose.

They quickly parked their rented Tahoe on the street. The three Team guys quietly checked their surroundings as they donned their backpacks. Kyle slung a bag with some additional firepower over his shoulder and checked the deep turquoise sky. Clear as a bell. There was a distant siren, but it could be going somewhere else. No one in the neighborhood stirred. There was little traffic.

Gunny stayed in the Tahoe as lookout, while Kyle, Cooper, and Fredo quickly climbed the front steps to the Victorian. Kyle silently dropped his bag on the porch. Everyone unholstered their sidearms. On Kyle's mark, all three breached the open doorway, fanning out in three directions. Cooper went right, Fredo left. Kyle went straight back to the source of the fire in the back.

A few moments later, they gathered back in the kitchen. Someone had left meat in a pan, and it had burned until the pan itself was red hot. The back door was open, so most the smoke had gone out that way. It made an excellent calling card. Kyle had shut off the gas to the expensive commercial range. He didn't want to alert anyone still in the house to their presence, so didn't turn on the fan.

Next, they mounted the stairs without a sound, Kyle leading the way. They heard labored breathing and shallow coughing. And then came a faint cry, "Help."

They were in the master bedroom. There were two bodies on the bed. An older man had been shot in the chest, and was having trouble breathing. Kyle thought it might have been a direct hit near his heart, but noticed the blood had pooled left and the gunshot was luckily on the right. The frail woman next to him looked like she could be his mother. She was clearly dead. Her shocked expression was permanently etched on her face. The back of her head was wet and soppy with dark blood. They'd punched her in the nose before they'd killed her. A trickle of blood ran down the side of her mouth, onto the flowered bedspread.

"Didn't even tie her up," Fredo said, and then he swore. "She was no threat to anybody." Kyle knew it made Fredo sick to his stomach to see the elderly, especially women, abused. Kyle pointed down the hall, asking for Fredo to check out the rest of the floor.

Stripping away the man's shirt, Coop applied an occlusive dressing to the wound with chest seals.

"Come on, buddy, don't give out on me now." Coop coaxed him

to stay conscious. The man's large eyes stared back, gasping for breath. The SEAL medic dug for his blow out kit, and then applied needle decompression to the right of the man's sternum, which relieved the man's breathing almost immediately. A hissing sound came from the 14-gauge needle. Coop re-checked the man's blood pressure.

"Coop?" Kyle asked. He needed a quick assessment.

"Pretty bad, but if he gets to the hospital, he'll be okay. I've stopped the bleeding for now, given some relief so his lungs don't collapse, but this is only temporary. He's bleeding on the inside and he's in a lot of pain, and weak. Don't think the bullet hit any other organ but the lung. We need an EMT. Can't risk moving him with this chest tube."

Fredo had returned. "All clear. You want me to call it in?" he asked.

Kyle gave a nod and Fredo dashed from the room.

"Don't touch anything except the phone, Fredo," Kyle said to his back. He looked down at their patient. His chest rose and fell, the tube hissing with each breath. "Can he talk?"

"Not sure. We can try." Cooper moved the man's head from side to side. "Hey, buddy, help's on the way. You gotta try staying awake. Can you do that for me?"

The man nodded his head. Sweat covered his forehead, but his color was coming back.

"Who did this to you?" Kyle asked.

The man's eyes opened halfway. He scanned the two faces in front of him and then focused on Kyle. "You're Christy's SEAL, aren't you?"

Kyle winced. God, he wished he were. "Where is she?" he asked.

"They took her."

"They?"

"Three guys. One was in uniform."

"Military?"

"No, khaki." He coughed and spit blood.

"Shit," Cooper said. He shook his head, looking at Kyle. "No more talking."

"They left you a note…" The man was fighting for every word. He raised a bloody finger and pointed to the bureau. His arm collapsed back onto the bed.

Fredo returned. "They're on their way. Someone else had already reported the smoke."

"She…" The man was struggling to say something to Kyle.

"Don't. Don't talk right now. The paramedics are on their way. Save your energy," Coop said tenderly as he brushed back the graying hair from his forehead and checked the man's eyes.

"She loves you." He wouldn't stop staring at Kyle. "Please. You must save her."

"Let's get the hell out of here. Nothing more we can do for him," Cooper said. He punched Kyle in the arm, which brought the SEAL back to reality. The man's body had gone limp again.

On the way out, Kyle picked up the envelope with his name written on it in Christy's handwriting. He looked at the man on the bed and said a little prayer for him.

A small explosion downstairs in the kitchen caught them all off guard.

This was not a good sign.

"Must've set a timed IED," Fredo said from behind as they were jumping down the stairs. Kyle was worried more timed devices were set. Was this a trap?

Gunny had the Tahoe running as the trio slid down along the stair railing, avoiding the stairs themselves. Sirens were coming from the bottom of the hill. They could see the red lights flashing. The big behemoth fire truck had to come up slow, honking and almost coming to a complete stop at each intersection along the way. Luckily, there were lots of intersections, even though the signs made cross traffic stop before proceeding across Stanyan. It gave Kyle and the crew barely enough time to get into the SUV.

Gunny stepped on the gas and almost killed the engine. Everyone else slid down in their seats, ducking under the lid of their caps, and waited. At last, the sputtering truck, romanced by the steady stream of filthy diatribes from Gunny, lumbered up one block. Gunny turned, but continued to swear at the vehicle, telling it that it lacked a soul, that its newness was its flaw. He extolled the virtues of his old but reliable truck back home.

"No special gas. Turns over every time. It'll be running circles around you while you're on your way to the junkyard."

They were headed down toward the bay, and then followed the meandering side street around a neighborhood dog park and then back down to 19th Avenue.

When Kyle was sure they weren't being followed, he sat up and others took his cue, doing the same.

"You gonna open that love letter, Kyle?" Fredo wanted to know.

Kyle's palm smoothed over the script on the outside of the cream-colored vellum. He would have put it to his nose, if he'd been alone.

His tongue flicked at his upper right lip as he carefully slit the letter open with his utility knife. He felt as if he were violating her, so he did it carefully. The quiet purr of the three-fifty V8 engine was the only noise Kyle heard. He didn't even hear his own breath as he unfolded the stiff paper.

Kyle,

I'm writing this at the request of the Scorpion Kings. Caesar asks, commander to commander, that you meet him, or he says he will do things to me that will make it impossible to identify my body, except through DNA. (His words).

He's left you a note in a Taco Bell bag in a garbage can at the corner of 19th Avenue and Kearney, just outside Starbucks.

You'll be watched, so come alone and no one will get hurt.

Christy—

He was holding evidence in his hands. Evidence he was bad for all the women in his life. Evidence that yet another person was going to pay the price for his lack of judgment. Because he couldn't get a grip on himself and just stay the hell away. He'd known getting involved with Christy was a mistake from the beginning. And now, because of his lack of control, his animal need, others were suffering. It was the heaviest burden he'd ever had to bear.

He vowed when all of this was done, he'd stay as far away from Christy as he possibly could. Maybe he'd request one of the East Coast Teams. Yeah. But then he'd be leaving Fredo and Cooper. He could do it. And maybe they could go together. But he had to get away from her.

He imagined how she was feeling right now. Scared to death. And his involvement with her had caused all this. He folded the letter without saying anything and tapped it against his other palm, looking out the windshield at pedestrians in the crosswalk as the vehicle stopped at a red light. It was an unusually warm San Francisco night.

They were sitting ducks, he thought. They had the all the firepower in the world, but were not able to use it. Even though there was always collateral damage, it was different here. These people he watched didn't sign on for this. The gangly kids and couples and seniors walking their dogs this night were the ones he was supposed to be fighting to protect.

The truck lurched forward, Kyle almost hitting his head against the windshield. When he turned to look at Gunny, he saw a pair of red, rheumy eyes staring back at him.

"You gonna leave me here holding my dick, or are we gonna go get these guys?"

"Keep your hands on the steering wheel, Gunny," Fredo shouted. "That ain't nothin' I wanna see in my lifetime."

Gunny ignored the insult and kept his gaze on Kyle. "Any day now. What'd they want?"

"I'm supposed to go pick up a note in a garbage can on 19th Avenue." Kyle turned to Fredo and Cooper. "By the Starbucks."

Cooper had his gloved hand outstretched. Kyle gave him the note.

Fredo was whistling from the back seat. "No way you're going alone."

"Have to."

"No fuckin' way, Kyle," Fredo insisted. "I'll set you up with a wire. You'll read their note out loud and we'll be a block away, hearing every word."

"First I call Timmons," Kyle said.

KYLE WAS SURPRISED to find Timmons in the office this late. He knew some brass were in the office with him, because his chief addressed him as Adele and said he was sorry the dinner plans he had with he and his wife were canceled. "That's real sad about your mom. Hope your family can be of some comfort to you. Be safe, okay? We can reschedule for next week."

"You got big timers there?" Kyle asked.

"Don't worry about me, honey. You just go be with your family in this time of crisis and I'll call you later."

Timmons hung up.

Kyle let the team know about the call. It was the closest to a green light he was going to get from the US Navy.

FREDO HAD KYLE fitted with a small Invisio earpiece with a micro-phone, so they could talk back and forth. The thing was so small, he didn't like to use it on missions because occasionally it would get lodged into his ear too far and hurt like a son of a gun pulling it out. It also made him a bit hard of hearing, and he had to be careful not to talk too loud when under cover. But in this case, this small earpiece was way safer.

Fredo had fashioned portable mikes mounted behind cheap, American flag pins he'd bought at a souvenir store on Coronado. He pinned one to Kyle's chest on the right side so Kyle's heartbeat wouldn't interfere with the reception. They were that good.

"This one is bait. They find it and think they've got the device, you feel me?" Fredo said.

Kyle nodded.

Fredo had gotten written up for pinning one of Carlisle's flunkies. The whole team listened and recorded the young MA banging a pro for fifty bucks. CDs of the incident earned Fredo enough to pay for all the equipment. But he got a letter in his file. The young MA got himself transferred to a ship, he'd been so hounded by Team guys.

"How many of these did you make?" Kyle asked as he tapped on the flag.

Coop jumped violently out of his seat, hitting his head on the roof of the truck. He pulled off his headset. "Shit, shit, shit. That thing is strong."

Fredo frowned and looked back at Coop as if to tell him to grow up, but didn't. He focused back on Kyle.

"If you need to, you put this thing in under your collar, or your breast pocket if you don't have time."

They dropped Kyle off at the corner, and he took a taxi the rest of the way to the Starbucks. He'd instructed the boys to stay several blocks behind, turn right before Kearney and park within view of the garbage can. Kyle asked the cab to wait, figuring he'd need transportation.

He fished through wrappers and wet semi-empty coffee cups. He found the bag down about a foot into the trash and pulled it out, earning him a scowl from an older, nearly hairless Chinese barber who watched him through the plate glass window of his shop.

When he opened the bag, he found another note, but this time it was written on a yellow Post-It.

"Keep the bag for prints," he heard in his earpiece.

"Go to the rear entrance of the Shoe Barn at 16th and Harrison." He turned the note over. "Nothing else."

Kyle gave the directions to the driver, a portly black man, who chewed on a toothpick. He folded and stuffed the Taco Bell bag into his backpack.

They arrived at the Shoe Barn, but the huge building, taking up a full city block, was boarded up. Half its windows were broken and replaced with plywood. However, some gaping holes remained. From the row of street people sitting out front with shopping carts filled with belongings and sleeping bags, Kyle realized this place was probably a makeshift hotel of sorts.

Was Christy held in this grimy warehouse with the drunks and filth?

Kyle instructed the driver to go around to the backside of the large building, where they found rollup garage doors spray-painted with gang graffiti and one metal exterior door.

"Look man, I don't want no trouble. This is a dangerous neighborhood," the cabbie said.

"No trouble. I'm supposed to meet someone here. But they might have left another note. Gotta be sure I don't need another ride."

The driver harrumphed and put the cab in park, shaking his head. As Kyle started to get out, the driver called to him through the opened driver's side window. "Hey, dude. How about I get paid for the two fares *now*." His palm was outstretched.

Kyle scanned the empty storage yard, pulled out his wallet, and handed the driver a couple of twenties. "Wait. If I don't come out in five minutes, you can take off," Kyle said.

As soon as he was paid, the cabbie revved the engine, his tires spinning loose gravel all over Kyle. The cabbie took off like his life depended on it.

"Fuck. Hope you guys are nearby. My driver just bailed on me. I'm behind the building." He inhaled, not getting a response in his ear. "I'm going in."

Still nothing. As he touched the silver knob of the door, he heard the crackle in his ear. "We're here."

The door was unlocked. Kyle stepped into a darkened expanse. Pigeons fluttered in the filtered light between a couple of dangling fluorescent fixtures. He heard water dripping somewhere, then the sound of a chair sliding on concrete. He heard footsteps as he unclipped his side arm, but didn't unholster it.

"Well, well, well. We meet at last." The figure of a man appeared from the dark shadows in front of him, and said, "If you value your life, you'll give me that weapon."

CHAPTER 35

K YLE WAITED UNTIL the man stepped into the light created by a
four-bulb fluorescent fixture that fluttered on one bulb. He was
shorter than Kyle by several inches, with a buzz cut and a deep scar
over his left eye that extended into a lopsided cavern in his cheek, as if
a bullet had been dug out with a spoon. It was a prison wound. His
neck and exposed forearms were covered in ink. Blurry and milky
tattoos. Not many of them professional.

Junkyard dog.

The man's upper torso was as hard as any of Kyle's SEAL Team
members, but the leathery skin was scarred and pockmarked. His
arms were longer than the rest of him proportionally. Well developed
guns, connected to gnarly fingers. He held a semiautomatic that Kyle
recognized as an FN 5.7, which could hold 20 armor-piercing rounds.
Across his chest was an AK-47 strap.

The guy was connected. And armed for bloody battle.

"Allow me to introduce myself. I'm Caesar Rodriguez." A muscled
forearm covered with tats of naked women extended, palm up. He
wiggled his fingers, indicating he wanted Kyle's gun.

Kyle gave it to him. Caesar looked to his left and a young boy
popped out of the shadows, grabbed the gun, and ran into the safety
of darkness.

"Now I will shake your hand," Caesar said, "for saving my brother's life."

Brother?

"Excuse me?" Kyle asked. He stepped back and heard the sounds of safeties being released.

"Stop right there, amigo."

Kyle did as he was told and froze in place. He was listening, searching for any small movement. He counted three, maybe four other breathing patterns.

"Any friend to my brother is a friend to me." Caesar extended his hand again, palm up. "We will finish the formalities, like two soldiers on the battlefield, then we will talk and determine if we are enemies."

Kyle shook his hand, which was hard as a piece of wood, callused and scratchy. This was a man who was used to fighting barehanded, without the use of the military-issue gloves.

Big box taught.

"And here I thought you cared for the girl." Kyle could see a flicker of panic in Caesar's eyes. "We got her some place safe. Not sure about the baby, though."

Caesar withdrew his hand and grimaced in spite of himself. He was missing several upper teeth. The gaping smile chilled Kyle. The man had no soul. That meant he had no limits.

"So who is your brother?" Kyle asked as he dropped his arm down by his side, resisting the temptation to wipe his hand on his pants.

"Blood brother, really. Armando Guzman. I believe you know him, yes?"

The creature was enjoying this too much, Kyle thought. His time would come. It dawned on him that's why Armando was probably still alive. And why they'd killed the guy who'd overdosed Armando on heroin. This thug and Armando were childhood friends. Kyle had been told about them, how Armando had fought his way out of the street and eventually joined the Navy after he relocated his mom and sister. Pieces were clicking into place as a familiar face walked around Caesar, holding two white zip ties in his right hand.

"We use these too, asshole," Deputy Hilber whispered to the side of Kyle's face. Before he could secure Kyle's wrists, Caesar bid him to stop. Hilber definitely looked disappointed, but obeyed.

"When you say *we*, you mean the San Diego Sheriff's Office, or your vast criminal enterprise here in San Francisco," Kyle said with mock respect.

"You'll see," Hilber said, pulling Kyle by the shirt.

"No need for that," Caesar interjected. "Get your filthy hands off my guest."

"Well, he's not *my* guest. I'd just as soon see these guys disappear." Hilber sneered at his ally, who spat on his shoes and got a face full of hatred for his efforts.

An unholy alliance. Divide and conquer. Kyle saw the power struggle already, and wondered who the warriors in the background were loyal to.

His eyes were getting used to the dark now. He glanced around and found a couple of dirty mattresses on the floor, some blankets drying on a clothesline, an ice chest, and a hospital gurney with the unmistakable body of Armando strapped to it, an IV inserted into his arm. Armando's eyes were closed.

"That Armando over there?" he asked his captors.

Caesar nodded, studying him. "Your brother too. More recent war. Now I hope we can all be friends."

Hilber swore.

"You proud of the fact that you kidnapped your own best friend?"

The man didn't move a muscle, but his mouth turned down in a sneer. He stared into Kyle's eyes without moving back and forth. Thinking. "Thank you, amigo, for understanding our connection. But no, I'm not proud of it."

Caesar motioned to have Kyle walk over. "I do what I must to be valuable to the organization." He placed his palm against his chest and bowed. "Please. You will confirm now that he is still alive. Everything you do next will ensure he stays that way."

Kyle looked at his Team buddy, sleeping soundly. But he noticed the left side of Armando's mouth twitching, which was the sign he was looking for. That meant he was fully awake, listening, and uninjured enough to fight. Armando's wrists were bound with zip ties, but Kyle saw Armando had already moved the flaps back and forth to break them with a sudden jerk.

"Has he suffered injuries? How'd you get him to sleep?"

"You saw it, Mr. SEAL man. We give him heroin." Caesar glanced over Armando's body. "He likes it now, man. Don't you, little Paco?" Caesar jammed his fist into Armando's thigh, but the SEAL didn't move. Kyle saw Armando's jaw tense, sending a flash to his temple, but the movement was so slight, he doubted anyone else saw it. But he sure as hell knew that grimace. He'd seen it before when Armando had caught a bullet in his back while he was bending over to pick Kyle up when Kyle had been wounded. Armando had got the wound looked at only after Kyle was safely in the arms of the medic.

"And what makes you think I would help you with all this, whatever it is?" Kyle spoke quickly to hopefully keep from earning Armando another blow.

"Come, my friend of my friend. We will talk like two generals." Caesar motioned to two dirty leather recliners on the cold oily warehouse floor, one losing its stuffing.

Kyle complied. He chose the chair facing Armando and noticed his buddy rolled his head slightly in his direction and smiled.

"We want to procure some equipment. Guns and shit like that. Armor. All that crazy shit you guys get to use every day."

"So you can use them against innocents?" Kyle asked, meeting Caesar's gaze head-on.

"Nah, mostly against people who have made promises they haven't kept. Officials that don't play nice. Other organizations who want a piece of our action. Sticking their noses where they don't fucking belong. We run a very efficient and profitable business here. It feeds people. Women and children too. It's *our* Stimulus Package. We require your services."

"You've got my gun. I presume you unloaded something from Armando too. You don't want a fight with our kind."

"On the contrary. I *like* your kind. I *respect* your kind." Caesar gave a quick look to Hilber, who squinted in reply. Kyle could tell the men hated each other. And the only reason Hilber was behaving himself was because they were on Caesar's turf. Not the other way around.

Caesar leaned forward, elbows on his knees.

"You see, I have two things you want. One perhaps more than the other. I'm not interested in just a couple of things here and there—I want to establish an enterprise that will make you and your friend, if he cooperates, very rich men. I want enough so that I feel protected. So my friends can do business in the manner to which they are accustomed."

"Selling drugs."

"I give my customers what they want."

"You steal their futures, their youth."

"They're bored. They willingly give it up. Lotta sick people around these days, you know? We don't bother anyone else unless they interfere, my friend. It reduces our overhead when we don't have to pay so much for protection." He nodded to Hilber, who crossed his chest with his folded arms.

"And you think I will do this because you have Armando here."

Caesar stood up and motioned for Kyle to follow him.

"I am going to ask much of you, I agree. This is a serious commitment you are going to have to make. But then, there is much at stake." He walked over to the rose-colored blanket draped over a white nylon cord and pulled it back with his heavily inked fingers.

Christy was tied to a chair. Her hair was tussled, eye makeup running down her cheeks, but other than that, she looked unharmed. She actually looked wonderful. Kyle couldn't believe how good it felt to see her. Alive and breathing.

Her eyes looked big and scared above the red bandana tied across her mouth a little too tight. Her eyes got even bigger when she saw Kyle.

Caesar walked over to her. "I believe you know this woman in, shall we say, the carnal way?" He smiled and slipped his hand under the hem of her red top and fondled her breast. Christy closed her eyes and suffered in silence. She didn't flinch. Kyle knew she wouldn't show her fear or her humiliation.

"May I speak with her?"

"Sure, sure." Caesar continued to fondle her, but motioned for Kyle to step closer.

Kyle could have killed him right then and there. The foul-breathed cretin leaned in and whispered in his ear, "Are her thighs as creamy? She has the smoothest skin." He brushed the fingers of his hand against her cheek, wiping the tears that had spilled down in rivulets, had dripped off her chin. Caesar touched the shiny droplets like they were diamonds. "Too perfect. Maybe I should take a bite, so you can remember me later when I let you fuck her and I get to watch."

Kyle's hands made fists.

"Watch it there, cowboy." Hilber reminded him he was still at his back. And a gun was trained at his head.

Kyle extended his hands to the side, watched Caesar nod at him, giving him the green light to speak to Christy. He knelt in front of her. He would do anything to protect her. When he put his hand on her knee, she jumped and opened her eyes. He gave her warm flesh a little squeeze, hoping it reassured her. She couldn't hide the terror trembling inside her.

"I'm sorry for this, Christy. I'm going to do everything I can to keep you safe. Whatever they ask, I will do it. Please don't worry. Just stay the course."

He thought about Mayfield's suggestion: "Become the bait." Yeah, he could do that.

Christy's face was still beautiful, despite the panic he read in her eyes and the dried tears that ran black down her cheeks. She needed him, clung to him, and, yes, wanted him. She'd been strong, holding out so as not to show emotion, but this touch on her knee opened the floodgates. Her lower lip quivered beneath the dirty bandana, but there was no sobbing.

"May I?" Kyle asked his captor, holding up the palm with teeth marks, now healing, as if to touch her face in a tender caress.

Caesar shrugged.

Kyle quickly lunged, grabbed Caesar's forearm, and from kneeling position, twisted it, and heard a loud crack as the two bones shattered. He jammed the broken bones up through the man's elbow joint and heard the scream. It echoed for several seconds throughout the warehouse.

Kyle felt the gun butt to his head the instant he saw Christy's horrified expression, and then blackness.

FREDO SAT UP. "Holy shit. He just brought hell down on all of them."

He explained what he'd heard to Cooper and Gunny. They had positioned themselves up the block so they could watch the back door with night-vision binoculars. The large warehouse/store complex was in a swale between two residential streets.

"I'm calling Timmons," Cooper said as he got out his cell. Gunny was on his phone as well.

Fredo tried to make out muffled talking, but Kyle had apparently landed face-down and the flag microphone was buried beneath his body, the Invisio slammed against the floor. One thing was for sure, whoever Caesar was, Fredo doubted the man would ever be the same. He could hear him screaming even without the microphone. It spooked several of the homeless guys leaning up against the wall and sleeping on the ground outside the compound.

Fredo hoped Kyle had broken some body part that would permanently cripple the dude. From the screams, whatever Kyle had done, didn't sound like this type of injury could go untreated for long. Caesar would have to go to a hospital, and soon. And that would mean one less bad guy. For now.

A dark van with blackened windows pulled up, and five heavy-set ex-military types got out and entered the warehouse door.

"Coop, Gunny. Get your asses over here," Fredo said.

He directed them to leave immediately. Neither wanted to. "Look, when they find the mike, they're going to be all over here."

"I'm staying. Gunny, you go," Cooper commanded.

Gunny looked between the two SEALs. "I'll be back in an hour. I've got some friends here, if there's time. Text me if it gets...if you can."

"Fredo will protect me," Coop said, throwing an arm around Fredo's neck. Gunny was given the keys and left.

"Shh!" Fredo whispered, throwing off Cooper's arm and scowling. "Something's happening." Coop pulled down his goggles and watched.

Fredo heard muffled scraping noises through the little microphone. He guessed it was from dragging Kyle's body across the floor. He thought he heard a faint, "left," from Kyle, but wasn't sure. That would mean that he was alive, and so was everyone else.

Fredo and Coop watched the five goons load a groggy, half-dead Armando into the back of the van. A second black SUV pulled up and two more characters got out and ran inside the compound. Next came Deputy Hilber. He stood out like a white worm with his khaki uniform that almost glowed in the night-vision goggles. He held the girl by the hair. She had her hands tied in front of her and was walking on tiptoes in ridiculous high heels that seemed way out of place. She was trying to wrench her head around to look at something. Fredo saw Kyle being dragged under both arms toward the other van.

Hilber pushed the girl into the SUV and came back to Kyle and bent over. Fredo listened as the microphone on the American flag was plucked from Kyle's shirt. Hilber scanned the surrounding buildings and streets, briefly hesitating over their position. He dropped the mike and Fredo heard the crackle, followed by silence as Hilber ground the thing into the asphalt.

"Flag Audio's gone."

Coop nodded, watching the same thing. "His Invisio still working?"

"Yessir, for now."

"But knowing you, there's another backup."

"Fuckin' A. We can track him."

The men loaded Kyle in the second van as Hilber barked orders to two men, who took off running as if it were a marathon. The vans left. The two men were headed right toward their location. Fredo recognized how quickly they tackled the incline, their speed most likely a result of years of military training.

"I'm itching for a burger," Fredo whispered while watching the ex-military types disappear into the neighborhood below. He presumed they were making their way up the hill and would be there within minutes. "Wonder if they got a decent place here, or if it's all tofu and grilled veggies."

Coop shrugged, then stowed his goggles, lifted the collar up on his jacket, and replaced his black cap with a Giants baseball cap he'd lifted from their ride. "I don't care, as long as you're paying."

To the average citizen, they would look like an ordinary pair of Joes on their way home from a late night shift. They ducked into the shadows along a back alleyway and disappeared.

GUNNY RETURNED AN hour later, as he'd promised, to the now-deserted spot and texted Fredo and Cooper, who were eating tacos at a canteen truck nearby. Fredo gave Gunny the address and five minutes later the Tahoe pulled up. It was filled with overweight, silver-haired guys who all looked just like Gunny.

"Whoa, we having a family gathering here?" Fredo barked. "Sure you got room for a little Mexican?"

Gunny introduced them to his friends, who were mostly retired police and firemen. Men he'd served with in Korea and Viet Nam. It wasn't lost on Fredo that these guys were looking for one last good fight. He could tell they missed the hunt.

He shook his head. "Hate involving innocents," he whispered to Coop, who just shrugged.

Coop leaned toward him and, out of earshot of the big guys in the front seats and said, "They're far from innocent. They heeded the call when you were in diapers, amigo."

Ain't that a fact? Fredo still didn't like it.

CHAPTER 36

MAYFIELD DECIDED IT was his turn to call the meeting with Timmons. He'd heard nothing from Kyle or Christy, though he'd placed a call to her. There also had been no answer at the house on Stanyan Street, which worried him too. Hilber wasn't available, and the office said he'd taken a couple days leave.

Sure he was. In the middle of a quadruple homicide?

Maybe he'd waited too long, he thought. Things had started coming unraveled and he was getting more and more uncomfortable with circumstances by the hour.

"This isn't an official meet and greet," he said to Timmons, on the phone.

"So then that means shots at Jimmy's."

Mayfield looked at his watch. Christ, it was nearly ten. Way too late for a meeting, but never the right time for shots.

"Can you be there in a half hour?" Mayfield asked.

"I'm here now."

He could hear the crowd in the background. It was Sunday, so it would be tamer than usual. "Okay. I'll be there as soon as I can."

"Take your time, man. I'm expecting a call from Fredo and the team at any time. I assume that's who you're gonna want to talk about."

"Yup."

"You coming alone?" Timmons asked.

"Of course."

"Then I'll wiggle out of my friends."

"I appreciate that." The last thing Mayfield wanted was a public viewing. Here he was conspiring with the Navy against one of his own. But that was what he was about to do.

Or he'd be on his way to no retirement at that little fishing village in Mexico, where he'd live until the ammo gave out. Forget about the pension.

The patio outside Jimmy's was warm, but a blazing fire pit at the center threw off a pleasant glow and heat that felt real good. Mayfield couldn't get the cold chill off the back of his neck that persisted in spite of the fire and the warm night air. Timmons was watching him from a table in the dark corner. The guy was so still, Mayfield almost walked right past him.

Cars slowly tooled past. An elderly couple in matching workout clothes walked their little white dog. The dog obviously thought he was leading.

Maybe he was, Mayfield thought. Not sure why it tickled him, but it did.

He sat in front of Timmons and in an instant was met by a young nubile thing with a low-cut white cotton smock shirt over an impossibly short skirt. She kneeled in front of him and he couldn't help but take a quick glance. Just a quick one. She had a wonderful rack. He murmured a forgiveness prayer to Maria.

"Sir? You want a beer, or something else?"

The something else came to mind, and Timmons grinned, picking up his drift somehow.

"Diet Coke."

"Coming right up." She rose and he had to follow those tanned long legs to the bar.

"How long's it been, Mayfield?"

Mayfield checked out his unmanicured fingernails, wiggled his fingers, which moved the little heart tattoo with "Maria" written in the center, emblazoned on his forearm, and answered, "I had a Coke for lunch."

Timmons was well on his way to being indecent in public. He tossed back another shot and winced like it was mouthwash, the kind that burned all the way down to your butt. He peered over at Mayfield in what looked like a challenge. He could see the officer wasn't having a good day.

And that probably meant Mayfield's day was shit too. But what the hell. He leaned in and asked, "I got a dead guy burnt to a crisp in a cabin we haven't been able to ID yet and two dead ex-deputies in the Palos Vega forest, and a dead personal trainer at one of our most exclusive condo complexes." He looked right and left, then behind him, then whispered and leaned further across the table. "Something's seriously out of whack. Everyone around this Lansdowne character is dying. And violently. Only a matter of time before one of your Team guys gets it too."

"You've got more to think about."

"Excuse me?" Mayfield knew he wasn't going to like the explanation.

"You've also—well, not you, but San Francisco—has a dead shopkeeper and a celebrity billionaire shot in the chest, almost dead. And a dirty cop. Name's Hilber."

Timmons stopped. Then it hit Mayfield. Hilber had gone too far and now the Navy was getting a whiff of his stink. But this caper was long beyond anyone's control now. Least of all his.

"Just thought you ought to know," Timmons added helpfully. Mayfield could see why the man was on the drunker side of conscious.

"And now I'm missing *two* of mine," Timmons added, holding up his fingers in the V sign.

Mayfield could see his retirement package going through a paper shredder. Shoot, at this rate, he'd have to hitchhike to San Felipe, carrying everything he owned on his back. This was a cluster fuck extraordinaire.

"I shouldn't have trusted your SEALs."

"Oh, yeah? Well, I understand you told Kyle to *be the bait?*"

The man was right. It was partially his fault too. "And so that's what's happened?"

"Yup. They've got Kyle. As far as I know, everyone's alive. Point is, we can't really go in there. We know where they are, but we have to let the locals do it."

"I can ask for a certain amount of cooperation from several departments, but that's only going to go so far. Pretty soon, they're going to link everything to Lansdowne, make him out as the one running the operation. And, as the man-hours keep ratcheting up in this time of economic crisis, they'll just come in blasting and sort it out later. You get my meaning?"

Timmons nodded.

"Someone's connected the dots real good. Got ATF, maybe the FBI on it too. This is becoming one giant fucking pile of shit, Timmons, and you know who is right in the middle of it."

"Warren Hilber," Timmons said.

Mayfield was going to swear loudly, but the nice young thing with the silky thighs brought his diet Coke, with a lime wedge on the lip for good measure.

Perfect.

He saluted her and took a long drag. Then he squeezed the lime over the top and took another. It seemed to ease his belly some, but not enough. "I don't even want to fucking answer my phone anymore." He took several ice cubes and ground them down quickly with his molars.

Timmons was nodding, staring at his empty glass. The girl hadn't asked him if he wanted another. That meant she could count pretty good, Mayfield thought.

"So, Timmons, tell me something that'll make me fucking feel better."

Timmons smiled lopsided and speared him in the eyes with a stare Mayfield knew was only the precursor to something bad. Really bad.

"Kyle and the team didn't get there in time." Timmons said.

"And?"

"Used her as bait, and now they have Kyle too, just like you instructed."

"Okay. Get to the point."

"They saved the billionaire's life. We have to get that word out there. But I've asked the two other members of Kyle's team to come in.

"And?"

"They refused."

Mayfield wanted to strangle the man, except they were on the same team and he was having his own share of problems. Of course, this news might convince a couple of his superiors that Kyle was more victim than perp, but it was a risk. He knew he'd waited too long to get additional help. He just thought these guys could handle it on their own. But the operation was exploding out of control.

"The one who is behind it all is Caesar Rodriguez, of the Scorpions. They—"

"I know who they are. They run guns and provide protection for the big Mexican gangs from San Diego. Got safe houses all the way from here to the border." Mayfield waved off down the strand. "Word has it, they use ex-military."

"No doubt," Timmons said, frowning. "Our training's the best." He sat back and looked into the night air, as if he were thinking about what to say. "We try to weed them out, but I'd be the first one to admit, we don't get them all."

"And the dropouts, the DORs?"

"Them too. They get just enough training to be dangerous, but we try to get into their heads right away and weed out the nut jobs."

"Or the ones with a higher calling."

"You know the drill. You were there."

That he was. Mayfield could remember the wet and sandy evenings, the chafing, the blood running down his leg under his uniform that Saturday after they'd passed Hell Week. He hadn't bothered to take off his clothes and had showered in the warm water, shampooed his face, and fallen asleep soaking wet on the cheap motel room bed. He'd woken up twelve hours later and was starving. They all ate together at a café that overlooked the ocean they had spent six excruciating days in. All thirty of them, less than a quarter of the original class, had walked as if they were crab-like creatures from the black lagoon. And when he finally had taken off his shoes, his feet had been green.

"How'd Caesar get to your guys?" Mayfield finally asked as he ground down another few ice chips.

"Childhood friend. Someone who knows the family. Got mixed up with Armando's sister off and on for years."

Timmons held his glass up and it was taken within seconds.

"I think your sheriff is there, in San Francisco," Timmons said.

"Good. I'll throw some shit his way. That I *can* do."

"And Kyle injured Caesar. He's probably going to need medical attention, from the sound of it."

"So we check the ERs. What kind of injury?"

"Fredo says he thinks an arm thing. The guy was screaming and passing out from the pain."

The girl brought two glasses. "Another?" she asked Mayfield.

"Sure." He was thinking about whom he could call to get the heat on Hilber, who was probably getting fairly desperate by now. "You know where they are?"

Timmons hesitated, and then tossed down the first of his two new drinks. "Yup. Know right where they all are. Kyle's painted."

"Painted?"

"We have a locator on him."

Mayfield understood. "Anything else I should know about?"

"Nope." Timmons grinned. "Well, if I told you, I'd have to kill you."

They both laughed at that one.

"You guys have some toys, I'll grant you that. Shoot, if we had your budget…"

"You'd catch more bad guys. I completely agree."

"Sometimes I think that's why I tried out for the SEALs," Mayfield said.

"Yup. Heard that one too."

Timmons was having a good time playing cat and mouse with him. Mayfield had to ask the question. "Your guys aren't actually thinking of going in there and getting him? Them, I mean?"

Timmons cocked his head and thought about it a minute. "Can't honestly say. I hope not, for the sake of their careers. Hell, for mine too. And you guys will never convince everyone in San Diego and San

Francisco, as well as the Feds, in time, either."

"We're fucked." Mayfield knew it. No way this was going to work out, unless…

"I'd put my money on my SEALs. Everything we need is inside that warehouse, or wherever the hell they are. The Scorpion King has no idea what or who they are dealing with."

"If he's still alive," Mayfield said.

"Oh, he's still alive. They both are. Trust me, if either one or both of them goes out, you and everyone else will know it."

CHAPTER 37

CHRISTY HAD BEEN placed on a blanket on the carpeted floor, but she still woke up stiff from the few hours' sleep she'd been able to snatch. She didn't recognize her surroundings. It was an apartment of sorts. She heard traffic and the ring of a cable car, so she knew she was still in San Francisco.

In a cruel twist of fate, she was on her side, nearly touching Kyle's sleeping form, the one person in the world she wanted to be sleeping next to. But he was hog-tied and her hands ached from the zip ties at her wrists in front of her. All night long she kept forgetting where she was and would try to force her arms apart, to adjust to a more comfortable position, but then realization of her situation would dawn and she'd quickly remember comfort and movement was useless.

She had to pee, though it had been hours, nearly twenty now, since she'd eaten or had anything to drink. That told her there was no real concern for her safety or her health.

No smell of coffee. No warm bed smelling of fresh lovemaking. No warm shower and lavender shower gel. No warm scent at the back of Kyle's neck that she could bury her nose in. No touch of his solid ass as he came alive to the caress of her thighs. No holding the man who was a god—perhaps too much of a god. Was it possible to love someone, to need someone so much? Was it a good thing or a very bad thing?

Death stared her in the face. Kyle looked at peace in his sleep.

What if Kyle died? What if she had to watch that? What if she died? On the scale in her soul, she knew her life wasn't worth half of his. This was the man who had touched her on the knee last night and told her everything would be all right. And she had believed him. He'd wanted to take the burden and the pain from her. She vowed if there were a chance, even if it meant sacrificing herself, she would provide a distraction. Somehow she would help set him free. That was the only thing she would focus on today.

What had he said before he'd been beaten? *Stay the course.* Not *have a nice life,* or *don't worry.* Those would have been useless words. Unrealistic words. No. He'd asked her to endure. Not give up. Not to think about it. Just go on.

She knew it all would happen today. There wouldn't be a long few days of torture. All she had to do was get through this next day, because she was certain there wouldn't be another one.

Time is of the essence. Just like what she'd learned in her real estate classes.

Madame M had had no time to prepare for her end of days, although Christy suspected the woman had not been entirely truthful with her. Christy had watched in horror as Madame was beaten and then shot. Caesar had put the gun to Tom's chest and got Christy to write the note to Kyle, creating the snare that would entrap him. And then the devil shot Tom anyway. Just for spite.

It's all my fault.

Tom? She'd heard the shot. Was he gone too? Her thoughts wandered. She allowed herself to explore what could have been her future. Could she have changed the course of his involvement in this drama? She said a prayer for him. God, she hoped he was alive. He didn't deserve this fate. It was hers. It wasn't his.

Forgive me, Tom. She had never meant to hurt him. Never meant to hurt Madame. And Marla. Was Kyle going to be next? Was everyone who cared about her going to die?

Tears flowed down her cheeks as she fluttered her eyelids so the blurriness of Kyle's handsome face wasn't lost to her. She would need that strong jaw line, those blue eyes that made her feel like some great Amazon warrior princess at his side. With this man, she could overcome anything. All he had to do was love her and she would be healed. She was everything she needed to be. She had everything she wanted to have. Even if it was for a day.

All she needed to do now was save him. Somehow. And today was the day it would have to happen.

Kyle stirred. A beam of early morning light had crossed the side of his face. The black stubble on his cheeks glistened, the hairs at his neckline rose and fell with his steady breathing. He wasn't like anyone else she had ever met. His body was a lean killing machine, but his heart was as full and tender as a child's. Full of life. Full of love. Full of hope—not just for her, but for a nation she knew needed him. A nation that would never be able to thank him the way he deserved. Who would never understand the heart of the man. The heart and dedication of a warrior. Being a SEAL was his true calling and always would be.

Another wave of tears shielded the view of him. He nestled his head against the floor and arched his back. His chest expanded and rose. Her fingers and lips had explored the length of that chest not nearly enough times. She hadn't heard his steady heartbeat enough. She needed to lay her ear against his breast and listen to life as it was meant to be. Until it was all over, the memory of those glorious moments in his arms would be all she would have.

And though it wouldn't be nearly enough, it would have to do.

It was all she had, after all.

And for right now he was lying next to her, in the morning, with the sun on his chest. And he was alive.

She fell to sleep dreaming of a life that could have been.

CHAPTER 38

KYLE WOKE TO a splitting headache. He felt like he was wearing a hatchet lodged in his forehead, right between his eyes. Eyes that refused to focus.

But when the fuzzy red spots in front of him cleared, he saw Christy's luscious shape. Her cherry red top was half slung over one shoulder and smudged. She was on her side, facing him, her hands bloody from struggling with the zip ties. But right now they lay relaxed and in repose. Like she was praying.

He looked at her strong arched eyebrows and her long smooth nose, ending with just a slight upturn guarding full rose-colored lips. A little of her red lipstick remained. He remembered everything about those lips.

He had no right to be thinking about them right now. Cooper and Fredo were right—those kinds of thoughts could get a good Team guy killed. That wasn't the hard part, he thought. He didn't want to make Armando and Christy sacrifice for his mistakes. That just wasn't going to happen.

Soft blond curls hugged the dark canyon along her neck. Her shiny shoulder, transected by a red satin bra strap, rose and fell with her even breathing. They hadn't beaten her, thank God. Her black, form-fitting pants hugged those long legs of hers, with one crossed over the other. His gaze followed down to her ankles with just a couple of blue veins visible at the top of her foot.

And then there were those heels.

They were still shiny, as if she'd been protecting them. Probably expensive, he thought. He fantasized what those bare legs would look like with the patent leather, spiked heels wrapped around his waist or flat up against the wall as he sunk himself deep inside her.

Not helpful, these thoughts. Dangerous. His package was coming to life. Oblivious to danger. Maybe because of the danger. What kind of thinking was that? It was gallows humor, for sure.

She was trying to turn over in her sleep. She arched her spine just enough so he could see the outline of her breasts under the top, the hint of shadow he could remember that played between her nipples those times when he buried his head there, those times when he tasted this gentle woman who had the heart of a lion in a siren's body.

Knowing her, it was the first time he'd found someone who could take everything he could dish out. All of it. All the lovemaking, all the moodiness and distances he had to maintain to keep sight of the mission, all of who he was. She was his equal in every respect, and perhaps superior to him in many. If it took every ounce of courage and life force, he would make sure she survived.

Maybe if he didn't survive and Armando did, his buddy would take care of her, protect her, and learn to cherish her like he had. Christy deserved someone in her life who would bring her a deep love that would rock her to her core, not something casual and brittle. Something deep, everlasting. Something worthy of her courage and strength.

If it can't be me, let it be someone like Armando.

Kyle did feel the pangs of regret and jealousy. Had he mentally agreed to give her up? Well, if he died saving her life, that is what he would do. She was worth it, after all.

He scanned as much of the room as he could see. And he listened. Hispanic music was playing outside on the street somewhere. The sound of traffic came from below, which meant they were in an urban neighborhood, most likely on a second or third floor. He could hear morning delivery trucks. An occasional car swished by. Doors slammed and motors revved, and then he heard the telltale ring of a cable car nearby.

He was in San Francisco. People were coming and going about their lives.

A cheap dresser with pictures stuck into the mirror frame was on the opposite side of the room. He could feel fabric and the metal band of a bed frame behind him. Someone was snoring on the bed. He hoped it was Armando, but after listening to the rhythmic snoring, he realized the pattern wasn't familiar. So one of his captors was with them.

Where was Armando?

He heard a door slam shut downstairs and footsteps get closer. They were heavy, like combat boots on wooden steps, two—no, three sets of boots. And whoever it was, they were big men. Like the ex-military types he'd seen at the warehouse.

So it was all starting now. He checked his heartbeat. No evidence he'd been drugged. But he had a dull ache at what probably was a big knob at the back of his head where he was sure he'd been gun-butted. Hilber's love tap, he thought. Kyle squeezed his fists and released them twice. Time for dealing with Hilber was soon approaching.

He wiggled the flap on his zip ties, twisting his wrists so a finger could move the flap back and forth like they'd been shown in captor training. In a few seconds the plastic failed, and his hands were free. Quietly, he rose up and took a quick peek at the bed. Sure enough, one huge guy dwarfed the bare twin mattress. He was fully clothed and a 9mm was laced in his limp fingers. It was too much of a risk to go for the gun.

Kyle worked the tie on his ankles and saw Christy's eyes open. He put a finger to his lips and she smiled. God, he would have to stretch, but he would kiss those lips. Slowly, quietly, he arched, lifting his torso in a one-armed pushup so he wouldn't drag over the carpet and make a sound.

She kept her eyes open when he kissed her.

"I won't let anything happen to you," he whispered. She nodded and looked at his lips again. When he kissed her again, she tried to arch her chest to his. Her sweet breath and kisses were furtive, desperate, strained at having to be kept quiet. Like she didn't think she'd ever get another kiss. He could feel the moan in her chest she wouldn't reveal. He smelled the perfume in her hair as her pulse points released her scent to him. She was his woman in every sense of the word. The better half of him. The half he would save. Even if the other half had to die.

CHAPTER 39

B Y NINE O'CLOCK in the morning, Mayfield made the calls to the IA Department at the San Diego sheriff's office, promising a full written report on Deputy Hilber and his involvement in the gang's swath of violence. As a courtesy, he also called the sheriff, who said he'd had his own suspicions about Hilber's extracurricular activities. There'd been rumors, he told Mayfield.

A politician's answer.

For jurisdictional harmony, Mayfield bought the story, for now. He didn't need another enemy just at this moment in his career. He knew the elected man was going to do everything possible to keep the dirty cop angle minimized.

Mayfield also alerted his chief, who pulled in the commissioner. One thing going for them was that it didn't look like any regular SDPD units were involved. And that was one hell of a good thing. At least the war was only on two fronts. Not like what Kyle and those poor bastards in the Navy had on their hands in Iraq and Afghanistan.

Arab Spring, my ass.

All he had to worry about now were the drug gangs and the rogue deputy's protection racket. He knew what they were after. And he knew they'd never succeed. He may not have trusted Kyle with his daughter, if he had one, but he knew the young man would rather die than resort to a life of crime and violence in the private sector. No guns for hire with this lot.

He believed Timmons's assessment that the two SEALs were still alive. No big explosions, shootouts, or vehicles bursting into flames had been reported. And it had been two days without another dead body turning up. Thank God for small favors.

He had no choice but to trust the men Timmons trusted. He wondered how Timmons was managing to keep the brass off his back.

Not my war. It's his.

Whatever private hell Hilber had created, the man wasn't going to be able to hide behind the badge anymore. Even if he survived, his days of running protection for the San Diego gangs were over. At least now the public could breathe a little easier.

Until the gangs found someone else. Hell, they probably had several eager candidates already lining up. Someone who needed money. Someone who felt they deserved a little extra special retirement package in exchange for their years of faithful service. The money was enough to tempt a saint.

Mayfield sometimes wished he felt the same way. Maybe life would be easier. Just sell out. But no, that would never happen. The system wasn't perfect. Lots of holes in it. But it was the only one around that made any sense, and, in general, the system improved the lives of the public. And they were his real bosses. Not the brass or the guys who signed his paycheck. He worked for those couples in the matching leisure suits out walking their dogs on a balmy San Diego night. The little people. The people who had families, went to work, paid their mortgages, and sent their kids to college.

He thought maybe Maria would like it if he went back to church. Maybe he'd get to spend more time with her there. He chuckled. She'd scold him. He'd been having some thoughts lately. And admitted for the first time, perhaps he was lonely after all.

No replacing you, Maria. Just saying a man has needs.

Maybe if he went to church and asked for help, she'd put her head together with Jesus and they'd find someone good for him.

Nah. Not going to happen.

He knew as sure as he was alive today that if he ever did that, he wouldn't be able to hear Maria scolding him any longer. Like she'd be gone forever.

And he wasn't ready for that. Not yet.

Mayfield called the SFPD's Office of Special Affairs, the ones who handled jurisdictional cooperation, and told them about Caesar and his injury. They promised to alert ERs in the San Francisco Bay Area. He knew SFPD would get Caesar. And he didn't mind that they would get credit for the collar. There was a need for San Francisco to show some toughness on crime, and this gave them that opportunity on a silver platter. Mayfield didn't need the medal.

He didn't even take joy knowing the DEA and ATF would send out hunting parties, rounding up gang members, weeding out their support system and wiping the slate clean for a time. He never really liked manhunts. Probably was a good thing he'd never made it through the SEAL program to earn a Trident.

Mayfield wondered how long it would be before Hilber would lose control over those gang members. He couldn't ever recall hearing Hilber speak Spanish. That was a real handicap. And if Hilber was no longer a deputy, he might be more of a liability, more of a loose end to the gangs than he'd ever figured he'd be.

Could be, sooner or later, Hilber would find himself a nice watery grave, if the gangs even bothered to find a grave at all. With Caesar out of the picture for a while, someone else no doubt would soon step up to fill his shoes. The new guy would need to do some housecleaning. And that would be bad news for the soon-to-be ex-deputy.

But it was also true that if Kyle and Armando wouldn't cooperate, they'd be loose ends as well. Mayfield knew from experience that the real leadership was in Mexico, hiding in plain sight, probably running operations right out of some territorial police captain's office, one or two steps from a prison term himself. Maybe even paid for by US anti-drug task force money.

Crime finds a way. It doesn't really pay, but for a time, crime always looks as if it's winning.

He checked his watch. Only nine-thirty. Today was going to be a big day, if his instincts were right. He decided it was time to do a little research in the field to help set up the next phase of hunting down the bad guys and putting them behind bars. That was his job, after all.

FELICIA GUZMAN WAS hanging laundry in her backyard when Sergeant Mayfield drove up in his patrol car. He saw her flowered dress and the braid wound up on top of her head, just like how Maria used to wear her hair. The sight almost took him back a step.

The house was painted bright yellow. Way too bright. An explosion of huge bursting dahlias and fragrant columns of pink and blue flowers grew all along the front of the stucco house. In front of the tall stalks was a profusion of low bedding flowers. In contrast to the rest of the neighborhood, Mrs. Guzman's house looked like the Fourth of July and Christmas all at once, only without the flags and twinkle lights. No way you could drive down the street and miss it.

The dark little woman wiped her hands on her apron and prepared to greet him. He could see she was steeling herself for some bad news. Didn't she know if bad news was being delivered, the Navy would be the ones to call and not some lowly San Diego police sergeant?

"Ma'am." He wore his badge on his uniform and she was staring at it. "I'm Sergeant Mayfield from the San Diego Police Department."

"You have some news about my son?"

She had a lined face that was full of character and resolution. The way she stared back at Mayfield almost made him embarrassed for some reason. Her large nut-brown eyes were soft but demanding. He didn't see any trace of the fear and concern he knew she felt.

A young, twenty-something woman came dashing down the front steps. She had a gauze pad taped to her forehead. She was stunning in every sense of the word. A total knockout. Her long dark hair and tanned limbs nearly took his breath away. She was a taller, younger, and thinner version of her mother. The mother was quite stunning as well.

"Mom. I'm going down to Gina's place for a couple of hours. She wants to help me pick out some clothes for the baby. We might go shopping, but I'll be home before dinner. You want me to get you anything?"

"No. Mia, I don't like you leaving the house." She frowned and addressed Mayfield. "Mia, this is Sergeant—I'm sorry, I don't remember your name…"

"Mayfield."

"Nice to meet you," Mia said as she extended her hand.

He saw the same strength her mother showed, but also saw defiance, especially directed at his uniform. What could be so attractive about the low-lives like Caesar when she had a home and a mother like this little woman standing next to her?

Mayfield shook her soft hand, very tentatively placed.

"You will stay home today, Mia. Have you no respect for your brother? Now go back inside. I need to discuss some things with the sergeant here."

"Oh, Mama. They probably think I'm in the hospital. Besides, if they were looking for me, they would never expect me to be with Gina."

Felicia Guzman dropped her gaze. "Mia, I am not happy about this. It isn't safe."

"You worry too much. He'll…" Mia looked up at Mayfield.

He blurted out, "I know about your brother. That's why I'm here."

Mia took her mother by the shoulders and leveled a gaze at her that translated to a rejection of Felicia's demand.

"He's going to be okay. You'll see. Armando always finds a way."

After Mia gave her mother a peck on her cheek, they both watched Felicia's daughter saunter out to her car.

"Armando's sister. You've met my son?"

"No. I have not. Heard a lot of good things about him, though."

"That's good. He's good to his mama." She pulled a pair of clippers out from her apron and began to deadhead a rose bush. "You have news, then, about my son?" she said to the bush.

"Not really. You'll have to be talking to the Navy about that. All I know is that he's still being held, but we believe he is alive."

She put her palm to her throat and closed her eyes. "Thank God." She crossed herself. "And Kyle Lansdowne? Is he safe?"

"Not quite. They are together. And the girl too."

"What girl?" She was alarmed.

Mayfield looked down the street and saw he was attracting some attention. "Would you mind if I grabbed a glass of water and discussed this with you inside? I have some questions I need to ask, in private."

"Oh, pardon my manners. Of course. Come."

Mayfield followed her inside, and it felt like he was going back in time to the early days of his marriage with Maria. When she had felt better. When she filled his life with sunshine and joy.

When she grew big showy dahlias just like Felicia Guzman's.

CHAPTER 40

KYLE HEARD AN argument going on in the next room, and it was getting louder. He was expecting the staccato of gunfire at any moment. He pulled a thin razor wire from the flap in his belt and cut Christy's ties. She rubbed her wrists together, showing him with her eyes how grateful she was. He motioned for her to stay down and she nodded. He was on his feet and had garroted the sleeping thug with the razor wire.

He checked the man's weapon to make sure it was operational. He found two clips he knew he'd need, and then rolled the body toward the wall, dumping a pillow on the man's head to hide the blood. He checked for an additional weapon and found one stowed in his groin. Kyle tucked it in the front of his pants under his shirt. He lifted a limp arm over the top to make it look like the guy had fallen into a deep sleep.

When Kyle turned around, Christy was watching him from the floor. She'd just seen him kill a man. He saw the twins: fear and acceptance. But there was more.

Admiration.

Not what he needed, but what she wanted to show.

He helped Christy up so she wouldn't stumble, but she did, and into his chest. He felt her breasts press against him and the brush of her hair under his chin. With his free hand, he clutched the back of her head and sunk a deep kiss, feeling her arms go up and around his neck. Her body went limp in his embrace.

But this was folly. He pulled her away and asked her with his eyes if she was ready.

Christy nodded.

That's my girl.

Kyle debated whether or not he should arm Christy with the 9mm and decided not to. He motioned for her to stay in the corner. A sliding closet door was opened, but not wide enough for her to slip into. He shook his finger at it so she wouldn't consider trying to enter. She crouched down in the corner, the shiny patent leather pumps dangerously delicious, even now. She looked like cat woman. He wanted to fuck her so bad it really did hurt. His package was rubbing against the blue steel of the weapon.

"How many?" he mouthed to her.

She looked up to the right, and then leveled back at him. She held up six fingers, then pointed to the man on the bed and turned a finger down. Five.

"Armando?" he whispered.

The arguing in Spanish stopped abruptly and Kyle tensed, then leaned flat against the doorframe. Christy pointed through the wall to the next room.

Armando was next door.

The Spanish conversations resumed, but the voices were calmer now. Kyle heard four distinct voices and the rustling of bags. He guessed the three returning boots had brought breakfast. And they'd want to share it with the dead guy.

Something was said in Spanish outside the door. Kyle and Christy waited.

The door burst open. Kyle let the gunman enter the room fully before he pushed the door closed, twisted the man's neck, breaking it instantly, keeping his palm over the man's mouth to muffle any sound.

Now Christy had seen him kill two men. In less than five minutes. He glanced in her direction and was thankful to see her staring at the floor. Killing was not something he was proud of, but if the odds were down to four versus two, not counting Christy, they had a damned good chance. If Armando was in any shape to fight.

The absence of the two gunmen was getting attention from the other room. The door was kicked open and then the room was sprayed with automatic gunfire, splinters of wood flying like a wood chipper. Someone breached the doorway and caught Kyle's rounds across the chest. Kyle hadn't been sure until that moment whether or not the ammo was hollow point, and thank God it was. The body, encased in a flak vest, crumbled to the ground.

The other two gunmen fanned out in opposite directions on the other side of the door, disappearing into the shadows of the hallway. Kyle hoped Armando was awake and ready. He kicked the door in with the heel of his boot and stepped into the living room, his weapon trained on anything that moved. Armando stepped up next to him. His teammate was weaving.

Kyle went to fish out his other 9mm, but Armando held up the captor's weapon.

"You okay?"

"Fucked, man, but I can do this blindfolded."

It felt good to hear Armando's voice after all this time.

Another hail of automatic rounds pierced the air, sending little explosions along the walls, shattering the window glass. Armando and Kyle pressed themselves to the floor until the firestorm subsided, then leapt through the doorway and swung an arc of fire across the room, cutting one man down but pinning the other one behind the kitchen counter. Armando was going to blast through the cabinets.

But that wasn't the real problem.

"Hey, asshole," came the familiar voice of Deputy Hilber behind Kyle.

Kyle turned and saw Hilber in his shorts and a T-shirt, barefoot, gingerly stepping across debris from the gunfight. He had Christy in a chokehold and had an automatic aimed at her temple. She was barely able to keep upright, Kyle saw. Her feet were slipping on pieces of door, furniture, and sheetrock as she and Hilber made their shaky path from the doorway into the living room.

Kyle and Armando lowered their weapons, but didn't let them drop.

"Aquí, aquí," Hilber said to the gunman behind the counter, pointing to Armando and Kyle with his forehead.

The two SEALs were disarmed. Kyle's gaze flew back and forth between Christy and Hilber. He and Armando spread out from each other, then slowly raised their hands and placed them behind their heads as they'd been instructed. They continued to turn toward Hilber and spread apart further. Kyle was slightly forward. Armando was closer to the other gunman, backing into the kitchen area.

"Not so fast, gentlemen. Stop right there." Hilber was having a hard time with Christy's balance. She was leaning into him, trying to get her footing on the uneven floor.

Christy's eyes were not wild and unfocused. She was trying to tell him something, but Kyle couldn't get it.

He looked at Armando, who twitched the left side of his lip. The gunman in the corner looked like he was about to pee in his pants. He was mumbling something Kyle couldn't understand, but Armando whispered a terse sentence back at him in Spanish, which made the man flinch and aim his weapon on him.

"I said knock it off, *a-mee-gos*. Or she gets it. *Com-pren-day*?" Hilber shouted. He looked ridiculous in his shorts. His one eye had taken a blow and was nearly swollen shut, but his good eye was darting all over the room, looking for danger in every corner. "Ever try talking to a bunch of Mexicans without their leader? No offense." He nodded to Armando.

"I'm Puerto Rican," Armando shot back.

Christy was still having difficulty balancing. Kyle watched her feet and ankles twisting over the debris.

"Will you fucking stop with the wiggling?" Hilber screamed at her and bent her backward. Kyle knew Hilber was past his breaking point and was highly dangerous. A sudden jerk could set his trigger finger askew and Christy's head would explode.

Christy's expression got wide, she was damn scared. Her gaze clung to him like he was her lifeline. She wouldn't take her eyes off him.

She glanced down quickly and then right back up to Kyle's face in a deliberate attempt to send him a message. That's when it hit him. He watched in slow motion as she fumbled to balance herself on one foot. One long black leg bent at the knee and rose up slowly. He knew what was coming next. He hoped Armando was ready because they were going to go on her mark.

Christy jammed her heel back into the fleshy portion on the inside of Hilber's right thigh. At least three inches of the deadly weapon ripped and tore away at his skin. The deputy screamed. Blood spurted across the room from Hilber's severed femoral artery.

Armando hit the other gunman with a roundhouse kick to the nose. The man's weapons clattered to the ground like pickup sticks.

He was dead before he landed on top.

The outside door burst open and a herd of hefty gray-hairs stormed in like elephants in musth. Guns drawn. Flack jackets flapping, unable to be fastened at the sides. Kyle was going to train his weapon on them when he heard Fredo's voice. "Hold it, Kyle. Friendlies."

Kyle was never so happy to see a bunch of overweight retirees in his life, even though one of them swore at having missed the chance to fire a weapon.

Cooper looked between Kyle, Armando, and Christy, and then kneeled to examine Hilber, who was trying to stop the bleeding by holding onto his thigh, but to no avail.

Gunny was there too. "Let the sonofabitch bleed out," he said to Cooper's arched back.

"Can't do that," Cooper answered. He quickly fashioned a tourniquet from his medic kit and the spurting stopped in mere seconds.

Christy stood in the middle of the carnage, still trying to get her balance. Her dainty pink toes were exposed on her right foot, her left still wore the stiletto. Kyle swept her up in his arms and took her to a corner, where he consumed every inch of her body he could touch with kisses.

Sirens were blaring outside as the younger version of the elephant squad arrived in full battle gear. Everyone silently began checking the dead, whispering among themselves. There was a lot of nodding of heads as whispers were passed around from man to man.

Kyle and Armando shook every hand that was outstretched. Armando made some comment about it feeling like an election, with the slapping on the back and the "Well done, sons," going around.

"Privilege, kid."

"It's an honor."

"Glad we could help out."

"Nothin' else to do," was Gunny's response.

Kyle grabbed the man and gave him a bear hug. The four Team brothers locked shoulders in a circle and looked to each other without uttering a word.

Damn good to be alive.

Just as quickly as the circle formed, they dropped their arms and stepped away, all of them focused on a spot behind Kyle's back. Kyle turned and saw Christy come up to the group. She slipped into the circle next to Kyle and wrapped her arms around his waist. And they let her stand there.

Just like one of the guys. Kyle was so proud of her.

"Now you're an honorary member of SEAL Team 3," Kyle said.

She threw her head back and giggled. "Yes! Accidentally."

CHAPTER 41

CHRISTY STUDIED THEIR faces. These were her new brothers. She was not their equal in any way, but these were brothers who would have sacrificed their lives for her. It was a family of brothers unlike any other family she had ever known or had heard about.

"Thank you?" Her expression came out like a question and she cursed to herself. "I really don't know exactly what to say. I'm so grateful to all of you."

"Oh, it's okay, missy," Fredo said. "Kyle has that effect on women all the time, don't you, studly?" Fredo winked at Kyle and got the finger for it.

"Sorry," Kyle whispered to the top of her head.

She answered him by clutching his body closer to hers. He chuckled and looked back down into her eyes. Their shared reverie was interrupted by groans coming from the other SEALs. But Gunny was grinning like he'd found a million dollars. Kyle shrugged.

Fredo announced they were getting out of the battle zone.

Kyle pulled Christy alongside him as they walked past the squads. There were smiles all around.

Christy heard Fredo shout out, "Kyle, for Chrissakes, would you two get a room?"

More bitching and comments bounced off the walls. The four

SEALs had their swagger back. Christy knew tonight they'd be celebrating—without Kyle, of course. She had plans of her own.

They loaded up in the Tahoe, Kyle pulling Christy into the third seat for some privacy. Christy felt her skin tingle as his thigh brushed against hers. He slipped his hand under her top and squeezed her breasts one at a time.

"Satin. Red satin," he whispered.

"What? What are you talking about?" she asked. But he covered her mouth and flicked his tongue over her teeth.

When he pulled away, he whispered, "You once asked me what kind of underwear I liked. I like you in red satin." One hand was finding its way down the front of her pants. She closed her eyes when his fingers rubbed over her nub and sought entry along the lacy opening at the top of her thigh.

When she opened her eyes, Fredo's chin was resting on his two fists stacked on the back of the second seat. He had a very intimate view of what Kyle was doing, and wasn't afraid to watch. Kyle hadn't seen him.

Yet.

"Do your nipples get hard when he does that? I've just always wanted to know, from a woman's perspective," Fredo asked with a clinical air. The Team guys burst into laughter.

Kyle raised his head and pushed Fredo so hard he almost slid off the bench seat.

Christy watched Kyle lean back, stretch, and look up to the headliner of the van. "We've got all night," she whispered to the side of his face. "And your presence is required the whole time." She smiled and saw her smile returned.

Gunny and Kyle shared a conspiratorial wink via the rear view mirror. They had something up their sleeve.

And Christy could hardly wait.

"Don't know what it is, fellas. He gets kidnapped, he gets us running all over California looking for him, and he gets the girl. Armando, you got kidnapped and beat up real good too. Where's your woman?" Fredo was merciless.

Armando flashed a big white smile behind to Kyle. They hand slapped their greeting.

"Yeah, thanks, man." Armando cocked his head. "I'm hoping Kyle will introduce me here to her cute sister."

The others chimed in, complaining about the lack of an introduction.

"Christy, this is the group. Fellas, this is Christy." Kyle pointed. "This one is Cooper. We call him Coop. He hangs out at the beach a lot when we're home."

Christy nodded her head to Cooper.

"He brings his bedroom with him so he's always ready," Fredo added.

More laughter. Christy didn't understand the statement and squinted.

"I'll explain it to you later, baby," Kyle said and kissed the side of her face. "This one, of course, is Armando. Saved my bones in BUD/S. Strongest swimmer on the team too. And, as he's already told you, he's from Puerto Rico."

"Nice to meet you, Armando," she said.

"Nah, man. The pleasure is all mine."

Armando could have easily been a cover model, or soap opera star, once his black and blue parts healed. His quiet demeanor and brilliant smile probably stole hearts on a regular basis, she thought.

"Wish I had a sister. But sadly, I'm the only one," she said.

"That you are, my dear. That you are." Kyle planted a long, languid kiss up the side of her neck, ending the kiss in her ear. "And I'm going to kiss every inch of you tonight," he whispered, but his words weren't exactly out of earshot.

She felt her cheeks flush as she watched the envious faces of Cooper, Armando, and Fredo. Even Gunny was watching in the mirror again.

The space between her legs ached and she was so ready to let Kyle do whatever it was he had in mind. As often as he had it in mind. "I'm going to hold you to that promise," she said as she winked at Armando. She tapped Kyle's lower lip with her forefinger and he sucked it into his mouth.

"So I'm the invisible Mexican now?" Fredo shouted. "No respect. This discrimination thing sucks, man. Really sucks."

"Christy, this is Fredo."

Fredo took her hand and, just like in a historical romance, brought it to his lips. "Alphonso Manuel Esquidido Chavez, mi lady."

"Whoa. Alphonso?" Cooper teased. "All this time I never knew that was your fuckin' name, man."

"You didn't ask nice," Fredo answered.

Everyone left Christy and Kyle alone again.

"What's the plan?" she whispered to Kyle's lips.

"Shower and bed. In that order."

"And then?"

"We'll see. We'll have to talk, Christy." He drew her to his chest. She could hear his heartbeat, at last.

CHAPTER 42

G UNNY DROPPED THEM off at a boutique hotel near the Ferry Building. The rest of the guys were staying elsewhere. Disappearing, Christy thought.

The familiar ache in her stomach came back, just like the first night she and Kyle had stayed up nearly the whole night. Talking. Kissing. Making love. Until they both had fallen asleep, exhausted, entangled in sheets. Entangled in each other's legs and arms.

At breakfast that first morning, she'd known her body was tired and that she had gotten so little sleep. But she'd willed herself to enjoy every minute in his presence. Just like today. She urgently needed a hot shower and then to feel Kyle's hard body on hers.

She walked barefoot onto the plush flower patterned carpet of the hotel lobby, holding her remaining patent leather stiletto. It garnered some worried looks, but she was beyond caring. She wondered why she'd even brought the darned thing along. Kyle had his backpack and duffel bag slung over his right shoulder.

Gunny had made the arrangements, Kyle told her. He was very tight-lipped about what he knew, if anything. The front desk clerk asked if they needed help with their luggage and they both laughed. If the clerk only knew what the bags contained: enough firepower to start a war. Arm in arm, they walked down the hallway to the elevators. Kyle was deliberately slow and Christy found herself dragging him a slight bit. He wasn't hesitant in any way. He was teasing her, looking at her with that crooked grin that hinted of things to come.

She walked backward, towing him, watching the way his beautiful body moved lithely at her command. At her beck and call. She blushed as she thought about what they would be doing shortly. Loving Kyle Lansdowne was way more than sex.

It was an art form.

"Remember that elevator ride from the model that first day?" she asked as she punched the elevator call button. The doors opened immediately.

Once inside, Kyle inserted the gold plastic room card above the bank of numbers on the elevator menu, and immediately the doors closed. "Of course I do." His eyes swept up her body. He owned her. She wanted him to see it, and he did. He stepped to her and pressed her back against the walls of the humming elevator box, clutching her hands above her head, rubbing his erection against her thigh. They kissed, Kyle teasing her lips open, his need mingling with hers.

The doors pinged open and they found themselves in a mini anteroom. Its large windows framed breathtaking views of the pier and the San Francisco Bay. The glassy sparkle of cities across the bay shot up from the horizon like copper crystals.

Only one set of double doors lead off of this reception area. Kyle put his key in the slot. Christy heard it click, and the doors were opened to a warm room done in peach tones with equally stunning views of the bay, the bridges, and beyond. On one end, a mirror hung above a gas-fired fireplace, fully flaming. On the other side, sitting atop a raised dais, was the largest bed Christy had ever seen. It was covered in a thick comforter of shiny rose pink satin and lace, littered with red rose petals and a smattering of multicolored silk pillows.

"Did you…" She couldn't get the question finished. His mouth was covering hers again, and she melted into his arms.

Kyle's hands found her flesh underneath her red top. He kneeled in front of her and pushed up the fabric to kiss her lower abdomen. His fingers kneaded her vertebrae at the back of her waist and then smoothed over her ass, finishing with a squeeze. He hugged her body, kissing and licking her belly button, making a wet trail with his tongue that went lower. He slid his palms down over her hips, hooking her black pants and panties along the way as he peeled her clothes down to her ankles.

She removed her top, tossing it aside, and stood before him, wearing only the expensive satin bra. She pulled his shirt up and over his shoulders and head. His fingers found the empty spot between her legs that needed to be filled. He slowly caressed the lips of her sex. Looking up into her eyes, he pressed two fingers inside her.

Christy melted, enjoying the sensation of being impaled by his fingers, which moved in a gentle rhythm. Practiced. Confident. Fingers she wanted all over her body.

She knelt down and joined him, leaning forward. She felt his chest against hers as flesh met flesh again. He hugged her tight, pressing her breasts against him.

Kyle's belt was undone. She quickly slid his pants down to his knees and placed her palms on his shaft, lacing his length with her fingers. They held each other while blending in a deep kiss that sent her spine tingling. His stiff cock got in the way.

"Will you bathe me?" she asked.

"With pleasure."

Kyle stood, bringing her up with him, and stepped out of his pants. They leaned against each other, fully naked. The honest look in his eyes told her she would remember this afternoon forever. There was nothing to run from anymore, and everything to savor and walk toward.

The bathroom was done in rich chocolate brown marble. Floors, walls, the massive roman tub and stall shower with dual heads were covered in the heavily veined stone. She entered the shower and turned on one spigot. Kyle took the other.

Under the warm water cascading over her body, she watched his muscled torso and his strong and thickly muscled thighs move under the steamy spray. His forearm with the little three-legged tattoo flexed as he poured shower gel into the palm of his hand and smoothed it down over his torso, and then lower to massage his thighs. He handed the plastic tube of gel to her.

She touched the tattoo. "What is this?"

"It's the footprints of a tree frog. Everyone on the Team has them."

She bent and kissed each footprint, one by one. Then she reached up and covered his mouth with hers. "I thought you were a SEAL." She fed from his mouth. His hands massaged her rear. His groan was delicious and made her spine tingle.

"We are. It's just what we do," he whispered in return.

"Well, sailor. What else do you do?"

"I do it all. Anything you like. For as long as you like."

She leaned back. His eyes roved over her hands as she massaged the soapy bubbled mixture over her breasts. She squeezed them together, then flicked her nipples. He licked his lips as his full erection lurched. Her hands traveled up around her neck, over her shoulders and down each arm, one at a time. She applied another generous dollop to her palm and rubbed her thighs with the gel, and then let her fingers play in and over her sex.

He was completely still as he watched her sluice her body with warm rinse water. She poured shampoo in the palm of her right hand and worked the suds through her scalp. He was fixated on her breasts that rose, her elbows above her head. She closed her eyes and let the warm spray cover her crown, working all the shampoo out of her hair. Kyle's hands were at her knees, gently prodding them to part. She looked down and saw he had kneeled, his mouth enveloped her sex, sucking and licking her slick petals. His hot tongue sliced a wedge between her lips and then found its way inside.

Her fingers curled in his hair as he ministered to her sex, lighting her whole body on fire. One of Kyle's palms was gently grazing her right thigh. The other hand pushed her lower torso onto his tongue, which swirled around her nub. She jumped with the burst of sensation. She felt his teeth rub against the flesh of her sex, pushing against her pubic bone. He pulled back, spread her lips with his fingers, and looked at her there.

When their eyes met, she saw the deep hunger he had for her. She cupped her hands under his jaw and drew him up to kiss him, giving him her tongue, tasting the juices of her own body on his lips.

He broke free. "God, Christy," he whispered in her ear. "I can't get enough of you. I don't want this to ever end."

She touched his cock, then wrapped her fingers around it and squeezed. She rubbed the lips of her sex against his thigh as their passion bloomed. He kissed the side of her neck, from the hollow of her shoulder to a place just under her ear.

She could spend eternity with him in the shower, until their skin withered away and their bones creaked. But she was listening for three little words. And she wasn't going to give up until she heard them.

"Tell me again." She smiled and squeezed his left nipple.

"I don't ever want this to end."

"Nor do I. Tell me again."

Kyle halted his massaging. With the warm water coursing down between both their bodies, he looked into her eyes. He pressed his hands over her cheeks, clutching her head, rubbing his thumbs over her lips. He pulled her to his mouth and kissed her tenderly. And then he looked at her again.

"I love you."

And there it was.

Her eyes filled with tears.

He kissed one eye, and then the other. "I love you, Christy," he whispered again. "I love you."

"And I have loved you, Kyle Lansdowne, ever since you tied me up and lay on top of me. I belonged to you that first day and always will."

CHRISTY DRIED OFF first, then ran to the bed and fell back among the rose petals. The plush satin coverlet was delicious under her warm, steamy flesh. She propped her head up with a light green pillow, put another under her rear, and raised one knee.

Kyle was there with something in his right hand. His fingers wrapped around her ankle as he raised her leg into the air. He kneeled on the bed and placed the black stiletto on her foot. He traced from her ankle down the inside of her leg until the finger teased the outsides of her lips. She needed that finger plunged deep inside her, but he smiled and rimmed her opening and around her nub in a figure-eight motion.

Christy was dripping wet. She could feel her internal muscles working in vain to try to draw his digit in. With his left hand and finger strategically left between her legs, he turned and kissed her ankle, holding her stiletto-clad foot around the ankle with a hand.

He kissed her twice on the backside of her knee, then once on the front. He guided her leg to bend over his shoulder. Christy was careful not to hurt him with the pointed tip, but then she forgot about it when he inserted his finger a mere half-inch. She was insane with desire for more.

Her pleading look generated a smile and he inserted another finger into her wet opening. He kissed her thigh, then lower toward her sex, and just before his tongue touched her lips, his two fingers slid easily to the hilt. She arched, presenting herself to him. She needed to be tasted. Needed him inside her.

Christy writhed on the bed as he played with her, as he slid the surface of his tongue up and down her opening, around her folds, and tasted her. Every time she opened her eyes he was looking at her, needing to see her passion.

"I need you inside me, please."

"Yes. Soon, Christy. I need to make sure you are ready."

"I'm ready now."

"Yes, soon. Before exertion you must loosen and warm your body up."

"I'm loose. I'm warm. Trust me, Kyle, I'm ready."

"Are you sure?" He plunged his tongue deeper.

"God, yes!" She grabbed pillows and squeezed them to her chest.

"No, no. You don't get to cover up. I must see those. I may need to taste them, too." He pulled the pillows away and shoved them under her rear. Her pelvis was now lifted off the bed. She clutched the satin coverlet at her sides, drunk with need.

"And something else," he whispered as he kissed her belly button. He climbed up over to the head of the bed. Under one of the satin pillows was a one-inch wide red satin ribbon. He held it up in front of her face, waving it back and forth.

"What are you doing?" she asked.

He smirked, grabbed hold of both her hands with one of his, and lay them gently up over her head. He wound the red ribbon around her wrists in a loose figure eight. Christy felt like she was going to explode inside.

"Please. Please," she begged.

"Yes. You like this?"

"Yes. I belong to you. All yours. Please, Kyle. Make love to me."

"Yes, you are mine. You always will be mine."

"Please. Fill me. I need you."

"Yes."

"I love you, Kyle. Please love me. Please never leave me again."

Kyle climbed over her body, holding his muscled torso with one hand over her, barely touching her flesh. With his other hand he placed her other knee over his shoulder. With her pelvis angled to meet him, he placed the head of his penis at her opening and smiled as she gasped.

"I have no protection."

"You are my protection."

"Are you sure?"

"Completely. You are my protection, Kyle. You are all I need, all I ever will need."

"And you are mine." With that, he thrust deep inside her.

He rocked gently at first, with back and forth motions that sent jolts of pleasure all over her body, radiating from between her legs. She saw his tanned, handsome face, the square jaw and full lips now forming a smile. Her fingers struggled and he gripped her wrists and the ribbon firmly as he plunged in deeper holding her in place, restraining her body, possessing her in every way possible.

"Love you," she whispered.

"Love you," he repeated.

He changed angles, rolling her to the side, repositioning her leg as he fucked her harder. She felt a long orgasm growing and wanted to match his, but couldn't wait. All of a sudden, spasms rocked her body. Her eyes fluttered closed as she arched her back. He used the new angle to plunge in deeper, which was exactly what she wanted, needed. She moaned as he filled her, as he rubbed his thighs against hers, as he pressed a thumb into her nub and watched her lurch.

Everything he did heightened her pleasure. Her orgasm was beginning to fade as he continued to pump her, then he'd stop, change a leg, or an angle and show her a spot he'd missed that sent her over the edge again.

He flipped her over on her belly with one arm as she presented herself to him, her hands out front, bound in the red ribbon.

She begged, "Please."

He first kissed the quivering lips, red-hot and still filled with need. Balancing himself on one knee and arm, he placed himself at her opening. She backed toward him.

He backed away. She turned to look at his eyes. She raised her rear up, over his erect penis, rubbed herself over his head, and laved herself against the delicious feel of his shaft.

And then she pushed herself onto him, moving up and down, back and forth, showing him how much she loved him there. She watched his face as he looked at the place where they joined. She wished she could see where they mated. She wished she could see him thrusting in and out of her.

He stuffed two pillows under her belly, then put two powerful hands on her shoulders and pulled her back onto his length. His movements became frenzied and again her insides began to explode. She moaned as the wave of contractions clamped down on him, milking him, driving him deeper. Just as she was losing the last ounce of control she felt the bonds of her ribbons loosen. All at once he shuddered, and then he moaned as his own spasms matched hers.

She wanted every drop of him.

She would take him all.

Forever. She would never give up loving him.

No matter what.

CHAPTER 43

K YLE FELT LIKE he was floating on a cloud. He wasn't used to it. He'd given himself permission to go over the edge with Christy, to let his guard down. And he knew she would gladly give him anything he asked.

He snuggled against her soft backside as she slept. He'd wrapped them both in the satin spread. Rose petals had gotten caught in her hair when he'd eased the silky surface over her body.

She had tied the satin ribbon around her neck in a bow.

She was smiling in her sleep. Oblivious to the world. Lost in a dream state of her own making. He hoped she was dreaming about him. He was sure daydreaming about her. In fact, he'd gotten hard again mere minutes after he heard her fall off into a deep sleep. He decided if she moved a muscle in his direction, he'd have his lovely way with her again. Her fingers would find him. Her legs would rub against his thighs and send him soaring.

He'd untie the ribbon and watch her come.

He'd never told a woman he loved her. But he'd told Christy several times this evening. And he couldn't wait to do it again. He kissed the back of her neck and pulled her into his chest again.

Please wake so I can have you again.

Two hours later, twilight had turned to darkness. Kyle was starved. Christy was now resting on his chest. After the second lovemaking, he had finally fallen asleep. And now he was enveloped in the scent of the lavender gel shampoo that lingered in her still-damp hair. The pillows were all over the room. He looked down her body, draped over his. She'd tucked his thigh between both of hers, as if she was making sure he wasn't going to leave.

No, he would never leave her. If she asked him, he would leave the SEALs. He never thought he'd say that. It would be a difficult choice. But his place was at her side now. Perhaps his days of running into and through trouble were over. Maybe he could join the ranks of the good cops like Mayfield. There was honor in that. Leave the Teams for the younger ones coming up from BUD/S. Give them a chance to show what they're made of.

It was strange to even think about leaving the Navy, though. He'd never thought anything but the Navy was his family. But now there was Christy. And she was his life. She had to be a part of his life, for however long that was. And women didn't like to be second best to anything. Not the military, not to duty, not to honor. They had to come first. And then there might be kids. Kids need a dad. Not some father who was vacant like his dad had been. He wouldn't do that to a kid.

Especially not his kid.

There she was again. Arching her body against him, squeezing his thigh high up against her wet sex. The little things she did to show him she was interested were such an unexpected thrill. He looked forward to learning all about the ways it would take to turn her on, keep her satisfied, and keep her wanting more. And the more he gave, the more he wanted to give.

And the more he had something to lose.

There were those fingers again, strumming the flesh around his left nipple. If he opened his eyes, she'd be kissing him in seconds. He'd be spilling his seed inside her in no time. It was just about the only thing he could think about.

"I know you're awake, Kyle," she whispered.

He let his lips tell her she was right as he allowed a smile to form. Sure enough, she was up and over him. She'd migrated her knee to over his lower abdomen, grazing his shaft that was standing at full attention. He loved the chance encounter with her soft flesh, no matter how brief.

He watched her wrap the satin ribbon around his left wrist. She was on her way to obtaining his other one.

"So you don't want me to use my hands, then?" he said as he watched his words register. While she considered her options.

She halted, and then removed the ribbon and tossed it off the bed.

She lowered herself on his legs and licked the length of his shaft. She sucked hard, and then licked the long length of him. Was this round three or four?

Did it matter?

He lay there and enjoyed her wanting to pleasure him. After only a few minutes, he was hard as a rock and about to come in her mouth as she moved up and down his length. He loved watching her mouth work him over. She flashed her big brown eyes up at him.

Ah, delicious. She was a wonder, all right. Long curls falling all over his thighs, those honest eyes that begged him to fuck her. Well, he'd deliver on that request as many times as she asked it of him. Happy to oblige, in fact.

She mounted him, slowly settling down on his cock, and was arching backward, holding her breasts, tweaking her nipples. Her eyes flashed open when he raised his pelvis up, placing a couple of pillows under his butt. It gave her a higher mount so she could ride him. And ride him she did.

He pushed himself deep inside her and she quivered, moaned. She held her hair up with her hands, letting it fall partially over her eyes as she looked at him. She turned in profile. He followed the line of her perfect torso and filled his hands with soft pillows of flesh. She licked her lips slowly and he lost it. Next thing he knew he was shooting inside her like a seventeen-year-old.

The woman was going to wear him out.

And he was going to love every minute of it.

CHRISTY LAY NEXT to Kyle. Both stared at the ceiling. She was enjoying the sounds of his heavy breathing. He laced his fingers through hers and kissed her hand.

"Are you hungry?" he asked.

Christy hadn't thought about it until just then, but she was. "Famished. Let's go walk some place close by."

"I was hoping you'd say that." He turned his head. She felt his stare on the side of her face. He raised himself up on one arm, outlining her nipples with a forefinger. He kissed her first on one side, and then the other. She couldn't escape those blue eyes softly bearing down on hers. "Christy, I'm thinking about leaving the Navy when my time is up this fall."

"Why?" His statement surprised her.

"Maybe it's time I grow up. I've been blowing things up, snatching and grabbing bad guys. Playing with really cool gear for ten years now. Can't do that forever." He was watching her reaction.

"But it's who you are, Kyle. Don't you love what you do?"

"Absolutely." He lay back on the bed and sighed. They lay in silence, Kyle's warm thigh against hers, as if they'd been doing this for years. As if it were a routine, the talking and then the lovemaking, and then the talking and then…it felt like life as it was supposed to be.

"Don't do it for me," she said finally. "I don't want to be the one responsible for taking you away from something that means so much. I love you for who you are. And who you are, right now at least, is a SEAL. You were born to be one. I want you to do what you love. And I'll be here when you come home."

She turned her head and saw he'd been watching her. Something deep in his eyes held her. It was devotion. She'd never seen anyone look at her that way before.

"If it wasn't for me, what would you do?" she asked.

"I'd stay in."

"Then that's what you should—no, that's what I *want* you to do."

THEY WALKED THROUGH the shops at Ferry Plaza, tasting wine, olive oil, and homemade chocolates along the way. Her feet were cold in the flip-flops he'd bought her in the lobby shop. Christy wanted to go to the oyster bar overlooking the Marin Ferry. They stayed inside and watched the twinkle of lights from the Bay Bridge reflected in the choppy waters of the Bay. She ordered a plate with three local varieties of oysters. They came smothered in garlic and simmering in butter.

Fog was beginning to roll in on the bay, covering the tips of the bridge arching high overhead, but the pier was still clear, and would be for another hour.

"Oysters are supposed to help your stamina," Christy said.

"You find something wrong with my stamina?" Kyle asked. He had butter and a piece of garlic stuck to his upper lip. She kissed it off.

"No. Not at all." She laughed. "I think perhaps *I* need it."

He curled his forefinger, motioning her to lean closer to him. "You are perfect just the way you are." He kissed her.

Christy glowed inside. The man could charm the pants off a...an oyster.

"So you like oysters?" she continued.

"I like eating anything around you. Everything tastes great."

With his fingers, he placed a stray lock of hair behind her left ear, and then held up her chin for another long kiss. His palm slid down her arm, over the fabric of her oversized San Francisco souvenir sweatshirt that matched his.

"And everything is good around you," he said in a raspy, dead-sexy bedroom voice.

She turned her stool and let his knee hit her pubic bone. She locked him there. "You know what I'm thinking?" she asked.

"I'm afraid to ask."

"Well, you've had your fortification. So, how many more times can we do it before midnight?"

"I should be good for one or two...but first I wanna have a little talk with you."

His face got serious. Christy held her breath. Every time there was a "serious" talk before, it had been bad news. Now what? Had their earlier discussion set off a chain of events that was now going to hurt?

Kyle fished something out of his San Francisco sweatshirt pocket.

He got down on one knee, and in front of the whole group of oyster-loving, beer drinking customers, held her left hand and said, "Christy Nelson. Would you marry me?"

Did he just ask me to marry him? She hadn't allowed herself to long for a proposal of marriage. She'd been planning on enjoying what was to come as long as he was there by her side.

"Absolutely," she answered. She couldn't believe it.

He put the ring on her finger.

The crowd took note of the proposal and burst into spontaneous clapping.

She looked at the costume jewelry ring he must have purchased at the hotel. It was the most beautiful stone she had ever seen, and it mattered not one whit that it wasn't real.

Her man was.

*   *   *

Here's an excerpt from Sharon's latest book, SEALed Forever, Book 3 in the Bone Frog Brotherhood, which releases 4-16-19. It's available to order here.

sharonhamiltonauthor.com/sealed-forever

Here's the first chapter for your reading pleasure!

Chapter 1 excerpt, SEALed Forever, Book 3 of the Bone Frog Brotherhood Series:

N AVY SEAL TUCKER Hudson squinted across the beach bonfire that roared taller than any of the men on his SEAL Team 3. He was back—at least in all the ways he could be. He was now forty years of age—a retread. He'd survived the landmines of past deployments, the vacancy of those years off the teams, as well as the grueling BUD/S training re-qualifying for his spot. He was ready for his first mission as a new *silver* SEAL, as the ladies called him. He was a Bone Frog, one of the old guys on SEAL Team 3.

He was ready for the do-over. Told himself he deserved it. But just to add a little gasoline to the fire in his soul, his childhood best friend, Brawley Hanks, was failing. And that's what ate at him.

Brawley had just spent six months in rehab while Tucker completed his SQT, SEAL Qualification Training. His Chief, Kyle Lansdowne, had misgivings about allowing Brawley to go on the next mission to Africa, but since Tucker would be there, he'd overruled a suggestion from higher up to sit him out. This didn't help Tucker's nerves any.

He knew it was his job to cover all that up and make those jitters disappear.

He watched the ladies dancing around the bonfire and looked for his wife of two months. Brandy cooed over Dorie and Brawley's little pink daughter while Dorie showed her off. The toddler was fast asleep. Several of the Team's kids jumped to get a look at the child until Dorie knelt and let them stand in a circle and check her out.

Their particular SEAL platoon tradition made them gather at the beach before a new deployment. All the wives, the kids, the close girlfriends and occasionally parents were there. But only those on the inside, in the know. Some had lost loved ones. Some had been injured. Some had suffered too much. But these were the people who held them all together—who would hold Brandy together while he was gone.

The past two years with Brandy had been the hardest but most rewarding years of his life. When he was a younger SEAL, sometimes the ladies made him nervous since he didn't have anyone to come home to. But now that he did, now that he could actually lose something dear to him, it made this little celebration all the more special. He'd missed those evenings under the stars in Coronado, surrounded by life and the promise of living forever.

No one would understand this kind of SEAL brotherhood, Tucker thought. You had to live it to know how it felt to be part of this family. You had to cry and celebrate with these people, tell them things would turn out, somehow. The miraculous would happen, because it always did. That's who they were. There wasn't any other group in the whole world he'd rather be a part of, and he'd tried doing without before. He knew better.

Tucker studied the beautiful, round face of his new bride, and all her other curves that enticingly called to him by firelight. It seemed she grew more and more stunning every day. Her eyes met his, and he glanced down quickly, embarrassed that he might look like a teenage boy. But that's the way he felt. He was back to being the big quiet kid the Homecoming Queen or head cheerleader came over to tease. It used to happen a lot in high school and he'd never gotten used to it.

Chief Petty Officer Kyle Lansdowne took up a seat next to him. His Chief was the most respected man on the team, even more than some of the officers, who were never invited to these events. Kyle had worked hard to make sure Tucker came to his squad. Although slightly younger than Tucker or Brawley, Kyle's experience leading successful campaigns through sticky assignments made him one of Team 3's most valuable assets.

"You nervous?" his LPO asked.

"You asked me that the day of my wedding, remember?"

Kyle nodded.

"I was nervous then." Tucker took a pull on his long-necked beer. "I know what I'm getting into this time." He smiled, which was reflected back to him.

"Well, you know what they say about leading men. Don't ask a question you don't know the answer to first." Kyle clinked his bottle against Tucker's.

They both watched the children fawning over Brawley's daughter, still sleeping by the firelight, tucked in Dorie's arms. Kyle's two were right in the middle of them. Brandy gave Tucker a sexy wave.

"You got a good one, Tucker. I'm really happy for you," Kyle whispered, continuing to follow the ladies.

"You bet I did." Tucker meant every word he uttered. He'd always liked women he could grab onto and squeeze without breaking half her ribs. Brandy had the heart he did and that fierce joy of living, which also matched his own. And she'd earned that because of how she'd fought for every ounce of respect she so richly deserved. She spoke her mind. She loved with abandon, and he was damned lucky to have her in his corner. He was also grateful she let him go off and be a warrior again, just when most friends his age had wives ragged on them to quit.

And that was okay too. The SEAL teams were a revolving door of fresh and old faces, and internal dramas played out every day all over the world. It was sometimes hardest on the families. Men had to consider all of that when they played Varsity.

Kyle searched the crowd.

"I haven't seen him in about twenty minutes," Tucker mumbled. It worried him, too, that Brawley wasn't nearby. "I think he might have gone to get more beer, but that's just a rumor."

He knew Kyle suspected he was making up a safe story, which is why he didn't say a word. Then his Chief slowly turned, facing him. "You let me know if he gets shaky, and I thoroughly suspect he will." Kyle's voice was low, avoiding anyone else's ears.

The two men stared at each other for a few long seconds.

"I got it, Kyle. He's not on his own."

"And you only risk a little. Don't let that go over the edge."

"We don't leave men behind." Tucker knew Kyle understood what he meant.

"No, we don't. I want you both upright. Both of you, Tucker."

"Roger that."

They gripped hands. Then Kyle broke it off and punched him in the arm.

"Dayam, Tucker. You can stop drinking those protein shakes anytime now."

Tucker liked that thought but dished some trash talk back. "Lannie, it ain't protein shakes. It's her," he said, aiming his beer bottle at

Brandy. "You should see how she works me out."

Kyle stood up and then murmured, "I can't unsee that, dammit," and disappeared into the crowd.

Tucker hoped Brawley would show himself soon. His "ghosting" wasn't a good sign. He should be at Dorie's side. Tucker kept searching and then finally spotted Brawley pissing into the surf, which meant he was drunker than he should be.

Come on, Brawley. You're gonna get us both killed.

Brandy was still occupied with the women, and Kyle was having a little nuzzle time with Christy while carrying one of his two on his shoulders. Tucker scrambled to his feet and strolled toward his best friend, who was now throwing rocks into the ocean. His jeans were wet, and he was barefoot.

Brawley Hanks grew up alongside Tucker's family in Oregon. He couldn't ever remember a time when they weren't best friends. Always competitors when it came to sports and girls, even enlisting in the Navy the same day, they attended the same BUD/S class. They'd planned on getting out after their ten years, but close to the end, Brawley met Dorie, and, well, the poor guy couldn't help himself and got hitched up. She had pushed for the re-signing bonus so they could buy a nice house in Coronado. A beautiful, classy girl with all the wildness Brawley had, Dorie was missing his self-destructive bend.

Tucker wondered at first if their marriage would survive, but as Brawley showed all the signs of getting seriously embroiled in a lusty kind of full-tilt love that made him go stupid and do dumb things like buy flowers, he became convinced his friend had finally been tamed and had given up his wandering ways.

Except that after his last two deployments, Brawley was back to being the bad boy he'd always been before he met Dorie. He drank and chased too much. And although they had high hopes for his rehab, he wasn't as convinced as Brandy or Dorie that his bad days were behind him.

"Hit any fish yet?" he asked Brawley.

"Fuck no," Hanks replied, slurring his words and letting go of another smooth, flat stone. It didn't skip like he'd been aiming to do.

"You know the more you hit the ocean, that ocean is gonna get you back, Brawley."

"I'm registering my complaint."

Tucker had to proceed with caution. He was at one of those turning points. But if Brawley lost it, at least he'd lose it here and save Kyle the trouble of having him sent home in shame. It sucked to be thinking this way just a day from deployment, but it was what it was. No sense sugar-coating it.

"I think your registration is going to the wrong department. Got your branches of service mixed up, Brawley. You should take it up with the man upstairs. Have you had that conversation recently?"

Brawley squinted back at him, as if the moonlight hurt his eyes. He did look like a big teenager, albeit a lethal one.

"I wear the Trident. Poseidon and Davy Jones are my buds. The man upstairs has given up on me."

His challenge hit Tucker in his stomach. *You dumb fuck. Where are you goin?*

He walked to within inches of Brawley's hulking form. Inhaling deeply, he worked to calm himself down so it would be effective. He knew he only could say this once, so he made sure Brawley didn't misunderstand his steely stare.

"I'm going to remind you that you just brought a daughter into the world. What kind of a world do you want her to grow up in, you old fart? You want her to grow up with an angry son-of-a-bitch for a father, like you did, Brawley?"

His best friend started to interrupt him, and Tucker grabbed his ears and spit out his message.

"Or were you thinkin' you'd check out over there in that shit African red clay, making Dorie a widow and your daughter fatherless? Maybe causing the death of one or more of your friends who have pledged their lives to save your dumb ass. You willing to take us all with you? You want to be that kind of best friend to me, Brawley? Or, are you gonna man-up?"

Tucker released Brawley's ears and pivoted like a Color Guard. He thanked his lucky stars he hadn't gotten clobbered with that delivery and called it good. Whatever Brawley did next was up to him.

It was just something that had to be delivered *before* they left for Africa. After they were there, it would be too late.

Tucker had done all he could.

If you enjoyed that excerpt, you can order your book here.
sharonhamiltonauthor.com/sealed-forever

But Wait!! There's more. Did you know Sharon bundles all her series books so you can enjoy binge reading? And, all these bundled books have audio books (which you can get at a discount if you have the digital copy by some retailers). If you already know you want to read more about the Brotherhood, Sharon's original SEAL series, here's how you can get bundled up!

Ultimate SEAL Collection #1 (Books 1-4 with 2 novellas) Order here.
sharonhamiltonauthor.com/Ultimate1

Ultimate SEAL Collection #2 (3 novels) Order here.
sharonhamiltonauthor.com/Ultimate2

Or, for those of you who just want to read one book at a time, in order, here's the next one. And don't forget to leave a review!

Continue reading the first chapter of the next book in the SEAL Brotherhood Series…

Fallen SEAL Legacy (Book #2) is available here.
sharonhamiltonauthor.com/SEALBro2

Book 2 in the Band of SEAL Brotherhood Series: Fallen SEAL Legacy

CHAPTER 1

A TORNADO SCRAPED the Nebraska landscape with deadly force, tasting contents of houses and farms, furrowing down fence posts and over pencil-thin crop rows like a tongue from Hell. It seemed to like the flavor of metal and sheetrock as well as the tender green stalks of corn, sunflowers and soybeans. Human and animal body parts spewed out to the sides, detritus from a bored gourmand.

Sirens wailed in the distance. The steamy ground hissed in response.

SPECIAL OPERATOR CALVIN "Coop" Cooper awoke and smelled cherries mixed with crisp morning sea air. He heard running water and then felt the steam, which had filled the entire motor home.

Daisy. In the shower. Slippery and soapy all over.

She'd spent the night in his love cave, which was usually parked by the beach. What a night it had been. He still wore a handcuff that dangled from his left wrist. Only Daisy had the key. He chuckled to himself.

His other SEAL Team buddies called his place the *Babemobile*. They could call it anything they liked, he thought. Coop was saving a ton of money by pocketing his housing allowance.

He'd have been pissed if it was one of his Team buddies using up all his propane taking a hot shower. But for Daisy he allowed the indulgence, since her qualities and talents made it so worth it. Besides, it was one of the greatest places to fuck. Maybe...

Coop scratched above his forehead as the handcuffs jangled and then slapped against his ear. His sparse light brown hair left his fingers sticky. And smelling of cherries.

That would be the gel she used on me last night. The gel I used on her, all over.

Daisy did have a job to get ready for, and God, yes, they *both* needed a shower.

Coop rolled over and placed his palms behind his head, disentangling the sweaty sheet from his long six-foot-four-inch frame. It had been a wonderful Coronado Island night. Daisy was the best pleasure partner a guy could want. Totally willing. Totally hot. She'd brought her costume bag filled with "cop props" as she liked to call them. She'd arrested him several times last night, and each time he was subjected to fierce interrogation which usually made her wind up in compromising positions. He loved her sex play.

"I have a thing for cops," she'd told him one day when she was working on a new tat.

"I'm not a cop," Coop had said.

"But you wear a uniform. I love uniforms, too. Got a whole closet of them."

He could only guess.

Everyone else wanted to bang her, too. But she, temporarily at least, had secretly chosen Coop to share her bed. Or rather, his bed. Daisy never brought anyone to her place. Cooper had occasionally dated other girls, mostly when they threw themselves at him. He wasn't really looking. They just seemed to find him.

Daisy was the one all his SEAL Team 3 buddies hired to do their tattoos. It was odd, with all the places they'd been sent, all the injuries they'd incurred, his buddies would only let one tattoo artist touch their delicate skin. Daisy was the best. In lots of ways.

Coop rubbed his groin, which was getting interested in chasing down the trail of thoughts his brain wandered through.

Down boy.

He usually parked his motor home at the beach, where the owner of the now-defunct trailer park was happy with the fifty bucks Coop gave him each month for his share of the water and power used. But tonight he'd parked in the lot at Costco so they wouldn't have any visitors. No sense having a sweet young thing calling on his door, thinking he was available, and him being kinda busy. Daisy had followed him there so he wouldn't need to take her home. She was a very practical woman.

"Hey baby," Daisy said as she paraded in front of him, sizing up his exposed torso. "We had some fun last night, didn't we?" She put two fingers in her pink-lipped mouth. Those lips would leave a ring, all right. Her makeup was done, and she was wearing one of those kid's tee shirts that showed off the frog tattoo around her belly button, which was pierced with a gold ring glinting in the morning sun. Her shorts were so short, if Coop slipped a hand up her backside, he'd be in clover before he got three inches in.

"You smell good." *You taste good, too.* Cherry wasn't his favorite flavor. He liked the way she tasted all by her little lonesome, he thought as he scanned her many alluring attributes. And he'd told her that one time, just before she exploded in his arms. Telling her things like that worked real well on Daisy. Like some of the girls in high school he had read scriptures to, especially the Love Chapter from 1 Corinthians. Make them hot as hell, and so willing to show it.

Her knees sunk onto the bed and crawled her way up to straddle him. "I'm gonna be late for work if you aren't quick."

By the time he gave his assent, she had already removed her Tee shirt and 38 DDD bra.

JUST BEFORE DAISY left, Coop had to remind her to remove his cuffs. Then, while he waited for the water to warm up again, he sat in his boxers at the nook, chowing down on granola and whole milk. He checked between the metal blinds in the window and watched a couple of early Costco employees arrive. That also meant it was time for him to leave.

His cell phone chirped.

"Coop here." He recognized the number belonging to his Chief Petty Officer Timmons.

"Mornin' Coop. Say, mind if we have a word?"

"Sure. When do you need me in by?"

"How soon can you get here?"

Something was up, and it wasn't good. "Can you tell me a little about it?" Coop asked.

"No, mister. I gotta do this eyeball to eyeball."

Coop hesitated a bit before answering. Timmons hadn't said it involved anyone else, so this wasn't a Team thing. Had someone complained about him parking the Babemobile at the beach? Some jerkoff do-gooder Ranger exerting himself on the community they loved to bust for littering and public drinking? *Only because the girls would rather hang out with me than some overweight guy with a green gabardine scout leader uniform and a chronic case of sunburn.*

"I can be there in a half hour, unless there's a jam-up on the highway."

"See you then, son."

Son? When his Chief called him son, it usually meant he was in trouble. Coop felt dark fingers dig into his spine at the back of his neck. Something wasn't right.

He called Fredo. "Timmons calling a Team meeting this morning?" he asked his Mexican SEAL friend.

"Shit if I know. What'd you do last night, Coop?"

Cooper fingered the vase of fresh flowers in front of him, and shrugged, like Fredo could see it.

Fredo whispered into the phone, "You better pray she's over 18."

"Not to worry, Fredo. I'm heading over there now. You want to meet me afterwards for some PT?"

"Sure, you go have your meeting with Timmons, get your strength back up, cowboy, and I'll kick your ass in a few." Fredo hung up.

He skipped the shower, anxious to find out what Timmons wanted. He doubted his Chief would notice Daisy's smell or the trace of cherry lube gel instead of his usual Irish Spring. If he ran into his Team leader, Kyle Lansdowne, he'd be ordered to get wet and sandy. Old married man Kyle, with a new baby, was a real hard-ass these days. But a damn good SEAL, and the best Team leader a guy could have.

He considered taking his scooter, but decided to drive the Babemobile instead.

He climbed over the bench seat at the nook, inserting his extra-long legs under the wheel of the beast and started her up. Coop had turned the beast into a regular fortress, installing a secret weapons compartment, a sophisticated GPS unit, a satellite tracking system with infrared, and a sound system worthy of a rock star. The entire blackened roof surface of the motor home was a solar collector. He'd rather spend his money on toys than housing, so he spent half of his paycheck on special parts and upgrades for gadgets he was constantly tinkering with. The rest he dutifully saved. Something his dad had taught him growing up on the farm in Nebraska.

Never too early to plan for a rainy day, his dad had always told him.

He opted for the *Gone Country* satellite channel, donned his sunglasses and departed for the check-in.

Coop rounded the corner to the Special Warfare base at Coronado, stopped at the guard shack and addressed the flunky on duty. A new one. Navy Regular. Clean cut. Cooper was thinking he might luck out and get on base without a wisecrack since the guy was new, but had no such luck.

"Well if it isn't the stud of Coronado and his limp dick pleasure palace."

Coop studied the new man's nametag, *Dorian Hamburg*. He and his Team guys could have fun with that name. And the look on the man's face told him he had a hair trigger. That was always fun. So the other regulars had told him about Coop's motor home. No problem. If the guy wanted to spar, Coop would spar with him, and make him pay for it.

"Nice to see the ladies've told you about it. That's why they won't lick your sorry ass." Coop watched his words punch Dorian in the face and make him redden. But the man was quick on his feet, unlike some of the other Navy regulars.

"I hear the health department wants to do a study of all the interesting cultures growing in that bat mobile, especially on the ceiling..."

"Nice try, asshole, or is it Dorian? If I were you, I'd go by the name asshole. Dorian sounds queer."

"You ought to know..." Dorian squinted at Coop's upside down nametag hanging at a slight angle. "Calvin."

Sticks and stones don't bust my balls...

"Well *Dorian*, you can call me Special Operator Cooper. But for your information, the only other Calvin I ever met was a real big black dude, and he *definitely* wasn't gay." Coop handed over his military ID.

"When are you gonna fix that rag on your head? Don't they pay you boys enough for a hairpiece or some plugs?"

"Lost all my hair going down. If the girl likes it, she kinda tugs. Hurts sometimes, get my drift?"

"Um hum." The sentry handed Coop back his card. "You be careful how you park, hear? And straighten that god-damned nametag."

The rumble of the engine left a thick cloud of black smoke in its wake. Happened every time Coop plastered his foot against the floorboard.

Timmons's office was all metal and no frills, except for the bright lime-green ceramic frog holding a surfboard that SEAL Team 3 bought him. It stood two and a half perilous feet tall, perched on top of a metal bookshelf. This was the replacement to the statue Timmons had destroyed on a rather ill-tempered day last year.

Timmons had bouts of anger, more frequently now, especially about procedural things. Coop knew the enlisted man was not longing for the forced retirement. It meant more time at home with a wife who publicly made fun of him. The Navy was his life, always had been. But that wasn't going to stop them from retiring him anyway.

"Chief?" Coop called out as he stooped under the doorframe to avoid hitting his head.

"Sit down, son," Timmons said, pointing to one of two metal folding chairs in front of his paper-strewn desk.

The cold chair matched the eerie chill that tingled up his spine every time his Chief Officer used the term *son*. He licked his lips and waited while Timmons looked like he was gathering strength. Whatever it was, it wasn't anything good.

"I'm afraid I've got some bad news. We've just been contacted by the authorities in Nebraska." He looked up at Coop with his watery light blue eyes. Coop held his breath.

"I'm not sure if you've heard it in the news, but there's been a tornado in Pender and parts nearby, and I'm sorry to say that your family and the farm are gone, son."

Cooper had been trained to deal with the death of a Team guy. He'd held them sometimes as the life force exited their bodies, rocking them slowly or telling them little jokes to ease their way home. But his real home, his roots in Nebraska, those always remained.

Gone? All of them? Gone? He never figured this could ever happen. *I'm completely alone?*

His body tensed as he came to terms with the reality of what was just spoken. One by one, every nerve ending began to shout, until the rage inside, the scream *Hell, no!* consumed all his energy. He dug his fingernails into his thighs and, without realizing it, had drawn blood through the green canvas of his cargo pants.

Timmons got up, which prompted Coop to stand as well, although he was weaving. If Timmons hugged him, he'd deck the guy and end his career for sure. But Timmons stood a healthy two feet away, which was close enough to smell the angst of the older man who nervously flexed and unflexed his fingers at his side. "I'm so sorry, son."

There's that goddamned word again. Coop took a deep breath and then felt the tears flood his eyes. *I'm no one's son any longer.* Mercifully, he couldn't see his Chief's expression. Coop's fists tightened, he stepped to the side and belted the frog statue, which crashed up against the side of the wall and shattered. Although his Team had recently replaced it for well over two hundred dollars, the green, glassy fragments exploded and fell in a satisfying tinkle all over the floor, the windowsill and Timmons's desk.

TIMMONS LOOKED OVER the mess in silence, nodding his head. He apparently thought the frog had suffered a good, honorable death, after all. Team 3 would have it replaced as soon as the donations came in. Next time maybe he should find a way to bolt it to the wall. But that could be dangerous.

For the wall.

Fallen SEAL Legacy (Book #2) is available here.
sharonhamiltonauthor.com/SEALBro2

ABOUT THE AUTHOR

 NYT and USA/Today Bestselling Author Sharon Hamilton's SEAL Brotherhood series have earned her author rankings of #1 in Romantic Suspense, Military Romance and Contemporary Romance. Her other *Brotherhood* stand-alone series are: Bad Boys of SEAL Team 3, Band of Bachelors, True Blue SEALs, Nashville SEALs, Bone Frog Brotherhood, Sunset SEALs, Bone Frog Bachelor Series and SEAL Brotherhood Legacy Series. She is a contributing author to the very popular Shadow SEALs multi-author series.

Her SEALs and former SEALs have invested in two wineries, a lavender farm and a brewery in Sonoma County, which have become part of the new stories. They also have expanded to include Veteran-benefit projects on the Florida Gulf Coast, as well as projects in Africa and the Maldives. One of the SEAL wives has even launched her own women's fiction series. But old characters, as well as children of these SEAL heroes keep returning to all the newer books.

Sharon also writes sexy paranormals in two series: Golden Vampires of Tuscany and The Guardians.

A lifelong organic vegetable and flower gardener, Sharon and her husband lived for fifty years in the Wine Country of Northern California, where many of her stories take place. Recently, they have moved to the beautiful Gulf Coast of Florida, with stories of shipwrecks, the white sugar-sand beaches of Sunset, Treasure Island and Indian Rocks Beaches.

She loves hearing from fans through her website:
authorsharonhamilton.com

Find out more about Sharon, her upcoming releases, appearances and news when you sign up for Sharon's newsletter.

Facebook:
facebook.com/SharonHamiltonAuthor

Twitter:
twitter.com/sharonlhamilton

Pinterest:
pinterest.com/AuthorSharonH

Amazon:
amazon.com/Sharon-Hamilton/e/B004FQQMAC

BookBub:
bookbub.com/authors/sharon-hamilton

Youtube:
youtube.com/channel/UCDInkxXFpXp_4Vnq08ZxMBQ

Soundcloud:
soundcloud.com/sharon-hamilton-1

Sharon Hamilton's Rockin' Romance Readers:
facebook.com/groups/sealteamromance

Sharon Hamilton's Goodreads Group:
goodreads.com/group/show/199125-sharon-hamilton-readers-group

Visit Sharon's Online Store:
sharon-hamilton-author.myshopify.com

Join Sharon's Review Teams:

eBook Reviews:
sharonhamiltonassistant@gmail.com

Audio Reviews:
sharonhamiltonassistant@gmail.com

Life *is one fool thing after another.*
Love *is two fool things after each other.*

REVIEWS

PRAISE FOR THE
GOLDEN VAMPIRES OF TUSCANY SERIES

"Well to say the least I was thoroughly surprise. I have read many Vampire books, from Ann Rice to Kym Grosso and few other Authors, so yes I do like Vampires, not the super scary ones from the old days, but the new ones are far more interesting far more human then one can remember. I found Honeymoon Bite a totally engrossing book, I was not able to put it down, page after page I found delight, love, understanding, well that is until the bad bad Vamp started being really bad. But seeing someone love another person so much that they would do anything to protect them, well that had me going, then well there was more and for a while I thought it was the end of a beautiful love story that spanned not only time but, spanned Italy and California. Won't divulge how it ended, but I did shed a few tears after screaming but Sharon Hamilton did not let me down, she took me on amazing trip that I loved, look forward to reading another Vampire book of hers."

"An excellent paranormal romance that was exciting, romantic, entertaining and very satisfying to read. It had me anticipating what would happen next many times over, so much so I could not put it down and even finished it up in a day. The vampires in this book were different from your average vampire, but I enjoy different variations and changes to the same old stuff. It made for a more unpredictable read and more adventurous to explore! Vampire lovers, any paranormal readers and even those who love the romance genre will enjoy Honeymoon Bite."

"This is the first non-Seal book of this author's I have read and I loved it. There is a cast-like hierarchy in this vampire community with humans at the very bottom and Golden vampires at the top. Lionel is a dark vampire who are servants of the Goldens. Phoebe is a Golden who has not decided if she will remain human or accept the turning to become a vampire. Either way she and Lionel can never be together since it is forbidden.

I enjoyed this story and I am looking forward to the next installment."

"A hauntingly romantic read. Old love lost and new love found. Family, heart, intrigue and vampires. Grabbed my attention and couldn't put down. Would definitely recommend."

PRAISE FOR THE
SEAL BROTHERHOOD SERIES

"Fans of Navy SEAL romance, I found a new author to feed your addiction. Finely written and loaded delicious with moments, Sharon Hamilton's storytelling satisfies like a thick bar of chocolate." — Marliss Melton, bestselling author of the *Team Twelve* Navy SEALs series

"Sharon Hamilton does an EXCELLENT job of fitting all the characters into a brotherhood of SEALS that may not be real but sure makes you feel that you have entered the circle and security of their world. The stories intertwine with each book before…and each book after and THAT is what makes Sharon Hamilton's SEAL Brotherhood Series so very interesting. You won't want to put down ANY of her books and they will keep you reading into the night when you should be sleeping. Start with this book…and you will not want to stop until you've read the whole series and then…you will be waiting for Sharon to write the next one." (5 Star Review)

"Kyle and Christy explode all over the pages in this first book, *[Accidental SEAL]*, in a whole new series of SEALs. If the twist and turns don't get your heart jumping, then maybe the suspense will. This is a must read for those that are looking for love and adventure with a little sloppy love thrown in for good measure." (5 Star Review)

PRAISE FOR THE
BAD BOYS OF SEAL TEAM 3 SERIES

"I love reading this series! Once you start these books, you can hardly put them down. The mix of romance and suspense keeps you turning the pages one right after another! Can't wait until the next book!" (5 Star Review)

"I love all of Sharon's Seal books, but *[SEAL's Code]* may just be her best to date. Danny and Luci's journey is filled with a wonderful insight into the Native American life. It is a love story that will fill you with warmth and contentment. You will enjoy Danny's journey to become a SEAL and his reasons for it. Good job Sharon!" (5 Star Review)

PRAISE FOR THE
BAND OF BACHELORS SERIES

"*[Lucas]* was the first book in the Band of Bachelors series and it was a phenomenal start. I loved how we got to see the other SEALs we all love and we got a look at Lucas and Marcy. They had an instant attraction, and their love was very intense. This book had it all, suspense, steamy romance, humor, everything you want in a riveting, outstanding read. I can't wait to read the next book in this series." (5 Star Review)

Made in United States
Orlando, FL
05 August 2022

20581808R00238